THE WILL OF TIME

J.B. Pierce

Songyard Publishing
A MULTIMEDIA MEDLEY OF IMAGINATION

THE WILL OF TIME
Copyright © 2022 by J.B.Pierce

ISBN:

10 9 8 7 6 5 4 3 2 1

First Edition: June2018

For information contact :
Songyard Publishing, Pittsburgh, PA
songyardpublishing@gmail.com

Cover design by J.B.Pierce
Cover photographs courtesy of: BK Photography & Jenn Davis

Through the years you watched me grow,
and taught me all I needed to know.

~ Mom

Prologue

A flash of light singed the evening sky. A slight rain fell to the ground. As Eldon Aires ran out of the house, he glanced down at one of the many watches attached to his wrist. *4:00 a.m.* Time was running out.

With a quick adjustment of his black derby hat, Eldon tightened his hold on a black, rectangular box in his hands and raced past a red barn and across an open field; his long jacket fluttering behind him. Like a thief in the night, he slipped further into the shadows. But Eldon was no thief; more like an angel, who along with six others called themselves NEVES (nah' vess).

From the moment of their first initiative, the NEVES have continued to bend the laws of time. They have pledged their honor through their convictions to justify the journey. They have defended the righteous and protected the greater good. Resilient in action and tenacious in word, their valor has remained rooted in their hearts to triumph over the rising NEFARIONS and their wicked hands.

Eldon ran toward a copse of evergreen trees through the blowing rain. He ducked under their bristly arms and stopped at a large, deserted chicken coop that stood next to a small, flowing stream: *Plum Run.* Eldon wiped the rain off his face, opened the coop's wooden door, and stepped inside. The hard-thrumming rain that pelted the wooden roof matched the blood thumping in his ears and the rhythm of his beating heart.

In the dimness, Eldon held up the black, rectangular box and ran his fingers across its leather binding, inspecting its metal latch-key, three round buttons, and small glass lens. His lips slowly curled into a smile. After all this time, he had finally found it – the missing piece of the puzzle; the camera.

Eldon opened his jacket. Leather straps of all sizes were fastened around his waist and secured to his grey pants. Various gears and compass faceplates were attached to his black vest. Eldon dug into his jacket pocket and pulled out a leather-bound journal. He flipped to the middle of the book and reread the five numbers on the page, memorizing their sequence. *Seven – one – eighteen – six – three.*

A gust of cold wind whistled through the thin cracks in the chicken coop's walls. The door squeaked open. Firm footsteps hit off the wooden floor.

Eldon closed the journal and slowly slipped it back into his pocket. He stiffened and shifted his eyes over his shoulder, straining to see behind him. In the doorway, highlighted by the flickering lightning, stood a tall man with red suspenders attached to brown trousers. Thick goggles decorated the man's black top hat.

Eldon relaxed his shoulders and sighed. "Fink? Geezus. What are you doing here?"

"I came to help," Fink said. "Wesley said you needed a hand."

Eldon furrowed his brow. "Wesley?"

"You found it," Fink beamed, looking at the camera in Eldon's hands. He moved away from the open door; one hand tucked behind his back. "Let me see it."

Eldon held the camera close. "When did you see Wesley?"

"Just this morning," Fink replied, all too quickly.

Eldon pressed his lips together and stared at Fink, looking hard into his brown eyes. Something about this whole situation felt wrong.

Soon after the war and the tragic events that struck NEVES, Eldon recalled assembling the group for a private session of time's unfortunate circumstances. After a heated discussion, a vote was taken, and a recovery mission was planned. For months, the group spent countless nights on the logistics of the execution. Codes were written, mapped out strategically, and held in highest secrecy; none of which included Fink, who had mysteriously gone rogue.

"The requisition of time," Eldon said. "What did it say?"

Fink strutted forward. "Oh, you know. Same 'ole, same 'ole: dates, locations . . ."

Keeping his eyes on Fink, Eldon slid his fingers to the latch-key on top of the camera and turned it one full rotation: counterclockwise. He then moved his fingers to a small round button and pulled. Little by little, a thin, white string emerged from deep within the camera.

"What's wrong Eldy-boy?" Fink flicked up his glaring eyes. Lightning flashed. "Don't you trust me?"

"I don't trust anyone anymore," Eldon sneered. "'Specially you."

Fink rubbed his narrow chin and cackled harmoniously with the crack of thunder. He brought his hand out from behind his back and aimed a long-barreled pistol at Eldon's chest. "Congratulations; for once, you're right. Now, give me that camera."

"I don't understand," Eldon said. "Why are you doing this?"

Fink jutted his chin and smirked. "I have my reasons."

"Don't you see? We can bring him back."

Fink leaned in close. "Who says we want him back?"

"Why you – "

"Ah, ah, ah . . . " Fink said, cocking back his gun. "Don't even think about it, or you'll end up just like him."

"I should've known. It's been you all along, hasn't it?"

Fink opened his arms wide. "What can I say? Life's a stage. It's my turn to hold the spotlight."

Eldon felt the camera's string go taut in his fingers. It was time. Time to make the jump.

Eldon reached up to his neck and froze. His heart stopped. His blood ran cold. He patted his vest and pockets. He scanned and searched the floor.

J.B. Pierce

"Looking for this?" Fink asked.

Eldon looked up. A long necklace with an oak tree medallion swung like a pendulum between Fink's gnarly fingers.

"My apologies, *brother*," Fink spat, "but it looks like you won't be going anywhere, except to your grave." He gave a snarky grin. "Say hello to your precious leader for me."

Lightning singed the earth, sending its light through the cracks in the surrounding walls of the chicken coop. A clap of thunder followed, breaking through the drumming rain. A gust of wind blew through the space, closing the door with a **BANG**.

"Hey!" Eldon pointed. "Who's that?"

As Fink looked over his shoulder, Eldon seized the opportunity and swung the camera up at the gun. *Smack!* The gun flew out of Fink's hand, discharging a bullet from its chamber, which punched a hole in the wooden roof.

With a roar of rage, Fink sprung forward and tackled Eldon at the waist. The two stumbled, head over heels, crashing through the back wall of the chicken coop and to the outside.

Wind tore through the nearby woods and chopped at the grassy fields, creating waves of green. The torrential rain caused *Plum Run* to overflow in a rushing current. Lightning bit the earth and played an intense game of cat and mouse as it dashed through the inky clouds. Thunder crashed in sonic cymbals.

With a mighty heave, Fink flipped Eldon onto his back. He grabbed a fistful of Eldon's jacket, reared back, and delivered a solid punch to the jaw. *Thwack!*

The blow was a sledgehammer; a sudden numbness of all senses. Eldon moaned as he withered on the sodden grass, his vision stained black.

Fink shook the rain out of his face and ripped the camera out of Eldon's hands. "You should have just handed it over. Now, look at you. What a pathetic excuse for a hero."

Eldon squinted through the rain and pain and watched as Fink stumbled away with both the camera and the necklace. *No. I will not let you win.* Fighting through the throbbing in his face, Eldon pushed himself to his feet. He staggered a few steps, regaining his balance. He clenched his fists and with a battle cry, he charged at Fink.

Before Fink could turn around, Eldon clutched Fink's right shoulder, wrapped his leg behind his knee, and pushed down. Fink howled like a wounded animal as his leg twisted out from under him. The camera fell out of his hands and tumbled across the grass.

"You will never," Eldon panted, taking back the necklace. "Never have the power of time." He swiped the camera off the ground, and remembering the sequence of numbers, popped open the oak tree medallion.

Turn to 7. Toggle to 1. Click each number: 18 - 6 - 3.

Eldon snapped the medallion shut and pointed the lens of the camera toward the opaque resin that sat beneath the oak tree. Slowly, it began to churn in an iridescent wave - around and around, distorting the sequence of numbers.

Eldon placed his thumb on the side button and closed his eyes. An icy liquid seeped out from the medallion and frosted his fingers. He took one last deep breath, anticipating the cold and the jump when a pair of wet hands wrapped around his own.

Eldon opened his eyes to find Fink - inches away - grinning from ear to ear. "You can't get rid of me that easily," Fink said, pulling at the camera.

A ball of light surged through the stormy sky. A soft, crackling static rolled across the field. As Eldon and Fink looked up, a bolt of lightning broke through the storm clouds and struck the camera's lens with a startling flash. Its voltaic current propelled straight through the glass in a searing explosion.

The charge threw the battling pair to the ground. The oak tree medallion flew out of Eldon's hand in a shower of shimmering, soft flecks of gold. Unable to move, he watched as the necklace soared through the opened door of the chicken coop, disappearing in the darkness.

Eldon shook on the ground, gasping for air in spasms. The heat pulsated in waves of energy while a high-pitched ringing pinged in his ears. When he opened his eyes, a dome of white light surrounded him. A whip of ice lashed out and nipped his fingers. He swallowed hard; unable to believe his eyes. Without the camera or necklace in his hands, how could he be transporting?

A shriek of terror rose against the thunderous symphony. A smell of sulfur permeated the rain. Eldon rolled onto his side and found Fink twisting and jerking about on the ground. He watched in wide-eyed horror as Fink's freckled skin shriveled and branched down the side of his face, neck, arms, and fingers. His brown curly hair streaked itself silvery-white.

"You," Fink growled with black eyes. "Look what you did to me!"

"You did it to yourself," Eldon struggled to say.

Using one hand, Fink dragged himself across the ground. He clutched Eldon's ankle and then brought his other arm forward; the camera stuck to his gnarly fingers. "See you on the other side."

Eldon's eyes went wide. "Fink! No!"

With a malicious laugh, Fink pushed the side button on the camera. The field blurred in a brilliant white light. A gust of frigid wind soared down from the sky and hit the ground in a sonic boom. Its force rolled out in a monumental wave and split the soil, shaking Eldon loose from Fink's boney hand.

The earth cracked and crumbled. It opened in a wide yawn around Fink's prostrate form and seeped into his veins. "Eldon," Fink cried as the ground swallowed him whole. "Help me."

As Eldon reached out his hand, a multitude of blazing tendrils shot out from the camera's lens, braiding themselves around his torso, arms, and legs. An icy glaze coated his body. He looked up at the churning clouds. They funneled and then parted, revealing a deep and hollow black hole in the sky. Taking a deep breath, he braced himself as the energy from the camera thrust him upwards and sucked him into a tunnel of darkness.

Chapter 1

FRIDAY, JUNE 12, 2009

F ifteen-year-old Will Marshall jolted awake. He grabbed his chest and blinked away the bright light that stung his eyes. Mismatched socks and t-shirts overflowed from his dresser. School exams, projects, and assignments sat unevenly piled on his desk. Even his collection of American Revolutionary War figurines buried under a thick coating of dust lay neglected atop a crooked shelf his mother insisted he put up.

Will breathed in through his nose and then exhaled, running his hand through his hair. *Get it together. It was just a dream - only a dream.*

Will plopped back down onto his pillow and closed his eyes, fighting to clear his mind. But no matter how hard he tried, the recurring and haunting images were still there. The high-pitched timbre ringing in his ears; the fire burning in his chest; the blurry vision of a young woman, long hair cascading around her shoulders, screaming out to him through thick fog as he strains to see her face.

A solid knock rapped against his bedroom door.

"Will, you up?" came a barking voice.

Will glanced over at the glowing lime green numbers of his alarm clock that sat on the nightstand next to his bed. 6:12 a.m. *Great.* He rolled over toward the wall and pulled the covers over his head.

Another knock. Louder this time.

"Will? You have to go."

"All right, geez. I can hear you, ya know?"

"Listen, Will - "The bedroom door swung open, stopping halfway against a pile of dirty clothes, soccer spikes, and cardboard boxes. His father looked down at the mounding clutter that blocked the way. "Are you ever going to unpack? You can't keep living out of boxes."

"Who says I can't?" Will asked, throwing the covers aside. He sat up and began kicking a random soccer ball back and forth between his socked feet.

"Hey! Cut the attitude. Your mother needs to have you and your sister at Nana and Grandpa's by nine-thirty, so – "

"Wait a second," Will interrupted. "Madi's coming to Nana and Grandpa's?"

"Yes, which means – "

"But I thought she was going to that summer camp she always goes to."

"Change of plans," his father said matter-of-factly. "So, for your mother to make her flight and get you both to Nana's on time, you have to be packed and out of the house in twenty minutes. Understand?"

"Hey, I know," Will said. "What if Madi goes to Nana and Grandpa's, and I stay home – here – by myself? I can keep an eye on the place for you guys while you're away."

"I don't think so."

"Oh, c'mon. I think I can handle three weeks on my own. I mean, in two months, I'll be sixteen. What's the big deal?"

His father started to close the door but stopped short, looking back down at the mound of clutter. "You really should clean up this room when you get back."

"Yeah, yeah, sure thing," Will quickly answered. "So, whatcha say? I can stay home, right?"

Will's father gave a straight-faced stare. "Maybe next year."

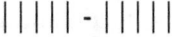

The late morning sunlight broke through the high clouds and gave a warm welcome to the tree-lined horizon of the Appalachians. For the past three miserable hours, Will sat silently in the front passenger seat of his mother's SUV; a prisoner of circumstance.

"I am so excited," came the shrill voice of Will's eleven-year-old sister Madi from the backseat. "Just think; we get to spend three weeks together."

Will shifted in his seat and hid under his baseball cap, sinking further into its leather. Central Pennsylvania. He had seen it all before; miles of cornfields; endless farms; vast green pastures.

The SUV slowed. Gravel crunched underneath its heavy tires. Will peeked out the windshield from beneath the brim of his baseball hat and groaned, knowing full well his summer nightmare was about to begin.

From beyond a copse of large, white oak trees, his grandparents' house and the hundred-year-old red barn came into view. Built in the early 1800s, the two-story Georgian colonial sat outside the small town of Gettysburg, Pennsylvania. Sometime during the Civil War, the homestead was abandoned. As the years went by, time and weather slowly deteriorated the structure. Paint curled and hung off the walls like ribbons. Shingles cracked – its roof a weathered patchwork quilt. It wasn't until the late 1950s that Will and Madi's grandparents bought the estate. Though the home showed its distress, the foundation was strong.

Over time, the restoration began. The siding was repainted with the original color of buttermilk yellow. Its large, wrap-around porch hugged the exterior of the home while black louvered shutters outlined each double-hung window. Straight rows of white clapboard and pilaster columns enhanced its facade, giving the house an elegant, yet sophisticated look. To this day, Will and Madi's grandparents continued to work on the outside and inside of the home, vowing to maintain its historical integrity.

Will's mother guided the SUV to the front of the house, following the curve of the governor's drive. She parked the car and turned off the ignition. "Now listen," she began. "I want you both to be on your best behavior and remember your manners."

"You know me, Mom," Madi said. "Unlike Will, I always behave."

Will glared over his shoulder at his sister, who sat with a full grin, dimples and all. "Yeah right," he said under his breath, turning toward the front.

Madi unbuckled her seatbelt and jumped forward, poking Will's shoulder with her perfectly polished nail.

Will spun around in his seat. "Cut it out, Madi."

"Make me."

"All right. Now, that's enough," their mother said.

"You're such a brat," Will sneered.

"At least I'm not a jerk like you," Madi retorted.

"Both of you just stop already," their mother shouted. She removed her sunglasses and threw them on the dashboard. "So, help me if I get a call from Nana or Grandpa saying you two are giving each other a hard time again, you will both be grounded for the rest of the summer."

"But he started it," Madi exclaimed.

"Do I make myself clear?"

Will met his sister's glowering stare.

"Yeah," Madi answered with a huff. "I hear you." She pushed herself back against the seat and folded her arms across her chest.

"Like it can get any worse," Will grumbled, playing with the straps of his duffle bag.

"I'm serious," his mother said, lightly smacking the side of his arm with the backside of her hand. "Now, let's go; I'm already late."

Chapter 2

*W*ill hung back as Madi and his mother got out of the SUV. He watched his sister drop her bookbag to the ground and run up the porch steps, throwing her arms around their grandmother, who rushed out of the house to greet her. Will grabbed the brim of his hat and looked away, reminiscent of their very first summer vacation at the farm.

|||||-|||||

Will had just turned nine and Madi four. He remembered being dropped off at their grandparents' house early one summer morning. No warning; nothing. In the car; three-hour drive, and here they were.

"What's going on? Where are you guys going?" Will asked, trailing behind his mother as she carried Madi up the porch steps.

"Your father and I have a meeting in Harrisburg to discuss our case study," she said. "We may have found an investor to help with our research. Do you know what this could mean?"

Will's father placed their suitcases on the porch, looked up at Will, and then headed back to the car without even a goodbye.

"We'll only be gone for a week," his mother continued, handing Madi over to Nana. "So, be good and look after your sister for me, okay?" She leaned into Will and lightly kissed him on the cheek. "We'll be back soon. I promise."

Will walked to the edge of the porch and stood next to Nana while Madi clung to her neck crying, pleading pathetically for their parents to come back. But for Will, as he watched them drive away, something came over him that he had never felt before; a strange contentment of happiness flooded his heart.

"So," came Grandpa's voice. He placed an arm around Will's shoulder. "Since your grandmother went inside to calm your sister down, what would you like to do?"

Will shrugged. "I don't know."

"Well, I just may have something you might like." Grandpa handed over a pair of safety glasses and a set of protective earmuffs.

Will scrunched his nose. "What's this?"

Grandpa met Will's eyes. "Want to see if you can shoot?"

A broad smile spread across Will's face. "Really?"

"Sure," Grandpa beamed. He walked off the porch and headed toward an old rusty Ford sitting idle in the middle of the driveway. "Just don't tell your mother," he threw over his shoulder.

"Wait!" Will jumped off the porch and shuffled quickly behind. He hopped into the truck, placing the safety glasses on his nose and the earmuffs around his neck. "Why can't I tell mom?"

Grandpa started the engine and drove around the house, heading toward an adjacent field. "Your mother . . . "He paused and looked at Will. "I'd say she was about your age when she shot her first gun."

"Mom shot a gun? What kind?"

"An 1863 Springfield muzzle-loading rifle. It was used right here during the Battle of Gettysburg. Guess that can be a bit intimidating for anyone."

"Hold up. You let Mom shoot a gun from the actual war?"

"You bet."

"Awesome," Will breathed.

"She was a quick learner," Grandpa went on, "but the moment it threw her plum on her backside, she never wanted to shoot again." Grandpa chuckled. He stopped the truck and shifted into park. "Made her a bit nervous I guess."

Will looked out the windshield. In the middle of the field was a makeshift firing range. Targets were made out of tin cans. Bottles on haystacks. A plywood bull's eye nailed to a tree.

A grin formed on Will's face; the glasses crooked on his nose. "Doesn't make me nervous."

Grandpa mussed Will's hair and smiled back. "I guess we'll find out now; won't we?"

| | | | | - | | | | |

A slight chuckle escaped Will's lips as he remembered that day and all the days spent here – with Nana and Grandpa. They meant so much to him; all he had learned and heard and experienced. Each breathless moment of laughter and adventure captivated him, and with each passing year, here was where he felt most at home.

Will stared down at his soccer ball near his feet. His shoulders fell, and his smile slowly waned. His emotions were divided; a war between his contented past and his undesired present.

A tap on the passenger side window startled him. It was his mother. "Let's go," she gestured. "Nana's waiting to see you."

Will opened the door and stepped out, meeting a thick, soggy rag of stagnant air. He took off his baseball hat and rubbed his brow. The sun filtered through the clouds and struck his sky-blue eyes, causing him to squint. He refitted his hat back on his head and grabbed his duffle bag. He took his iPod and earbuds out of the car's cupholder and shoved them both in his shorts pocket.

"Hello, William," Nana said sweetly.

"He likes to be called Will now," his mother said.

"Oh," Nana said surprised.

"Seriously, Mom?" Will snapped.

"Well, that's what you tell me," she replied.

Will swiped his soccer ball off the floor of the car and walked over to his grandmother. "Hi, Nana," he said, accepting her embrace. "You can still call me William if you'd like."

Nana pulled back and smiled. "Will sounds wonderful to me."

She squeezed his hand. "I'm so glad you're here."

"Me too."

"How are you? Your mother told me that you might take up soccer at your new school."

Will adjusted the strap of his duffle bag on his shoulder. "Yeah, I might." He dropped his soccer ball to the ground and held it in place with the tip of his foot.

Nana lightly cupped his cheek. "I'm so proud of you. I know how hard it can be to start over again."

"Thanks, Nana."

"William, my boy!" came a booming voice.

"It's Will now, David," Nana said, putting her hands into the pockets of her yellow apron, which was, as usual, dusted in flour. "He likes to be called Will now."

"Oh. Well, okay then. Will it is," Grandpa replied.

Will turned around to find his grandfather walking up behind him carrying a long-barreled gun against an open plaid button-down flannel that revealed a white, oil-stained undershirt. "I've been waiting all morning to show you this new muzzleloader."

Will's mother shifted on her feet and turned away. "Oh, I've always hated those things."

Will took the gun out of Grandpa's hand and inspected its construction – barrel band, serrated trigger, and two initials – *TS* – which was carved into its wooden stock. "1884 Springfield trapdoor," Will said.

Grandpa raised his eyebrows. "Impressive. Good eye, son."

Will placed the rifle against his shoulder. "Carbine; single shot." He peered down its long barrel. "Pretty sweet. Where'd you get it?"

Grandpa wiped the sweat off his neck with a rust-colored handkerchief and then tucked it in the back pocket of his faded blue jeans. "At a gun show that came through town a few weeks back. I saw it and had to have it, so I traded in a few I had lying around."

Will handed back the rifle. "You do have a lot."

"Isn't that the truth?" Grandpa laughed. "Maybe once you're all settled in, we can go out in the field and give it a run; see if you grew a bit rusty since last year," he said, patting Will on the back.

"Ah, yeah, maybe." Will tightened his grip on his duffle bag's strap. "I should – ah – I should probably get my bags first."

"Sure thing," Grandpa said. "You're here for a few weeks. We have plenty of time to catch up."

Will left his soccer ball on the ground and made his way to the back of the SUV. He pushed the button on the back hatch and grabbed his black suitcase.

"Hey, Will," Madi said, leaning over the porch railing. "Grab my suitcase for me, okay?"

"Come get it yourself!"

"Will, grab your sister's suitcase," his mother said. "What's the big deal? You're right there."

Will mumbled a slew of vexes under his breath as he snatched Madi's polka-dot suitcase out of the back hatch. Before he closed it shut, a stream of sunlight spilled through the panoramic sunroof and highlighted a familiar garment bag packed with his Civil War uniform, shoes, and accessories.

"She didn't," Will groaned. He narrowed his eyes and looked over at his mother, who was standing by the porch, talking to his grandparents. Sometime this morning and without him noticing, she must have put it in the car along with his suitcase. Will shook his head and closed the back hatch. *Not this year.*

"You get everything?" his mother asked as she typed a text message on her cell phone.

Will lifted his arms, dangling both suitcases from his hands like two piñatas before dropping them to the ground with a hard *thud.*

"William James," his mother shrieked. "Was that necessary?"

Will ignored his mother and the suitcases and walked to the

nearest hickory tree, kicking his soccer ball in front of him. He hiked his duffle bag strap higher on his shoulder and then leaned against the ancient tree, staring out at the adjacent road.

A small twig breaking snapped in his ears. He glanced down and recognized his mother's shoes. "You know. You didn't have to do that," she said.

Will turned away with a huff.

"I know you're mad at me. It's just - "

"You don't get it, do you?" he said, cutting her off. "Ever since we moved, *again* - "

"We had to."

"Says who?"

"The moment that independent firm picked up our case study your father - "

"You mean Charles?" Will interrupted.

"Now stop. You know that when we were given the offer . . ."

Will stared blankly at his mother as she rambled on. Though her lips moved, he couldn't focus on the words. Each one spewed from her mouth and gathered in his ears in a collection of misaligned tones.

Charles and Christine Marshall - acclaimed historians - traveled and studied extensively in every Civil War state that dotted the East Coast. For as long as Will could remember, his parents' lives - more so his mother's - were devoted to finding the hidden secrets of a sub-cultural society, whose motivations were entwined before, during, and after the Civil War. Most of the time, their focus was there and elsewhere. Cell phones or laptops added their own personal touch to every birthday celebration and at any school function or sports event. Drive-thru or reheated leftovers became a dinner routine, and as the years went by, Will couldn't help but notice how much they sacrificed family for their own special interests and gains.

Somewhere behind the house, Grandpa's table saw cut through a piece of wood. A flock of birds fluttered in the tree overhead and mixed with a drawn-out moo from the cow in the barn.

"How could you do this to me?" Will mumbled.

His mother stopped short. "What's that supposed to mean?"

"You go behind my back; agree to move us to God knows where." Will's voice grew louder with each word. "I had to leave my friends and start a new school – not once but twice – where I had to make new ones, and you do whatever you want to do without even thinking or considering *my* feelings. All you care about is your stupid study about some stupid people from like the 1800s and her!" Will jabbed a finger at Madi, who was sitting on the porch steps, talking with Nana.

"Now, that's not fair, and you know it," his mother said.

"What is fair, Mom? You tell me."

"What would you like me to say?"

Will kicked at his soccer ball. "Never mind. What's the point anyway?"

His mother gave a heavy sigh. "I'm sorry. I'm sorry I haven't been spending much time with you like we used to when you were little. I'm sorry we had to move again, where you had to start a new school and make new friends." She moved closer. "Look. Sometimes things happen in our lives we have no control over. It's like life shoves us forward and chooses a path for us, saying 'here you go' or 'go there'. Change is hard and unfortunately, sometimes we have no other option than to – to accept the change and try to make the best of it."

"Bull," Will spat. "We *all* have control to choose."

The ringing sound of a cell phone cut through the tension. "I got to go if I'm going to catch my flight," Will's mother said.

He stood unmoved.

She stepped closer; the car keys jingling in her hand. "How about this . . .after my conference in Antietam, I'll switch my flight time and come and pick you up. That way we can spend some time together –

you and me – before I drop you off at home. Yes, you can stay by yourself. What do you think?"

"Actually, that would be really great," Will said with a smile. He grew serious, narrowing his eyes. "But I'm not getting my hopes up."

Will turned back toward the road. He closed his eyes and pinched his lips together until they were nearly numb, trying to hold back all that circulated inside his head. How? How could she not see what was happening to their relationship over the last few years? What was so important about this case study? And why did she continue to push him away? All he ever wanted was to feel important and loved. Not from teammates or coaches or friends that come in and out of his life, but from his mother; the one who meant the most to him.

Will heard the car door shut followed by the sound of the SUV's engine. He opened his eyes and watched his mother drive away, wanting to believe her this time, hoping she would prove him wrong.

Chapter 3

Will stepped away from the tree and kicked his soccer ball with a hard *thwack*. It soared upward like an airborne missile, cutting through the trees over the driveway before disappearing underneath a blooming rosebush near the front porch.

Perfect.

Will made his way toward the house, kicking at the gravel driveway with the tip of his shoe; each footfall a bitter dig. His neck flushed, and his cheeks burned. Sweat beaded underneath his hat, and like a vice squeezing his temples, he felt a headache coming on. He wanted to blame it on the heat, but that would be a lie.

Will knelt down near the rosebush and stretched for his soccer ball careful not to jab himself on any thorns. When he stood up, he found Nana staring at him through the living room window. Will spun the ball in his hands and quickly looked away, hoping she didn't take notice of his ranting bitterness. After a few anxious seconds, he stole a quick glance back toward the window and found that she was gone.

Will puffed out his cheeks and exhaled. He adjusted his baseball hat and narrowed his eyes against the blazing sun. Directly above the covered porch, a sheer, yellow curtain fluttered carelessly outside the opened window with the soft, summer breeze. Will picked up his suitcase and smiled to himself. *At least I'll have my own room.*

The interior of his grandparents' home was immense and filled with character. Intricately layered mahogany woodwork outlined the expansive door frames and the multitude of windows. Hardwood floors shone with a deep, rich glass-like finish. White crown moldings bordered high ceilings while wall colors of baby blues, dusky rose, corn yellow, and milky whites completed the historic design.

As Will stood in the foyer, a pungent odor of varnish bit his nose. He looked in the living room and found it sitting empty; no couch or end tables – only the lace curtains hung from the opened windows. He could only assume his grandparents had started another one of their restorations.

Will peered down the long, narrow hallway that led to the kitchen. There he found Nana shuffling from the oven to the table, a pie in her oven-mitted hands. He breathed in deep and made his way up the grand staircase, relishing in the aroma of flour, sugar, and apricots that wafted out of the room.

Will stopped at his bedroom door, relaxed his shoulders, and let out a sigh. *Finally.*

"Well, well, well. Isn't this your lucky day?" came Madi's squeaky voice as the door slowly swung open.

"Tell me this is not happening," Will moaned.

"You won't believe it," Madi said, standing in the center of the room; a silly grin framing her small face. "Looks like I'll be bunking with you. Isn't that great?"

Will rubbed his forehead, struggling to find words. "No –I – I must be hallucinating."

Madi flicked her hair over her shoulder. "You and me. We're going to be roomies." She unlatched her polka-dotted suitcase. "We're going to have so much fun together."

Will dropped his suitcase to the floor and threw down his soccer ball. It thumped across the wooden floor and bounced to a rest under the window. With heavy footsteps, he stormed out of the room and whipped around the banister, stumbling awkwardly into Nana.

"Oh, William; I mean Will," she said, startled. "I was just coming up to see you. I'm guessing you found Madi in your room."

Will was tongue-tied. What was he to say?

"I know it's not what you expected," Nana went on. "But with the living room floor being varnished and the carpenter having a family emergency, it pushed everything back with the remodeling of your sister's room. You understand, don't you?"

Will held onto his duffle bag and tensed his arms, pressing them hard against his body.

"I'm sorry, but it's only for a couple of days, maybe a week at the most," she said. "After that, everything will be back to how it should be. Promise."

Will forced a smile. "Yeah. Sure thing, Nana. It's – it's fine."

She gave Will's shoulder a slight squeeze and started down the stairs. Will pinched his eyes shut and balled his fingers into a fist, wanting to scream. "Oh, and one more thing," Nana said, stopping halfway down the staircase. "Supper's at five."

Will clutched his duffle bag and trudged back to his room, stopping short of the doorway. There, he found Madi fluttering around the room busy as a bee, singing to herself as she stuffed tanks and shorts in the dresser. She lifted her arms above her head and gave the drawer a hip-check, closing it shut before pirouetting away from the dresser like a ballerina.

"Will," Madi said with a start, "You scared me. I didn't see you standing there." She smiled and then skipped over to his side, batting her eyes up at him. "Miss me yet?"

Will was unmoved.

"Oh, relax; I'm just kidding," she said with a light-hearted wave. "Anyway, roomie. I call the bed by the light switch 'cause you know, being in the dark scares me. Well, only sometimes, like during thunderstorms and . . ." She looked back at Will, who was standing stiffly in the doorway. "Aren't you coming in?"

Will hesitated. He tried to conjure up an excuse, think of another option to get him out of this situation, but the unrelenting pounding in his head blocked any ideas.

"Come on. This bed's all yours," Madi said, patting the blocked pattern quilt that was draped over the twin bed.

Grimacing, Will picked up his suitcase, walked into the room, and shoved everything far under his bed.

"Aren't you going to unpack?" Madi asked.

Will snapped around. "Look, as you can tell, I'm not exactly thrilled with this arrangement. So, here's the deal. Since we have to share *my* room, you're going to stay on that side and leave me to mine. Got it?"

Madi threw up her hands. "Alright. Geez."

"Good. Now that that is settled; leave me alone."

Will tossed his duffle bag on the floor and plopped down on the mattress. He pulled out his iPod and earbuds from his short's pocket and plugged his ears. He closed his eyes as the music flooded his head. The rhythm of the song calmed the churning storm inside him and drowned all his thoughts; all his thoughts except one that continued to float to the front of his mind. How was he going to survive the next three weeks with Madi by his side?

Chapter 4

he early morning sun crept lazily across the bedroom walls. Will flipped onto his stomach and pressed his pillow down around his ears, trying hard to muffle the penetrating noise that filtered in through the open window.

For the past eighteen days, his grandparents' rooster, Marvin, would perch on the top of the split-rail fence in front of the house and crow into the dawn. To make matters worse, the carpenter, who was to finish the crown-molding job in Madi's room, ended up breaking his arm, further delaying the project.

So much for my own room.

Will peeked out from under his pillow and glared at his sister. There she slept, dead to the world, sprawled out on the twin bed with half of the sheets lying on the floor. Her mouth – partially opened – emitted a soft snore while a thin stream of drool ran onto the sheets. Will rolled his eyes. How she continued to sleep through the bird's infernal racket was one of the world's biggest mysteries.

Marvin ceased his crowing, and the morning was filled once again with a serenade of tweeting birds and fading crickets. Will stretched out his long legs and sank into his pillow. Just as he was dozing to their calming melodies, a soft knock tapped against the bedroom door.

"Will, son? You up?" It was Grandpa.

"Yeah. I'm awake."

"I didn't mean to bother you," Grandpa whispered, peeking into the room. "But Mr. Stevens is holding the reenactment meeting this morning, so I won't be able to cut the field today. With all this rain, it's grown a bit. Would you mind going and – "

"I'll go now," Will said, sitting up.

"No rush. Whenever you're ready. The tractor's all gassed up."

Will laid back and placed his arms underneath his head as his grandfather quietly shut the door. He stared at the intricate swirls molded into the plaster ceiling and thought about his grandparents' homestead – the house and the barn and the forty-plus acres.

Compared to other farms in the county, the farm was small with limited agriculture and livestock, but it kept his grandparents busy nonetheless. Every year, they would harvest sweet bread-n-butter corn and pick the plump apricots grown in the orchard, selling the produce at the local farmer's market. The animals they had on the farm consisted of a few prized dairy cows, a flock of chickens, Marvin the rooster, and a chestnut-brown quarter horse named Misty, who was bought from a horse auction upstate for Madi's seventh birthday.

Will remembered the day Grandpa brought Misty home to the farm. Madi immediately took to the stallion and begged for lessons. So, during each summer vacation at the farm, she trained extensively with an instructor, and on occasion, Will found himself joining in on the lessons. Now with four years under her belt, Madi was a moderately skilled equestrian for her age, riding through the wide, open fields without a care in the world.

A mumble and slur of words. A squeak of the bed springs. A stirring of the sheets.

Will forced himself out of bed and quickly dressed. He grabbed his baseball cap and iPod off the dresser and tip-toed across the wooden floor. That's all he needed was for Madi to wake up and follow him around all day again.

Outside, a seeping layer of fog wrapped itself like a scarf around the mountaintops as a thick wave of morning heat collided with the night's cool air. Sunlight peeked through the trees and glided across the front porch. Will pulled the brim of his baseball hat lower on his head and made his way to the barn, following a worn path through the small grove of apricot trees. As he walked through the orchard, the sweet smell of the plump and juicy fruit made his stomach rumble. Will reached up and plucked a large, ripe orange-red apricot from its clustered bunch. After a quick wipe with the base of his shirt, he sunk his teeth in the fruit, savoring the taste of its sweet nectar.

When he finished, Will tossed the apricot's seed into a scorched metal burn barrel that sat outside the 150-plus-year-old barn. He licked his fingertips clean, wiping any sticky remains on the front of his shirt and then took hold of the two heavy metal rungs that were secured to the barn's faded red doors. He gave a hard tug and threw the doors wide open, sending a flood of sunlight streaming inside.

The dairy cows and Misty paused from their morning breakfast, eyeing Will cautiously from their stalls. "Relax," he said, covering his nose from the mixed scent of animals and hay. "It's just me. I'll be out of here in a minute."

The expansive interior was lined with rough wood with a few new boards sporadically placed alongside the aged timbers. Two single-paned windows, gummy with a mixture of humidity and microscopic granules of grain, sat crooked in the wooden walls. Loose pieces of straw and feed lay carelessly about, wedging themselves in every nook and cranny while bales of hay – twined together – were stacked in towering columns in the last stall.

Will walked past Grandpa's workbench, wiping his sweaty hands on his shorts as he eyed the rickety, old ladder that led to the high and narrow loft. In the corner of the barn, Grandpa's vintage John Deere lay in waiting. Will climbed on the tractor and turned the key.

The engine coughed to a start then settled into a consistent rumble. Will placed his earbuds in his ears and turned on his iPod, giving a quick adjustment of the volume. He fixed his hat, put one hand on the steering wheel, and shifted into gear. With a push of the pedal, Will guided the tractor through the red double doors and drove away from the barn, heading to the wide-open field.

The sun hung high like a suspended light bulb and the heat laid flat across the farm like a weighted blanket when Will finally finished. He parked the tractor back inside the barn and then made his way toward the house. As he cut back through the apricot orchard, he caught sight of Madi with her riding helmet on, sitting in the saddle atop Misty.

Will watched as the cantering horse made her way alongside a white picketed fence, through the opened gate, and onto a field adjacent to the house. Shortening the reins in her hands below Misty's mane, Madi stood up in the stirrups and brought her elbows close to her knees. Then, like a spring under pressure, the horse sprang forward, and the two rode off, disappearing across the wide, open field.

Will started back toward the house but stopped short. A young man in a black, derby hat and jacket was standing just beyond the fence in the center of the field.

"Hey," Will yelled. "Can I help you?"

A stream of sunlight broke through the moving clouds and struck Will with its harsh glare. He stepped out of its light, blinking away the orange and yellow spots that stained his vision and looked back at the field. The stranger was gone.

What the - where did he go?

Will turned himself around and scanned the tree line that bordered the woods, but after a few minutes, he shrugged it off, assuming his eyes and the heat were playing tricks on him.

Back inside the house, Will stood in the quiet of the kitchen with the refrigerator door opened. With no air-conditioning, he closed his eyes and savored the moment, letting the cool air hit his face. After a refreshing minute, Will searched the shelves. His stomach was an empty pit; his throat like sandpaper.

On the bottom shelf, a white ceramic dish covered with a piece of tinfoil had a small handwritten note sitting on its top. Will ran his finger over the written words and smiled.

Thanks for helping Grandpa today. I'm sure you're hungry. Enjoy your lunch. Love, Nana.

Will lifted the tinfoil: his favorite - sliced turkey and Swiss cheese on a sweet, hotdog bun. He took the plate and swiped a soda from the refrigerator door, and then sat at the kitchen table. With each bite, he reminisced all the notes and pies and hugs Nana had given him over the years; the little things she did - and Grandpa - had always made him feel loved and appreciated.

Will finished his sandwich and chugged down the rest of his soda, belching his contentment. He shuffled up to his room, threw off his grass-stained shirt, and pulled out a clean, green soccer t-shirt from his duffle bag. As he slipped it over his head, Will caught a glimpse of his reflection in the mirror. He moved closer, staring at the slightly faded five-inch scar that ran down the center of his chest near his heart. Lightly, he traced its raised and ridged imprint. The story his mother had told him replayed in his head: the storm; the tree; the accident; she said it was a miracle he survived at all.

A shiver ran down Will's spine. He shook the words out of his mind, pulled down his shirt, and collapsed on his bed. His breathing became steady; his body relaxed.

Halfway to sleep, the hardwood floor shifted and creaked. A muffled giggle niggled at his ears. Will opened his eyes and nearly jumped out of his skin at the sight of Madi and her friend, Cassie - the girl from the next farm over. The two hovered over his bedside like two pesky crows. "Argh, I should have known," he moaned. "What do you two want?"

"I know you said you didn't want to be bothered," Madi said sweetly, "but Cassie and me; we're wondering if you could help us?"

"With what?"

"See, there's this board that needs . . ."

Will tuned Madi out as she rambled on and looked up at Cassie. Twelve-year-old Cassie Baines, with her hazel eyes, full eyelashes, and glittered lip-gloss, stared back at Will. She twisted her long, sun-streaked hair between her fingers all while blowing pink bubbles between winks and smiles.

Three years ago, Will and Madi met Cassie when her family moved from New York City due to an unexpected inheritance. Even though the Baines family was affluent in the 'Big Apple', they were sent to a dilapidated Federal-style home adjacent to Hickory Lane and forced to live in the house by a binding will. So, in less than a year, Cassie's parents transformed the estate – both inside and out – with a complete overhaul of luxurious restorations. The home's exterior rose two and a half stories and was painted a sulfate gray. White shutters adorned each window and a total renovation of the grounds surrounding the house rejuvenated the overgrown landscape and driveway.

Cassie moved a piece of her layered hair off her face. "Hi, Will." She popped a bubble. "Nice tan."

"So, you see," Madi said, "these last few boards are too heavy for us. That's why we need your help."

Will lifted an eyebrow. "For what? Your playhouse? Aren't you getting a bit old for that?"

Madi folded her arms across her chest. "It's not a playhouse. It's a clubhouse. Yours and mine, remember?"

It was about five years ago. Will remembered he and Madi were coming back from their daily hike in the bordering woods. The sky was painted in streaks of warm marmalade, and the temperature hovered near-boiling by mid-afternoon. They stepped out of the tree line and crossed over Plum Run - a small stream that cuts through the woods and ran across their grandparents' property.

"Why did we have to come back so early?" a six-year-old Madi protested, jumping over the bubbling stream.

Will, who had just turned eleven, leaped across the water and knelt down in front of his sister. "You said that you were tired."

"That was before. I'm fine now. Let's go back."

"Maybe next time, squirt. It's getting late."

Madi folded her arms across her chest. "Not fair."

"Hey . . ." Will nudged her arm and smiled. "Last one to the barn is - "

Madi perked up. "- a rotten egg!"

The pair took off in a roar of high-pitched laughter, chasing after one another, weaving in and out of a copse of evergreen trees when Madi suddenly disappeared.

Will slid to a stop. "Madi?" He looked all around. "Madi? Where'd you go?"

"Over here," came her small, muffled voice.

Will turned around and found her caught up in a lattice of thick ivy and overgrown bushes like a fly in a spider's web. He rushed over to her side and quickly untangled her legs and feet. "Are you okay?"

"Yeah," she said with a sniffle, rubbing her bruised ankle. "I was running when all of a sudden it felt like something grabbed my foot and . . . wait, what's that?" She pointed.

Tucked deep beneath the evergreen trees stood a vertical, wooden board covered in knotted vines and weeds. Will took a step closer and pulled at the cluster of greenery, revealing a wall of aged and worn wood.

"What do you think it is?" Madi asked.

Will looked down at his little sister. "Want to find out?"

For the rest of the afternoon and into the early evening, the pair pulled and ripped at the overgrowth, creating piles of thick branches and twigs. When they finished, they stepped back and took in the sight they unwrapped – a small, run-down rectangular structure, sitting on four, short square posts. Will went over to its crumbling door and gave a slight push.

The door squealed open in contempt and fell off its rusted hinges, sending up a puff of dust. The smell of mold and ancient grain wafted in the air. Inside, weeds grew out of the floor planks and through the disintegrating wallboards. A cluster of ivy and evergreen branches hung down from the bowing roof that had a small hole in one of the boards.

"It's a secret clubhouse," Madi said, clapping her hands. "It can be ours; right, Will?"

He didn't answer.

"Will?"

||||| - |||||

Madi snapped her fingers. "Hello? Earth to Will? I'm talking to you."

Will blinked a few times; his daydream slipping from his mind. "Huh . . . what? What happened?"

Madi stood with her hands on her hips; her foot tapping on the hardwood floor. "So, are you going to help us or what?"

Will grabbed his iPod out of his shorts pocket and brought it to life. "I already told you no. Now, beat it." He plugged his ears, turned up the volume, and closed his eyes.

"Will!" Madi shouted, smacking his arm.

Cassie leaned close. "Let's just go. We can do it ourselves."

"No," Madi said. "He's helping us if he likes it or not." Quietly, she inched forward, carefully took hold of the loose earbud wires lying on his chest, and yanked.

"Hey!" Will snapped. "Give 'em back you brat!"

Madi balled the free cords in her hands and held them hostage behind her back. "No. Not until you help us."

"I'm not gonna help you, Madilyn! Now, leave me alone."

"Yes, you are! Nana said you had to."

"Nana?"

Madi cocked her head. "Yes. *Nana.*"

Will jumped to his feet. "You're lying."

"Am not."

"I swear Madi, give me back my earbuds or else . . . "

She stuck her arm out the opened window; the cords dangling in the wind just above the porch roof. "Or else what?"

Will stepped closer. "You wouldn't?"

"Try me."

Will grabbed Madi's wrist and pulled her close. "Hey! Let me go," she wailed in his face.

Will pried her fingers loose, taking back his earbuds and released his grip. Madi stumbled, falling backward into the dresser.

"Madi!" Cassie shrieked. "Are you okay?"

Madi stormed over to Will and threw her hands hard against his chest, pushing him down onto the bed. "I am so sick of you!"

"Me?" Will said, sitting up on his elbows.

"Yes. You. I – I can't take it anymore. You're so mean to me."

"No, I'm not."

Madi snorted a laugh. "Yeah, right. That's all you are is mean and blame me – *the brat* – for everything."

"Whatever."

Madi grabbed at her hair. "Argh. Don't you get it?"

"What are you talking about?"

"I'm talking about all the times we used to spend together. Like playing games or taking hikes through the woods or even building the clubhouse, the one that *you* helped start. What's going on with you, huh? I don't even know you, anymore. You're not the same Will I remember."

Will stood up and glared down at his sister. Madi met his stare with tears brimming in her eyes. "Why?" she whispered, "Why are you pushing me away?"

Will walked over to the window, ignoring Madi and pulled back the curtain. The half-built clubhouse sat just beyond the barn. They spent years together fixing the structure under the burning sun or moonlit sky. They shared Peanut Butter and Jelly sandwiches, Goldfish crackers, and cold lemonades on a blanket beside the flowing waters of *Plum Run*. They made up songs and told jokes to one another, grabbing their stomachs as they cried with laughter. So, what had happened? Where did it go wrong? And when?

Will clutched the lace curtain and lowered his head. "Just – just get out of here, Madi."

Chapter 5

o, what's the deal with your brother?" Cassie asked, stepping into the clubhouse with a thin piece of wood in her hands.

"What do you mean?" Madi said. She walked over to a collection of tools and rummaged through a can of random nails.

"Well, other than being pretty cute."

Madi glared up at Cassie, who was leaning against the doorframe of the clubhouse, twirling her hair between her fingers; eyes glazed over in bliss. Madi coughed, rousing the girl from her daydream.

"Well, he is," Cassie said, tossing her strand of hair aside.

"Let's just drop Will, okay? He's not worth talking about." Madi pushed the can of nails out of her way and stepped out of the clubhouse door. She plopped herself down on a pile of rough lumber and pulled at the hair tie holding back her ponytail, letting her dirty blonde hair fall slowly on her lean shoulders. She put her head in her hands and let out a sigh, staring back at the half-built structure.

"Is it done yet?" eight-year-old Madi asked, walking up to Will as he hammered in the last two nails on the sidewall of the clubhouse.

"Yep," he answered.

"Really?"

Will spun the hammer in his hand, slipped it through his belt loop, and smiled. "Sure. One done. A hundred more to go."

"A hundred?" Madi whined. "That will take forever."

Will looked in the direction of the house. "Come on. We better get going. The porch light is on."

"Can't we stay just a little bit longer? I can still see."

Will wrapped his arm around her small shoulders. "Don't worry, squirt. We'll get it done."

"Promise?"

Will smiled. "I promise. We have all the time in the world."

Madi squinted against the sun that reflected and bounced off *Plum Run.* On the other side of the stream, a robin pecked arbitrarily at the ground. Unlucky in its search, the bird bent its legs, spread its wings, and took flight, following the curve of the crystal clear, trickling brook, disappearing into the woods and down the trail she and Will used to walk.

"Madi?" came Cassie's voice. "Look, I didn't mean to – "

"It's okay," Madi said, drying her eyes.

"No, it's not. You're my best friend. I can tell that you're upset."

"I'm fine . . . really."

Cassie sat down next to Madi and wrapped an arm around her shoulder. "Look, everything going on between you and Will sucks. But it won't last forever. He'll come around sooner or later; you'll see. Everything will work out in the end."

Madi looked over at her friend. "I'm not so sure about that." She pulled away from Cassie, wiped her nose with the back of her wrist, and redid her ponytail.

For the past two years, Madi wanted to believe things would change between her and Will – go back to how it used to be, but who was she kidding. Things change; people change. Will has changed.

"Come on," Madi said, "let's get this place finished."

Back inside the clubhouse, the girls continued working, moving boards and scraps of lumber. Cassie picked up a hammer and looked up. "By the way, I forgot to ask, who fixed the hole in the roof?"

"Grandpa," Madi replied. "He patched it for me last week. Funny thing is it was the only board on the roof he could save . . ." She scanned the pile of tools scattered on the floor. "Did you see where I set the hammer?"

"You mean this hammer?" Cassie said holding out the tool.

Madi gave a quick grin. "Yeah. Thanks."

As she took the hammer out of Cassie's hand, its bulky wooden handle fumbled between their fingers and fell to the floor, puncturing through the rotted piece of wood. The girls dropped to their knees.

"Oh no," Cassie said. "I'm sorry. I should've - "

"Eh, don't worry about it," Madi reassured, sitting back on her legs. "That board needed to be replaced anyway."

"I'll go get another piece," Cassie said.

As he stood up, a ray of sunlight streamed in through a split in the clubhouse's wall and shot into the darkened void in the floor. A shimmer of gold reflected out of the hole and penetrated Madi's blue eyes in a swirling bokeh of light.

What the heck?

The light flickered again.

Madi shuffled closer and slowly slid her fingers through the break in the wood. Pieces of cracked lumber scraped and cut her skin like little jagged teeth. "I know I saw something," she whispered.

Madi pressed herself to the floor, lowering her hand and arm further beneath the board. The soil underneath the clubhouse was cold and slimy and gathered in clumps under her nails. As she blindly probed the space below the board, her fingertips skimmed something hard. With one final dig, she closed her fingers around the object and drew it out of the hole.

Madi jumped to her feet and ran out of the clubhouse and over to *Plum Run.*

"Wait for me!" Cassie called out.

Madi fell to her knees at the edge of the stream and plunged her hands into the warm water, disturbing a small school of minnows. With the help of the current, years of compounded grime and earth were washed away. Madi backed away from the water's edge and turned the object over in her dripping hands. She slowly ran her thumb across its top, pushing away a thin layer of mud.

"Wow," Cassie breathed. "Would you look at that?"

An embossed oak tree, with twisted branches, sprawled around an antique face of what appeared to be an old pocket watch.

"Where do you think it came from?" Cassie asked.

Captivated, Madi stared down at the oak tree medallion, which hung from a burnished, gold chain; its iridescent resin glistened amber in the sun's radiance. "I - I don't know."

Chapter 6

Will stirred as the scorching rays of the late afternoon sun pierced his sleeping body like hot knives. He yawned and wiped away the tiny droplets of sweat that formed on his forehead and ran down the bridge of his nose. Somewhere under the sheets, he heard a faint beat of drums.

Will sat up and dug his hands in the rumpled mess, coming up with his buzzing earbuds. As he turned off his iPod, a cold breeze made its way through the room, whipping the yellow chiffon curtain in a fit of fury. Will walked over to the opened window and pulled back the curtain. In the distance, he caught a glimpse of Madi and Cassie, running out of the clubhouse and over to *Plum Run*.

Will shook his head at the sight of the girls and dropped the curtain from his hand. He turned around and jumped, finding his grandmother standing in the doorway. "Nana? I . . . umm . . ." he let out a dry cough. "I didn't hear you knock."

She opened the door further and walked into the room. "I didn't me to startle you, but your mother – "

"She's here?" Will beamed. He swiped his iPod and earbuds off his bed and placed them in his short's front pocket. "You know, I was wondering what was taking her so long. Honestly, I thought she wasn't coming this time."

Will grabbed his suitcase from under his bed, then zipped his duffle bag shut. He turned around and met a solemn expression on Nana's face. Will's smile faded; his heart along with his duffle bag slowly sank to the floor. "She . . . she's not coming, huh?"

"Your mother feels awful; she told me to tell you –"

Will dropped his things to the floor and rushed out of the room.

"Will," Nana called out. "William, wait."

Will whipped around the wooden banister and ran down the stairs, two at a time. He threw open the screen door and jumped off the porch steps, landing hard on the driveway. The rubber soles of his tennis shoes hit the uneven stones, pitching him forward onto his knees. The sharp edges of the rocks nicked his skin and gouged the palm of his hand.

Will regained his footing and thrust himself upward; the gravel crunching loudly under his feet. As he ran, an unusual cold wind blew his hat off his head and whistled in his ears. He turned off the driveway and onto the adjacent road, losing himself in the vastness of Central Pennsylvania.

Once far enough away from the house, Will moved onto the shoulder of the road and collapsed in a cluster of tall grass near a battered stock-rail fence. His legs tightened and burned. His lips were parched and yearned for a drink. His lungs constricted in a vise-like grip with each breath he took.

Will placed his hands on his chest and stared down the endless blacktop. Somewhere out there, beyond the cornfields, further than any paved road could take him, was a life that he longed for; one of stability without conflict; a genuine family rather than one of convenience, where promises eliminated disappointment and truth surpassed lies.

Will stared up at the passing clouds. They were always moving; always changing; never in the same spot for very long. They reminded him of his life - especially the time around his thirteenth birthday.

It had started that summer when Will was forced to move yet again. He had begun to notice a distance slowly growing between him and his mother. It wasn't accidental but more so intentional. Yes, he pushed her away like any typical teenager, but she pushed him even further with each passing day, either working late or disappearing whenever it would storm, and Will could never understand why.

As for his father - Charles -something had been missing from the very beginning. Like a lion shunning his cub, they never really bonded like a father and son should have. Each and every day, they combated one another about this and that, deepening the ever-growing battle wounds.

And there was Madi. With each passing year, a wedge of contempt implanted itself deeper and deeper between them. At first, it fragmented the foundation, disrupting the typical ebb and flow of a sibling relationship. But then, as if foredestined by some unknown force, the very core of their once-close relationship was severed and broken into pieces.

For Will, it was so easy to find blame in his family for the growing resentments he felt and the distance he created. But in reality, maybe deep down, it wasn't them but him; perhaps he was the one responsible; the one that was actually changing.

A rise of chanting voices spilled onto the road. Will hoisted himself off the ground and quickly climbed a nearby fence shaded by a tall oak tree as a crowded and rowdy school bus wheeled by. One player, with shoulder-length hair, stuck his head out the back window and screamed, "Go Wildcats!" A vinyl banner was tethered to the back of the bus. "Eastwood Soccer Club."

Will pulled at a strand of tall grass that hugged the wooden post of the fence and ripped the blade into small pieces. One by one, he threw each fragment to the ground, remembering his old soccer team and that fateful last day of school.

| | | | | - | | | | |

Will slung his backpack over his shoulder and carefully walked to the front of the bus as it rolled to a stop at the corner of Independence and New World. The doors whooshed open, fanning his face with a blast of summer heat. He lowered his head, fixing the brim of his baseball hat, and smiled to himself. In one fluid motion, he whirled around, threw his fists into the air, and shouted, "Go, Warriors!"

The crowded bus erupted in a chanting chorus. "Mar-shall! Mar-shall!" Feet stomped and hands clapped in a thumping rhythm, repeating his name over and over again. Even the usual quiet bus driver joined in on the excitement.

"Catch you later Beesly," Will said, giving a light jab to a blond boy's shoulder. "You better be ready for my surprise kick attack when I see you at practice in a few weeks."

The boy smirked. "Ha. Prepare yourself for the Beesly Burn, Marshall."

Laughing, Will gave the boy an elaborate handshake and then hopped off the bus. As he headed home, he relished the sound of his chanting name fading in the distance.

School was out. Summer was officially here. Will's first real year of high school and all that it came with had been one for the books. He handed a championship victory to his school, East Central for the first time in twenty years. His coach promoted him unexpectedly to the captain of the varsity soccer team (not many incoming freshmen can land that job). And as for his band of friends, they continued to grow with each passing day.

It was unthinkable, really. In the course of the year, Will had become a legend on and off the field. He was a fighter known to win, a champion. His name was emblazed all over the school. Everywhere he went, everyone followed, and he couldn't seem to get enough.

Will walked up the porch steps and opened the front door. "Hello?" A wave of excited chatter floated out from the kitchen. "Mom? Madi? Where are you guys"

Will threw his book bag on the floor next to the metal coat rack and headed down the hall.

"There you are," his mother said as he walked into the kitchen. "How was your last day of school?"

Will stopped short of the doorway, seeing his mother, father, and sister sitting around a spread of desserts on the table. He pointed. "What's this?"

"Chocolate chip," Madi replied with a mouthful of the cookie.

"What would you like?" his mother asked. "I can get you a - "

"I'm fine," Will said, cutting her off. "Apricot pies? You only make them when something's wrong or when it's my birthday, and it's obviously not my birthday. So, what is it?"

Will's mother hesitated. She slowly sat back in her seat, organizing a stack of printed leaflets and leaned into her husband, who was typing away on his laptop. "Do you want to tell him?" she whispered.

His father looked up from the screen, mumbling something under his breath.

Will glanced at Madi and then back at his parents. He shifted on his feet, growing impatient. "Will somebody just tell me already!"

"We're moving," Madi blurted, swiping another cookie from the plate.

Will did a double-take. "Hold up. Tell me she's kidding. You know, end of the school year joke."

"Well," his mother began, "your father and I received a phone call last week from that independent firm we've been working with." She smiled. "It finally happened. They approved our research case; you know, the one I - we - have been working on. Can you believe it? After all this time."

Will sank into the kitchen chair. He felt the walls closing in; a claustrophobia of memories - past and present. Everything he knew; everything he held onto - his friends he finally had made; his team and coach, who made him feel important and wanted - was about to be ripped out from under him by no choice of his own.

Will rested his elbows on the table and lowered his head in his hands. "When do we leave?"

"In about a month," his mother replied.

"Just wait 'til you see the house Will," Madi said. "It's so big!"

Will glared at his parents. "You told her, but not me?"

"When we got the call," his father answered as he continued to type away on his computer in a rhythmic tapping of keys, "we weren't sure of anything; who exactly was taking on the study, where we would move, or when the funding would be distributed. It wasn't until last week that we got the go-ahead."

Will pushed himself back in the chair and sat rigid, taking in the news. His face flushed. His head began to thump. He clenched his jaw, feeling his emotions swell and morph into a white-hot rage. With both fists, he slammed them against the table and kicked back his chair, sending it crashing into the wall. "I can't believe you're doing this to me! I – " Will glowered at his parents. "As a matter of fact, I can believe it. I should have seen it coming. It's so typical of you guys. You never consider me or my feelings. You're always thinking about yourselves and her."

"Me?" Madi yelled, throwing her cookie onto the table. "What did I do?"

"Give me a break, Madi. What don't you do?"

Will's father slammed the lid of his laptop shut. "Alright. That's it; I've had about enough of you."

"The feeling's mutual, Charles," Will sneered.

The room erupted in an all-out argument.

Will's father jabbed a finger at Will, who had pushed the stack of leaflets off the table, which fluttered down like confetti to the kitchen floor. Madi stuck her tongue and grabbed a handful of the broken cookie, throwing the crumbs across the room.

"Stop," Will's mother yelled above the escalating banter. "Everybody just stop!"

The room fell silent.

Somewhere outside a neighbor's dog barked; the kitchen faucet *dripped against the porcelain sink; the doorbell rang.*

"Look," Will's mother said, taking in a deep breath. *"I know how hard this is for you, but – "*

"No, you don't," Will interrupted. *"You don't know anything about me anymore; not like you care anyway." He threw the chair into the table and then stormed out of the room, making his way up the stairs, slamming his bedroom door shut.*

| | | | | - | | | | |

Will jumped. He looked up and found Grandpa's old pickup parked on the soft shoulder of the road; its engine idling; the driver's door wide open.

"Will!" came Nana's voice as she stepped away from the truck.

Will threw the last strand of grass out of his hand and hopped down from the fence. Nana rushed to his side and hugged him tightly.

"Oh, thank God, I found you. You had me so worried." She pulled back and put his baseball hat on his head. "Come on. Let's go home."

Once on the road, the old pickup gained momentum. Its pistons clanked and popped in a rhythmic pulse. Its rusted doors and hinges squeaked with each bump in the road. Will adjusted his hat and stared out the open window. Farms, barns, hills, and valleys. As the truck passed a large wheat field adjacent to his grandparents' farm, a silhouetted figure, standing next to a lone oak tree, tipped his black, derby hat and threw Will a wave.

"Him," Will muttered, craning his neck as they drove by.

"Will? Is something wrong?" Nana asked.

"No, I – " Will turned toward the front, but not without looking back one more time. "I – I just thought I saw something, that's all."

Nana steered the truck off the road and onto the gravel driveway; its frame bouncing against its worn-out springs. She shifted the truck into park and turned off the rattling engine. Will took the door handle in his hand. "Umm . . . thanks."

"I understand how disappointed you are," Nana said.

Will met her eyes. "I don't think you do." He pushed open the door and headed toward the house.

"Will. Wait," Nana called out., chasing after him. "William. Just give me a minute. Please. I just want to talk."

Will stopped at the bottom of the porch steps, stuffing his hands into his pockets. Nana took a deep breath and adjusted a bronze chain around her neck. "Many years ago," she began, running her thumb over its round ornamental charm, "I knew someone who was just like you - lost."

"But I'm not - "

"They were angry at life," Nana went on, "devastated by an unexpected and unfortunate circumstance. It hit them hard, knocked them down, and refused to let go. They fought through a storm of anguish and pain, armoring themselves in strength. But unfortunately, it came with a price. They lost a bit of themselves in order to endure; they hardened their heart and lost sight on how to forgive." Nana took Will's hand. "You have every right to armor yourself when you must and have cause to push through the dark shadows where you can. You're tough; a fighter - always have been and always will be. But never forget where true strength lies. In here," she said, tapping his chest. "The strength of heart."

"It's not that easy," Will said.

"No one said it will or ever be," Nana said. "We all are faced with choices to make, but it's up to you - and you alone - to do with them what you will. Remember, 'nothing can get into a closed fist'." She gave Will's hand a slight squeeze and then walked up the porch steps, disappearing inside the house.

Will slumped down on the top porch step and took off his hat. He ran his hand through his hair and let out a heavy sigh. All these years – out of everyone in his life – Nana was the only one who guided him along and picked him up when he fell; she accepted him for who he was – no questions asked. So, why was he pushing her away, too?

A warm breeze of scented lavender sailed through the air. Will placed his hat on his head and leaned back on his hands. The tips of his fingers brushed against a cluster of thin grooves dug into the worn wood. He lifted his hand. Carved deep into the top step were three small capital letters; the middle letter crossed out.

W B̶ J

Chapter 7

WEDNESDAY, JULY 1, 2009

*T*he pickup slowed to a rolling stop at the entrance of the reenactment site. Will looked out the side window and watched as crowds of people from all across the country milled around the reenactors' encampments. Row after row of white canvas tents, designated for artillery, infantry, and cavalry dotted the fringes of the campgrounds. Inside two large pavilions, a group of spectators sat in white folding chairs, most likely listening to a ghostly tale of historic Gettysburg.

Off in the distance, in the middle of a large field, was a vendor area, consisting mostly of general mercantile and sutlery tents. Authors of all ages and cultures would sell their historical novels or biographical narratives. Skilled men and women would ply their needles and fashion authentically replicated Civil War period clothing and uniforms. Historical games like marbles, Jacob's ladder, and Bilbo Catcher— a wooden spindle with a ball attached to a string, entertained children of all ages. But rising above it all was the massive grandstand that faced the battlefield. Its bleachers remained empty, eagerly waiting to be filled by the thousands of spectators expected for the day.

Grandpa inched the truck forward into the parking area and stopped at the raised hand of a middle-aged man dressed in a navy-blue uniform and foraged hat. "Morning, David. Dorothy Jean," the man said, walking up to the window.

"Mr. Jacobs," Grandpa replied with a nod. "How'd you do?"

"Fine, thank you." Mr. Jacobs dug his hand into a tan, canvas sack that hung off his shoulder and handed over a few sheets of blue paper. "Here are some fliers of today's events for you folks, and if you keep going straight, then make a left at the fence, you'll see Mr. Bowman directing the cars for our infantry group."

Grandpa tipped his hat. "Sounds great! See you soon."

Mr. Jacobs returned the gesture with a smile and then moved on to the next vehicle waiting in line.

As the truck bounced over the uneven ground, Nana passed back two fliers to Will and Madi. Without so much as a glance, Will crumpled the paper into a ball and tossed it out the window and into a wired garbage can as they drove by.

The parking lot was a beehive of activity. Men, women, and children roamed the fairgrounds, displaying their patriotic pride in colors of red, white, and blue. Reenactors paraded the area in their Civil War attire of bonnets and hoop skirts, uniforms and suits. Even President Abraham Lincoln himself walked through the crowds under the watchful eyes of his secret service man – Allen Pinkerton.

Over the loudspeaker, an enthusiastic commentator broadcasted the day's events and called for all Yankees and Rebels to move to their designated units. Will leaned back on the truck, stuffing his hands in his pockets. *Today's going to be a long day.*

"Will! Hey, Will," came Madi's screeching voice.

Will looked over his shoulder and found his sister and Cassie skipping toward him, arm in arm, giggling and carrying on. Cassie smiled and threw him a wave.

"Oh, Will," Nana called out. "Would you come here, please?"

Will pushed himself off the truck and headed toward his grandmother, who was standing near the wooden fence; the girls, still giggling, followed closely behind.

"Since I know how much you enjoy participating in the reenactments," she began, "I sent Grandpa with Mr. Stevens to find you a uniform to borrow for the day. I'm sure someone here has an extra."

Will rubbed the back of his neck. Every year, the theatrical extravaganza held at Gettysburg showcased the most authentic portrayal of the war fought during those three days in 1863. For Will, all those reenacting years, alongside his grandparents – the excitement of the day, the spirit of the battles, and the emotions revealed through every reenactor – was a pastime he truly enjoyed. But that was then, not now.

"Nana, I-" Will paused. His grandmother, who stood in her signature costume; a long, chocolate brown and green plaid dress, layered petticoat, and black boots, had a small pendant in the shape of a twisted oak tree pinned to her lace collar. The morning sunlight reflected against its bronzed leaves and branches.

"Oh, look." Nana pointed. "Here they come now."

Grandpa, suited as a Union officer, was talking, walking alongside Mr. Stevens – a man with a stocky build, and who sported a prickly, overgrown brown beard that complimented his Confederate gray uniform. In his meaty hands was a smaller uniform dangling from an old wire hanger.

Will pulled at his shirt collar, already feeling the uniform's itchy wool fabric around his neck. In all the years he'd participated in the reenactments, the suffocating weight of the costume, especially in the July heat, would cause him to perspire by the bucketful.

"William, my boy. I mean Will," Grandpa said with a jolly smile. "You remember our old neighbor, Mr. Stevens? Comes all the way up from South Carolina for our great reenactment."

"Ah, yeah," Will said, extending his hand. "How are you?"

"Great actually. Perfect day for a reenactment." Mr. Stevens ignored Will's gesture and gave a heavy-handed smack on the back. "I'll say you sure have grown since I saw you last; matured actually. Ms. Dorothy Jean, what's happening to this boy?"

Nana answered with a slight giggle; her gloved hand covering her mouth.

"How old are you now, son?" Mr. Stevens asked.

Will looked away, feeling his cheeks flush with annoyance.

"You found it!" Will heard Madi shriek. He looked over at the girls and watched as Cassie pulled out a long, bronze chain from her small purse.

"I don't know, David," Mr. Stevens went on, holding up the uniform to Will's chest. "The jacket may be a bit too small."

Will moved away from his grandparents and Mr. Stevens as they debated the uniform's size and tuned in to the girls' conversation.

"Where was it?" Madi asked.

"In the toolbox," Cassie said, snapping her purse shut. "Remember, you put it in there while we were cleaning up. You must have forgotten to take it with you when Nana called you in for dinner."

"So that's where it went," Madi said. "I thought I lost it."

"Here. Put it on. That way you won't lose it again."

As Cassie placed the necklace around Madi's neck, a blast of cold wind parted the clouds and soared through the fairgrounds. It careened through the crowds and hit Will like a tidal wave, striking him with its icy energy. *Oof.*

Will buckled at the knees and braced himself against the rail fence, recoiling under the penetrating pressure and intensity that was pushing all around him. His chest began to burn (icy-hot). His heart began to race, and his body grew numb.

Will closed his eyes and gritted his teeth, fighting against the roaring gale that swarmed his body. "Nana. Madi," came his distorted cry. "Help . . . me!"

The wind stopped. The pressure ceased. The burning flame flushed away from the center of his chest. Will held his eyes shut and didn't dare move. His shallow breathing and pounding of his heart in his ears were all he could hear against the sudden eerie silence. Slowly, he let go of the fence and opened his eyes.

Everything – and everyone around him – was mysteriously warped in suspended animation. Cassie stood smiling at Madi, who looked down at the necklace in the palm of her hand; his grandparents and Mr. Stevens pointed in his direction as they sized him up for the costume. Reenactors and spectators were paused in conversation. Horses and cars were stopped in momentum. Flags and birds were stiff in flight.

Will blinked and rubbed his eyes. *What the . . .*

With slow and careful steps, he meandered through crowds. He passed the girls and his grandparents, waving his hands in front of their faces, snapping his fingers, or calling out their names. Nothing. Not a flinch or a blink of an eye. Somehow, time had stilled for everyone. Everyone that is, except for him.

Will made his way back toward Nana. A crescendoing whir – like that of a train whistle – bounced off the air. He grabbed his ears and closed his eyes, grunting under the earsplitting noise.

"Will?" came Nana's muffled voice.

The earth tilted.

Will grasped for the fence, nearly toppling to the ground. His fingers brushed against its rough top rail, and he grabbed tight.

"Will, what's wrong?" Nana asked.

The whirring noise stopped.

Will gulped in a breath, feeling his palpitations slow. With a glassy stare, he scanned the fairgrounds, searching for the source of the phenomenon. But nothing – no person, even those on mounted horses – appeared affected. They all seemed unaware of the strange ripple in time.

"Did – did you feel that?" Will muttered.

Nana stepped closer. "William. You're scaring me. Are you sure you're, okay?"

Will's eyes grew wide. He stumbled back and pointed at the lace fabric on Nana's dress. It was sticking straight up against the side of her chin. "Your – ummm – collar." He gulped down a breath. "It moved."

Nana reached to adjust the oak tree pendant but quickly pulled back her hand, feeling a sharp pinch. "Ow." A circle of blood formed on her thumb, staining her white lace glove. With a lightning thrust, she seized Will by the wrist; eyes wide. "You have to promise me something," she said.

Will was taken aback. "Promise? Promise what?"

"I need you to promise me that wherever you go today, you stay with Madi. Don't let her wander alone. Don't let her out of your sight, even for one minute. And whatever you do, don't let her talk to anyone. Do you understand?"

Will stood speechless.

Nana tightened her grip; the line of blood trailed down her glove and onto the cuff of her dress. "Do you understand?"

A rhythmic pulse thumped in Will's wrist, causing his fingers to tingle. "Yeah. Sure thing. What – whatever you want."

Nana quickly dug into her apron pocket and pulled out a small cloth change purse. "And here," she said, passing Will a fifty-dollar bill.

He put up his hands. "What? No . . . I can't take this. I mean, it's way too much."

Nana pressed the money into his palm. "Don't argue with me, and just take it. You'll . . . " She cleared her throat. "You'll need it."

Will tried to pull away, but Nana yanked him close and hugged him tightly, holding him for a silent moment. "I love you, William."

Will hesitated; he stood rigid; his arms pressed against his sides. "I – I love you, too Nana."

Nana let go and stepped back. She patted her cheeks with her gloved hands and took a deep breath, composing herself. "You'll be back. One-thirty. The artillery show."

"Yeah. We'll be there."

Will placed the bill in his front pocket and then took off in a light jog toward Madi and Cassie, who were already walking away.

"William!" Nana called out. "Whatever you do, do the right thing," she said, clutching the oak pendant pinned to her collar. "And please . . . don't ever forget!"

Chapter 8

*W*ill propped his feet on the white folding chair in front of him. For the past half hour, he sat next to Madi and Cassie amongst a crowd of Civil War enthusiasts, watching a group of reenactors present the devastating events that led up to the Battle of Gettysburg.

Will took his baseball cap out of his back pocket and shaped its brim, staring absently at the grass below his feet. He couldn't help but think back to everything that had happened - the frigid surge of wind, the stop in time, and Nana. How could it be that he was the only one who felt the anomaly? Where did it come from? And what was up with his grandmother, acting so strange?

A roll of applause rose from the audience. Will placed his hat on his head and forced himself up and on his feet. As the morning dragged on, he trailed behind the girls at a snail's pace. Lunch - courtesy of Cassie - consisted of corn dogs and warm funnel cakes sprinkled with powdered sugar. And by the early afternoon, he found himself in the activity tent, watching the girls participate in Civil War life demonstrations and play historical games like Graces — a wooden ring and stick game that he found oddly entertaining.

"Hey, Will," came Madi's screeching voice. She skipped over to her brother, who was tying his shoe. "Check out what we did while you were in the bathroom."

"Geezus Madi, what did I tell you? You can't keep running off. Nana said - "

"Relax, I'm fine. Here, take a look." Madi handed Will a photo strip of four small square pictures, showcasing both her and Cassie in a series of silly expressions.

"You can have one, Will," Cassie said with a wink.

Will handed back the photo strip. "I'm good. Thanks." He checked the time on his watch. *1:11 p.m.* "Come on, Madi. We have to go or we'll be late."

Madi shuffled her feet and kicked at the dirt path. "Well. . .I was thinking that maybe we could get our pictures taken, you know? You and me."

"Thanks, but I'll pass."

Madi took her brother by the arm. "Really quick, huh? It will be fun. I promise."

"Madi, I don't think – "

"Please."

Will rolled his eyes and looked at the passing crowd. He thought the whole idea was childish and dumb, but at that moment a faint scent of lavender hit his nose and he thought back to yesterday when Nana brought him back home. 'Nothing can get into a closed fist,' she had said. Will looked down at his smiling sister. "Oh, alright. Why not?"

"Yay." Madi clapped her hands excitedly and dragged him inside the photo booth.

The air that filled the cramped space permeated an odor of sweaty sneakers that reminded Will of the locker rooms at school. He put his hand up to his nose. "Let's hurry this up, huh, before I change my mind."

Madi took her place next to Will on a narrow metal seat and tugged the red velvet curtain shut. She quickly inserted two dollars into the machine and pushed start. The screen flashed to life. Without wasting any time, she started making funny faces. Will sat unmoved.

Madi nudged his arm. "Oh, come on. Smile."

The automated voice began to count down.

Six.

Five.

Madi furrowed her eyebrows and puffed out her cheeks.

Four.

She gave Will bunny ears.

Three.

She crossed her eyes and stuck out her tongue, touching the tip of her nose.

Two.

Will coughed, holding back from his rising laughter as he looked at Madi's contorted face.

One.

Flash . . . Flash . . .

Flash . . . Flash . . .

| | | | | - | | | | |

Cassie, who was peeking inside the photo booth, leaped back as Will and Madi shot out from behind the curtain in a burst of laughter. A few seconds later, the photo strip popped out into a metal tray.

Madi took the photo strip in her hands and snorted a laugh. "See," she said, handing it over to Will, ". . . fun, right?"

Will glanced at the four pictures and smiled. "Yeah. It was fun."

Madi slipped her arms around his waist and squeezed. "Thanks, Will. You're the best."

Will raised his eyebrows and twisted his lip. Ever-so-slowly, he wrapped his arms around her thin frame. With all that had happened over the past few years, not to mention the past few weeks, what has been broken between them somehow was restored for that brief moment.

Will looked over at Cassie and found the girl, swaying from side to side; a flirtatious smile on her face. He cleared his throat and unlocked his embrace. "Okay, okay. Nana wanted us back for the reenactment, remember? We can't be – "

At that moment, a robust and crisp breeze blew through the fairgrounds swiping Will's hat off his head. He started after it but froze. Resting up against a white fence stood a young man in a peculiar vintage costume. Small industrial gears and chains were attached to a vest underneath his long, black jacket, and a leather-bound journal was in his hand.

At first, Will didn't think anything of the stranger, until the young man placed the journal in his back pocket and set a black, derby hat atop his light brown hair. *It's him.*

The derby-clad young man adjusted his hat and then headed toward a large, cream-colored canvas tent with a nylon sign that read: *The Battle of Gettysburg and its Stories In-between.*

Will stuffed the photo strip in his front pocket, picked up his hat off the dirt path, and shadowed the young man, forgetting about Nana and the reenactment and leaving Madi and Cassie behind.

The young man picked up his pace, weaving through the crowd. He sidestepped a group of teenagers near a hotdog vendor and entered the tent. Without hesitating, Will followed. He lifted up the weighted canvas of the tent's entrance and stepped inside.

"Why, good afternoon!" came a cheery voice. "You're just in time." A middle-aged, pudgy man with splotchy red cheeks and glasses, whose lenses were as thick as bottles, stood with a broad grin on his face. His hair tucked under his smashed hat was a salt-n-pepper greasy mop, and his dirty, faded blue Civil War uniform, with its tarnished gold buttons, bulged under the pressure of his potbelly.

"Oh, I – I'm sorry," Will stuttered, feeling twenty pairs of eyes from the crowd staring at him. "I didn't mean to interrupt."

"Nonsense," the man said, pulling on his too-short sleeves that rested inches above his wrists. "The tour hasn't started yet."

"Thanks, but I should – "

"Oh no, no, no. There's always room for one more." The curator shuffled Will to the front of the group. "It sure is a hot one today," he went on. "I mean, these uniforms are the worst. It'd be nicer if we had air-conditioning, but what am I hem-hawing about? They were nice enough to install portable fans."

Will looked up at the three spinning machines that were fastened to the tent's metal skeleton.

"Those fans," the man said, pulling out a yellow-stained handkerchief from his back pocket, "they may help maintain a consistent temperature for the artifacts, but whooey, not me." The curator wiped the dripping sweat from his brow. "Leave it to the Confederates to bring the heat along with the war." The man gave a hearty laugh and elbowed Will in the ribs, throwing him sideways.

"Yeah," Will said with a half-hearted chuckle.

"Well, here you go," the curator said, handing over a folded brochure. "It maps out the display cases you'll see here. You'll also find a story about a secret sub-cultural society that was formed right here in Gettysburg just before the war broke out. Wait until you hear that one." The curator whistled through his teeth. "It's a doozy."

"Um, thanks," Will said, accepting the brochure.

The curator raised his arms and waved them over his head. "Ladies and gentlemen, if I can have your attention. Our tour is about to begin. Please do not be shy in asking any questions as we move through the tent. I encourage you – without the use of your flash – to take as many pictures as you wish. You never know . . . you might find a few extra 'ghostly subjects' in the photos." He raised an eyebrow and twisted his face into a quirky smile.

The crowd stirred in a chorus of excited chatter, reaching for their cameras and cell phones. Will scanned the faces behind him. At the back of the group, he caught sight of the young man in the derby hat, pointing forward.

"Alright ladies and gentlemen, if you'd be so kind as to follow me this way," the curator said with a wave.

As Will turned to confront the young man, the swarm of visitors forced him forward through two flags—a replicated 36-star Union banner and a 13-star Confederate – the infamous Northern Virginia battle flag. They both towered nine feet tall and were capped with shiny, brass spears. Their cotton material was swagged back and tied at the bottom, allowing the crowd to duck below their thick fabric.

Will struggled against the flow of the crowd like a fish swimming upstream to reach the young man, but with the forward momentum, he had no choice but to make his way through the first part of the tour: a narrow maze of artifacts on display.

Rectangular glass cases held various weapons, an assortment of discharged bullets, decks of cards, pans used to cook hardtack, mismatched shoes, and long-forgotten personal diary notes. Soiled with sweat, torn by strength, or stained with blood, each artifact presented the true nature of the Civil War, hinting at their untold stories.

Will continued with the movement of the crowd to a collection of grainy black-and-white photographs that hung on the sturdy canvas walls. Captivated by their history, he walked from picture to picture, transfixed by the timeless images. Field headquarters and hospitals, distended with the multitude of patients, illustrated the war's medical advances or lack thereof. Battlefields, with their horrific aftermath, showed the decomposing exteriors of departing souls. Resolute poses of soldiers and the vacant stares of the Gettysburg civilians displayed the true nature of the time.

"Ladies and gentlemen," the curator spoke up. "We are now at the last part of our tour. This way if you please."

Will followed the crowd to a large open area. Near the front of the tent sat a small, rectangular table with skinny metal legs. A bare vintage bulb spotlighted a photo album with an oak tree emblem, a leather pocket journal, a laminated newspaper clipping, a wooden picture frame with beveled glass, and a black camera with a round glass lens, three metal buttons, and a turnkey.

"Picture it," the curator began, pushing his glasses higher up on his sweaty nose.

The crowd moved closer, forming a semi-circle around Will and the table, snapping pictures and murmuring to one other.

"July 2, 1863. Total destruction all around. A haze of smoke from the days of battle seeps across the land. Two secret groups meet outside the confines of Little Round Top. Three brothers are reunited in those early morning hours. Upon their reunion, there is an exchange of words, a rise of tempers, and then . . . "The crowd fell silent and inched forward in anticipation. "BANG! Shots were fired," the curator yelled, throwing up his hands.

"Goodness me," shrieked an elderly woman with a crop of curly gray hair.

The crowd broke out in a chuckle. Will raised his eyebrows and shook his head amused.

"Now, now, now." The curator waved his hands, quieting the group. "No one really knows what actually transpired, but many believe a young man by the name of William James Parker was killed by the hands of his younger brother."

"It wasn't his younger brother," shouted a confident voice from the back of the tent.

Simultaneously, the crowd and Will turned around. Above the heads and shoulders of the audience, Will noticed the top of a black derby hat.

The curator coughed. "Excuse me, ladies and gentlemen, if I may direct your attention to this journal, you see here . . . "

As the crowd turned back toward the curator, who was holding up an old journal in a protective, plastic sleeve, Will slowly slithered through the crush of people, making his way to the young man.

"Each page inside," the curator went on, "documents the web of events that unfolded before, during, and after that fateful day. However, the ink, which is extremely faded - most likely from age and water damage – fails to point out its rightful and true owner."

"That's because part of it is written in code," the voice said again.

The curator huffed; his voice slowly rising. "Which is why many historians search for the missing clues to solve the cryptic syntax."

"Who are those people in the photograph?" a middle-aged woman in a <u>Gettysburg, Got Ghosts?</u> t-shirt asked. "And why is that young man wearing a necklace?"

Laughter rose from the crowd. Will stopped in his pursuit and shifted his position to get a better look at the photo.

The curator scratched the skin beneath his bearded chin. "Ah, yes. To answer your first question, the young man you see here in the long, navy jacket holding the rifle is indeed William Parker – the one killed by his younger brother. Now, as for the other young man and young lady pictured here, unfortunately, there has been no known records of their existence."

"Has anybody found out who they are?" the woman interjected.

"Afraid not," the curator said. "Though they are not known by name or record, legend has it that they both were a crucial part of the secret society along with William Parker."

An older man in the middle of the crowd held up the brochure. "NEE - NEEVEES?" he asked, stumbling over the word.

The curator folded his hands across his rotund belly. "One would think that is how you say it; it is, however, pronounced – "

"*Nah-vess*," Will whispered to himself as the young man in the derby hat said it loud enough for the crowd to hear.

As the words escaped Will's lips, he dropped the brochure from his hands suddenly feeling lightheaded. He threw out his arms and planted his feet firmly on the ground, steadying his woozy head.

"Watch it," barked a tall, slender man, annoyed by Will's sudden episode. He let out a huff and stepped away.

"And from what I know," continued the young man in the derby hat. "Those two individuals and the secret society you are discussing are not legend, but in fact the truth. And that, I assure you, is no necklace around William Parker's neck, but a very rare and remarkable timepiece."

"Young man," the curator said. He pushed back his sleeves and made his way through the crowd. "I don't know where you came from or who you think you are, interrupting and spouting out – "

"Facts," the young man said sharply.

"Theory," the curator shot back. "I'll have you know many historians have dedicated countless years of their lives to locate that rare and remarkable piece of history."

Historians? Will thought, regaining his balance. *Countless years?* He knew exactly who the curator was talking about – his parents, especially his mother, who for years have been chasing after stories and theories and conspiracies of the Civil War.

"But you seem to know more than all those prestigious historians combined," the curator said with a hint of jovial sarcasm. "So, do share. Enlighten us. We're all ears." The curator stopped at the back of the tent. "Young man?" He spun around. "Where'd he go?"

Will stood on the tips of his toes in an attempt to get a better look, but everyone continued to block his view.

"Amateurs," the curator said. "Well . . . " He clapped his hands. "That – ladies and gentlemen – concludes our tour. I would like to thank you for your time and attention. Enjoy the rest of your day."

A multitude of hands shot into the air with comments and questions. Will made his way to the exit but stopped short by a strange pungent odor – the scent of rotten eggs and burnt hair. He wrinkled his nose and brought his right hand to his face, trying to block the putrid smell. He looked up at the fans, thinking maybe their motors were burning, but they moved via a pulley system and somehow ran without electricity. He looked around the tent and on the ground. No garbage cans were in sight or any piles of litter that would cause the foul stench.

A faint red light glowing against the lens of the black camera caught Will's eye. With his hand still cupped against his nose, he walked up to the table. Confused, he scanned the crowd. Was it a trick? A laser pointer? Some kind of portable light? No; not a person was looking his way; not even the curator. They were all caught up in their own conversations, reading brochures, or taking pictures.

Will shrugged and started for the entrance of the tent when the photo album, with its metallic ornament of an oak tree, flipped open to an outdoor portrait of two young men standing on a staircase, poised and straight-faced. The one wore a black, derby hat and held the black camera in his hands; the other, in the long navy jacket, held a rifle and wore the timepiece around his neck.

Will leaned in closer. A chill ran down his spine, and his knees grew weak. "No. It - it can't be," he stuttered, looking at the young man in the navy jacket staring up at him from the page. He stepped back and stumbled hard into the curator.

"What in tarnation?" the man said.

Will grabbed his knees and focused on the ground, trying to steady his spinning head.

"Son? Is everything alright? You - ah - you don't look too good," the curator said.

"The - the picture - how - how can- " Will heaved in and out. He gulped down a breath and slowly looked up. Standing near the entrance to the tent was the young man in the black derby hat.

The curator stepped closer, blocking Will's view. "Is the heat getting to ya? You need the paramedics or something?" The curator faced the thinning crowd. "Anybody here a doctor?"

"I am," came a woman's voice.

A cold gust of wind ripped through the tent. It soared through the crowd and hooked Will in its icy clutch, doubling him over. "Ah," he cried. At the same moment, the young man adjusted his black, derby hat and then quickly ducked out of the tent.

Fighting through the pain, his onset of vertigo, and rising nausea, Will thrust himself against the icy current and ran after the derby-clad young man, leaving behind a bewildered curator, doctor, and crowd.

Chapter 9

Will raced down the path, weaving in and out of the throng of people. "Move. Out of my way!" He glanced over his shoulder, feeling the icy wind's tentacles nipping at his shoes and biting at his clothes.

POW. The impact nearly knocked him off his feet.

"Will!" came Madi's shrill voice. "What the heck?"

Will shook the stars out of his head and blinked a few times, finding his sister sprawled on the ground. "Watch where you're going, huh?" she yelled, rising to her feet.

Will coughed, catching his breath. He looked back at the tent. A few spectators were exiting, shaking their heads and murmuring to one another as they walked by.

Madi stormed over to her brother, rubbing her bruised elbows. "What's your problem, huh?" She squatted down in front of him. "Hey, you okay? You sick or somethin'?"

"No. It's ah . . . it's nothing," Will said, drying the bridge of his sweaty nose with the bottom of his t-shirt.

"You sure? Because – "

"I'm fine," he snapped. "Alright?"

"Geez. Sorry, I asked," Madi mumbled. She reached around her neck and fixed the bronze chain of the oak tree medallion.

A reverberation of cannon blasts echoed off the terrain. Billows of white smoke rose above the grandstand and touched the sky. "Perfect," Will moaned. "The reenactment started. Let's go, Madi."

Together, they walked in silence, heading toward the battlefield. The quiet gave Will time to think. He took off his hat and rubbed his forehead, trying to make heads or tails of each bizarre anomaly – the reappearance of the young man in the black, derby hat, the sharp and

J . B . P i e r c e

rancid smell, the unexplainable photograph, and the sudden gust of cold wind that, once again, only he could feel.

Will stopped in mid-stride. "Wait a second. Where's Cass – " He turned to talk to Madi but found her standing alone in the middle of the dirt path, staring at the adjacent tree line. "What now?" he asked, coming up beside her.

A round of gunfire popped in the air. Madi pointed. "That."

Will followed the direction of her finger. Stretching out and away from the main path was an abandoned, dirt trail. Towers of oak trees lined its narrow path while a canopy of thick foliage and vines created a mesh of hazy shadows. Broken tree limbs and withered leaves dotted the untraveled ground like confetti. It wasn't the trail that struck Will odd but the wooden table in the middle of the path piled high with a hodgepodge of antiques and collectibles.

Madi started forward. "I want to go look."

Will latched onto her arm and pulled back. "I don't think so."

"Come on. I'll only be a minute. I promise."

"No. We're leaving. Nana and Grandpa are going to wonder where we are."

A faint rumble of thunder thrummed in the distance as Madi continued on with her pathetic protest. Will looked up. A shelf of greyish, green clouds were rolling in from the west. They crept across the landscape like a giant blob, swallowing every inch of the blue sky.

"You know what? Fine," he said, letting go of Madi's arm. "Do whatever you want. Not like you listen to me anyway. I'll see you back at the reenactment."

Will started to walk away but quickly glanced down the path. The derby-clad young man was standing behind the wooden table. At that moment, Nana's words replayed in his head. *I need you to promise me that wherever you go today, you stay with Madi.*

Will looked at his sister as she stepped onto the dirt trail. "No, Madi. Stop."

The young man in the black, derby hat adjusted the lapel of his black jacket and took off, disappearing into a rising fog that began to consume Madi, the path, and its thick foliage.

Will crossed onto the secluded trail and stumbled on his feet, narrowly falling to the ground as his body collided with an invisible wall of wind and ice. It numbed his fingers and toes and shrouded his arms and legs. All around, the towering trees, with their thick and dense branches, groaned in pain with each wave of cold wind.

Will hugged himself tight, trying to control his shivering body. He craned his neck, struggling against the stinging gale, and looked back toward the fairgrounds. "H-h-help!" he called out to the few people that walked by. "H-h-help m-m-me." No matter how loud he screamed, no one seemed to hear his pleas.

Will staggered forward. He reached out a trembling hand. As his fingertips hit where the trail began and fairgrounds ended, the air rippled like skipping stones on a vertical pond, creating small circles as it bounces across a calm lake. Will's eyes grew wide. Somehow, the trail had magically transformed into a two-way mirror, and he couldn't get out.

"M-M-Madi . . . " Will said; his breath a cloud of frosty dew. "I think we sh-should get out of here; something's not right." He turned back around to find her at the wooden table, rummaging through a pile of tarnished and rusty memorabilia. "M-M-Madi. Do y-you hear mm-me?"

Will came up behind his sister and lifted his trembling hand. As his fingers brushed against her arm, a blast of cold energy shot down from the trees, spearing his entire body. The force traversed from the top of his head and ended at the tips of his toes, rooting his legs to the ground; his hand hovering near her shoulder.

Madi picked up a black, rectangular box and stepped back from the table, bumping into Will's outstretched hand. She turned around and curled her lip. "Ummm, why are you standing like that?"

Will couldn't move; couldn't answer. With an exasperated huff, Madi took his hand and pushed it down. A surge of warmth washed over his body. His temperature rose; his muscles relaxed, and he could move once again.

"I don't know what's up with you," Madi said, letting go of his hand. "But you're acting really weird."

Will ripped off his baseball hat and threw it to the ground. He slumped against an oak tree and breathed in deep.

Get it together, Will. You can fight this.

A stream of sulfur entered his nose and tingled the inside of his nostrils. Will coughed, choking on the putrid scent. He bent down to retrieve his hat and froze. A pair of wrinkled feet cupped inside a pair of toeless and worn-out boots stood at the edge of the woods. Wide-eyed, Will slowly stood up.

A tall and menacing stranger emerged from the towering trees. He wore a long, black cape on his bony shoulders. His tattered brown pants were singed with holes and frayed at the seams. His thin neck was wrapped tight in a high collar, which was decorated with two, small metal gears, and a brown hood with a transparent, black mask concealed most of his scarred face.

The man leaned forward, rubbing his chin with his bony hand. "I know you," he said in a drawn-out, monotone voice.

Will recoiled at the sight of the man's hollow eyes.

"Okay, we can go now," Madi said, stepping away from the table. "It's nothing but a bunch of junk, anyway."

"Why hello, Madilyn," the man said.

Madi swallowed hard and stepped closer to her brother.

"Ah, yes," the man said. He coughed, breaking up a pool of mucus in his lungs. "Now, I know who you are. I knew you looked familiar." A sly grin formed on his face. He leaned in close to Will and whispered, "Hello, William."

Shocked, Madi looked at her brother and then at the stranger.

"That's pretty cool, mister. What are you, some type of magician or something? How'd you know our names?"

The man cackled and clapped his hands together amused. A bright, white flash sparked in the distance.

Will watched as the electrical impulse of light ping-ponged at hypersonic speed through the canopy of tree branches that loomed overhead. He closed his eyes and grabbed his temples, grunting from a low, explosive surge of energy that resounded and pierced his ears.

Will gritted his teeth and fought hard against the unearthly power, struggling to reach Madi's hand. When their fingers met, he latched on and quickly pulled her away.

"What's your hurry, William?" the sinister stranger asked, suddenly blocking their way.

"Move," Will demanded.

"I see we got off on the wrong foot. Let's start again, shall we?" The man straightened his crooked body in a popping melody of cracking bones. He slowly drew out his right hand from underneath his cape. "The name is Fink."

Will ignored Fink's outstretched hand and started back down the path. "Will," Madi shrieked as she was towed along. "Where are we going?"

"What's it look like?" he puffed. "I'm getting us out of here."

"Why?"

Will slid to a stop. "Take a look around you," he said, throwing out his hands. "I don't know what's going on or who that guy is back there, but everything about this place is just wrong."

"Oh, c'mon," Madi said. "So, the guy's a little creepy."

Will coughed a laugh. "A little creepy? And this is coming from someone who is afraid of a little storm."

A crack of thunder rumbled above the trees. Madi recoiled against the sound. "My point exactly," Will said. He looked toward the fairgrounds.

Beyond the threshold of the trail, the once bright and yellow hue of daylight grew to an unhealthy shade of green. Crowds, huddling in one another's arms, rushed by in haste. In the intensifying wind, vendors covered and tied down personal effects.

Lightning flashed. Thunder clapped. Trees that lined the dirt trail shook and began to sway. Leaves ruffled against the torrent of wind and quivered in its wake. At the end of the trail, two large oak trees simultaneously wilted and folded into one another, barricading their only way out.

"What the – "Will let go of Madi's hand. "See. This is what I'm talking about. How can this even be happening?" He looked back at his sister, who stared blankly back at him. "Madi? Are you even listening to me?"

Somewhere in the wake of the storm, a faint serenade of a woman's voice, with its soft tone and rich melody, floated in on the cusp of the wind and hit Will's ears.

Out of the darkness, down from the stars,
Your light guides me both near and far.
Through storm and rain, by land or sea,
I shall never fear when I follow thee.

"Wait a second," Will said. "That song. I – I've heard it before."

A warm breeze blew down through the woods and wrapped him in a scent of rich lavender. Will breathed in deep. He hummed along with the continuous tune, searching the trees for the source of the sonorous voice. "You hear that, don't you, Madi?"

Will spun around and found her slowly walking back toward Fink, who was standing in the middle of the path raising and lowering his hands as if orchestrating the symphony of swaying trees.

"Madi?" Will fought to push the sweet-sounding aria out of his head. He ran after her and reached for her hand but immediately pulled back as an icy bite shocked his skin. "Ow," he yelled, shaking out his throbbing hand.

The hypnotic melody continued to float in the air, luring Madi closer and closer to Fink. Will covered his ears, trying to muffle the song that repeated over and over in his head. "Madi. It's the song. Don't listen to it! The song!"

Fighting through the force, Will threw out his left hand, reaching for her shoulder. Fink flicked his eyes up, raised his right arm, and snapped open his hand. An emission of white light shot out from his palm, sending a jagged spear of lightning straight to Will's chest.

The last thing Will felt before Fink had Madi in his wicked hands was the back of her tank top slipping out of his fingers.

Chapter 10

*A*bove the trees, lightning pulsed like a heartbeat. A percussion of thunder ticked like a metronome, keeping time with the continuous melody playing from the trees. The fog dispersed amongst the trees and sent a wave of misty air down the path, whipping strands of Madi's hair across her face.

"Hello, child," Fink said warmly.

Madi blinked and tucked the loose pieces of hair behind her ear. "Hello, Mr. Fink."

Fink brought his hands together, each fingertip lightly touching the other. "I see that you have found what I've been searching for."

Madi followed Fink's ravenous stare to the necklace around her neck. She placed its bronzed, oak tree medallion in her hand. "This?"

"Why yes. Open it child and see for yourself."

Madi hesitated.

"Don't be afraid," Fink said. "You'll find it simply fascinating."

Timidly, Madi pushed down on the medallion's top button, popping it open with a *click*. Inside was a beautiful and unique face of a watch, unlike anything she had ever seen. And though its primary face displayed the numbers 1 - 12, the watch had an additional three small-scale clocks; their numbers ranging from 0 - 9 on the first two clocks and 01 - 24 on the third. A separate square sat in the middle of the watch with an analog number in its box.

"What does it do?" Madi asked.

"Do you see those three tiny buttons, key, and toggle gear on its bronzed band?" Fink indicated.

Madi turned the medallion on its side and nodded.

"Working together, they each do something quite *incredible*." Fink curled his lips in a ghoulish grin. "Give 'em a try?"

"Ummm – I don't think I should," Madi said.

"Oh, go on," Fink urged. "It won't hurt you."

Slowly, Madi pushed down on each of the three buttons, turned the key slightly, and toggled the gear. Mesmerized, she watched as each individual clock on the watch advanced their hands to a different number. The analog number in the square box flipped last. She looked up at Fink. "They moved," she whispered.

Fink smiled with icy satisfaction. A brilliant flash of lightning wove through the looming clouds and crashed down to the ground.

Madi released the necklace and covered her ears. Her legs trembled with the thunder that vibrated the earth. Through the fading quake, she could hear a faint call of her name.

Will.

"Is something wrong, Madilyn?" Fink asked.

Madi snapped the medallion shut. "I . . . ah . . . I gotta go."

"Oh, Madilyn," Fink called out as she started to walk away.

Madi stopped and watched as Fink glided across the ground; his cape and brown cloak skirting just above the dirt. He hovered in front of her and extended his bony hand that was jeweled with a tarnished, bronze ring in the shape of a skull. Its ruby eyes twinkled against the lightning and winked at Madi. "It was a pleasure to finally make your acquaintance," he said, slipping her small hand in his.

"Ow." Madi pulled back her hand. "What – what did you do?"

Fink bowed his head. "My apologies. It was not my intention to shock you."

Madi raised her trembling hand in front of her face. Her fingertips pulsated like a second heartbeat, and they burned as if prodded by hundreds of tiny electrified needles. She curled her fingers into her palms and held them close to her chest. "Get – get away from me."

"If you would be so kind and forgive me."

"No," Madi whimpered. "Leave me alone."

J.B. Pierce

Fink dug into his cloak and pulled out a black, rectangular object. It had three metal buttons — one on its side; the other two on its top. A thin silver latch that resembled a winding key from a music box sat near the back, and on its front, directly in the middle, was a circular piece of glass partially hidden by an oval shutter.

Madi sniffled and shyly moved closer. "What's that?"

"Why a camera," Fink said.

Madi wiped her dripping nose with the back of her hand. "I've never seen a camera like that before."

"That's because this is no *ordinary* camera, my dear," Fink said as he slowly slid his hands over its three metal buttons and latchkey. "It's actually quite extraordinary."

"What's that supposed to mean?"

Fink leaned into her ear. "Would you like to find out?"

The wind returned and whistled through the trees. The branches bowed and strummed against each other in a legato chorus, repeating the hypnotical melody.

Spellbound, Madi uncurled her aching fingers and accepted Fink's camera. As it hit the palm of her hand, a current of liquid crystal seeped out of its leather seams and began to coat her fingers. Madi inhaled sharply and held her breath. "What - what's happening to me?"

The frost traveled from her hands, over her wrists, and up her arms, stopping at her neckline. The opaque resin below the oak tree medallion began to churn in an earthy-colored cyclone, draping Madi in an amber glow. She tried to drop the camera and run - run far, far away from Mr. Fink and this place, but the cold quickly stiffened her body, holding her captive.

"It works," Fink cackled with sheer delight. "After all this time, it still works."

"Please," Madi begged. "Please make it stop."

Fink floated in front of Madi and cupped his scarred and

74

blistered fingers around her hands. He held tight and looked deep into her frightened, blue eyes.

> *"Now listen, my child, and hear me well,*
> *for all that I am about to tell.*
> *The secret has been buried, but as you can see,*
> *by the hands of time, Madilyn, you now hold the key."*

"Take it back," Madi demanded, withering in his hold. "I don't want your camera. Just – just let me go."

Fink narrowed his gaze. "I'm afraid it's too late, my dear."

An abrupt burst of light cut through the trees, singeing Madi's vision. Fink let go of her hands and righted his crooked frame. The wind surged in a roaring cyclone, and the music swelled in a musical romp. Over and over, his black cape wound itself in a heap of fabric around his skeletal frame. A rush of wind parted the trees and then engulfed Fink in an upward cyclone of dust and pebbles.

A flash of lightning speared the earth.

Madi pinched her eyes shut and screamed Will's name against the puncturing voltage.

Chapter 11

rilliant beams of light flashed through the black clouds and crashed to the earth, shooting fiery, iridescent icicles up and into the air. The torrent of wind whipped at the trees and washed over the ground, scooping up fragments of dirt and leaves.

At the end of the path, Will strained to see through the sleeting soil. No more than ten yards away, he found Madi immersed in a glowing amber sphere.

Will grunted and groaned, fighting against the spectral force that held him hostage, trying with all his might to break free.

"Well, well, well," came Fink's ominous voice out of the gale. His blurred figure pushed through the electrical storm; his black cape flapping wildly in the wind. "Looks like you got yourself in a real jam there, William."

Will looked down. A whirlpool of earthly powder swirled around his feet and rose with each rotation. It was unthinkable; he was sinking.

"Stop whatever it is that you are doing, and let me go," Will demanded.

"I could if I wanted to," Fink said as he circled Will like a hungry lion eyeing his prey. "But, then again, why would I?"

"Who are you? And what do you want from us?"

A wicked glow lit Fink's shrouded face. He chortled in a loud, baritone voice. "I – I can't help but be amused, William; I thought you, of all people, would have seen through the illusion by now."

Will furrowed his brow. "Illusion? What illusion?"

Fink opened his arms wide and calmed the tempest with a simple gesture of his hands. He toyed with the skull ring on his index finger and shifted his eyes up to Will. "The illusion of your life."

A flash of lightning split through the trees. The earth rumbled underneath Will's feet, scattering the rising dirt. Like an unstrung puppet, he collapsed hard to the ground in a puff of choking dust.

Will heaved in and out. His face flushed and a rush of adrenaline spiked through his veins, hearing Fink's rising cackle. Will narrowed his eyes and dug his fingers into the dirt. A knobby tree branch jutting out from the edge of the path hit his palm. Keeping his eyes on Fink, he tightened his grip around the branch and sprang forward.

Fink whipped around. "Not so fast."

With commanding power, Fink thrust his hands up then outward, sending a gust of cold wind down from the trees. Will fell back from the blast and cowered against a giant oak tree.

"What did you honestly think you were going to do?" Fink sneered, drifting across the ground in a towering rage. "Hurt me?" He extended his right arm toward the woods, curled his fingers into a fist, and pulled. A thick vine spiraled out from the foliage and like a snake, coiled itself around Will's neck, hanging him high.

"P – put me down," Will gasped, clawing at the vine. "I can't – I can't breathe." He coughed and blinked. The path, the trees, even Madi faded behind the splashes of black spots that painted his vision. "I'll – I'll do whatever it is you need me to do. Just – just let us go."

A narrow-lipped smile slowly formed on Fink's face. "Of course, you will," he said. "And do you know why?"

Will shook his head, struggling to breathe.

"You think you're a fighter," Fink began, "but in truth," he relaxed his fingers and opened his clenched fist.; the vine unwound itself, dropping Will harshly to the ground. "you're weak."

Will grappled at his aching neck. "Why . . . why are you doing this?"

Fink unrolled his skeletal arm, revealing a pile of powdery dust sitting in his palm in the shape of a knotted oak tree.

"Long, long ago, cast down by the stars.
An enchanting piece of time fell from afar.
It merged three lives and rooted them through
Bonds of brotherhood and trust that developed their view."

A beam of sunlight sliced through the trees and divided the darkness of the dirt trail, illuminating Fink in a sphere of light.

"I was basking in the spotlight; reciting sonatas of words.
Until the curtain fell and my voice ceased to be heard."

"What are you even saying," Will said, shielding his eyes from the intense light.

"You were the voice; the warrior to call.
You set it in motion and started it all."

"Me?" Will said. "You're crazy."

Fink twisted his fingers. The powder swirled in his hands, transforming the figment of the oak tree into the camera.

"There is no turning back; the prophecy has come to pass.
For the time is now William; you were found at last!"

Fink smacked his hands together, smothering the dust. He shot up into the air with the sound of a sonic boom, spawning a tremoring wave of dirt and debris.

Will scrambled to his feet and took off, running toward Madi. He stole a glance over his shoulder and found Fink's earthly tsunami gaining momentum.

Will propelled himself forward; his determination to reach his sister shifted into overdrive. As he reached for her hand, the wave of soil bit at the soles of his sneakers and grabbed at his heels, twisting his feet out from under him. His knees hit the packed earth first, then his shoulders, and then the side of his head.

The last thing Will saw before everything went black was the terror on Madi's face.

Chapter 12

The bump in the road woke Will with a start. He sat up dazed; lethargic. He winced; what a headache. A droplet of water fell onto his right hand, tickling his skin. His hair was saturated, and his hat was missing. Even his shorts and t-shirt were soaked through and clung to his skin. A shiver ran down his spine.

Will wiped the lingering moisture from his face. *What happened?*

Three repetitive drawn-out tones, followed by a computer-generated voice hit his ears. The National Weather Service in Adams County Pennsylvania has issued a severe thunderstorm warning for . . .

"Can you believe this?" Will heard Nana say as she turned up the truck's radio.

. . . at 2:48 p.m. Eastern Daylight Time, the National Weather Service Doppler radar indicated a severe thunderstorm capable of producing quarter-sized hail and damaging winds in excess of . . .

"It's okay, Dorothy Jean," Grandpa said. "We're almost home."

"I know. It just reminds me of – "

"I know, I know," Grandpa soothed, patting her hand.

Will looked over at Madi, who was staring out the truck's side window. Her leg bounced rapidly, and her fingers were wrapped tightly around the straps of her bookbag, turning her knuckles white.

"Hey," Will whispered, pushing down on her bouncing leg.

Madi jumped at his touch.

"What's going on? How did we get here?"

Madi offered up a blank look from behind her tangled and soggy hair and shrugged her shoulders before looking back out the side window.

Will sat back and ran his hand through his wet hair. *What the heck is going on?*

| | | | | - | | | | |

The usual twenty-minute ride home took nearly an hour. High above the passing trees, thick thunderclouds wrestled in a swarming heap. Jagged bolts of lightning lit up the raging sky like lightsabers in battle. Giant globs of rain assaulted the truck, bursting like water balloons upon impact. Small creeks crested and turned roads into rushing rivers. Broken tree branches and fallen debris turned the asphalt into sooty ponds.

Will looked up at the sky. Everywhere Grandpa guided the truck, the storm seemed to follow them home like a relentless serpent.

"David! Watch out!" Nana yelled.

Grandpa gripped the steering wheel and slammed on the brakes. Nana reached for the dash. Madi screamed as the truck fishtailed and slid across the water-logged road. Will grabbed onto the headrest and stared – wide-eyed – through the windshield as the white fence that lined the entrance to the driveway came up fast. He closed his eyes and braced himself for impact. At the last second, the big tires gained traction and bit at the road, jolting the truck to a stop.

The wipers swished across the windshield, pushing away the pinging rain. Will opened his eyes and slumped back into his seat, placing his hand on his chest. In the stunned silence, he looked out the windshield. Illuminated by the beam of the headlights, he saw the same young man in the black, derby hat from the fair standing in the pouring rain.

The two locked eyes.

Will grabbed the door handle and jumped out. "Hey," he shouted through the blowing rain. "What's your deal, man?"

"Will?" Nana said, rolling down her window. "Where are you going? Get back in the truck."

The young man adjusted his black, derby hat and then took off down the gravel driveway, running toward the house.

"Hey! I'm talking to you," Will yelled, rushing toward the front of the truck.

Nana turned toward her husband. "David. Stop him."

Grandpa put the truck in park and whipped open the door. "Will? Son? Get back inside."

A sharp crack snapped through the storm. Will looked up and watched in horror as one of the oldest oak trees that lined the driveway split down the center of its trunk. The tree creaked and leaned, teetering on its round massive base. "Watch out!"

Will seized Grandpa by the shoulders and pulled him out of the way and onto the grass as the two-hundred-year-old oak slammed to the ground.

Lightning flashed. Thunder crashed, and with that, the storm stopped.

Nana jumped out of the truck. "David! Will!"

Madi quickly followed.

Will slowly stood up and helped Grandpa to his feet.

"Are you two, okay?" Nana asked.

Will surveyed the scene. Thick branches clogged the entire span of the driveway with shattered limbs and scattered leaves. Shards of bark protruded in all directions from the massive base, creating a deadly ring of impaling swords.

"We're - we're okay, Dorothy Jean," Grandpa said, wiping the mud off his Civil War uniform.

"Will?" she asked.

"Yeah," he answered, staring down the driveway toward the house. "I'm okay."

Strange as it was, if it weren't for the young man in the black, derby hat jumping in front of the truck, causing Grandpa to slam on the brakes, the tree would have fallen on the truck's roof and crushed them all.

"I don't think I'll be moving this anytime soon," Grandpa said, rubbing the back of his neck. "At least not tonight."

"Well," Nana began, "let's get inside before the rain starts again, shall we?"

The four made their way down the long driveway to the house. When they reached the porch steps, the telephone rang. Nana quickly unlocked the front door and rushed inside.

A shrill whinny resonated out from the barn.

"David," Nana said from behind the screen door. "Mr. Stevens is on the phone. He asked if you needed help with the tree."

Surprised, Will looked at Nana and then over at his grandfather.

"Now, that's strange," Grandpa replied, walking into the house. "How would he – "

Another whinny split through the air.

"Misty," Madi said. She took Will by the arm and pulled him around the side of the house and to the edge of the back porch. "She's afraid. The storm must have scared her."

Will shrugged out of Madi's hold. He looked past the apricot trees and over at the barn. "I'm sure she's . . ." Off in the distance the young man in the black, derby hat sprinted across the open field and disappeared inside. Will clenched his fists.

Him!

Another whinny. Louder this time.

"Misty!" Madi yelled. "I'm coming, girl." With her book bag in tow, she ran down the steps of the porch and over to the barn.

A bolt of lightning set fire to the sky, illuminating the landscape beyond the fields. Enormous thunderclouds changed the remaining threads of daylight into a murky green. Will took off after Madi but stopped in his tracks. His stomach knotted. His breath quickened.

Just beyond the clubhouse stood a tall, ominous man; his black cape flapping in the torrent of wind.

No. It can't be.

Will didn't know how, but Fink had found them.

"Madi," Will yelled. "We have to get to the house. Now." As he turned toward the barn, a cold rush of air looped around his neck and yanked him to the ground, nearly cracking his spine.

Fink stepped out from the trees, chortling together with the symphony of the thunder. He raised his hand toward the clouds and propelled himself upwards. Little by little, he grew, sprouting taller than the trees. His arms and hands became sharp streaks of lightning, and his legs turned into violent vortexes of dirt and debris.

Will rolled over and stared in stark terror – his body and senses numbed – as Fink marched forward.

The multitude of trees that lined the farm hung their crowns, bowing to Fink's commanding power. Their branches snapped off their trunks and plummeted to the ground in a synchronized, cascading thud. Leaves were plucked like rose petals and swirled aimlessly around the grass caught up in his cyclonic legs.

Will coughed, choking on the shredded particles that rained down from the sky and covered him in a cloud of heavy dust.

Fink threw back his head and cackled in the midst of Will's asphyxiation. "What's the problem, William?" his voice boomed.

Will scrambled to his feet and raced toward the barn. A droning noise like that of a locomotive hit his ears. He turned toward the sound; his face fell and his eyes grew wide. "Oh my god."

An earthly blizzard of grass, bark, and hay consumed the sky. Sparks of lightning traversed away from Fink's skeletal tendril hands and ignited the clouds. A spear of light, brighter than the sun, struck the earth and bit the ground, throwing dirt and rocks into the air in an explosion of thunder. A torrent of cold wind tore through the farm, ripping a barn shutter off of its metal anchor.

Will covered his head and cowered to the ground as the shutter sailed into the sky and then crashed through the barn's thin roof.

"Nana! Grandpa!" Madi screamed, running out of the barn. "Will!"

Hearing his name, Will jumped into action. He ran over to his sister and latched onto her arm. "We have to get inside," he warned, closing the barn's first door.

"I thought the storm was over!" Madi yelled; her hair flailing about with the wind.

"It's not."

Will rushed to the second door and pulled. Stuck. He tried again and again but to no avail; something was holding it back. Will fell to his knees and noticed one of the door's exterior metal locking latches was bent in half and jammed deep into the mud. Frantically, he searched the saturated ground and came up with a sharp stone that littered the grass.

"It's a tornado," Madi panicked as Will dug away at the earth.

Will looked over his shoulder. Fink and his storm were gaining ground. Faster he dug, scooping and flinging the soil aside. Finally, the door broke free and swung open in the wind.

Will grabbed Madi by the shoulders and pushed her inside the barn. "I want to go to the house," she cried.

Using both hands, Will grabbed the door and pulled, fighting hard against the howling gale. *Come on you stupid* – With one last strain of muscle, the door closed.

Will slid the emergency metal latch into place and secured the lock. He took Madi by the arm and dragged her to the center of the barn away from the doors. "We – we shouldn't be in here," she protested. "We should be in the house; down in the basement."

"There isn't time," Will explained.

A bolt of lightning struck the ground outside the barn; its fiery bones flooded the gloomy inside with its light. A crackling explosion boomed. Madi screamed and cowered into Will's arm. The boards beneath their feet vibrated as the thunder rolled in waves. Misty paced inside her stall and whinnied along with the cows, who mooed their distress.

Then, everything went silent.

Madi opened her eyes. She loosened her grasp on Will's arm. "Is – is it over?"

Will walked over to the gaping hole in the roof where the shutter smashed through and looked up. A ball of ice fell from the sky and whizzed past his face, shattering like a glass bulb on the wooden floor. The walls of the barn began to rattle like an earthquake, shuttering the boards and beams. Sporadic plopping sounds tapped on the rooftop.

"I'm going to the house," Madi said. She marched over to the barn doors and reached for the latch. "And no storm or you can stop me."

Will felt the hair on the back of his neck stand straight. He turned around and watched as the ravaging storm punctured through the barn with a *bang*, plucking Madi off the ground and tossing her hard on the wooden floor.

Chapter 13

"Madi!"

Through the dense gale, Will could see his little sister struggling to get up. Gritting his teeth, he shielded his eyes with his arm and forced himself straight through the swirling, blinding squall. The deafening wind whipped at his clothes and thrummed in his ears. Loose pieces of hay pricked like needles and sliced his skin, burning the surface of his face, arms, and legs. He winced through the pain but foraged on.

"Madi! Give me your hand!" he yelled.

A collection of dirt and hay entered Will's mouth, causing him to gag. He coughed up the gritty phlegm and spat it out on the floor.

"I . . . I can't," she cried through the whirlwind of debris.

Will covered his mouth with his shirt and extended his arm into the lashing barrage. "Yes, you can! Now, come on!"

Madi raised a trembling arm. She strained against the pressure of Fink's storm and searched for Will's outstretched hand. As their fingers met, a monstrous roar shook the barn, shifting the floor. Will stumbled back, losing Madi in the turbulent storm.

Fink floated through the two open barn doors and landed in a helix of black and brown fabric. Electrical impulses of light sparked in an upward shower behind him. He raised a spiny hand and threw a stream of fiber-optic light straight toward Madi. She screamed against its shock and, like a rag doll, collapsed to the barn floor, vanishing amongst the spinning debris.

"NO," Will bellowed. He glared at Fink. "Get away from her you creep."

"What did you call me?" Fink asked. He caught two handfuls of the swirling dirt and pitched it at Will.

Will ran to the back of the barn, tripping on his feet as the debris rushed toward him. He fell against Grandpa's workbench and closed his eyes, preparing himself for the atomic wave that was about to bury him alive.

"Get back!" a strident voice ordered through the thunderous slosh.

Will opened his eyes to find the young man in the black, derby hat, blocking Fink's violent wind and debris with a circular, metal shield that fanned out from the center of a leather arm cuff.

"You?" Fink roared.

The young man gave a smug smile. "Surprise."

With an ear-piercing howl, Fink snatched the end of his black cape and folded himself in its fabric. A cluster of electrical tentacles mushroomed his warped form, and he and his storm retreated out of the barn, slamming the doors shut.

In the sudden calm, Will watched as the young man pressed the center button on his shield, retracting the metal armor back into the cuff. He dug into his jacket and handed over a similar arm cuff to Will. "Quick. Put it on," the young man instructed.

Will furrowed his brow. "What?"

"Slip it over your wrist, press N - E - V - E - S, then brace yourself."

Will stared down at the silver metal cuff. Its faceplate resembled a compass engraved with three of the four cardinal directions: north, east, and south. West had been replaced with the capital letter V.

Will threw the cuff to the ground and grabbed the young man by the jacket. "Who are you? And why do you keep following me?"

"Please. William. You must remain calm."

Will let go of the young man and took a cautious step back. "How do you know my name?"

A low baritone hum cut through the silence. Will buckled over and grabbed his ears as its deep reverberation bounced remnants of

Fink's storm against the wooden floor like kernels of popcorn.

"What's going on?" Will asked the young man, who seemed unaffected by the booming noise.

The sound crescendoed three octaves to a sustained drone. Like a cork under pressure, the barn doors and stalls and all its windows exploded out of their frames against the ear-splitting timbre. Wood chips turned to flaming embers. Shards of glass sprayed in all directions in mini, star-like flares.

Instant combustion.

"We've got to get out of here!" Will said in a panic as Misty and the cows ran out of the burning barn.

The young man knelt back down next to Madi. He placed the oak tree medallion in his hand and popped open its cover. "Everything is quite alright, William. Trust me."

"Trust you? I – " Will coughed into his sleeve from the dust and smoke. "I don't even know you!"

The young man looked up and smiled. "It's me, Eldon."

A rushing river of rocks, mud, and grass cascaded over the broken window frames from the outside and slid down the barn walls in a stream of earthly molasses. It hit the floor and then inched its way forward, rolling through the growing flames.

Will took Eldon by the arm and pointed. "What is *that*?"

"Fink. I'd thought we'd have more time."

"What do you mean, Fink? How is that even possible?"

Eldon closed the medallion. He rose to his feet and pulled Will over to an empty stall. "Fink thinks he can hurt us, but he can't . . . well, not technically, anyhow."

"What do you mean, not technically?"

"Long story."

"Look, buddy," Will said. "I don't know what game you're playing, but in case you haven't noticed – "

"Fink may have the upper hand this time around," Eldon

interrupted. "He may even think he's going to win this battle – "

"Battle? This is insane," Will said, running both hands through his hair. "No. You're insane. I'm getting my sister and getting us the hell out of here."

"Wait," Eldon said, seizing Will by the arm. "There's no time to explain everything now, and I apologize for that. But you must listen to me and listen to me clearly. When the time comes – and you'll know when – run, and I mean *run* straight toward Madilyn. Don't stop until you have a hold on her and hold on tight no matter what. That's the only way it will work." Eldon let go of Will's arm and headed for the barn doors.

"What do you mean work?" Will shouted.

Eldon pointed at Madi. "Run, grab on, and don't let go."

A crack of kindling. A dancing pulse of light.

Will looked behind him. Rows of fierce flames licked the walls and webbed its blaze around the support beams of the barn, sending pieces of wood falling to the floor. The seeping current of rocks, mud, and grass slithered its way up and through Grandpa's John Deere. It glided off the seat and filtered itself through the tractor's front grill, gelling in the tall shape of Fink.

"You got to be kidding me?" Will muttered.

Eyes glowing, Fink stepped out of the roaring flames and stretched out his long, congealed arm toward the front of the barn.

"Eldon, look out!" Will yelled.

Fink clamped onto the back of Eldon's jacket with his gnarly hand and tossed him into a stack of smoldering hay.

Will wheeled around. "You son-of-a-"

Fink lifted his hand and propelled a thin strand of debris across the barn, scraping Will's forearm like sandpaper. "What were you thinking, William?" he said. "That you honestly were going to beat me . . . win?"

Will bit his bottom lip and grabbed his stinging arm. Beneath his trembling hand, a thin line of blood seeped between his fingers.

"I've been waiting years for this very moment," Fink said.

Through a mounting wall of fire and sparks, Will saw the leather arm cuff Eldon gave him lying in the middle of the barn. He looked at Fink and then at the cuff. He could make it.

With a silent count to three, Will rushed past Fink. He leaped over the small flames and slid across the floor, snatching up the cuff.

"Get back here!" Fink roared.

Will jumped to his feet and fumbled with the cuff, fighting through the burning pain in his arm. He looked over his shoulder and found Fink floating through the mounting flames. It was unbelievable; nothing was slowing him down.

The cuff clicked into place. Will pressed each letter in sequence. *N - E - S - V.* Nothing. *E - N - V - S.* "Come on. Think."

What did Eldon say?

Will glanced over at Fink, who was rising like a cobra above the flames, ready to strike. Suddenly, Eldon's words echoed in Will's head.

NEVES.N - E - V - E.

"S," he said out loud, pressing the last letter on the cuff.

With a sharp click, the cuff fanned open one section at a time, snapping quickly into a round, metal shield - three feet in diameter. Will spun around and raised his weighted arm just as Fink struck down with his surge of debris. Like a rushing waterfall, the current fell over the sides, disappearing into the thin space between the floorboards.

Will grunted against its driving force - the soles of his sneakers slowly sliding across the floor - as it pushed him into Misty's empty stall.

Fink retreated and regenerated. He threw his hands to the sides and then to the front, summoning a collection of flames forward.

Will quickly pressed the S a second time on the compass, which retracted the shield back into the cuff. He rushed forward but cowered back as Fink's electrical, flaming fence barricaded him inside Misty's stall.

"You will never stop me," Fink bellowed. "You hear me, William? Never."

Will frantically searched Misty's stall through burning and watering eyes. Hanging in one corner was a woolen saddle blanket. He ripped the blanket off its hook and covered his head and shoulders. Through the smoky haze and scorching flames, he watched as Fink knelt by Madi's unconscious body and reached for the chain around her neck.

"Leave her alone you monster," Will shouted.

Snap. A thin bolt of lightning shot out from the necklace and zapped Fink's fingers.

Hissing with rage, Fink turned red eyes on Madi. He dug his hand inside her book bag that rested near her feet and carefully removed a black, rectangular box – the camera.

One by one, he peeled back her fingers and placed the camera in her open palm. He pulled the top silver button and gripped the camera's metal key, turning it once. A beam of light shot out of the camera's lens and draped her body in a veil of white.

"Madi!" Will screamed through the rising temperature.

Fink craned his neck in the direction of Will; a venomous smile spread across his face. "Say goodbye, William."

Will narrowed his eyes and set his jaw.

I don't think so.

With the blanket wrapped tight around his body, Will hurled himself through the burning flames and landed beside Madi just as Fink pushed the small silver button on the side of the camera.

An intense flash lit the barn in a solar flare.

Will grabbed Madi's free hand, closed his eyes, and held tight. He didn't hear her scream but felt it through the surge of icy liquid that rushed across both their hands, linking them together. Her body jerked against the subzero substance flowing from her hand.

Will gasped and choked on the swirling and smoldering debris that consumed him.

Lightning sparked like fireworks gone awry. Deafening claps of thunder rocked the earth. The barn rattled and swayed. Wooden beams buckled and snapped like hollow trees. The roof and walls slowly collapsed in a cloud of rubble and smoke, engulfing Will and Madi in its wake.

Chapter 14

Darkness.

Will inhaled sharply. A scent of smoke stung his nostrils, and a weighted hug of heat smothered his body as if swallowing him whole. He flailed his arms and kicked his legs, throwing the woolen saddle blanket up and off his back.

Will breathed in a wave of stale air and coughed. His throat instantly went dry, and a knot cinched his stomach. He wrapped his arms around his waist and groaned. Saliva puddled in his mouth.

Will scrambled to all fours, arched his back, and heaved, vomiting a toxic mixture onto the barn floor. His whole body shook, and a relentless thumping pounded inside his head.

"Will?" Madi rasped. "Will, where are you?"

Will slowly opened his eyes. Blotches of red, yellow, and orange stained his vision. Through the fading spots, he found Madi stirring in the middle of the barn floor. He wiped his dripping chin with the back of his hand and crawled to her side.

"What happened?" Madi said, sitting up. She grabbed the side of her head and winced.

Will stared at his sister. Above her left ear a purplish bruise spidered down from her hairline. Beneath a thin layer of dirt, small cuts were etched on her skin.

Madi gasped. "Will, your arm. It's - wait, what's that you're wearing?" She pointed.

Will looked at his arm and found the leather cuff still attached to his wrist; its compass faceplate cracked down at its center. He writhed about, pulling at the contraption until it unfastened with a *pop*. With a mighty toss, Will hurled the cuff across the barn, sending it into a towering pile of discarded hay.

"What *was* that?" Madi asked.

Before he could answer, the crowing of a rooster echoed throughout the barn. Madi gingerly stood up, dusted off her clothes that were dotted with fragments of hay, and then made her way to the barn's entrance.

The rooster crowed again.

Will pushed himself off the floor and stood on shaky legs. He ran his hand through his hair and scanned the barn. Beams of sunlight filtered in through two clean windows, lighting the interior space in a sparkle of dust. He blinked and rubbed his eyes hard. "Ummm . . . Madi. Some – something's not right here."

The wooden planks that lined the towering walls were smooth and like new. The hole in the roof caused by the flying shutter was mended. Even the four-square stalls tacked with rusty metal hinges on either side of the barn were full of animal life – the horse and the cows unmoved. After all that had happened – the storm and Fink, the fire and collapse – amazingly, the barn sat unscathed.

Madi pushed open the barn's door. A slight breeze dipped to the floor and then soared upward, tossing pieces of hay up and into the air. The cold draft sailed straight to Will and skimmed over his feet. It rushed up his body and bounded his chest, tightening with every rapid breath he took.

Will threw his hands out to the sides, feeling a sudden surge of vertigo. "Madi," he murmured. "Shut the – "

Madi quickly closed the door. "Ah, Will. You – uh – you might want to take a look out there," she thumbed.

Will swallowed down the puddle of nausea rising in his throat and staggered across the barn on wobbly legs. He fell against the door and drew in a deep breath through his nose. He placed his sweaty palms on the individual grooves carved into the wood and then slowly ran his fingers down to the smooth iron handle.

A muted babble of excitement – short, shrill voices – filtered in from the outside. Will glanced over at Madi. She shook her head and sank into the shadows of the barn. Will turned back to the door. With a slow hand, he cautiously lifted the latch and pushed.

The blazing sun spilled through the small gap, forcing Will to raise his arm to his forehead. A sea of steaming fog from the morning dew rose from the landscape. Across an open field stood a grand house with dark wooden shutters and yellow siding. But oddly, the old hickory trees that once towered over the home's roof were mysteriously gone. Even Nana's apricot trees, the ones used in her pies and that separated the back of the house from the barn, were nothing more than mere seedlings.

The earth pulsated in a distorted wave of heat. Will buckled at the knees and grabbed onto both doors, trying to keep from falling over.

"Mama," shouted a small voice. "Mama. Look here."

Will struggled to lift his head from the weight of the heat pushing down on him.

"Mama watch. Watch what I can do."

Will looked back at the house. A little boy in a checkered blue and white shirt was standing at the edge of the large wrap-around porch. He pushed back his shaggy light-brown hair that covered his forehead, and then with a small butterfly net in his hand, he ran across the porch in bare feet, chasing after a giant, red-winged dragonfly that seemed to dance with a fluttering Monarch.

"I think you have to be a wee bit faster, my love," sailed in a gentle voice carried by the wind.

In the pocket-sized grove tucked between the house and the barn, Will found a young woman in a baby blue, floral printed dress. She tucked a piece of her curly hair behind her ears and then dove her hands into a wooden bucket filled to the brim with sudsy water. Up and down, she worked a cream-colored shirt against the metal grooves of a washboard. After a quick minute, she wrung the water out of the fabric and hung the shirt on a taut rope that stretched between two oak trees.

Will held onto the doors and stared down at the ground. *Where are we?*

A loud nicker clipped the open air.

Will looked toward the sound. Coming up on the horizon was a tall and strident man; a stately brown stallion trotted beside him. Will watched as the man guided the horse through a green field and over to a bale of hay piled high against a worn corral fence.

"No bother tending the chickens," the man called out as he harnessed the horse to a tall post. "I shall see that Benjamin takes care of his own chores."

"Yes, Father," came a courteous reply.

Madi came out from the shadows of the barn and huddled in the nook of Will's arm.

"Get back," Will whispered, waving her away. He closed the door slightly and peeked through its thin space.

A young boy, appearing no older than twelve, stopped just beyond the entrance of the barn. He set down two metal buckets brimming with chicken feed and wiped his hands down his brown trousers. The boy took off his baker's boy cap and ran his right hand through his tousled, sandy-brown hair.

"Son," the man called out again as he searched a wooden bin next to the fence. "Have you seen my auger? It seems to have gone missing."

"I believe I saw Benjamin playing with it earlier this morning, digging at the trees."

"And where is he now?"

"*Plum Run,*" the boy replied. "No doubt throwing rocks again."

"Run to and fetch him for me. It's time I'd talk with that boy."

"Yes, Father." The boy placed his hat back on his head and then dabbed the bridge of his sweaty nose with the front of his white shirt.

He picked up the two buckets of chicken feed before walking away from the barn and out of sight.

Will quietly shut the door and rested his forehead against its cool wooden panel. His mind was a speeding locomotive as he tried to put together everything that has happened in the last few hours. *The storm. The fire. Nana and Grandpa. The apricot trees. Misty and the cows. The tractor. Even Marvin, the rooster.* Each thought thrummed in his head in a rapid pulse as he searched for a connection or any logical answer to their sudden disappearance.

"Will," Madi said in a timid voice, "what's going on?"

Will stepped away from the door and walked to the center of the barn, rubbing his throbbing temples. He needed to sit down. He needed a minute; needed to think.

A clink of metal and a groan of expanding wood hit off the walls. Madi rushed to Will's side and seized his hand. Together, they held their collective breath as the barn door slowly swung open. A scrawny, calico tabby, with white paws, scampered through the opened door.

Madi let go of Will's hand and exhaled. "It's just a cat."

As the tabby chased its flicking tail, a rhythm of skipping feet hit off the wooden floor. Will looked up and watched as the little boy from the porch bounced his way into the barn; his arms full with a pair of unlaced boots, four wooden sticks, and a large ring. He was humming to himself and skipping to his happy tune unaware of Will and Madi standing in the center of the barn.

When the song and dance were over, the little boy plopped down to the ground, dumping his items on the floor. The cat meowed its approval, and then with a precocious gate, waltzed over to the little boy and rubbed his head against his arm.

"I see you, Mr. Jinx," the little boy said with a playful giggle. He took one of his shoelaces and hung it above the cat's head. "Be happy you have paws," he said as the cat toyed with the string. "Mama says I have to learn how to tie these silly boots. So, shoo, we'll play later."

While the little boy struggled to tie his bootlaces, the cat strolled over to Will and rubbed its face against his leg.

"Scram," Will hissed, pushing the cat away with his foot. The cat hopped back but quickly returned, purring. It pawed at Will's feet then rolled onto its back, curling its paws and showing its tummy.

Madi breathed in fast. A burst of air shot through her nose. "Achoo!"

Startled, the cat rolled onto all fours and scampered away, disappearing between bales of hay. The little boy jumped to his feet and stared – mouth open.

"Way to go," Will said through clenched teeth.

"I couldn't help it," Madi whispered.

Without a word, the little boy turned on his heels and quickly closed the barn door. He grabbed his four sticks and ring off the floor and shuffled over to Will and Madi; his boots still untied. "Hello," he said; a wide grin spread across his face. "Do you want to play Graces?"

Instead of answering, Will studied the boy's face. There was something unique and strikingly familiar about him – especially the color of his eyes. The right one was sparkling blue; the left, a sweet honey color, rimmed in dark chocolate.

The little boy tilted his head. "Can you not speak?"

Will muttered a course of inconsistent syllables. "Ah . . . I . . ."

The boy grabbed Will's free hand and placed two of the wooden sticks in his open palm. Upon contact, the wash of vertigo rushed back through Will's head and punched at his stomach. He curled his lips together and slumped against Madi's shoulder. "What's wrong?" she asked, buckling under her brother's weight.

Will breathed in deep. "Nothing. I'm – I'm okay."

"Maybe you should sit down?"

"No," he said, steadying himself. "I'm fine. Really."

"Are you ready *now*?" the little boy asked impatiently, pointing at the sticks in Will's hand.

"I – ah . . . I really don't know how to play this game," Will said, setting the sticks down on the floor.

The little boy stomped his foot and folded his small arms across his chest. "But I want to play."

"Okay then, my sister will play."

"No. No. No. No girls allowed."

Will looked to Madi for help. She shrugged. "Just go with it."

Hesitant, Will held his breath and slowly picked up the two wooden sticks. They reminded him of the pair of drumsticks he had stashed away with his dismantled drum set in the attic back at home.

"Here it comes!" the little boy yelled out from a few feet away; the wooden ring dangling over each of his catching wands. With careful aim, he crossed his two sticks into an X and cast off the ring.

As Will watched the ring soar through the air, the walls of the barn faded and morphed into a grove of trees held back by a white picket fence.

Confused, he looked all around. A warm breeze hit against his cheeks, and a round of laughter popped in his ears. Through the brilliant sunlight that pierced through the collection of clouds, he saw, not Madi, but a young boy standing across from him, laughing all the same. Will stepped closer, trying to see the boy's face, but the harsh glare obscured his vision and burned his eyes. He blinked.

The déjà vu vanished. The ring was falling fast.

Will stabbed at the air with both sticks, catching the ring perfectly. Without stopping, he crossed his sticks over one another and cast the ring off in return.

The little boy dove after the falling ring but missed, landing on his backside. "Wow!" he exclaimed as the ring clattered on the floor. "You play very well."

A sharp clanging – metal against metal – rang out, startling both Will and Madi. The little boy scrambled to his feet, dropping his catching wands and rushed out of the barn.

Madi nudged Will's arm. "Hey, how do you know how to play that game?"

Will looked at the sticks in his hand. A haunting sensation stung his palms and quivered up his spine. He threw the sticks to the ground and backed away, feeling the barn walls droop and compress with each breath he took.

"Will?" Madi's voice tunneled through his ears. "Will? Are you okay?"

"Excuse me," the little boy called out as he peeked inside the barn. "Are you two hungry? Mother's made corn griddle cakes."

Will shook his head clear and slowly took Madi's hand in his. "Uh . . . thanks, but we – we got to go."

"Oh, that's too bad," the little boy replied with a pout. He looked up at Will and smiled. "Maybe next time."

Chapter 15

ive-year-old Jeremiah Parker ran out of the barn and splashed through a small puddle, scaring away a few robins who were taking their morning bath. He dashed across the yard and threw up his arms, smacking the laundry with his small hands. He rushed up the porch steps and opened the wooden screen door that led into the kitchen. It slammed with a *bang* against its doorframe, startling his mother, who stood at the table kneading dough. "Jeremiah, your hands," she called out after him as he ran past her and into the adjacent room.

Eager to eat his breakfast and return to the barn, Jeremiah settled down on a wooden bench around the dining table where his two older brothers and father were already eating. He rubbed his hands over his shirt, wiping them clean and then grabbed the ceramic pitcher, with small, intricate purple flowers, which was filled high with maple syrup. He tilted it on its side, dousing his pile of hot griddle cakes with the warm, sweet liquid. Satisfied there was enough, Jeremiah set the pitcher down, snatched his fork off the table, and began shoveling his breakfast into his mouth.

His father, Stephen Parker, who sat at the head of the table, looked up from his breakfast and watched his youngest son with keen interest. "Jeremiah? Why such a hurry to inhale your food this morning?"

Jeremiah, chin level with his plate, shifted his eyes and shrugged.

"I say, slow yourself down, boy."

"Yes, Father," Jeremiah replied with a mouthful.

Mr. Parker quietly set down his fork next to his breakfast plate. He rested his elbows on the table and folded his hands together. "It's the swine again? You want to go back and play; don't you?"

Jeremiah swallowed down a piece of griddle cake and quickly shook his head.

"For aught I know Father, he does," said Benjamin, the middle child. His hooded cold, coal eyes glared at Jeremiah from behind a lock of his dark brown hair. "He's always in that pen." Benjamin leaned in and sniffed. "He smells like them, too."

"Do not," Jeremiah cried.

"It's probably that *stupid* cat of yours who always paws at my feet," mumbled nine-year-old William, the oldest of the three. "He never leaves me alone."

"Boys," Mr. Parker said. "There shall be no banter of ill words around the table. Understood?"

"Yes, Father," the boys replied.

"Now, Jeremiah," Mr. Parker continued. "If it is not the swine, then what is the explanation for your hurried behavior?"

Jeremiah turned back toward his father. "I can assure you it is not the pigs, nor Mr. Jinx." He took another bite of griddlecakes and swallowed. "I *so* want to play Graces in the barn with my new friends."

Mr. Parker dropped his fork and rolled his eyes, lolling his head to the side. "Young man, how many times do we have to go through this?"

"Now, now, now, Jeremiah," came the soft voice of his mother, Meredith, as she entered the room with another helping of hot griddle cakes. She set down the plate and took her seat next to her husband, tucking her dress under her as she sat. "Those that you think of in your head are not real, my love, but imagined."

"Yes, Mother, but . . ." Jeremiah picked up his cup of milk and took a huge gulp. He wiped the white mustache off of his upper lip and went on. "But they are not imagined. They're real!"

"How many times have I told you?" Mr. Parker barked. "There is to be no storytelling. It's wrongful to make up tall tales."

"But I'm not making up stories, Father. I saw them—a boy and a girl in the barn. The boy and I played Graces. He was really good at it, too!" Jeremiah turned on his seat and faced his older brother. "Almost as good as you, William."

"That girl game?" Benjamin sneered with spiteful eyes. "You're such a liar, brother."

"Am not!"

"You are to and you know it." Benjamin chuckled. "How many times have you been caught lying with your made-up stories?"

Jeremiah stood up and leaned toward Benjamin. "Better a liar than a thief."

Benjamin jumped to his feet and pushed Jeremiah on the shoulder. "Bite your tongue."

Mr. Parker slammed his free hand onto the table. "Sit down," he commanded. "The both of you. Now!"

The two boys lowered their arms and slowly took their seats.

"There shall be no more out of the both of you today, understood?" Mr. Parker turned to Benjamin. "And you, young man, as I told you earlier, which it appears I must tell you yet again, be mindful and steadfast, especially like young William here. Heed the deed. Your constant running off with no concern, disregarding your chores and free speech is something I will not tolerate any longer. Do I make myself clear?"

"Yes, sir," Benjamin mumbled.

Mr. Parker composed himself, adjusting the suspenders on his broad shoulders. He turned his attention back to Jeremiah. "This boy and girl, who you make the claim that is in our barn, if I may ask, what are the names of these two friends of yours?"

Jeremiah felt his cheeks flush. He sank further into his chair, holding back his rising tears as he looked at each face around the table. "I – I don't know, Father."

Benjamin tilted his head toward Jeremiah; a sly grin framing his face. "Clod," he mouthed.

Jeremiah jumped up from his seat, dropping his fork to the floor, and ran out of the room. He rushed down the hall and out the front door, plopping himself down on the top porch step. He sat quietly for a moment and then with his little fingers, traced three ridged letters carved deep into the wood:

W – B – J.

| | | | | - | | | | |

"Today brothers," a seven-year-old William said as he scraped a small hunting knife across the top porch step, "we make a pact. A pact bonded in a brotherhood where even time itself shall never erase."

"What's that supposed to mean?" asked an annoyed six-year-old Benjamin, who stood tossing rocks beyond the dirt drive.

*"Only together, rooted like the strong oak, shall we be fierce and defend with courage," William said as he finished chiseling out a capital letter **W** into the wood.*

"Like the story of the Musketeers," a three-year-old Jeremiah blurted.

"Precisely." William smiled. He turned to Benjamin and held out the knife. "Your turn, dear brother. Do you stand with us or not?"

| | | | | - | | | | |

Jeremiah put his head in his hands and stared out at his mother's laundry that swayed back and forth in the warm morning breeze. Tears ran down his chubby cheeks, remembering the day he and his brothers dug their names into that very piece of wood. But unlike the *Musketeers,* the pact for them – Benjamin and William – had diminished over time, and their honor to one another faded into a washed-out memory.

The screen door squeaked open. Jeremiah quickly wiped away his tears and rose to his feet, meeting the smiling face of his mother.

"I know you still must be hungry," she said, pulling out a folded white cloth napkin from her apron pocket. She placed it in his little hand. "Just in case you and your friends are hungry."

Jeremiah smiled down at the cloth. He leaped into his mother's arms, laughing and giggling as she hugged him tightly, nuzzling his cheek into hers, which smelled of flour and maple syrup.

| | | | | - | | | | |

Madi let go of Will's hand and made her way toward the barn doors. He rushed over and pulled her back. "Where do you think you're going?"

"What does it look like?" she said, putting her hands on her hips. "I'm going to the house, to Nana and Grandpa, and find out what the heck's going on around here."

Will brought her closer. "Are you nuts? You can't."

Madi met his stare. "I can do anything I want."

"Take a good look around you, Madi. In case you haven't noticed, 'we're not in Kansas anymore'."

She rolled her eyes and scoffed a laugh. "What are you talking about? We're in Nana and Grandpa's barn."

"Then who are those people out there, and what about that kid, and the cat, or did you suddenly forget?"

A low snort bounced off the walls. Madi cowered behind Will, grasping the fabric of his shirt. "What was that?"

"It's called a pig," Will said.

"When did Grandpa get a pig?"

Will threw up his arms. "That's *exactly* what I'm trying to tell you." He walked over to a wooden stool and sat down with a huff, placing his head in his hands.

Madi curled her fingers into her palms and stepped away from the door, scanning the interior of the barn. The first stall consisted of animal harnesses, a few bundles of frayed ropes, and a collection of gardening tools. A canvas bag and a worn blanket shared a long wooden bench. Four fresh bouquets of wildflowers hung upside above a wooden spoked wheel that rested against the back wall. Different from Grandpa's typical array of odds and ends, but not all that unusual.

Madi made her way to the second enclosure. A few rays of sunlight snuck through the thin cracks in the walls, casting slivers of light onto the barn floor. Inside the small stall lay a fat, pink pig fast asleep, unaware of her six hungry piglets snorting around her prostrate form. Penned in the third stall was a red cow that chewed on hay from a narrow trough and swished away the hovering, pesky flies with its tail.

A roiling panic slowly grew in Madi's stomach. She stole a glance over at Will, who was still sitting with his head in his hands. Madi stuck her head inside the final stall; an airy gasp escaped her lips. A heavy-boned and muscular horse stepped out of the shadows; ears flat. Its midnight mane blended into its dark hair. Madi closed her eyes and held her breath as the horse sniffed her face. With a snort, it blew air out of its muzzle before retreating back into its stall.

"Do you believe me now?" Will said.

Madi backed away on stiff legs and ran over to her brother. "Where are we?" she demanded, clutching the front of his t-shirt. "What happened to Misty? To Nana and Grandpa?"

"Calm down, will ya?"

"What do you mean, calm down?" she yelled.

Will pushed her hands aside and stood up. "Look, I'm just as confused as you are. But there's no sense in getting all worked up. We have to think."

Madi threw her hands to her chest and breathed in and out with long, panted gasps. "I want Nana. Grandpa. I want to go home!"

The barn door creaked open, spilling a splash of sunlight across the floor. "Oh good," came the sweet voice of Jeremiah. "You are both still here." He shut the door with the sole of his boot. "I brought you both something."

Madi watched as the little boy juggled a pile of clothes in his arms that towered higher than his shoulders before dropping them onto the floor. "What's all that?"

Jeremiah rocked back on his heels. "I took them from mother's line. You may want to dress before you leave."

"What do you mean dress?" Will asked. "I *am* dressed."

"Yes, but you can't wear that," Jeremiah said.

Will cocked an eyebrow. "And why not?"

Jeremiah stepped up to Will and raised himself on his tiptoes. Using his finger, he traced over the embossed lettering and numbers in the center of Will's t-shirt.

"What – what are you doing?" Will said, shooing the boy away like a fly.

"I have never seen anything such as that before," Jeremiah said with a puzzled look.

Madi stepped closer. "You mean the words?"

The boy nodded.

"It says *National Eastern Conference - Soccer Champions*," Will replied, pointing at each word.

"And that's the year," Madi said. "2008. Well, that was last year."

Jeremiah's eyes grew wide. "2008?" He grabbed his stomach and bent at the waist, letting out a hearty laugh that echoed throughout the barn. "I – I like you. Even though you're a girl."

Madi exchanged a worried look with Will.

"Hey," Will snapped. "What year is it then?"

Jeremiah suppressed his amusement. "*Everybody* knows that, silly. It's the 26th of June. 1848."

Chapter 16

Will threw up his hands. "Whoa, whoa, whoa! Hold up. What do you mean, 1848?"

"I mean 1848," Jeremiah replied.

"Listen, kid, I got this shirt last year when my high school team won the National Championship 2 - 0 - 0 - 8!"

Jeremiah tilted his head and studied the white lettering. "Well," he began, folding his little hands together, "it is a very peculiar garment you are wearing, but I can assure you that it is 1848." He paused and looked down at the pile of clothes near his feet. "Oh, I almost forgot." He bent down and pulled out a folded cloth. "Here."

"What's this?" Madi asked, accepting the tiny bundle.

"Griddlecakes. You will surely enjoy them. Mother makes the best around."

Madi slowly unwrapped the four corners of the cloth. The smell of powdered sugar, sprinkled atop the cakes, swam up to her nose, sending her stomach in a rolling rumble.

"Well, thanks," Will said, taking his sister by the hand. "But we have to go. Come on, Madi."

"Is that your name?" Jeremiah asked.

"That's what most people call me," Madi answered, rewrapping the warm, flaky pastry, "but my real name is Madilyn."

Jeremiah looked up at Will. "What's your name?"

"Will," Will answered all too quickly. He grabbed his forehead with his fingers. "Wait . . . this – this is crazy." He turned to Madi. "Why are we still talking to this kid?"

"My name's Jeremiah, and I'm five," the little boy said, holding up his small hand, fingers wide. "I'll be six real soon. My brother, William; he's nine, and Benjamin's eight. You should meet them.

They're – "An ingenious smile took shape on Jeremiah's face. "Yes. Why didn't I think of that before?" He jumped up and down, clapping his hands. "Wait right here. I shall go and get them. They'll have to believe me now."

"No," Will called out as Jeremiah rushed out of the barn. "I don't think that's a good i – dea." Will stopped in his tracks. "Perfect."

Madi knelt on the floor and took two of the cotton shirts in her hands. "It – it can't be 1848." She looked up at Will. "Can it?"

Will glanced over his shoulder and raised his hand. "Just . . . just hold on a minute."

A wash of panic prickled Madi's skin. She dropped the shirts to the floor and grabbed at her neck. A series of interconnected links brushed against the tips of her fingers. From beneath her tank top, she pulled out a long, metal chain adorned with a familiar oak tree medallion. *The necklace*, she whispered, thinking back to Fink and the fair. *It couldn't . . . could it?*

Madi flipped the medallion over in her hand and ran her thumb across its embossed oak tree. She pressed the small button on its top, popping open its cover. Inside, the antique faceplate showed three little clocks whose hands pointed to a specific number: 18 on the first clock; 4 on the second, and 8 on the third. The hand on the primary face pointed to 6, and the small square fixed above the three small clocks showed the analog number as 26.

Madi brought the medallion closer and studied the rim of its bronze casing, which had a small key, a toggle gear, and three small valves. Curious, she pressed the second and third valves a few times.

From a dark corner of the barn, a glowing, flickering light caught her eye. Madi snapped the lid shut and walked toward the glimmer unaware that the hands on the second and third small clocks slowly began to change. The number 4 moved to 6, and the 8 changed to 3. The face of the primary clock stayed at 6, and the first small clock remained at 18. The analog number, 26, sat unchanged.

"All right," Will said, closing the barn door. "I think I found a place for us to hide out for a bit. We just need to sneak out of here before that kid comes back and head for the bordering woods. That way we can sit down and try to figure all this out."

Madi stood in the back of the barn at the mound of hay, staring down at the flickering light that lured her in like a moth to a flame. She let go of the oak tree medallion and dropped to her knees.

"Madi," Will said, coming up beside her. "Did you hear . . . what are you doing?"

Ignoring her brother, Madi dug her arm deep into the straw and drew the object out of the hay. Will looked down at her hands. "It's the – "

"The camera," she whispered.

Without thought, Madi took the thin, metal key on its top and turned it one full rotation clockwise. A blinding light shot out of the camera's glass lens and illuminated the barn in a halo of white.

"Ah! Madi!" Will shouted, shielding his eyes. "What did you do?"

"I don't know," she yelled back, fumbling with the camera.

"Well, turn it off!"

Madi turned the key again. Nothing. She pushed down on its top button. Nothing. She pulled the button. Little by little, it moved between her fingers, revealing a small white string that was tucked deep inside the camera. It stopped with a loud ***pop,*** filling the air with the scent of rotten eggs.

Will stumbled blindly about – arms flailing. "Stop messing around and give it here."

"No, I can do it," Madi insisted. She spun away from Will and brought the camera close.

The blinding light reflected off the oak tree medallion hanging loosely around her neck and fanned out around her in a dome of crystal white. An icy glaze began to coat her fingertips, and like a snake, it slithered across her hands, over her wrists, and up her arms.

"Will," Madi rasped against the frigid and invisible vise that slowly constricted and numbed her entire body. "What's happening to me?"

Will latched onto her free hand and grabbed for the camera. With a heavy thumb, he accidentally pushed its side button.

Crack!

A loud ping hit the air like a spoon striking against crystal glass. A bright burst of white light fanned open like an umbrella and sent a shimmering veil onto the floor. Gusts of frigid winds soared down from the rafters, whipping hay and dust in all directions.

Madi looked up and watched in horror as the barn's roof disintegrated and opened to a wide and hollow black hole. Before she could scream, a flowing force of blazing tendrils shot out from the camera's lens and latched onto her fingers. In rapid succession, they wrapped themselves around her torso, arms, and legs. With a force of a geyser, she was shot upwards into the cold, dark abyss, losing her hold of Will.

| | | | | - | | | | |

"Hurry! They are in here," Jeremiah said, leading the way for his brothers, William and Benjamin. "Wait until you meet them. You will surely – "

The trio stopped just inside the door and stared into a silent and empty barn.

"What a waste of time," Benjamin said. "No wonder no one ever believes you."

"But, but. . . They were right here," Jeremiah said.

"But, but . . ." Benjamin erupted in a fit of laughter and pushed Jeremiah harshly to the floor. "Go play with the pigs; at least they are still here."

William grabbed Benjamin and pulled him back on his shoulder. "Leave him alone."

As Benjamin whirled around, his opened palm flew backward through the air and smacked William full in the face. *Slap.*

With a battle roar, William sprung forward, tackling Benjamin to the ground. The two rolled about the loose pieces of hay and dirt, yelling and cursing, throwing fists into shoulders, arms, and faces.

"Stop," Jeremiah yelled, scrambling to his feet. "Stop. Stop. Stop." He wedged himself between the pair and threw out his hands, pushing on their chests.

"Boys," came Mr. Parker's loud call. "What's going on in there?"

Hearing their father's stern voice, Benjamin and William froze. They glared at one another, nostrils flaring, heaving in and out.

"You're – you're always defending him," Benjamin panted.

"And why should I not?" William puffed.

"Just you wait, William," Benjamin said, taunting with a pointed finger. "You will see. You're not always going to be the hero." He turned on his heels and rushed out of the barn.

Jeremiah walked over to William and tugged at his sleeve. "You believe me, don't you?"

William combed his hair with his fingers and then fixed his twisted shirt. He crouched down, looked Jeremiah in the eyes, and smiled. Then, without a word, he turned away and walked out of the barn, closing the doors behind him.

"Will . . . Madi?" Jeremiah called out to his new friends. "Please come out! There is no need to hide."

High and low, Jeremiah searched the barn. He looked behind his father's tool bench and around the towering bales of hay. He scanned the stalls and rummaged through the loft above. With a giant leap, Jeremiah hopped off the last rung of the loft's ladder and sat on its narrowed piece of wood, placing his chin in his hands; the lowing sounds of the animals in their stalls floated to his ears.

Mr. Jinx jumped quietly from his perch in the barn's rafters and strolled over to Jeremiah. He lowered his furry head and ran it against the boy's leg, purring. "You saw them," Jeremiah said as he patted his four-legged friend. "I know you believe me."

A ray of sunlight broke through a slit in the barn's wall and crept across the floor. Deep within in the corner of the barn, a bright white light flickered. "Did you see that?" Jeremiah asked his cat.

Led by a curious Mr. Jinx, Jeremiah walked to the light shining from a large pile of hay. He dug his hands inside the loose bale and pulled out a black, rectangular box – the camera. "Wow," Jeremiah breathed, looking down at the strange object in his small hands. "I wonder what it could be."

"Jeremiah," came the loud voice of his father. "Come here, son!"

Jeremiah ran to the very first stall just inside the barn doors and fell to his knees in front of a small wooden bench. He set down the camera and carefully wedged his little fingers between two pieces of the floorboard that sat askew from the rest. With a slight grunt, he pulled at the board until it came loose.

Jeremiah smiled as he stared down at a pile of his prized possessions that laid deep inside his earthly vault: a collection of metal American Revolutionary soldiers given to him by his great-grandfather, a leather bag full of marbles he found in the nearby woods, and a small book given to him by his mother.

"Jeremiah!" his father called out again. "Time does not wait!"

Quickly, Jeremiah pushed the items aside, making room for his new treasure. He set the camera inside the hole and buried it with dirt. He replaced the floorboard and hammered each of the loose nails in place with the heel of his boot. He slid his shoe back on his foot and then ran out to his waiting father, leaving the camera and the secret of his friends hidden deep beneath the barn's floor.

Chapter 17

A full string of broken and deep melodic clangs resounded through the air. Madi inhaled sharply as a bottomless warmth smothered her chest. It streamed across her arms and rolled down her legs, driving away the inundating cold that once coated her body. She rolled onto her back and coughed, opening her burning and watering eyes to a film of white haze that masked her vision. A ball of fire behind milky clouds met her eyes.

Madi slowly rose to her feet. The ground tilted; the air rippled. She threw her hands out to the sides and bent her knees, steadying her wobbly legs.

Beyond a rickety fence sat a white brick building with a large porch and numerous shuttered windows. An octagon tower, with a large bronze bell in the middle of the roof, rhythmically swayed back and forth on its wooden headstock. In the distance, rolling mountainsides rose into the sky. Modest homes, impressive buildings, and grand farms tucked themselves between the wide and open valleys while giant evergreen trees - surrounded by patches of tall and uncut grass - dotted the landscape.

"No," Madi whispered, shaking her head. "Where . . ." She spun herself around. Everything that once was - the little boy, Jeremiah, the barn, the animals, Will. They all were gone.

Madi cupped her hands around her mouth. "Will," she shouted, "Will, where are you?"

Above the tolling bell rose an uproar of frenzied cries. Madi turned around and found a group of young girls, in cotton dresses and black ankle boots, rushing away from the white brick building and heading in her direction. She dashed behind the trunk of a large tree and watched as they ran past.

One by one, the young girls made their way through the plotted evergreens that ran parallel to a white fence. No one said a word to one another but glanced nervously over their shoulders as they ran. A little girl with a crop of braided red hair hurried past the tree and slipped on the wet grass.

Instinctively, Madi jumped out from behind the tree and caught the girl by the arm before she fell to the ground. A telltale of pure shock masked the little girl's face. Her cheeks were pale; her wild eyes red from crying; even her lips quivered as she spoke. "Please, let me go. I must go home."

"What's going on?" Madi asked. "Why are you all running?"

"Sarah, go!" a voice yelled.

As the little girl wiggled herself free, a teenage girl with a crop of short, brown hair grabbed Madi by the wrist. "Come," she said. "It is not safe out in the open."

"Wait," Madi shrieked as she was dragged through the field. "Stop. Where are you taking me?" Using her free hand, she plucked the girl's fingers from her wrist, stopping them both in their frantic dash.

"You're making a terrible mistake," the teenage girl panted.

"What do you mean?" Madi asked, rubbing her aching wrist. "What mistake?"

The teenage girl gathered the front of her long maroon-colored dress and continued toward the trees. "Go home," she shouted. "Go home before it's too late."

"I know. I want to, but . . ."

"They're coming," the girl yelled.

"Who?" Madi asked. "Who's coming?"

The teenage girl pointed at the southern horizon. "The Rebels!"

A rush of soaring wind filled Will's ears with a deafening flutter. Needles jabbed at his arms and sliced at his face as gravity pulled him down to the earth. He threw out his arms and grasped blindly for something, anything, to stop his fall. When his hands finally caught, he grabbed tight and howled through the searing, fiery pain that ripped at his palms as he slid to a stop.

A pungent smell of pine entered his nose. A hazy multicolor of greens and browns morphed together and created a tapestry of branches and twigs. Will closed his eyes and braced himself against the thick trunk of the evergreen he suddenly found himself in. His heartbeat thumped in his ears and his sticky palms grew clammy as a warm wind blew through the boughs of green fur. Will sucked in his bottom lip and exhaled through his nose, fighting against his fear and the idea of falling straight to the ground.

A bell clanged. A roar of shrieks sifted through the swaying branches. Will forced himself to look down and nearly lost his grip on the rough bark in his sweaty hand. Fifteen feet below, a group of young girls rushed by in frantic haste sparking a single thought in his mind. *Madi.*

Will steadied his balance and looked through the branches of the tree, calling out her name. After a few nervous seconds and with no reply, he knew his only option was down. With arms like wet noodles and legs like jelly, Will took hold of the nearest branch and gave it a slight tug, testing its strength and his courage. He closed his eyes and took a deep breath. *A ladder. It's just like a ladder.*

Left Foot. Step down. Right Foot. Step down. Left Hand. Right Hand. Repeat.

Will repeated the process, clinging to the trunk as he descended into the bowels of the evergreen, building his confidence with each step. Six feet from the bottom, and with no other branch to grab onto, he swung himself off and out of the tree, falling straight into the path of a teenage girl.

The unexpected collision sent Will flailing. He grabbed hold of the girl's waist and held on, sending them both crashing to the ground. *Thud.* The back of his head smacked off the hard terrain, painting his brain with a splash of supernova colors.

Will shook the stars out of his head and found a pair of angelic eyes, staring down at him. Half-dazed, a smooth smile spread across his face. "Hi," he said.

"I beg your pardon," the girl said, struggling in his arms. "But get your hands off of me."

Will blinked. "Oh, I'm - I'm sorry," he said, unwrapping her from his hold.

The young girl staggered clumsily to her feet, tripping over Will's legs and the fabric of her maroon-colored dress. With a half-hearted smirk, she tucked a loose piece of her hair behind her ears, and then without another word, ran off toward a small town that sat beyond the row of evergreens.

"Hey!" Will said, jumping to his feet. "Wait a second!"

The girl stole a quick glance back but continued running. Will chased after her, zipping through the cluster of trees. At an arm's length away, he grabbed her by the shoulder and spun her around.

"I say, are you mad?" she said, twisting in his hold.

"No . . . I just - "

The tolling of the bell grew urgent. The girl looked past Will's shoulder. Her body began to tremble in his hold and tears filled her doe-brown eyes. "Release me," she demanded. "Now!"

"Okay, relax," Will said. "I just want to know what's going on."

The girl took a wary step back. "You must go home and hide. Hide, and don't come out until it is safe."

Will furrowed his brow. "Hide? What are you talking about?"

The girl met his eyes. "They're coming!" she said with an icy quiver in her voice. And with that, she turned and ran away, disappearing into the town below.

| | | | | - | | | | |

A layer of clouds slowly began to paint the sky in a chilling shade of gray. A cool breeze dipped onto the field and chopped at the clusters of tall grass, creating waves of green. Madi shivered and rubbed her hands up and down her bare arms as she scanned the open field. She turned herself around and froze. The white building. *Will.*

Madi dashed across the field and ran through an opened gate attached to the rickety fence. She bounded up the porch steps and peered around the front door that sat slightly opened on its hinges.

"Will?" Her voice echoed off the dark paneled walls of a large foyer. "Will, are you in here?"

Down a dimly lit hallway, a shaft of light spilled out from an opened door and illuminated the floor. Barely making a sound, Madi tiptoed toward the light. The tick, tock of a grandfather clock, with its brass pendulum swinging back and forth, kept time with her light footsteps. Madi stopped at the opened door and peeked into the room.

A single desk with four drawers and a matching swivel chair sat front and center. Smaller desks with iron legs and slanted wooden tops made two horizontal rows. Feathered quill pens dripped their dark liquid across the desktops and onto the seats. Thin paperbound books and yellowed papers scattered the floor. Several long and narrow windows lined one wall and draped a glow of gray daylight across a slate chalkboard that spanned the front of the large room.

Madi slowly ran her fingers across the dusty chalk ledge, reading each section of the cursive script.

Teacher's name – Mrs. Eyster; ten arithmetic problems; a numerical list of reading pages designated for different age groups; and a 'golden rule' for the day – "*One's choice justifies the journey.*"

In the center of the chalkboard was a six-line poem.

Take thy step,
Which may not be desired.
Hence, you shall see.
Beyond that open door,
Forevermore;
You shall find the key.

"I say, child - " came a sharp voice.

Madi ducked behind the teacher's desk and peeked above its wooden top. A woman in a long twill skirt and a white, high-collared blouse with cotton ruffles and pearl buttons stood in the opened doorway. Her blonde hair was knotted tightly in a bun, which pulled back on her oval face.

The woman placed her hands behind her back and walked further into the room; the heels of her boots tapping against the floor with each firm footstep. "Did you not hear my instructions? You were to go home immediate - " The woman stopped short and tilted her head as Madi slowly stood up. "What on earth? Where are your clothes, child?"

Madi took stock of her tank top, shorts, and flip-flops she was wearing and gave the woman a weak smile.

"Who are you?" the woman said, eyeing Madi up and down.

Madi shifted her eyes to the opened door.

"No . . ." the woman said with a pointed finger. "Stay right there. Stay right - "

Madi sprang out from behind the desk and burst out of the classroom; her feet hitting hard as she pounded down the hall. She rushed out of the front door, startling a flock of crows in a nearby oak tree by her wild intrusion and jumped off the porch steps. She ran to the picket fence, threw herself against its white slats, and screamed Will's name against the bell's clamor.

Chapter 18

*T*he clanging bell resonated through the bending and bowing branches of the evergreen trees. Against a cool wind, Will heard a faint call of his name. He closed his eyes and focused, straining to hear the muted voice above the din of the bell. There it was again; to his right.

Will ran toward the sound of his name - up the hill, past the evergreens, and through a wide, open field. His eyes met a towering schoolhouse enclosed by a rickety fence and, "Madi," he shouted.

Like a jackal, Will took off, leaping over the fence and into the schoolyard. He rushed over to Madi and threw his arms around her waist.

"Oh, Will," she cried into his chest. "Thank God you're here. I didn't know where you were."

"Where did you go?" he said, taking her by the shoulders. "It's like one minute you were - "

"Me? What about - " She grabbed his cheeks. "What happened to your face?"

"I fell in a tree."

"You mean you fell *out* of a tree!"

"No - in." Will held up his hand and shook his head, silencing his sister. "Look, it doesn't matter what happened. We need to figure out what's going on."

"But you're hurt," she said, examining his scratches and brush burns.

Will pushed her hands aside. "I'm fine, okay? We have bigger problems than some cuts on my face."

The tolling bell stopped.

Against the sudden silence, its lingering hum sustained a

monotone drone that slowly faded with the growing cool breeze.

Will made his way to the fence that divided the schoolyard from an adjacent dirt road and stared into the hazy distance. *Where are we?*

"Will?" Madi came up beside him and slipped her trembling hand into his. "I'm scared. What happened to Nana and Grandpa? And what about the house and the barn; even that little boy?"

A rolling rumble shimmied the ground. Will looked up. On the dust-dotted horizon, a blurred line moved in a layering wave, like a mirage stretching across the desert sands.

Madi let go of Will's hand and tugged at his arm. "Maybe we ah –we should get out of here."

"Hold on," he said, brushing her off.

"No. You don't – "

"Just give me a minute, all right?"

"We don't have a minute," Madi argued. "See, this girl . . . I don't know who, dragged me through that field over there and told me to go home because the Rebels were coming."

Will whipped around. "What did you say?"

"This girl dragged me – "

"No, the other part."

"She said to go home?"

Will grabbed his forehead. "Argh, no; the last part."

"Oh," Madi said, nodding. "She said the Rebels were coming."

A round of quick and sharp popping sounds sliced through the air. Will dropped to the ground, yanking Madi down with him.

"Gunshots?" she cried, pressing her back against the fence. "Those were gunshots, right?"

The tolling bell, with its bronze voice, began to ring in a new urgency. Will raised himself ever-so-slightly and peered between the slats of the fence. The line – nearing the road – fanned open to form a battalion of marching men dressed in gray and butternut. Wagon wheels and clopping hooves shook the ground and shimmied the fence. Cups and cutlery that hung from canvas knapsacks pinged against each other with a metallic jingle as if keeping time with the approaching soldiers.

Will turned back around and stared blankly at the schoolhouse. It was unthinkable. No, impossible. How? How could they be here?

Another rapid round of gunfire struck the air. A chortle of shrilling yells followed the discharging barrage; their dog-like yips pierced through the humid air in a bone-chilling chorus.

"We need to hide," Madi said in a panic.

"Come on." Will crawled over her legs and followed the perimeter of the fence, stopping at its opened gate.

"Wait," Madi cried, tucking the oak tree medallion inside her tank top. "Where are we going?"

Will looked across the open field beyond the evergreen trees and pointed. "There."

"The town? But what about the schoolhouse?"

"We can't."

"Why not?" Madi pleaded.

Will took her by the shoulders. "Listen, something big is about to happen here, and I have a pretty good idea what it is, but staying isn't an option."

Madi looked at the band of marching soldiers and then at the town in the near distance. "But I don't think- "

"We'll make it," Will said.

Madi hesitated.

He extended his hand. "Trust me."

Madi bit her bottom lip and looked into his fixed and serious eyes. Slowly, she slid her trembling hand into his.

"On the count of three," Will began. "One . . . Two . . ."

Chapter 19

Will towed Madi across the open field and past the row of evergreens, zigzagging around their trunks and ducking under their lowing branches.

"Wait," she puffed, losing her flip-flops somewhere amongst the tall grass. "Slow down! You're – you're going too fast!"

Together, they broke through the evergreens and ran onto a dirt road; each of their thumping footsteps leaving a cloud of dust in their wake.

Will slid to a stop and let go of Madi's hand. He lumbered forward – tripping, blinking – unable to believe his eyes.

Two and three-story homes, some built with bricks and others constructed of wood siding, lined the street. In the distance, a general store, bath and washhouse, hotel, and tobacco shop outlined the town square.

"What is this place?" Madi asked, coming up beside him.

Everywhere Will looked, townspeople were running in a frenzy, closing shutters and locking doors. Farmers were driving out their livestock. Families were hurrying along, loading their wagons and carriages with personal belongings and priceless possessions.

"Hey, you," Will called out to a scrawny teenage boy with a burlap sack slung over his shoulder.

The boy, who was heading in their direction, paused in his stride and looked up from beneath his straw hat.

"What's the year?" Will asked.

Without a word, the boy shuffled back on his feet, wheeled around, and scampered away.

"Come on," Will said, taking Madi by the hand.

Keeping his eye on the boy, Will led Madi through the growing

123

crowds, whose frantic and inaudible babble seemed to match their hurried pace.

A two-horse team, pulling a carriage full of passengers, turned onto the dirt road and nearly collided with the boy. On instinct, the driver yanked on the reins. The horses whined and reared back, kicking up their front legs. The passengers shrieked as the carriage jerked to a stop, blocking the boy in his escape.

Will grabbed the boy by the back of his muslin shirt and whipped him around. "I was talking to you."

The boy spat at Will's feet and gritted his teeth.

Will stared down at the glob of spit on his sneakers and watched as the phlegm slid off his shoe like a slimy egg yolk.

With a rash thrust, Will grabbed the boy by the collar, knocking the straw hat off his head. "I asked you the year."

"M-m-my satchel," the boy whimpered, ignoring the question. "It's yours. Mother only gave me a few coins for the journey, but – "

"I don't want your bag or money," Will said. "I just want to know the year."

The boy didn't answer; his stark green eyes were fixed on the white letters and numbers written across Will's soccer t-shirt.

Will yanked the boy closer. "The year!"

"Eight . . . " the boy muttered. "Eighteen sixty-three."

Will stood solid; the boy clutched in his rigid grasp.

The clanking of wagon wheels, clopping of horses' hooves, and voices of the townspeople flooded the street from all directions, piercing Will's ears in a chirping chatter of hysteria. A crackling clatter rippled homes and buildings, bowing their walls at their foundations while a wave of energy rolled and curled the road beneath his feet.

"Will," Madi shrieked, pushing down on his arms. "Let him go!"

Will blinked.

A winding whir crescendoed.

He released his hold and stumbled back, sending the boy to the ground. He rocked on his heels and grabbed his knees, fighting hard to breathe. *1863?*

"You two – " the boy said, scooting away on his elbows. "– you two are crazy as loons." He snatched up his straw hat and satchel and then took off down a nearby alley, disappearing amongst its growing shadows.

"Will . . ." came Madi's drifting voice. "Can you hear me?"

"How?" Will mumbled, staring at the ground. "How can we be in1863?"

The road flattened. The homes straightened on their foundations. The voices dropped to a frenzied hush.

"Will, you're scaring me," Madi said. "What's wrong with you?"

A clip-clop reverberated through the town. Popping sound of gunshots bounced off the houses and buildings. Will slowly lifted his head in the direction of the noise. A cloud of dust was rising to the sky from beneath a team of horses making their way into town.

Will quickly scanned both sides of the road. Up ahead, two red-brick homes sat adjoined by a small, black wooden door. He seized Madi by the hand and yanked her forward.

"Wait," she shrieked as he dragged her along. "Where are we going, now?"

Will rushed over to the door and pulled at its handle. Locked. He planted his left foot and kicked hard just above the handle. *Snap.* He kicked at the door again. *Crack!* The door broke open, splintering a section of its frame.

Will grabbed Madi by the shoulders and shoved her into the dark alcove. He closed the door, crouched down, and held onto the broken latch and splintered wood.

"Will, please," Madi demanded. "Talk to me. What's going on?"

"Shut up, Madilyn," he snapped. He lowered his voice and peered through a pocket-sized hole that was notched into the door. "They're here!"

The Rebels were a dirty, disheveled group of men. Though a small troupe in number, their unruly display didn't go unnoticed as they stormed the town. They yelled and cackled and fired their pistols in the air like cowboys from a Wild West show. One by one, they hopped off their horses and bullied their way through the streets, pounding on doors and demanding provisions and the whereabouts of hidden slaves or any Union soldiers, taking anything or anyone in their greedy clutches.

One Rebel, a slender man with a pistol in his dirty hand, stopped his horse on the side of the road. He removed his feet from the frayed stirrups and slid off the gaunt and languid animal like a slug. Tugging at his sagging gray trousers and whistling to himself, he strolled toward the wooden door Will and Madi were hiding behind.

Will gripped the splintered wood and waved Madi to get back. The small amount of light that filtered in from the notch disappeared and a tired, bloodshot eye peeked through the space. It darted back and forth, straining to search the darkness.

"Anything, Shelton?" a rough voice asked.

"I can't see a bloody thing," Shelton answered in a thick, southern accent. "It's too dark."

Madi placed her hands over her mouth and cowered into Will's back; her rapid breathing hitting hard against his spine.

"Why don't you try opening it, you nitwit?" the rough voice barked back.

"Hmph, why didn't I think of that?" Shelton said. He backed away from the door, sending a stream of light back into the alcove.

Will felt a sharp tug at the door.

"It's stuck," Shelton shouted.

"Well, try harder," the rough voice ordered.

Will wiped the sweat beading on his brow with his shoulder and gripped the latch with both hands. With each yank, the splintered piece of wood burrowed itself deeper into his skin. Will closed his eyes and bit his lip as a shard of wood snapped away from the door and bore deep into his clammy palm.

"NOOOOO!" a young girl's voice sailed through the air.

"Shelton," the rough voice called out. "This way."

"But sir, I think I saw . . . "

"Move it, you lunk! We have other gems to conquer."

Shelton released the handle and scurried back to his horse, muttering under his breath. He hoisted himself back onto the animal and galloped away.

Will let go of the broken latch and lifted his shaking hand in front of his face. The jagged piece of wood stuck out from the middle of his palm like an impaling sword. Grimacing, he slowly pulled out the serrated splinter. A thin stream of blood ran across his hand and down his wrist.

"Leave us alone," the young girl's voice yelled.

Will inched the door open.

"Wait," Madi said, taking him by the elbow. "You're not going out there, are you?"

"I need to see what's going on," Will said.

"Then, I'm going with you."

Will closed the door. "No. You're going to stay right here."

"But – "

"But nothing. Just stay here and stay quiet. Got it?"

Will inched the door open and peeked out. Up the road, a small group of Rebels, all dressed in gray, were jumping off their horses. Like a pack of wolves eyeing their prey, they stomped across the street and circled a teenage girl in a maroon-colored dress and her family.

Will couldn't believe his eyes. It was her; the same girl he fell onto when he jumped out of the evergreen.

"Please," he heard the girl cry. "He can't, Father. Please, tell the man no."

A bulky man with a full beard pushed through the family and

retreated to the back of the house. A few minutes later, he returned, pulling a reluctant white horse.

Will watched as the young girl broke out of her mother's holding arms and lunged at the burly man, screaming and pounding her fists against his back. The man threw out a strong arm and pushed the girl aside, sending her to the ground. He rocked back on his heels and laughed loudly; his band of soldiers chimed in with amusement.

The girl's father puffed out his chest and yelled, pointing his finger at the beastly man. In a graceful arc, the man pulled out his revolver and aimed, sending the family cowering back. After a few inaudible words, the man spat on the ground and then made his way to the house across the street with his rowdy bunch of soldiers.

Will slipped back into the alcove and closed the door. He placed his bleeding and throbbing hand against his shorts and slumped against the brick wall.

"So? What did you see?" Madi asked. "What's going on?"

Will looked past his sister and stared blankly at the brick wall across from him. *1863. The Rebels. Gray uniforms. The town raided.* His thoughts raced in all directions as he tried to put it all together; each element a piece of the bigger puzzle.

Madi crouched down in front of him and shook his shoulders. "Don't just sit there. Say something!"

Will locked wide eyes with his sister. He couldn't believe what he was about to tell her; couldn't believe it himself.

Madi let go and slowly sat back. "What is it?"

"I think – " Will swallowed hard. "I think we just found ourselves in Gettysburg, right smack in the middle of the Civil War."

Chapter 20

"What?" Madi shrieked. "What do you mean *the* Civil War?"

"At first, I didn't realize it," Will began, "but when I started to put it all together. 1863. Everyone running and hiding from the *Rebels* –Confederate soldiers."

Madi snapped her fingers. "You're right; I can't believe I didn't figure it out." She grew serious. "So, what are we going to do?"

Will rubbed the back of his neck. "I don't know."

Madi went for the door. "I think we should leave."

"Are you crazy?"

"Well, we can't just stay here. We need to find a way to get back home."

"And you think that I don't know that?"

"Then what are we waiting for?"

Will jumped to his feet, blocking the way. "Think about it Madi. We can't just waltz out of here and walk down the street."

She folded her arms across her chest. "And why not?"

Will plucked the strap of her black tank top. "Ah, hello . . . Our clothes, genius, for one. Last time I checked, not really fitting for 1863. I mean, you saw how that kid looked at us – at me with my soccer t-shirt. Plus, there is a –"

"Wait a second," Madi interrupted. She ducked under the nook of Will's arm and pushed her ear up against the door. "Hear that?"

"Hear what?"

"Nothing," she said. "It's quiet."

Madi eased the door open on its hinges and stepped out of the alcove and onto the street. "Everyone's gone," she whispered.

Will came up beside his sister and looked up and down the road.

A light drizzle had started to fall and tinted the once chaotic town in a calm, silvery mist.

"This – this isn't good," he said, shaking his head.

Madi tapped Will's arm and pointed across the road.

Will followed the direction of her finger to a team of horses standing in front of a wood-sided home. One horse, a white steed, was secured to a lone post by a thick, braided rope. It nickered and pawed nervously at the dirt with its hoof.

"No way," Will said. "You know I don't know how to ride."

Madi rolled her eyes. "Oh, stop. You know you can; you just don't."

Will twisted his lip and stared down at his sister. He couldn't argue the point. She was right. With every riding lesson at Nana and Grandpa's over the years, he always joined in and quickly and surprisingly caught on.

Will remembered it was a few years back. After a long day on the field with Madi and Misty, he overheard the instructor telling his grandparents that in all her years of training young equestrians – "*I've never seen someone, like your grandson, so natural at the sport.*"

"I don't know," Will said, pushing his damp hair off his forehead. "It's been forever since I've been on one of those things."

"Oh hush," Madi said with a wave. "And they're not things. That beauty is our ticket out of here."

Will looked over his shoulder and scanned the deserted town. "Honestly, I think it's best if we head back the way we came. That way we could retrace our steps and figure out how to get– "

When Will turned back around, he found Madi making her way across the road toward the lone and disgruntled horse.

"Hey there, beautiful," Madi said.

The horse cocked its head; its ears hard-pressed forward.

Madi cautiously walked closer. She slowly raised herself on her toes and carefully extended her hands. "It's okay," she soothed as the horse cowered back and let out a sharp neigh. "Shhh . . . I'm not going to hurt you."

Gently, she placed one hand near the top of the horse's back and the other on its belly. She brought her hand forward across the horse's hair and then softly rotated her hand upward. After a few calming strokes, Madi went back to the front of the horse and met its watchful eyes. "There, there . . . you're all better now; aren't you girl?"

The horse lowered its face and nuzzled its muzzle against Madi's cheek.

"Let's say we get you off of this post."

Will was ten strides away from his sister – his mouth open to protest – when a rise of barking voices broke the silence. A wild band of Confederate soldiers – arms overflowing with loaves of bread, canned goods, and glass jars – stumbled out the front door of the small home and onto its covered porch.

Will ducked behind a large wooden barrel, sitting on the side of the road and peered over its top. He watched as the soldiers plopped down on the porch steps and traded their tattered shoes for the ones they had just stolen from the house. To Will, they were hyenas; their raucous laughter pricked at the air as they poked fun at one another and passed around a brown bottle – most likely whiskey – chugging back its dry, distilled liquid.

The screen door burst open with a *bang*, breaking off its weak hinges. A beefy soldier, sporting a gruff-looking beard, exited the home; his heavy boots hit firmly against the wooden porch. He was a brick house – thick legs holding up a solid torso that bulged against the seams of his gray Confederate uniform.

"Well, boys," the soldier bellowed, trampling through his cheering comrades and down the porch steps. "I'd say we've done mighty fine for ourselves this time."

Will looked over at Madi, who was struggling with untying the horse's rope. "Hurry," he hissed.

The rope fell slack.

Madi looped the excess twine around her hand and cowered under the neck of the horse, leading the animal away.

Will glanced back at the house. The burly man stood at the bottom of the steps, a revolver in his hand. He pointed the gun at the sky and pulled the trigger, silencing his ragtag band of soldiers.

Will recoiled.

Madi jumped.

The horse shrank back with a squeal and a nicker.

The burly man swiped the bottle of whiskey out of the hands of a mangy soldier and took a giant swig. He wiped his dripping lips with the sleeve of his dirty jacket and struggled to pull up on the belt that was secured around his protruding waist. "I say we go get ourselves some Yankees."

The group broke into a high-pitched cackle of yips and yells as they made their way toward their team of horses. The burly man – in all his crudity – pranced backward in an awkward dance and chugged back the whiskey, making a spectacle of himself for his band of soldiers. Using one hand, he reached for the rope that held the white steed to the post and froze. With a grizzled growl, he spun around and launched the bottle against the house.

Smash!

The bottle exploded in a shower of glass fragments, which sent streams of whiskey running down the siding on the house.

"Who's been toying with my horse?" the burly man bellowed.

The group of soldiers stopped. They looked at the man -- confused, scratching their heads and mumbling to one another.

"I said -- "

"Ah, sir?" interrupted a slender soldier with long, greasy brown hair jetting out underneath his black slouch hat.

"What now, Shelton?" the burly man spat.

Shelton pointed a shaky finger. "There'd be your horse!"

The burly man turned on the heels of his boots. "Where?"

"Right there! Walking away with that wee girl, who's wearing some strange-looking undergarments."

"Well, I'll be damned," the burly man said, holstering his gun.

With a strident gait, he marched over to Madi; his Confederate cronies shadowing his wide gait. "Well, well, well lookie, what we have here? And what do you think you're doing there, little lassie?"

Madi stopped and quickly dropped the thick rope to the ground. Slowly, she turned around and met the man's narrowed gaze. "Nothing," she answered all too sweetly.

"Doesn't look like nothing to me, now. Does it boys?" the man asked his group of soldiers. They all nodded and answered in unison with a series of murmured noes.

With a mighty swipe, the burly man seized Madi by the arm and lifted her high off the ground.

"Hey!" she cried, kicking her feet. "Let. Me. Go!"

"Maybe you should have thought that before taking what's not yours," the man growled.

"Please, mister. You're -- you're hurting my arm."

A rush of adrenaline surged through Will's veins as he watched his sister hang helplessly in the clutches of the burly man. He clenched his fists and stepped out from behind the barrel. "Hey, you. Bushy Beard. Let my sister go!"

Bushy Beard whirled around; Madi dangling limply in his vise-like grip. "Who said that?"

Will sized up the man amazed at his bulky proportions. He swallowed hard and stood his ground. "I did."

With Madi in tow, Bushy Beard stormed over to Will, heaving in and out like a raging bull. "Who are you to give me orders?"

"She didn't mean anything by it. She's just a kid. Let her go."

Bushy Beard looked at Madi; her eyes brimming with tears. "You know . . ." he said, setting her feet down on the ground. "You're right. What has gotten into me today?" Bushy Beard shoved Madi forward, sending her into Will's arms. He took off his hat and gave a curt bow. Fluttering his thick eyelashes. "My apologies, little lassie. Laddie. You two have a mighty fine day."

Will wrapped his arm around Madi's shoulders. "Come on," he whispered, looking back at Bushy Beard and his soldiers, who crowded together in the middle of the road like a band of bandits. "Let's get out of here."

"I'm sorry," she said. "I thought that I could've – "

Madi's scream sliced her words like a knife as she was ripped from under the security of Will's arm.

"Will!" she cried. "Will, help me!"

Will spun around and watched as two of Bushy Beard's comrades drag Madi across the road. He sprang forward – intent on war –but immediately fell back as Bushy Beard drew out his weapon and took aim.

"I don't think so," the brute sneered, cocking back his gun.

Every capillary in Will's body chilled as he stared down the dark barrel of the revolver that was pointed at his face.

Will raised his hands in surrender. "Look, I'm sure we can work this out. Just give me a – "

Two strong hands grabbed Will by the arms and yanked them behind his back. "Hey!" he demanded, twisting in their firm hold. "Let me go!"

A rough-looking soldier in a butternut Confederate uniform dug through Will's front pockets, tossing out the photo strip and keeping the money Nana had given him at the fair. "Whooey, would you lookie here?" the man said with a smile full of yellowed teeth. "Not sure what it is, but it looks like fifty dollars to me!"

Another soldier ripped the bill out of the man's hand and studied the paper. "That's no money. It's phony; see?"

"Whatcha mean phony?" the soldier asked, taking it back.

"You noodle brain," bantered another. "This here green paper has General Grant's face on it."

"I say, Buford," Shelton said over the bickering bunch. "Never seen undergarments like this before; all decorated n' such." He plucked at the cuff of Will's soccer shirt and read the logo on his sleeve. "Ah-diy-daus. Must be French?"

"It's Adidas, you moron," Will mumbled under his breath.

Bushy Beard haltered his gun. He strutted forward – a sly grin on his hairy face – and snatched the bill from his comrade. With the tips of his chubby fingers, he tore the money in half and flicked each piece to the ground. He grabbed Will by the shoulder, reared back his meaty fist, and let it fly.

Oomph.

Will buckled over and reeled back before falling straight to the ground.

"Leave him alone you . . . you bully!" Madi yelled above the soldiers' rowdy and intimidating laughter.

"Someone shut her up," Bushy Beard commanded.

A dirty hand smothered Madi's feeble protests.

Will rolled on the ground, coughing and gasping for air; his stomach contracted; his vision blackened around the edges. He closed his watering eyes and found himself *suddenly surrounded by an abundant cluster of towering trees and vines. A young woman with long, dark wavy hair, was running toward him, yelling his name. She fell to her knees and grabbed his hands; her eyes full of tears. She leaned in closer, blocking the golden sunlight, which cast a soft glow behind her thin form.*

Will winced, feeling himself being hauled to his feet. He opened his eyes and found himself back on the road; the young woman and the trees vanishing in the misty rain that continued to fall on the town.

"You a Yankee, aren't ya boy?" Bushy Beard asked.

Will blinked, focusing on the man's dirty, menacing face. "I'd rather be a Yankee than some stealing, bully, Johnny Reb like you."

Bushy Beard's eyes blazed cold. "What did you say?"

Will set his jaw and bit down on his tongue, preparing himself for a punch to the face. But instead of the hammer blow, Bushy Beard grabbed Will by the hair and pushed the muzzle of his revolver under his chin.

"Hard case, I see," Bushy Beard scoffed; his breath a foul stench of whiskey. "Quick with the tongue, too. How's you say you become my prisoner?" He glanced over at his two comrades. "Take 'em both."

"Noooo . . ." came Madi's smothered scream behind the soldier's grimy fingers as she was towed away.

"Stop! Take me," Will pleaded, fighting to break free from Shelton and Jasper's hold. "Please! Let my sister go. Let her go!"

"Colonel Mills!" a strong voice called out above the commotion.

Shelton and Jasper stopped in their tracks.

Will looked over his shoulder. A young man, mounted on a brown stallion, was galloping up the road.

"Colonel Mills," the young man said, "a word with you."

Bushy Beard tilted his head. "What are *you* doing here?"

The young man pulled back on the reins and steadied his horse. "Your presence is requested immediately."

Bushy Beard stepped away from Will and his soldiers and lowered his voice. "A bit early, aren't we?"

"It appears things have changed."

Bushy Beard pursed his lips together and grunted a nod.

"So, I suggest you finish up whatever it is you are doing here," the young man said, taking in the scene. "The boss wouldn't appreciate knowing that – " He paused and stared down at Will with hooded, coal-colored eyes. "Do I know you?"

Will looked at the ground and shook his head.

The young man commanded his horse closer; its breath hit against the side of Will's face with a hot puff. "Are you certain? You look very familiar to me."

"I've never seen you before in my life," Will muttered.

The young man sat back on his horse and adjusted his tan suspenders that were decorated with gears and chains. "Hmm . . . I would have bet the farm I knew you. Oh well." He guided his horse around the group and pointed at Bushy Beard. "Make haste, brother; time does not wait."

With a slap of the reins, the young man and his horse took off down the muddy road, disappearing in the misty rain.

"Well, ain't you lucky?" Bushy Beard said to Will. "Seems as though I have other – important – business to attend to. But, let me tell you this though." He hocked up a wad of nasty phlegm and spat it at Will's feet. "You better be watching your back boy, 'cause next time . . ." He flicked his nose and leaned in close; a collection of rain dripped off the brim of his hat. ". . . you won't be so fortunate."

Bushy Beard smirked and lightly slapped Will two times on the cheek. "All right boys," he said as he heaved himself onto his stolen white horse. "You heard the man. Let's ride."

Shelton and Jasper threw Will to the muddy ground and kicked at his arms and legs, howling in a fit of laughter before joining the rest of the entourage.

"Will!" Madi cried as she was released. She lunged forward and trampled through the mud-laden road in her bare feet. She fell to her knees and wrapped her arms around his waist, holding him tight. "I'm sorry, Will," she wept against his chest. "I'm so, so sorry."

The light drizzle grew to a consistent shower, which sent a damp, muggy chill through the air.

Will closed his eyes and tilted his head back, letting the rain hit his face as Bushy Beard and his wicked assembly disappeared down the road, yipping and cursing with pistols blazing.

Wake up, Will. It's time to wake up.

Chapter 21

"*I* - I want to go home," Madi whimpered.

Fighting through the pulsating pain that tortured his stomach, Will slowly rose to his feet. He looked down at his sister's worried face as the cool summer rain dripped off the tips of her wet hair and ran down her bare arms. "I know," he said, pulling her close. "Come on. Let's go find someplace dry."

"Little girl! Boy!" came a soft, yet urgent voice.

Will wiped the rain out of his eyes and scanned the road.

"Over here," the voice called out again.

Across the street, standing halfway out of the front door of a red brick home, Will saw the teenage girl in the maroon-colored dress, waving them over.

"It's her," Madi said. "She's the one I was telling you about."

"Come quickly," the girl yelled.

Madi started across the road, but Will pulled her back. "No, Madi. We can't."

"Why not?"

"Because we don't belong here."

"And you think I don't know that?"

"Hurry. I fear there is not much time," the girl urged.

Madi looked up at Will. "Where do you expect us to go?"

Will hesitated. He looked past his sister, searching the desolate town for an answer. He sorted through all the possibilities, all the places to hide and take refuge from the weather and the rising hostilities, but Madi was right. Where would they go?

Exhaustion plagued Will - mentally and physically; he needed to think; figure everything out. Not to mention, they both were filthy and soaked to the bone.

J.B. Pierce

Will looked over at the house and then back down at his sister, who stood hugging her shivering body. "All right," he said with a heavy sigh. "Come on. Let's go."

|||||-|||||

Will and Madi stepped into the house but stopped in their tracks from a sour and pungent aroma that hung heavy in the air.

"What's that smell?" Will asked, breathing into his wet t-shirt.

"Yeah, it's horrible," Madi said, covering her nose.

"Salt," the young girl replied. "And smoke from corn cobs."

"Salt?" Madi asked.

"Why, yes. It preserves the quality of meat," the young girl said.

Will and Madi looked at one another confused.

"Father's town's butcher," the young girl continued as she locked the front door. "The smell is strong at first, especially with this heat we've been having, but you'll get used to it in no time."

Will peered past the girl's shoulder and into the adjacent room. A long wooden table, with a cast iron scale and three stackable weights, took up most of the space. Knives and cleavers, with sharp points or curved metal, hung beyond a wooden pocket that ran alongside the table. Hooks in the shape of an S dangled from a six-foot metal rod that hung out from the wall. A rectangular chalkboard declared: "Salted Pork Special - $.10 a pound!"

The young girl gathered the front layers of her dress. "If you may," she said. "This way."

Will and Madi took each other's hand, lacing their fingers together, and closely followed the girl down the hall.

The end of the hallway opened to a large but modest kitchen with an iron cook stove and a table for kneading dough. On one side of the room, six wooden shelves were built into the wall and held various bottles - some clear, others brown, green, and yellow - all of

140

which were corked closed. Tin cans and canvas bags were labeled and neatly placed in alphabetical order on the top two shelves. Ceramic bowls, kettles, pots, and other cooking utensils rested on the bottom shelf. Parsley and basil hung in clusters from the rafters.

The back door opened and in walked a middle-aged woman, wearing a long, plaid dress with a basket full of ripe apples. She closed the door and slipped a cream-colored apron over her head, tying its cotton ties behind her back.

"Goodness me," the woman said with a start as she turned around. "I didn't see you there, child. You gave me such a - " The woman glanced at her daughter and then over at Will and Madi, who stood soaking wet beyond the threshold of the door. "Matilda, who, may I ask, are these two children standing inside our home?"

"Oh, Mother. You couldn't imagine," Matilda began. "As I was looking out our front window for Father's return, I saw these two stranded on the road, standing in the pouring rain. With all that is happening to our town, I took it upon myself to provide them shelter. As you have told me before, the greatest bounty that one shall receive is in those we seek to help."

"Yes, my dear, you are correct, and I applaud you on your charity, but - " Matilda's mother stopped and stared harshly at Will.

Will felt the woman's eyes burning holes in their clothes as she scrutinized their appearance. "We - ah - we should go," he said, lifting his bloody hand in protest. "Thank you, but we don't- "

"My heavens," Matilda's mother exclaimed. "Whatever happened to you?"

Will looked at his wound. "This? It's nothing really. Just a scratch."

Matilda's mother walked over to Will and examined his hand. "I can assure you, young man, that hole is certainly no scratch."

"I shall go fetch your elixirs, Mother," Matilda said, rushing out of the kitchen.

Will pulled back his hand and took Madi by the elbow. "Really, I'm fine. Thank you for your concern, but we – "

"Hush now," Matilda's mother ordered. She folded her arms across her chest and sauntered closer. "How old are you?"

"Fif-" Will cleared his throat. "Fifteen."

"And she, I imagine, is your sister?"

"Yes, mam."

"Your parents? Where can I find them?"

Will looked over at Madi, whose red and puffy eyes peered out from behind strands of stringy hair. What was he to say? That their parents are more than 150 years in the future, unaware that both their children were magically thrown into the past by some mysterious and unexplainable power. Will could barely believe it himself; how could and why would this woman accept the truth?

Madi wrapped her arms around Will's waist, burying her head in his chest and started to cry.

"Oh, please child. No need for tears," Matilda's mother said. "It was not my intention to upset you."

"It-it's okay," Madi mumbled, wiping her eyes dry.

"No. It's not. It seems that ever since the War has found its way North to our little town, I have to remind myself that what was once familiar and comfortable around here swiftly has changed." Matilda's mother placed a comforting hand on both Will and Madi's arms. "Let me restart by saying that inside these walls you are safe. There shall be food to fill your stomach and a place to lie down until you can move on and find your family wherever they may be. Wherever you two have traveled from, I can plainly see that it has been quite a journey. Now, please, have yourselves a seat."

Will allowed himself – and Madi – to be ushered further into the room. Together, they sat down at the kitchen table on a narrow wooden bench. Matilda's mother came up behind them and shrouded each of their wet shoulders with thin, woolen blankets.

"Thank you," Madi said, pulling the ends of the blanket close.

"You are quite welcome," Matilda's mother replied.

Will sat under the warmth of the blanket and watched as Matilda's mother placed a small jar of apple butter, a knife, and two plates on the table. She took a pan of warm biscuits out of the oven and set it in front of him.

Will's stomach rumbled, smelling the sweet aroma of baked dough. He thought back to the last time Madi and he had eaten. The Independence Day Fair. Will remembered he had a corn dog, and they both split a funnel cake. How much real-time has passed since then? And did it continue to move forward with each passing hour and day, or did it stop, waiting patiently – paused in limbo – for their return home?

A tea kettle sitting over a small flame on the cast iron stove whistled in complaint against its rising temperature, pulling Will from his musing.

"Please," Matilda's mother said. "Help yourselves."

Without hesitation, Madi grabbed a biscuit from the top of the pile and began to eat.

Will sat unmoved, mulling over their journey so far; the supernatural obstacles they fought; the imposing powers and strength they stood up against. He looked down at his wounded hand; even his own pain he endured. Will glanced over at Madi. By some design of twisted fate, they both had been thrown back in time without any choice of their own and held in its sticky web.

"Eat." Matilda's mother urged. "I'm sure you are hungry."

Will gave a casual nod and then took a warm biscuit in his hands. He brought it to his lips and stopped, wondering. If he succumbed to the hunger ravaging his stomach and took a bite, would it confirm the reality of this alternate place and altered time?

"Go on," Matilda's mother gestured.

Will pushed the question out of his mind and bit into the biscuit.

He sighed as the flaky dough hit his mouth – buttery and moist. His shoulders relaxed and the burdens of this time and place seemed to disappear for the moment. He took another bite and another, relishing in the biscuit's sweet flavor that reminded him of the crescent rolls Nana made with the summer dinners around the table.

Will dropped the biscuit and quickly pushed it aside.

"If I may," came Matilda's voice.

Will looked up from the table and found the young girl standing beside him, a metal box in her hands. "I'm fine. Really," he insisted.

"Oh fiddlesticks. It will only be a few moments' time."

Matilda pulled out a chair and tucked her skirts under her before sitting down. She opened the box and then took Will's injured hand in hers.

Will's heart skipped a beat, feeling her petite, soft hands moving slowly against his own.

"I say," Matilda began as she dabbed his wound with a white cloth. "How awful it must have been to be in the hands of those horrible Rebels."

"What did you say?" Will asked.

Matilda looked at her mother, who was tending to an assortment of jars and tins on a nearby shelf. She leaned into Will and lowered her voice. "I saw the man, the one with the bushy beard."

"The one who stole your horse," Will whispered back.

Matilda nodded. "Moments after, I overheard Mother speaking with Father and found that he went in search of the Rebel general in hopes to get our horseback. With everything going on here in our little town, I fear my faith has gone asunder." The girl blinked back her tears, composing herself and continued, "But you . . . you truly cannot fathom how fortunate you are that they let you go." Matilda scrunched her eyes and picked at a dark spot on Will's hand. "How on earth did you manage to injure yourself?"

"Long story," Will replied, averting his eyes.

Matilda gently pulled out a lingering splinter, and then with a piece of clean cloth, wiped away the blood that puddled in the palm of Will's hand. She grabbed a brown, glass bottle with a cork top labeled – iodine, opened it, and poured out its orangey liquid.

Will winced under its sharp sting.

Taking a deep breath, Matilda pursed her lips and softly blew onto his hand, cooling the irritation. She locked eyes with Will and smiled.

Will swallowed hard and quickly looked away, wondering if she noticed the flush on his face.

Across. Over. Around. Underneath.

With intricate detail, Matilda bounded Will's hand with a long strip of cloth. "Just another wrap. A quick tie, and . . . there," she said, completing the knot. She gathered her belongings and tossed Will's bloody cloth in a wicker basket that sat in the corner of the kitchen. "You'll see. In a few days, you shall be as good as new."

Chapter 22

After Matilda had returned and bandaged Will's hand, he barely finished his biscuit. He couldn't help but think there was something very familiar about her as she scurried around the room, helping her mother fill empty mason jars with berry preserves. Was it her natural beauty; the way she spoke? Or was it the kindhearted nature she showed in tending his wounded hand? Will shook his head. No; it was something else, something bigger; if only he could remember.

"Goodness me," Matilda shrieked, nearly dropping a half-filled jar onto the table. "With everything that has happened this morning, my manners have slipped past me. I didn't even ask you your names."

"Madilyn," Madi replied with a mouthful of biscuit. "But people call me Madi, right Will?"

Will gave a weak smile.

"Well, then," Matilda said, brushing a loose piece of her hair off her forehead. 'Will. Madi. It is a pleasure to meet you both." She smiled. "As you already know, I'm Matilda. And this is Mother, Mrs. Margaret Pierce."

"How do you do?" Mrs. Pierce said.

Pierce. Will thought. *Matilda Pierce.*

Slowly, he ran his fingers across the white cloth of his bandaged hand, repeating the girl's name over and over in his head. His fingers froze and his breath caught in his throat as a chill shocked his spine. All the pictures he had seen in books. All the stories he had heard from his grandfather; the courageous first-hand account of tending the wounded and dying soldiers at the Weikert farm during the Battle of Gettysburg. It was her; it had to be.

"Tillie?" Will said. He met the girl's surprised eyes.

"How – " Tillie said, setting down a fresh basket of biscuits on the table. "How do you know that?"

Before Will could answer, a loud pounding rattled the back door.

"Good Heavens," Mrs. Pierce shrieked. She wiped her hands down the front of her apron and peeked through the sheer curtain hanging from the kitchen window. With a sharp gasp, she spun around on her heels; her hand clutching her chest; her eyes wild.

"Mother, what's wrong? Who's at our door?" Tillie asked.

"Rebels," she whispered.

Madi dropped her half-eaten biscuit to the table and scooted closer to Will.

"What could they possibly want now?" Tillie asked. "They already have taken our horse."

"Oh, how I wish your father was here," Mrs. Pierce said, nervously knotting her fingers together. "I warned him not to go."

Will slid the blanket off his shoulders and raised himself just enough to see outside. Beyond the curtain and wavy glass, a group of Confederate soldiers milled around the back of the house, gawking up at the windows and poking fun at one another. In the middle of the bunch was an impatient, bulky man, with a cruel smirk behind a full growth of facial hair.

Will felt every hair on his body stand on end. He rose from the table, pulling Madi up with him. "Will," she said as he pulled her to the farthest corner of the room. "What are you – "

"He's here," Will breathed.

"Who?"

"Bushy Beard."

Another knock.

"I know you're in there," the brute snarled from behind the door. "I can see ya all moving."

"We need to hide," Will whispered to Tillie and her mother.

"Hide?" Mrs. Pierce asked confused. "Why on earth would you need to . . ." Her eyes grew concerned. "You have done something, haven't you? How dare you bring – "

"No. It's nothing like that. It's just that – "

Bushy Beard knocked louder.

"Please," Will insisted. "I know you don't know my sister or me for that matter, but I promise you on my life that I have done nothing that would bring harm to you or your house."

"Whatcha, y'all waiting for?" Bushy Beard bellowed.

Tillie looked at Will and then over at her mother with urgent eyes, who was standing at the back door; her hand hovering above the doorknob. "Mother, please."

Mrs. Pierce looked at Will and Madi and let out a reluctant sigh. She nodded toward the hallway. "Quickly now, Tillie," she said in a whisper. "You know the place."

"Yes, Mother. Will. Madi. This way."

Tillie gathered the front of her dress and scurried down the hallway.

Hand in hand, Will and Madi rushed out of the kitchen, following the girl to the front of the house.

The back door opened, creaking ever-so-slightly.

"It's about bloody time," came Bushy Beard's rough voice.

Will glanced back toward the kitchen. There the brute stood in the doorway surrounded by his troupe of Confederate soldiers, who look more like a pack of begging dogs.

"Well . . ." Bushy Beard huffed, towering over Mrs. Pierce. "Aren't you going to let us in?"

Will turned back around and followed the girls into the butcher room; the sharp, smoky, and salty smell hit his nose once again. "You're kidding, right?" he said to Tillie. "Where the heck are we going to hide in here?"

Tillie didn't answer. She hurried across the room to a lone

bookshelf that sat flush with the plaster wall. She knelt down and lifted a tarnished, tin box on the bottom shelf, revealing a small notch that sat an inch higher than the rest of the board. Using her thumb, she pressed down on the notch, drawing the circular button even with the floor. *Click.*

"Father . . . " Tillie said with a low grunt as she pulled the shelf away from the wall. ". . . added this to the house a few years back when the abolition movement began. He was adamant to help those that needed a place of refuge on their journey North to freedom. One cannot tell, but it sits opposite of Mother's shelf in the kitchen."

Will stared in awe. The hidden space appeared to measure no more than three feet tall and four feet wide. Its sides and floor were lined with rough wooden planks, and the ceiling was constructed of loose mortar and two timbered beams. "It's amazing," he said.

Tillie smiled. "Quite so."

A loud bang startled the trio.

"Hurry now," she warned.

Will and Madi crouched down and slipped into the darkness. Dust and dirt sat in-between the thin and tight niches in the wooden planks while silvery cobwebs strung themselves like streamers across the worn beams and corners of the space.

"My apologies for the awfully close quarters," Tillie said in a hushed voice as she sealed Will and Madi inside. She slipped her fingers through a small slit between two boards. "You will be safe. I can assure you; they will never find you in here."

Will adjusted himself in the tiny space and lightly squeezed her fingers. "Thank you."

Tillie drew back her hand and replaced the tin box on the bottom shelf. "You won't be able to open it from the inside, so I'll return when all is safe."

Will squinted through the narrow gap and watched as Tillie stopped at the butcher table. She took one of her Father's knives, gripping it in her hand and looked back one last time at the bookshelf before making her way out of the room.

In the semi-darkness, Will felt his heart begin to race. The stale and stagnant air, mixed with a dusting of salt and smoke, became a thick, suffocating blanket, pushing down on him with each passing minute.

Will closed his eyes and took a deep breath. He pictured himself kicking around his soccer ball on the field at school or riding Grandpa's tractor across the open field, trying anything to alleviate his escalating anxiety.

"I hate the dark," Madi muttered through the stillness.

"Shhh . . . "

"There are probably bugs in here."

"Quiet," Will whispered.

"They're going to crawl all over us or bite us and – "

"Knock it off, will ya?"

Madi sat back with a huff, wrapping her arms around her legs. "I'm just saying."

"So am I. Now, shhh."

Will closed his eyes again, straining to listen beyond the walls, but all he could hear was the rhythmic pulse of his heart thumping in his ears.

Breathe. Just breathe.

"What if she never comes back for us?" Madi continued.

"She will."

"But maybe she won't. We'll be stuck in here forever then. Run out of air; starve to death – "

"I shall say – " came Mrs. Pierce's muffled voice. "That's a thing to ask after taking one's horse."

"But we're hungry," a soldier's shrill pleading voice.

A collection of canned conversations and heavy footsteps penetrated their way through the layer of wood, plaster, and paint that separated the secret hiding space from the kitchen. To Will, it sounded more like a herd of wild boars than people as the soldiers stormed into the kitchen. Even the chairs screeched in protest as they were dragged along the wooden floor by the unwelcome visitors.

"Gentlemen, if you would be so kind as to wait outside," Mrs. Pierce said. "That way I can – "

"Outside?" Bushy Beard snarled loudly. "I say, Madam, that doesn't sound too hospitable to me?"

"I need to see what's going on," Will whispered, bumping into Madi as he shuffled around the cramped space.

Will placed his back against the shelf and extended his arms to the wall in front of him. Little by little, he probed at the boards, searching for a gap or crack. His index finger slid between a narrow divide of two boards, sending a sliver of light – the size of a dime – slicing through the darkness.

Adjusting his eyes to the sudden light, Will peered through the thin opening, looking past a small stack of ceramic dishes. He watched as Bushy Beard waltzed over to Mrs. Pierce, who was standing near the back door.

"You wouldn't be hiding anyone?" the brute asked. "A teenage boy and a little lassie, maybe?"

"No, sir. It's just me and my daughter," Mrs. Pierce answered.

"And where would she be at the present moment?"

"That sir is none of your business."

Bushy Beard leaned in close, inches from Mrs. Pierce's face. "Says who?"

Mrs. Pierce drew back slightly and stared up at the towering brute unyielding in her stance.

Bushy Beard curled his lip, letting out a loud grunt and then made his way around the kitchen. With a heavy hand, he lifted lids off of pots and slid dishes off their shelves, sending them crashing to the floor. His Confederate cronies, who were assembled around the table stuffing their faces with biscuits and globs of apple butter, hooted and hollered as each plate shattered to pieces.

Bushy Beard made his way to the corner of the kitchen and stopped. "Where is he?" he growled, staring down at the wicker basket near his feet.

The room and everyone in it fell silent.

"I beg your pardon?" Mrs. Pierce asked politely.

Bushy Beard bent down and reached inside the basket. He stood up and lifted his hand, showcasing the white cotton cloth stained with Will's blood. "If I recall, you claimed no one else was in this household other than your daughter, who is conveniently not present at the moment. So," Bushy Beard said, eyeing up Mrs. Pierce, "seeing you with no visible wounds – *pardon me, Madam* – but how on earth can you explain this?"

A shooting pain speared Will's calf. He grabbed his cramping leg and hit the top of his head against the ceiling of the enclosure, sending a cluster of loose dirt sprinkling down his forehead. The dust tickled his nose. He breathed in deep, and . . .

"Ah-choo!" Will cupped his mouth to silence his sneeze, but it was too late.

"Who was that?" Bushy Beard asked.

Idiot. Will cursed himself inwardly. How stupid could he be? He looked over at Madi and saw the whites of her eyes staring back at him in the obscurity of the secret space.

"Goodness me, gentlemen," came Tillie's voice.

Will peered back through the opening in the wall and found Tillie entering the kitchen, wrapping her hand with a white bandage that slowly began to stain red.

"That was *you?*" Bushy Beard jeered with a curl of his lip.

"Not one of my best traits, I must say," said Tillie, lightly wiping her nose.

"Matilda, goodness child, your hand. You have to be more careful when handling Father's knives," Mrs. Pierce said, looking at her daughter and then over at Bushy Beard.

Bushy Beard drew out his pistol from his waistband, the bloody cloth still clutched in his hand. "I'll have you know, lying to opposing generals during wartime or fostering persons of interest places you and your household in grave danger. Now, you have thirty seconds. Where is he?"

Mrs. Pierce stepped forward, shielding her daughter. "How dare you?" she seethed. "You push your way through our town, take our horse, storm into our house and eat our food, and now you draw your weapon upon us, demanding the whereabouts of some teenage boy and child. What would your Confederate officers think of your actions?"

Bushy Beard stepped close. "What makes you think I care?" he sneered. "Eddie," he called over his shoulder. "You stay with them. The rest of y'all, with me."

The soldiers didn't move but continued to stuff their mouths.

"I know you heard me," Bushy Beard said. "Quit acting like pigs at slops and get a-movin'. Find that boy."

Like a master puppeteer controlling all his marionettes at once, the soldiers rose to their feet and quickly dispersed. Will followed the harsh sounds of their footsteps out of the kitchen, down the hall, and throughout the house. He turned himself around and looked through the slats of the secret shelf. He watched as a pair of rugged boots stepped into the butcher room.

"Buford. Hey, Buford," yelled a soldier. "Come quick."

Madi grasped Will's arm. "They found us," she said with a quiet quiver to her voice. "They found us, and it's all your – "

Will covered her mouth, smothering her words. "Shut up or they will," he huffed into her ear through clenched teeth.

Bushy Beard stormed into the butcher room. "What is it, Shelton? You find him?"

"No," Shelton answered, stuffing his face with Madi's half-eaten biscuit. "That there sign says <u>Salted Pork</u>." Shelton jumped back out into the hall. "Excuse me, ma'am, but do you by chance have any salted pork left?"

Bushy Beard clamped his meaty hand down on Shelton's shoulder and yanked him back. "Shut your trap, you lunk; where's your brain, huh?" he said, tapping the top of Shelton's head with the muzzle of his gun.

"I'm sorry Buford," Shelton said, recoiling with each blow. "I'm just hungry; that's all."

"If we find that Yankee the boss told me about," Bushy Beard said, "we'll get more than just salted pork."

Shelton finished the biscuit and licked his fingers clean. "What's ah - what's he look like again, Buford? My memory hasn't been serving me too well since the start of this war."

Bushy Beard pulled out a small tintype photograph from his front pocket.

"Whooey! That's him all right," Shelton said, rubbing his bruised head. He followed Bushy Beard further into the room. "I can't believe it. You had the lad right there in your hands, and you let 'em go."

Bushy Beard grabbed a fistful of Shelton's shirt. "What you implying?"

"Ah, nothing Buford. It - it's a shame, really."

Bushy Beard shoved Shelton back into a wall. "Find him."

"Yea. Sure thing. Right away, Buford."

Will leaned forward, keeping his eyes on Bushy Beard. The brute stuffed the photograph back into his shirt pocket and made his way across the room. As he passed the butcher table, he extended his gun from his meaty hand and slowly ran its barrel against the hanging knives; their metal blades clinked like raging wind chimes.

"I don't think he's in here," said Shelton, looking inside a small copper pot.

Bushy Beard stopped at the bookshelf. He knelt down and pushed aside a few of the items. He squinted and peered between the thin, dark spaces between the boards.

Holding a collective breath, Will and Madi pressed themselves hard against the back wall and huddled close.

"Sir?" came a rich southern voice.

"What?" Bushy Beard spat over his shoulder.

"We searched everywhere, Colonel," the soldier said. "The woman's right. The house is empty."

Bushy Beard let out an unsatisfied huff. He looked back at the bookshelf with beady eyes unaware that beyond the smoky shadows, Will stared back, hiding a mere three feet away.

Chapter 23

*W*ill emerges from a dark and dense forest. He runs across an open field of tall grass, but stops, hearing a round of laughter; its high-pitched vibrato trilling against the warm breeze. He looks over his shoulder. The sun rises above the tree line and pierces his blue eyes.

Will takes a step forward and feels his feet slip out from under him, burying him in the sea of tall grass. He rubs the back of his head and blinks. Above him, the face of a young woman slowly comes into focus. Her skin appears translucent; smooth as porcelain; her lips red as a rose.

Who - who are you? Will struggles to ask.

The young woman giggles at his question and smiles down at him with enchanting sable eyes. She offers her hand and helps him to his feet.

A field sparrow, somewhere in the distance, whistles and trills its song. Another returns the call with a short, cricket chirp.

The young woman wraps her thin arm around Will's waist and pushes close. I'm so happy I found you, she whispers in his ear.

Her soft cheek brushes against his and a gust of wind swirls her long brown hair up and onto his shoulders, sending a scent of lavender sailing through the air. She pulls away and laces her soft and delicate fingers into his. Come, she says. This way.

Under the warmth of the setting sun, they walk together through the field. No words are spoken; no sound is passed between them; an evening of serenity surrounds them in still harmony. As they near the edge of the field, the young woman stops and points down an ethereal, deserted dirt path.

There, she says, is where the truth lies.

Truth lies? Will asks. *What does that –*

The ground tremors in a low grumble. Trees bend and groan in distress. A current of wind rumbles down the path, tearing leaves away from their stems.

Will grips the young woman's hand but feels her slip out of his hold through the growing turbulence. He fights through the storm to reach her, but she quickly vanishes within the colors of the approaching dusk.

A biting timbre punctures the air and shatters the setting sun into pieces. Will closes his eyes and shields himself from the shower of topaz fragments plunging from the sky. His body twitches as they scrape and scorch his skin.

The air thickens with smoke, casting a gray screen over the field. Screams and moans sail on the cusp of the wicked wind. All around soldiers – young and old – materialize before him from beneath the tall grass. They reach their bruised and bloody hands, begging for help. Will tries to run from the dissonance of death but finds his bare feet submerged in a thick pool of blood.

A thundering roar rattles the earth. A round metal orb soars overhead. It slams into a nearby tree and shatters its trunk in a fiery explosion, tossing Will to the ground.

The woods grow quiet except for the small crackling of burning and breaking tree branches. Will slowly rises to his feet. He wipes the dirt out of his eyes and watches a very, tall young man with a black top hat push through the smoke and raining debris.

The man smirks at Will, aims a gun, and . . .**Bang!**

Will buckles from the bullet's force as it penetrates through his jacket and pierces his skin. He places his hands over his heart and slumps to the ground, feeling a pang of fire surge deep within his chest. Blood seeps through his fingers. He trembles and struggles to breathe. As he closes his eyes, he hears the distant voice of the young woman screaming his name.

|||||-|||||

Will jerked awake in a cold sweat, hearing his name. Through a flickering orange glow, the face of Tillie came into focus; an oil lamp resting in her hands.

Tillie shuffled back from the bookshelf. "Come," she said. "The Rebels have finally left."

Will ran his hand through his damp hair and licked his dry lips, making no attempt to move. The dream. He had it again. But this time, it was all too real. He could still see her beautiful face and sultry eyes looking at him. He could still smell her lavender scent and feel her body wrapped in his arms.

Will winced, pinching his eyes shut. *The wind. The blood.* All the dying men, lying in the field, clawing at his feet. *The acrid smoke; the man; the gun; the bullet; the pain.*

"I assure you, it's quite all right," Tillie said.

Will shuddered. He pushed the images aside and buried them deep in his mind. He turned to Madi and lightly nudged her shoulder. "Madi. Wake up. It's time to go."

With a drawn-out yawn, Madi crawled out of the dark space.

Will wobbled to his feet and stretched his stiff, cramped body. "What time is it?" he asked, looking around the sepia-shaded room.

"Half-past ten," Tillie replied.

10:30?

"After the Rebels searched the house," Tillie continued as she closed the shelf, "let's just say they extended their welcome longer than Mother and I would have liked. We stood in the doorway and prayed silently for them to leave, but it was apparent they could not suppress their gluttony. It was only when Father returned – and without our horse – that they finally left." She gathered the front of her skirt. "Come. I will show you both to your room."

"Thanks, but we should go," Will said, bringing Madi close.

"You and your family have done enough for– "

"You can't," Tillie insisted. "Mother says it's much too dangerous out."

"But the gate is closed," Madi babbled as she nuzzled herself against Will's chest. "Misty can't go that far."

Tillie placed a gentle hand on Will's shoulder. "There is no shame in rest before you both can move on."

Will looked down at his sister, who stood half-asleep in his arms. "I guess you're right. Just for tonight. Tomorrow, we leave."

Tillie bowed her head slightly and then led Will and Madi out of the butcher room and up a mahogany staircase to a second-floor bedroom that was tucked into the corner of the house.

Will shuffled Madi over to the only bed in the room and pulled back the covers. He laid her down and slipped her legs under the cotton quilt.

"I must say," Tillie whispered as she carefully lifted the glass off her oil lamp and used its flame to light a latent candle that sat on a wooden desk near a curtained window. "I never saw anything quite so captivating."

"Excuse me?" Will asked.

"Your sister's necklace," Tillie said, coming up beside Will.

Will looked at the oak tree medallion that rested on Madi's chest.

Tillie gently sat down at the edge of the bed. "It happened a few years ago," she began. "I was walking home from my daily session at the Seminary for Young Ladies – that's where I attend school – but instead of following my usual path through the field, I made my way through town, heading to the mercantile for Mother. As I passed by Mr. Wills' house and turned down Baltimore, I suddenly stopped at the sight of a tall, young man." She shook her head. "No, he was unusually tall – almost as tall as the gas street lamp he was leaning against."

"I urged myself to move on, but I found myself oddly fascinated by his casual demeanor and peculiar attire. His black top hat had thick glasses attached to its fabric, and his belt and shirt had small metal buttons and tiny wheels and gears like those they use in factories. But the strangest of all was how he wore his red suspenders, which hung over his gray vest and fastened to the outside of his brown trousers."

Will sat down on a wooden captain's chair in the corner of the room, listening to Tillie's story.

"A carriage wheeled between us," she went on, "And before I could look away, the young man glanced up from a playbill he was reading and caught me staring in his direction. Dreadfully embarrassed, I quickly started home but stopped when he called out to me."

Tillie met Will's eyes; the flicker of the orange and yellow flame highlighted her face. "He called me by my name."

Will leaned forward in his chair. "He what?"

"Can you imagine?" Tillie said with a slight laugh. "A perfect stranger – one I never saw in our little town – speak my name. By any means, the young man closed his playbill and then strolled across the road in a casual air as if he had no care in the world. He removed his top hat and took my hand in his, which – strange in itself – felt unusually cold for such a hot day."

"At that moment, I knew I should have gone straight home, but I couldn't will my feet to move; there was something about the way he *looked* at me. His eyes were haunting and a bit frightening, but mesmerizing all the same. When he leaned in close, my breath caught in my throat as he whispered his name in my ear."

"For a brief moment, I felt weak; succumbed to his power as if lost in his trance." Tillie grew rigid. She folded her hands together and stared past Will as she went on.

"His words were velvet; his voice a spellbinding song. I listened intently to his story, a story he told me of seven vigilantes, who with a turn of a key and the press of a button had the power to travel through time. He claimed these seven, with the strength of an oak, had vowed to protect the ill-fated and help those in need."

Tillie blinked and smiled to herself. "Funny. His story took me back to when I was a child and sat on Father's knee, listening to the heroic folktale of Robin Hood. And the more he continued in his elaborate manner, I was further drawn in."

"Like a moth to a flame, I was captivated by his story. In all my years, I've never encountered someone so persuasive to have me listen. And then, through it all, I heard Mother's voice."

"Matilda," came the muffled call of Mrs. Pierce from somewhere down the hall.

Tillie rose from the bed and quickly closed the door. "I turned around and there she was beside me, rightfully angered by my behavior. Mother seized me by my arm and sternly pulled me away, but not without scolding the young man that towered over her for filling my head with nonsense. I tried and tried to tell her it was nothing that he meant no harm, but she dragged me down the road saying: 'Matilda, a young lady should never converse with strange men and listen to such hogwash' – gibberish, which she says taints the soul with fear and gives nothing but false hope."

"As Mother walked into our home, I secretly held back. I could not resist the urge to take another glance at him. And when I did, the young man tipped his hat and bowed in my direction. I looked away, feeling my heart flutter for he was quite fashionably handsome, and I was smitten by his mysterious allure. And yet again, I found myself tempted to see him one more time. But when I looked back up the road, the charming Mr. Fink was gone."

Will jumped up from the chair. "Who did you say?"

"Matilda, what's taking you so long, child?" Mrs. Pierce called with an impatience to her voice.

"You and Madi," Tillie whispered. "You're one of them? One of the seven vigilantes."

"Us?" Will sternly shook his head. "No."

"But Fink's story. must be true. She wears the oak he spoke of."

"I'm sorry, but you're wrong."

Tillie moved closer and met Will's gaze. "Whether you believe me or not, you must promise that none of what I have confessed to you is spoken to Mother or anyone else for that matter. You are the only person I have ever told."

"Matilda."

Tillie opened the door. "Coming Mother." She looked back at Will. "Please."

"Yeah," Will said. "Sure thing."

"Thank you." Tillie gave a smile and then rushed out of the room, closing the door quietly behind her.

A muffled clatter of wagon wheels pulled by galloping horses filtered into the room from the outside. Will walked over to the window and pushed back its long, lace curtain. Through the fog that painted the glass, he saw a sliver of the full moon breaking through the lingering rain clouds.

Will wiped the moisture off the single-paned window with his bandaged hand and looked down at the street. Muted shadows of a few civilians, who braved the night, were guiding their families and livestock up and down the road, fleeing from the imminent danger. In the distance, small patches of yellow and orange dotted the dark horizon. *Fires,* Will thought, knowing Union and Confederate soldiers lingered on the fringes of the small town.

He dropped the curtain and looked over at Madi, who was fast asleep. A small glimmer of light shimmered from the face of the oak tree medallion. Will furrowed his brow. The medallion flickered again.

It can't be true, can it?

Will went to Madi's bedside and stared down at the medallion; its opaque resin reflected shades of iridescent amber against the candle's light. Hypnotized, he reached for the necklace. As his fingers brushed over the raised metallic branches of the oak tree, a small web of lightning shot out from its center and nipped hard at his fingertips. "Ah. Ow."

Will pulled back from the jolt and looked down at his throbbing hand. His pulse quickened and sweat beaded on his forehead as a thin sheen of ice began to glaze his burning fingertips in an icy lattice design.

What's happening to me?

The room warped in a bending arc. Elongated yellow spheres of light from the candle, entwined in its own shadows, danced sporadically up and down the walls.

Will staggered across the room and fell back into the captain's chair. He clutched its armrests and dug his fingernails into the wood as the fiery frost infused his fingers. He fought to breathe as the liquid ice traveled across his palms. He watched as it braided up his arms and shrouded his neckline with choking hands.

Will bit down on his lower lip and threw back his head, stifling the scream that violently rose in his throat as a rapid montage of vintage images flashed in his eyes and tainted his memory and mind.

Chapter 24

adi woke to a scent of sweet cinnamon and sharp salt. She rolled onto her side and sat up, yawning wide. From behind a pair of lace curtains, a golden hue of morning light struggled to push its way into the room.

Madi brushed away a thin layer of her hair that covered her face and rubbed her bleary eyes with her fists. She peeled back the quilt that blanketed her legs and stood up; her dirty, bare feet hitting the cool, wooden floor. Half asleep, she shuffled over to the window and drew back the curtain.

Slices of the sun slid through homes and buildings throughout the town. On the street below, men were gathered in small huddles, conversing. Women, with baskets in hand, strolled up and down the sidewalks; their young children shadowing behind them. A dog barked. The children's laughter filled the air.

Madi turned her attention across the road. A young man in a black, derby hat stood leaning up against a white-sided home, intently reading from a small book. He turned the page, looked up at the window, and waved.

Madi quickly dropped the curtain and grabbed the necklace around her neck, looping its chain over and over her finger.

"Where did you get that?" came a groggy voice.

Madi jumped, finding Will sitting on a captain's chair in a shadowed corner of the room; his elbows on his knees; his chin resting on top of his folded hands. "Will. You – ah – you scared me."

"That necklace. Where did you get it?" he asked again.

"How long have you been sitting there? I thought you were – hey, are you okay? You don't look so well."

Will ran his bandaged hand down over the dark circles that hung under his puffy eyes. "I couldn't sleep." He shifted in the chair. "You didn't answer me. Where did you get that?"

A light knocking, followed by a groan of oil-thirsty hinges rang off the bedroom walls. "Will? Madi? Are you awake?"

Tillie pushed open the door and walked into the room, carrying an armload of clothes and shoes. "Good morning," she said. "I did not mean to disturb you both, but I arose early and took the liberty of getting you both fresh new garments."

Madi watched as the girl walked over to the bed and carefully laid out two outfits: a peach, ankle-length jumper with short sleeves, an ivory petticoat, thin white stockings, a pair of blue trousers, a white linen shirt, suspenders, and brown cotton socks.

"Soap and hand towels are underneath the washstand," Tillie said as she poured water from a porcelain pitcher into its matching bowl. "And I fashioned a few clean bandages for your hand."

"Thanks," Will replied.

"Once you both are settled, come and join us for breakfast," she said. "Mother's made ham, eggs, and griddlecakes with powdered cinnamon." Tillie smiled and then walked out of the room, closing the door behind her.

"So, tell me," Will began. "Where did you get that necklace?"

"Underneath the clubhouse," Madi answered, running the dress' silky, lace belt through her fingertips.

"When?"

"The day Cassie and me asked you to help us outside."

Will stood up from the chair. "Open it."

"What?"

"I want to see the inside."

Madi sat down on the edge of the bed and placed the oak tree medallion in her hand. She pressed her thumb hard against the top button, popping its cover open.

Will sat beside her. "I've seen something like this before."

"You have?"

Will nodded. "One large faceplate, three small clocks, and a flip-clock, whose number changes with each rotation. So, other than the square flip-clock box, which reads 26, every other clock has its hand pointing to a different number. 6 – 18 – 6 – 3."

"What do you think it means?" Madi asked.

Will rose to his feet and paced the floor, mumbling the numbers over and over again. He stopped in midstride. "A date."

"A what?"

"It's a date." Will sat back down. "Look. . . the number in the flip-clock and each other clock represents a different number in a calendar year. Twenty-six is the day. Eighteen, six, and three are the four digits of the year, and six is the month."

"Really?" Madi said. She brought the necklace closer and studied its components.

Will stood up and rubbed the back of his neck. "But it still doesn't make any sense. After the Independence Day Fair and the storm, we ended up in the past, but somehow still in Grandpa's barn, where we met that kid with the two-colored eyes."

"Jeremiah," Madi interrupted.

"Sure. Whatever his name was," Will said, pacing the floor. "But remember what he told us? He said the date was June 26, 1848."

"That's right," Madi agreed. "And when you asked that kid on the street yesterday what the year was, he said it was 1863."

"Which means," Will went on, "at one point while we were back in 1848, the year on that necklace was changed, and it brought us here."

"But how? And who could have changed it?"

Will thought for a moment. "You," he whispered.

"Me?"

"You changed it. You brought us here."

Madi shot to her feet. "No, I didn't!"

"Who else could it have been? It certainly wasn't me."

"Who was the one who started this whole crazy adventure in the first place, huh?"

Will balled his fingers into a tight fist. "Fink."

"That's right," Madi spat. She snapped the medallion shut. "He did this to us . . . him *and* that dumb camera of his."

Will's eyes flashed open. "That's it." He held out his hand. "Give it to me."

Madi reached for her neck. "No. Not the necklace," Will said. "The camera."

"Don't look at me; I don't have it."

"What do you mean you don't have it? Where did it go?"

Madi shrugged. "How should I know?"

"What happened to it, Madilyn?"

"I don't know."

"Well, you were the last one to have it."

"Well, I don't have it now, okay?"

"No, it's not okay." Will fumed. "How do you expect us to get back home?" He walked over to the desk and gripped the back of the chair.

"Maybe we don't need it," Madi said, walking up behind him.

Will whipped around. "Yes, we do. It's a very vital part of time travel. Without the camera, it won't work!"

Madi took a cautious step back. "How – how would you know about that?"

Will grabbed his forehead. "Ugh. Don't you get it?"

"No. No, I don't."

Will slammed his fist against the wall. "Dammit, Madi. Because of you, we've been bounced through time, not once, but twice."

"Stop it!" she shouted.

Will stormed forward, sending her cowering backward with each word he spat. "And now that *you* lost the camera, we're stuck in 1863 in Gettysburg, of all places, right before the biggest and deadliest battle of the Civil War!"

"I'm done talking to you" Madi turned away.

Will grabbed her roughly by the arm and brought her close. "How could you? How could you do this to me?"

"Stop it, Will!"

"It's all your fault. Ever since you found that necklace and took Fink's camera everything started happening!"

"Let me go. You're hurting my arm," she cried.

"Where's it at, Madilyn? Where's the camera?"

"I don't know," she seethed. "Just like I don't know where my flip-flops are or Nana and Grandpa! Now *leave . . . me . . . alone!*"

Madi twisted out of Will's hold, swiped the dress Tillie left for her off the bed, and threw open the bedroom door.

"Wait," Will called out.

Madi froze in the doorway; her breathing quick; her body shaking in rage.

Will sighed. "Look . . . I'm . . ." His face twisted. "What I'm trying to say is . . ."

"Is what?" Madi cut in. She stormed over to Will and glared into his eyes. "Why don't you do us both a favor and think hard, think *really* hard about everything that has happened to us. Then, take a good long look at yourself. 'Cause maybe, just maybe, *you're* the one to blame for all this."

Madi stormed out of the room, slamming the door in Will's face. She fell against its wooden frame and slid down to the floor. Amongst the stillness of the hallway, she buried her face in the fabric of the dress and cried, wanting nothing more than to go home and for this horrible nightmare to be over.

Chapter 25

From the bedroom window, Will watched as a torrential rain swamped the streets of Gettysburg. For hours, it continued to flood the town alongside the advancing and growing numbers of Confederate and Union troops. Households remained on edge and vigilant to all warnings concerned about the well-being of their families, farms, and businesses. But as each day passed with minimal conflict and then with the arrival of General Buford and his Union cavalry, Will noticed the town's citizens slowly became desensitized to the onset of an all-out war. They were convinced that the war would never, could never, seep through the boundaries of their little town.

Will turned away from the window. It made him sick to his stomach, knowing the grim fate that awaited Gettysburg and its people. He wanted to warn Tillie and her family of what they would witness and endure. He wanted to protect them all from the history that was about to be written, but he knew it wasn't his place. *Madi.* She was all that mattered.

Ever since their fight – four days ago – Will felt an insurmountable distance growing between them. All the words they said and actions they acted upon dug deep resentments that built an unbreakable wall of contempt. And as each day passed, they remained sheltered in their tiny, borrowed bedroom, keeping to themselves without saying a word to one another.

For Madi, she would lie on the bed and stare at the oak tree medallion in her hands with tears streaming down her face. As for Will, each night he wrestled through the same tortured dream only to wake in a cold sweat, heart racing, gasping for air.

~

One evening, while the household slept, Will found himself staring absently at the ceiling and walls. With a squinted eye and pointed finger, he constructed linear paths with each crack in the plaster. When the schematic diagrams ended in a roadblock, Will tried counting sheep, but the sheer thought of sleeping through another fitful dream played havoc on his already restless mind. So, without making a sound, he snuck out of the bedroom – careful not to wake Madi or the others – and tiptoed downstairs by candlelight.

Will entered the kitchen and sat alone at the table. The iron stove released a cloud of radiated heat from a day of baking by Tillie and her mother, who insisted on giving biscuits and water to passing Union soldiers.

Beyond the opened window, a soft, high-pitched trill of crickets chirped their songs. A great horned owl hoo-hoo-hooted into the night. Will set his elbows on the table and placed his head in his hands, sorting through all the logical explanations of their journey so far. After a few tense minutes and an assortment of blank conclusions, he decided to go back upstairs and try to get some – if any – sleep.

As Will made his way to the staircase, he noticed a large writing desk inside the front parlor. Quietly, he walked over to the desk and flipped through a collection of letters and banknotes. He searched arbitrarily through drawers and scanned the columns of dates, names, and accounts payable on an opened ledger, not knowing who or what he was even looking for.

Attached to the back of the desk was a wooden hutch with six smaller drawers – three of which were locked. The first two unlocked drawers housed four used quills, a glass bottle of writing ink, a stick of wax with a monogram seal stamp, a pile of stationery, a fountain pen, and a small, rectangular journal – unused. It was the last drawer where Will found two folded maps – one of Pennsylvania and one of Gettysburg – circa 1840.

The ceiling creaked. Footsteps – heavy and sluggish – slid across the floor. Will quickly gathered the maps and the unused journal, stuffing them under his arm. He shut the drawers, snuffed out his candle, and then dash back upstairs, making it inside his room before Tillie's father entered the hall.

~

Will grabbed the apple from his breakfast plate and sank his teeth through its tough, red skin. With a turn of a key and a press of a button, life – as he once knew it – changed. Yet, regardless of everything that has happened and has come between Madi and him, he knew one thing to be true: nothing would stand in his way to get them out of town safely. It was up to him – and him alone – to get them both back to where they belonged.

Will opened the small, rectangular journal and reread his notes. The word TIMELINE was written on top of the page with a list of bulleted points:

TIMELINE
*Friday, June 12, 2009 –
Arrived at Nana and Grandpa's

*Tuesday, June 30, 2009 –
Saw a stranger wearing a black hat in the field; Madi found the necklace under the clubhouse

*Wednesday, July 1, 2009 –
Independence Day Fair (cold wind blows by – only I felt it)
Stranger in a black hat (person from the field?) – appears to be following me; Met Fink on the path (knows us by name); Fink gives Madi the camera

*Storm comes

*Met a guy named Eldon in Grandpa's barn (He is the stranger wearing the black hat; who also knows our names & said to trust him)

*<u>Jumped to 1848 – June 26, 1848</u>, to be exact –
Met a little boy named Jeremiah, strangely familiar (two-colored eyes)

*<u>Jumped to June 26, 1863</u> – fifteen years later –
Met Tillie Pierce (her story of Fink???)

*Necklace, Madi is wearing, with its one large clock, three smaller clocks, and number in box = date (Month, Four-digit year, and Day)
*Camera is the missing piece!!!
*It all begins here →

Will curled his lip and tapped the top of the fountain pen on the desk, looking for a link between each event.

<u>June 26, 1848</u> – the day of their first jump.

He circled that date then three words *barn, Jeremiah, camera*. With a curved line, he connected each bulleted detail.

Will took another bite of his apple and leaned back against the back of the chair, rubbing the base of his neck. Something about all these events had to connect, but how? He looked back at one of the oldest maps of Gettysburg spread out in front of him and repeated the three words. *Barn, Jeremiah, Camera.*

Starting again at the top, Will studied and scrutinized the map's rough topography and primitive landmarks, hoping that something would jump out at him and steer him in the direction to find the camera and get them home.

Will rested his head in his hand. His eyelids grew heavy and his head drooped. Exhaustion had drained him both physically and mentally. With less than twelve hours of total sleep in the past four days, he needed to lie down and maybe get some rest, so he could start the process all over again with a fresh and clear head.

Will finished his apple, set its core on the plate, and pushed back on his chair. As he stood up, a marking on the Gettysburg 1840 map caught his eye. There in the bottom corner – an outline of a small stream south of Gettysburg that he hadn't noticed before. The line – traveling from the north of town southward – cut through an illustration of thick foliage and ran alongside a small family farm: *Parkers.*

Will ran his sleeve across his mouth, wiping the apple juice off his lips and slowly sat back down. He pushed his hair out of his eyes and carefully ran his index finger along the depression of the jagged line imprinted on the map and down to two washed-out words that were barely readable: *Plum Run.*

As the words left his lips, an image of a lush forest flashed in his head. The small bedroom – with its painted walls and traditional furniture – faded and he saw himself with a younger Madi, walking out of the woods. She gave him a smile and then ran off, giggling. As she splashed through a small, sparkling stream, a white light – brighter than the sun – sparked in the sky.

Will dropped his apple to the floor and grabbed his forehead, squeezing his eyes shut from the light. He grunted from a sharp pain that stabbed the front of his head as the image of Madi crystallized and shattered in a shower of fragmented flares. Each piece sparkled and fanned out in a glittering arc before morphing into a little boy with a crop of dark brown hair. The boy jumped through the shallow, crystal water, splashing and kicking. He plunged his hand into the stream, snaring minnows with his bare hands. He stood up, looked over his shoulder, and . . .

173

"Will," came Madi's shrieking voice.

Will flicked his eyes open, startled by the sound of his name, and teetered back in his chair, nearly falling to the floor. Beyond the bedroom walls, he could hear a distant roar swelling in his ears. A short, muffled blast rattled a framed picture that hung near the window. The desk shimmied under the vibration, toppling the lit candle onto the map.

Will jumped to his feet, sending the chair crashing to the floor as the fire furiously licked the paper. Using his hand, he smacked at the flame, extinguishing the small blaze.

The bedroom door flung open, smacking off the wall.

"Will," Madi cried, running into the room. "Something's happening!"

Will pulled back the curtain and strained to see through the river of rain that remained on the wavy glass. On the street below, a few soldiers dressed in Union blues with muzzleloading rifles in their hands dashed past the house.

Will pressed his face against the cool glass and scanned the horizon. His stomach tensed. A column of white smoke was rising above the buildings on the northern edge of town. He dropped the curtain and fit his suspenders up and onto his shoulders. "What's today's date?" he asked.

"How should I know," Madi answered.

The house trembled again, followed by short bursts of popping sounds from outside.

Will quickly folded the two maps, stuffing them, along with his journal, into his pants pocket. "Come on," he said, taking Madi by the arm. "We gotta get out of here."

"Wait," she protested as he dragged her out of the room. "What about our clothes?"

"Leave them. There's no time."

As they reached the bottom of the stairs, Will heard a frantic voice coming from across the hall. He stopped short and ducked behind the wooden posts of the staircase, pulling Madi down with him.

"The war . . . " a woman's voice quavered. "The war has commenced."

Will grabbed his forehead, thinking back to the very first day they met Tillie. *June 26. Add four days.* He did a rapid calculation. *July 1.*

Will looked over at Madi, barely blinking. "We're – we're too late."

Chapter 26

Beyond the threshold of the parlor, a woman with a round face and a rotund figure stood with Tillie and her parents. Two little girls, with sad eyes and dark brown hair set in curls, clutched the sides of the woman's skirt. Will peered through the railing and listened closely.

"So, my good neighbors if you may," the woman continued. She wrung her hands together and slid them down the front of her rumpled heap of green gingham. "I have come to ask permission for Tillie to accompany me and the girls to my father's home on Taneytown Road."

"But why would you risk venturing out, knowing the war surrounds us?" Mrs. Pierce asked; her voice wavering with concern.

"What you speak of is true. But with George serving with Cole's Cavalry, I do not feel safe at home being all alone."

"Yes, Mother. Father. Please let me go," Tillie said.

The group stepped further into the room.

"We shall be three miles out of town," Will heard the woman say.

"You hear that Mother? Father," came Tillie's voice. "Certainly, you would agree that I shall be far safer there than staying here."

"She's right, Margaret," Mr. Pierce spoke up. "You would agree that Matilda leaving town is for the best."

There was a lull in the conversation. A slight reverberation shook the house. The front door opened slightly on its loose hinges, spilling a faint band of light across the foyer. Will looked beyond the open door to the road outside. A plan began to take shape in his mind.

"Alright, yes," Mrs. Pierce said. "Hurry now, Tillie. No time to dawdle. Go and gather your – "

A sharp blast of a cannon shell exploded outside the home, sending an eruption of hysteria throughout the house. Seizing the opportunity, Will took Madi by the hand and led her through the open door.

"Wait," she quietly protested, pulling back on his arm. "Where are we going?"

Will stepped outside the Pierce home and froze.

The once quiet and small town of Gettysburg was encased in sheer pandemonium. The war – and all its clamor – was spreading like a wildfire. Men, young and old, guided women and children to safety as Union officers ordered the civilians to take cover in their cellars. Wagons abandoned by their fleeing owners were overturned on their sides; their contents lying haphazardly on the road. Bushels of hay and burlap bags burned in the middle of the street; the flames of the fires inching their way to awaiting kindling.

From all the stories Will had heard, one thing was true: nothing is ever what it seems unless you experience it and see it with your own eyes.

"I'm going back inside," Madi cried.

"No, you're not," Will said, squeezing her hand.

"Yes, I am. I don't want to be out– "

A round of gunfire punctured the air with a rapid **pop, pop, pop.** Will pulled Madi down the steps and dragged her into the firestorm of war.

"Stop," she screamed, struggling to stay on her feet. "Please, I want to go back."

A chorus of muffled shouts echoed above the din of warfare. Will looked up the road. A swarm of Union soldiers – their smoking rifles clutched in their dirty hands – were retreating from the center of town

Will pulled Madi out of their way and held her close as they rushed by in their filthy and blood-stained blue uniforms.

"You there," one soldier yelled. He stopped in his pursuit, loaded his rifle-musket, and fired blindly toward the center of town. "Find shelter. Now," he instructed.

A sudden crescendoing roar soared above the rooftops. Will grabbed Madi by the shoulders and pushed her hard up against the nearest brick building.

"Keep your head down!" he shouted, shielding her body as a cannonball slammed into a nearby house.

KA-BOOM!

Will squeezed his eyes shut as serrated pieces of brick and shingles pummeled the ground in a confetti of debris. A high-pitched timbre from the explosion left a buzzing residue in his ears.

"Why?" Madi screamed, choking on the dust as she pounded on his chest. "Why did you make me leave?"

Will caught her flying fist and stared into her frightened eyes that were ringed with a layer of powdered rubble. "Because I'm getting you home!"

Will yanked Madi back onto the street and ran, placing as much distance between them and the center of town. Footfall after footfall their feet sank deep into the mud-laden road, splattering muck up onto their clothes and creating a thick layer of sludge on their shoes. With each *poomb* of discharging cannons in the distance, the ground vibrated in an earthquake of violent tremors. Gunpowder mixed with clouds of dirt and seeped between the homes and buildings, blanketing the town in a grayish haze.

Will looked to his right and slid to a stop spellbound at the structure that stood before him.

A red-bricked building with a center arch towered two stories. From its top broken windows, almond-colored curtains precariously swayed in and out with the wind. A white slated gate ran along the front of the property while an array of tombstones dotted the grounds; each family plot nestled inside pockets of wrought-iron fences.

"Evergreen Cemetery," Will whispered.

As if magnetized by some unseen force, Will let go of Madi's hand and passed beneath the building's bricked archway, crossing to the other side. The earth tilted on its axis. The landscape warped and compressed. High grass drooped. Tombstones narrowed and funneled together.

Will planted his feet and threw out his hands, fighting against the fierce force that lassoed around him like a tether. He closed his eyes and clutched his stomach from a tidal wave of motion that towed him into another dimension.

Gritting his teeth, Will thrust himself forward, breaking through the rotating current.

An abrupt calm. A gentle peace.

Will regained his balance and expelled a breath of icy dew. He opened his eyes and turned around, finding himself halfway through the cemetery. Near the edge of the road just beyond the gatehouse, he saw Madi; the oak tree medallion around her neck glowed brightly through the smoky air.

The drone of a prolonged bugle call resounded. A round of gunfire punctured the crisp air. And a bullet whistled past Will's ear; its curling trail of sulfur sailing past his nose.

Acting on reflex, Will tucked his head into his arms and dropped straight to the ground.

Chapter 27

*T*he moment Will dragged Madi out of the house and into the firestorm of the war she begged to go back inside. In a matter of four days, the once peaceful town of Gettysburg had turned into an all-out war zone. Soldiers plowed through the streets shouting orders as they arbitrarily fired their weapons in the direction of the rising battle. Citizens ran about in frantic haste, clinging to one another for support and comfort as the horrific assault on their little town grew deep in battle.

A brutal roar clipped the rooftops. A blast of atomic thunder rattled the ground.

Madi clutched Will's shirt and buried her face in his chest, screaming in unison with the blast that assaulted her ears as a nearby home blew apart in an explosion of rubble. Her ears buzzed; her body shook.

Madi squeezed her fingers into tight fists and pounded on Will's chest in a rage of fury and fear as tears ran down her cheeks. How could he – why would he place her in such danger?

Madi took a final swing. Will grabbed her by the arm, looked deep into her tear-filled eyes, and said the one word she has been longing for . . . *home.*

Hand in hand, they ran away from the center of town, slipping and tripping on the muddy road that converted itself into a soupy concoction of dirt and grit from days of torrential rains.

As they approached the gates of the town's cemetery, Madi felt Will let go of her hand. She stood – stuck in the mud – and watched as he walked onto the hallowed grounds, leaving her behind.

"Wait," she called out. "Where are you going? Come – come back."

From the valley below, a barbaric chorus of yips, yowls, and howls filled the air. Explosions thundered and vibrated the ground in violent tremors as Union soldiers converged on the cemetery and positioned cannons along the fringes of the graveyard.

Madi covered her ears, muffling the traumatizing timbres of the growing commotion and yelled for Will.

What was wrong with him? Why was he ignoring her?

Madi trudged through the mud but stopped as an icy thread of wind snaked through the cemetery in a wicked whine. Tops of tombstones eroded, spilling their stone to the ground. Tallgrass furiously fluttered in its wake and fell flat with the earth. Wrought iron fences – solid and strong – bent like paper straws under its power.

Madi pinched her lips together and pushed through the torrent, struggling to hold down her dress as the brutal wind toyed with its hem. Loose pieces of her hair masked her eyes and a sulfuric haze from the firing artillery covered the cemetery, making it hard to see.

As Madi neared the arched building of the gatehouse, a spear of the cold wind nipped at her neck and branched downward toward the opaque resin that sat beneath the oak tree medallion.

The wind vanished. A drape of silence.

Madi placed a warm hand on the cold spot on her neck. She frantically searched for Will through the haze as it slinked itself through the wisps of tall grass. There he stood; halfway through the cemetery.

"Will!"

A collection of canned trumpeted notes rang out in a soft echo. A rapid wave of sporadic gunfire popped from all sides.

Madi watched as he fell hard to the ground, disappearing into the shafts of tall grass.

"No," she cried into the crossfire.

Madi lunged forward but fell back from an unexpected bite on the cheek. She gasped and bent at the waist, cupping her face that ignited like a red, hot ember. A groan escaped her drying lips. A shockwave of stabbing pain ran down the right side of her jaw and neck.

Madi brought a shaky hand forward. "No," she said with an airy breath as she stared at her blood-soaked fingertips.

Black spots dotted her vision. Her heart slowed in a rhythmic lub-dub. Madi stumbled on weak knees. Her head lolled on her shoulder, and like a puppet cut from its strings, she collapsed on the muddy ground.

| | | | | - | | | | |

Will opened his eyes to a sea of fog drifting above him. He staggered to his feet, wiping his dirty hands on his pants and turned back toward the cemetery entrance. His stomach knotted. "Madi!"

Will raced back through the graveyard, squishing and sinking into the sodden grass. He slid to the ground and cradled her lifeless body in his arms. Her head fell limp against his chest, revealing her ashen face; her cheek oozing in blood.

"No," Will said, blinking back his growing tears. "Oh, God. No. This can't be happening. Wake up, Madi. I need you to wake up."

A discharge of cannon fire broke out in rapid succession, tremoring the ground with each blow.

Will looked beyond the iron gates.

Columns of smoke rose toward the looming sky. Hordes of soldiers began to swarm the area from all sides.

Gritting his teeth, Will rose to his feet, hoisting Madi up and off the field. He looked left then right in search of a place they could take refuge. Then, he saw it, about a quarter of a mile away, peeking just above the horizon.

Will adjusted Madi in his arms. "Just hold on," he said. "I'm going to get you help."

Contending with mud, rocks, and tall grass, Will struggled under Madi's dead weight on the uneven terrain. He trekked across the soggy field, ignoring his throbbing muscles and the stream of sweat that ran down his face and burned his eyes.

Fifty feet.

Thirty.

He could see it now; a one-and-a-half story, white-sided home.

Will reached deep down into his very core, harnessing a hidden reserve of energy. He screamed through the last ten feet, stumbling through the opened gate of the picket fence that outlined the property.

Will dropped to his knees, heaving in and out. He brought Madi close and held her tight. *I should have listened to Nana; kept a better eye on you at the fair. Then, you never would have taken that camera from Fink, and none of this would be happening.*

Chapter 28

Will carried Madi up the stone steps of the tiny house and knocked on the front door with the tip of his shoe. The iron handle clicked and released its hold, swinging the door slowly open.

"Hello?" Will called out. "Is anyone home? My – my sister needs help."

Madi fluttered her eyes open and winced, whimpering under his slight movements. "Will?" she murmured.

"Shh . . . don't talk," he said, adjusting her in his arms. He closed the door with the bridge of his foot. "I got you. You're safe now."

A wave of heat rose from a pile of waning embers in the firebox of a large fireplace, creating a warm stagnant cloud that hovered below the wooden beams that supported a low ceiling. A wooden table with three chairs sat in the middle of the room; its plates and mugs empty, waiting to be filled.

Will walked through the tidy kitchen and into an adjacent bedroom. He carefully laid Madi on a straw-filled mattress covered with a linen pillow top and tucked a clump of her tangled hair behind her ear. A trail of tears puddled onto the sheets.

Madi breathed in deeply then exhaled a heavy sigh.

"I'm going to get you home," Will reassured, taking her hand in his. "I promise. I'm getting you home."

Will scanned the room. The bedroom floor sat bare except for a small collection of books, a pile of wooden blocks, and two cloth dolls with yellow dresses and white aprons. Near the foot of the bed rested a wooden rocking chair with a railroad pattern quilt. A mahogany chest – its drawers partially open – sat across the room near a muntin window.

Will hurried over to the dresser and rummaged through each drawer, hoping to find something to clean and comfort Madi's face. After the fourth and final drawer, he came up empty.

An unending lowing of shouts and gunfire bled through the wooden casements and drifted into the house. Will looked beyond the curtained window at the growing haze of smoke. He knew full well the path of death and destruction that would soon swallow Gettysburg whole. Husbands and wives, sisters and brothers – families – whose lives and futures would be ripped apart by the deadly tsunami of war.

Will turned away from the window. He caught a glimpse of Madi in an oblong mirror hanging on the bedroom wall. A trail of fresh blood seeped out from a two-inch gash of scraped and charred skin and ran down her face as she slept restlessly. Her once soft and fair complexion was damaged. Her innocence and youth were marred by the hands of this war.

Maybe Madi was right. Maybe I am the one to blame.

Will clutched the dresser – his knuckles whitening – and stared at his reflection. He kicked at the bottom drawer once, twice, three times, closing it shut. He wanted to yell out at the person he saw at the person he allowed himself to become over the years. Through his own confusion and mounting anger, he had created an armored isolation that pushed everyone – his mother and father, Nana and Grandpa, and Madi – so far away.

Will hung his head and sighed. Everything he said; everything he did or didn't do only caused more bitter disappointments, dissolutions, and discontent. And how could they blame him?

A report of gunfire ricocheted off the surrounding terrain in a rattling assault.

Will let go of the dresser. He threw back his shoulders and drew his brows together. *I'm not going to let it happen; not with Madi; not this time.* Though the past had been written; the future still remains. *And nothing's gonna stop me.*

"Mrs. Leister? Lydia?" came a soft voice. "Children? Are you home?"

Startled, Will quietly rushed over to the bedroom door and peeked into the other room. A young woman and two little girls – their shoes and skirts muddy – were standing just inside the kitchen.

"I fear they are not here," said a young teenage girl as she walked through the front door.

"Tillie?" Will said, stepping into the room.

"Will?" the girl replied in surprise. "Whatever are – "

"You?" the young woman said with a harsh glare.

"Mrs. Shriver," Tillie began, "you remember Will. Mother and I introduced him and his sister, Madi, to you just the other day. They both have been staying with us until they could move on."

"I see he already has," Mrs. Shriver said through pursed lips.

Will quietly closed the bedroom door. "The house was empty, and my sister needed – "

"So, conniving your way into one home encourages you to make use of an abandoned one?" Mrs. Shriver interrupted.

"No. It's not like that."

"Then what is it *like*, young man?" Mrs. Shriver asked. She walked over to Will; arms folded tight across her chest. "Obviously, you are not fighting in the war, nor are you from around here; so, I say, who are you, *really*? What has brought you to our town?"

The bedroom door swung open, smacking off the wall with a *bang*.

Tillie's hands flew to her mouth, smothering a sharp gasp. Mrs. Shriver cowered back and pulled her two children close, hiding their eyes in the pleats of her dress.

Will spun around to find Madi standing in the doorway. Her pale and dirty face was speckled in blood that oozed out of her wound and ran down her neck.

"Will?" Madi said. "Where are. . ." She took a wobbly step

forward and then slumped against the doorframe.

A thunder of cannon fire shook the walls of the wooden-framed house. The two children covered their ears and screamed.

"Mollie. Sadie. Quickly now," Mrs. Shriver said. "Tillie. Come. Away from this horrid sight and into the other room."

Will rushed over to Madi and took her into his arms. He guided her over to a rickety chair and helped her sit.

Madi raised a weak hand to her face and lightly touched her injured cheek. Her shaky finger slid against the drying blood and dipped into the opened gash of blistered skin. Her eyes grew wide; her body twitched. With an inarticulate scream, she jerked back in the chair, thrashing her arms and legs wildly.

"Help," she cried." Get me out of here! Get me out of here!"

Will caught her flailing arms by the wrists and lowered them to her lap. "Madi. You're okay."

"They're shooting," she said; her eyes shifting back and forth. "They're shooting!"

"Look at me," Will demanded. "You hear me? Look at me."

They locked eyes.

"Breathe," he soothed. "You need to breathe."

Madi inhaled then exhaled.

Will felt her body relax. "There you go," he said, loosening his hold on her wrists. "You're safe. No one can hurt you in here."

Madi threw her arms around Will's waist and held tight. "I want to go home," she cried into his chest; her cheek bleeding onto his shirt. "I want to go home."

Will wrapped his arms around her small frame that shook with each fallen tear. "I know," he said, closing his eyes. "I know."

Home.

Will knew it was out there. Somewhere in time; and like Madi, he longed to be there. Longed for its warmth and smells; its joys and laughter; its safety and comfort within its four walls.

One thing was undeniable: there is no place like home.

Will felt a light tap on his shoulder. He looked up and found Tillie holding out a frayed square patch of muslin cloth.

"To help slow the bleeding," she said with concern.

"Thank you," he said.

"Tillie?" came a tiny voice.

Stealing a peek from behind the girl's dress was the youngest of Mrs. Shriver's two daughters.

"Is that girl going to die?" she asked.

Tillie knelt down and took the girl's small hands in hers. "Good heavens no," she said with a comforting smile. "Madi. . . well, she ran into a bit of trouble on her journey. She'll be fine, but needs - "

"Matilda?" Mrs. Shriver called out from the bedroom. "Bring Mollie back here at once."

"Yes, ma'am." Tillie turned to Will. "I should - "

"It's okay," he said.

"Will you - "

"We'll be fine. Thanks again for the . . ."

"But of course."

Tillie gave a soft smile and then shuffled Mollie back into the bedroom.

Will took the muslin cloth, folding it in half and began to wipe Madi's cheek. She drew in a sharp breath and recoiled under his touch.

"Sorry," Will said.

Madi bit her bottom lip "I want mom," she said with a sniffle.

"I know." Will adjusted the patch in his hand and started again, lightly dabbing at her face. "Soon. I promise."

A report of rapid gunfire popped in the air. A bursting of shells grew louder with each powerful detonation, rattling the small home.

Madi grabbed Will's hand, lacing her trembling fingers around his.

"It's okay," he said, cleaning the dried blood off her neck. "I told you; you're safe."

Madi wiped her dripping nose dry with her dirty hands. She tilted her head and gave Will a befuddled look.

"What?" he asked.

"Something's different about you."

"What do you mean?"

"I don't know. You just look – "

"Tired," Will said, finishing her sentence. He handed Madi the small muslin cloth. "Hold that on your cheek. I need to show you something."

Will reached into the back pocket of his pants and pulled out the leather journal and maps he took from Tillie's house.

Madi scooted forward in her chair as he unfolded the 1840 map and spread it out across the table, flatting its aged paper. "What's this?" she asked.

"I know where – " Will glanced over at the bedroom door. He lowered his voice. "I know where the camera is."

Madi's eyes grew wide. "You do?"

"Well, I think," he said. "Okay, you see this?" He pointed. "Well, this is us, and this . . ." Will slid his finger down to the bottom corner on the map. ". . . is where we need to go."

"Parker Farm?" Madi asked. "That doesn't make sense."

"No. It does. Look here," Will said, indicating a rough, sketchy line. "What does that say?"

Madi squinted and read the faded script. "*Plum Run.* Wait a second! That's the same stream that runs through Nana and Grandpa's backyard."

"Yes," Will whispered. "And the barn, which sits on the Parker Farm, is Nana and Grandpa's barn. It was the first place we jumped to and the last place you had the camera, so I figured that's where we need to go."

"But fifteen years have passed since then," Madi began. "How do you know it's even still there?"

Will shrugged. "I don't," he said as he began to refold the map, "but I figured it's worth a try."

"No," Madi said, shaking her head. "I can't. You - you can't make me go back out there."

"Look," Will said. "When Mrs. Shriver first mentioned the name Leister, it didn't dawn on me why it sounded so familiar, but I remember now. When the war broke out, Mrs. Leister and her children were told to leave this house, and luckily, she did. Because by tomorrow night, General Meade, commander of the Union army, makes this place his headquarters, and everything you see surrounding this house and farm gets destroyed."

"Please," Madi pleaded quietly. "Isn't there another way? I mean, can't we . . ."

"There's no stopping this war," Will said. "Unfortunately, there are some things we can't change."

"But wonder if I - " Madi's voice trailed off. She lowered her head and rubbed her fingers against the coarse bloody cloth.

Will lifted her chin and met her worried eyes. "There's no other option. We have to do this."

A tear slipped out of Madi's puffy eyes and dripped to the floor.

"I know you're scared," Will said, taking her hand, "but you're strong, and I'll be right beside you the whole time."

Madi tightened her hold on his hand. "Promise?"

Will smiled. "Always. I'll never leave - "

The front door burst open, nearly breaking off its hinges.

Will shot to his feet and blocked Madi with his body as a brawny Union soldier with a few days of beard growth rushed inside.

"Ladies, we have found a- " The soldier stopped in his tracks, taking account of Will and the open map lying on the table. He raised his weapon and took aim. "Freeze."

"Don't shoot," Will said, throwing his hands up; the journal clutched in his bandaged hand.

Tillie and Mrs. Shriver rushed out of the bedroom followed by Mollie and Sadie, who were huddled close together.

"Private Donovan?" came the voice of another soldier, who bounded through the open front door. "The wagon is read – " He stopped short, taking in the scene and raised his weapon.

"Wait a second," Will shouted. "This isn't what it looks like. Just give me a minute and let me explain."

Private Donovan grabbed Will by the collar and hurled him face-first against the wall.

"Stop it," Madi yelled. "Let him go!"

"Quiet," Private Donovan barked. He pushed the barrel of his gun against Will's back and ripped the journal out of his hands.

"Deserter?" the other soldier asked.

"More likely a spy by the looks of it," Private Donovan said as he flipped through Will's journal.

"You can't be serious?" Will said over his shoulder.

Private Donovan stuffed the journal into his jacket pocket and shoved Will further into the rough, plastered wall. "Shut your mouth, rat."

Beyond the opened door, gunfire ripped through the air and a cascade of cannonballs pelted the ground, burying the home in a dome of dirt and smoke. The war was now playing out in full symphony; its ensemble amplifying the small space.

"Sir, we need to get these civilians out of here," the soldier said. "The wagon is waiting, and the Rebels are fast approaching."

Private Donovan nodded. "Alright, you heard Sergeant Collins; everyone move." He turned a jaundiced eye at Will. "Not you."

Mrs. Shriver clung to her daughters and quickly ushered them out of the house. Tillie gathered the front of her dress and followed closely behind.

"Wait," Will said.

Tillie stopped just inside the door; her eyes averted.

"You – " he lowered his voice. "You can't just leave."

"You know this traitor?" Private Donavan asked.

Tillie looked at the soldier and then at Will; her eyes stark and distant.

"Tell him," Will whispered. "Tell him. Please."

Tillie turned back to Private Donovan. "I never saw him before in my life," she muttered with a quivering lip.

"What? No," Madi shouted. "She's lying. You're lying!"

Tillie clutched the front of her mud-spattered dress and scurried out the front door, leaving Will in Private Donavan's clutch.

"Let's go," Sergeant Collins said to Madi. "Get a move on."

"No," Madi said.

The Sergeant took a step closer. "Listen here, little missy. You better get yourself go – "

"I said no," Madi interrupted harshly. "I'm not leaving without my brother."

"Unfortunately," Private Donovan said. "Your brother, be a spy or deserter, has committed a capital offense by the state of the Union, and for that is punishable to death by hanging." He nodded to his comrade. "Get her out of here."

Will watched as Sergeant Collins lifted Madi off the ground in one gigantic swoop and threw her up and over his shoulder.

"Stop. Put me down," Madi wildly protested as she pounded her fists against Sergeant Collins' back. "Will! Will, help me!"

Will turned blazing eyes on Private Donovan. "You're making a big mistake."

"Oh, really now?" the soldier said. He gave a haughty grin. "We shall see about that."

Chapter 29

"Let. Me Go," Madi wailed as she was carried out of the Leister house.

Sergeant Collins tightened his grip and ran on, weaving through the mighty wave of war.

Madi inhaled sharply and coughed, feeling her lungs compress against his muscular arms. The bloody cloth dropped from her hand and floated to the ground like a weighted leaf.

"Will," she cried. "Will!"

Outside the Leister home, giant brushstrokes of smoke and fog painted the landscape. Hundreds of Union soldiers, covered in dirt and soaked with sweat, howled and shouted as they raced across an open field, loading and firing their weapons. Men, young and old, were fighting, dying, suffering in droves; and in the center of this horrific and unfathomable savage display of war . . . Madi.

A cannonball thundered overhead and slammed into the ground, splitting the picket fence in a fiery explosion.

The blast shook the earth.

Madi felt Sergeant Collins stumble back, loosening his hold on her waist. She twisted about and wiggled free.

"Hey, little lady! Get back here," he yelled as she ran blindly into the firestorm. "It's – it's too dangerous."

Madi grabbed her ears as a discharge of shelling crashed to the ground in an earth-shattering *phoomb*. In every direction, gun barrels blazed in orange sparks and dispensed puffs of white smoke. Bullets popped like fireworks and zipped through the air like buzzing hornets toward their intended targets. A thunderous beat of deadly projectiles punctured through the cloudy, afternoon sky and fell to the ground in a succession of sonic – *boom, boom, boom.*

The force of each blast knocked Madi off her feet, tossing her sharply into the dirt. She cradled herself and covered her head, shielding her body from the flying and falling debris. Smoke choked her throat. Tears stung her eyes. Her cheek ruptured in a ring of fire.

Two robotic-like claws reached through the smoky haze, latched onto Madi's arms, and whisked her off the ground. Up and into the air she sailed – weightless when *thud*, she landed hard smacking the back of her head.

"Will," she screamed into the deafening barrage

"Get them out of here," commanded Sergeant Collins.

The world jerked forward with a harsh rattle.

Madi opened her watery eyes. An old man with a crooked smile chiseled between two tanned and weather cheeks was staring down at her.

"Just you hold tight, now, little lady," he said with a rasp to his voice. "Mr. Jamison is the fastest teamster here in Gettysburg. He'll have this here wagon far from this place in no time."

Madi pawed at her neck and clutched the oak tree medallion, which felt warm in her cold and clammy palm. A flash of fire ignited an atom of courage hidden deep inside her very being. There was no way this wagon or war would keep her from her brother. They were going to make it back home together.

Madi pushed away her tears and swallowed down the pain that radiated in the back of her head and throbbed in her cheek. She crawled over clusters of shoes and a tangle of legs, making her way to the back of the wagon. With all her strength, she climbed onto the wagon's narrow wooden bench, squeezing herself between a rotund woman and her pudgy daughter.

"Goodness gracious, child," the plump woman said. "I insist you sit down!"

Madi ignored the woman and watched – wide-eyed – as a mushroom cloud of fume and fire encased the once blue sky, erasing all that was left of the Leister home. Madi steadied herself against the wooden sideboard. She closed her eyes, breathed in deep, and silently counted. *One . . . Two . . .*

"Are you mad?" the plump woman shrieked, tugging at the bottom of Madi's dress. "You're going to fall plumb on your head."

Three feet below, the wagon rolled through a thick, murky stream that was once the road. It veered right and bounced left, sending its heavy wheels deep into a buried rut. In a spraying stream, a collection of mud flew into the air and coated each passenger in a thin layer of slime.

Madi slipped. losing her hold on the sideboard. Like a rag doll, she sailed backward, smacking the plump woman full in the face with the bridge of her knuckles.

The woman yelped and cupped her nose. "Look – look at what you did," she said as a thin stream of blood ran down her upper lip and onto her fingertips.

"What's all the commotion about?" Mr. Jamison yelled over his shoulder as he guided the wagon down the bumpy road.

"My nose," the woman said to Madi. She turned to the stunned crowd. "I think she broke my nose."

"You're crazy," Madi blurted, wiping the mud from her eyes.

"Watch your tongue young lady," bellowed a scruffy, gray-haired man.

"He's right," taunted a passenger.

"Yeah," heckled another.

Madi rose to her feet and dove for the side of the wagon, reaching for its sideboard with outstretched arms. Before she plummeted to the road below, the scruffy man seized her by the waist and pulled her back.

"Get off me," Madi shouted, thrashing about. "Let me go!"

"You best settle yourself," the man growled in her ear as the wagon raced on. "I'll hold you the whole way if I have to."

Madi let out a feverish huff and glared at each passenger. Each one stared back with flinty eyes; their stark faces carved in scorn or drenched in fear. It was her against them all. She was lost in two worlds and stuck in two wars.

Madi wiped her dripping nose. She looked to the driver but locked eyes with Tillie, who sat next to Mrs. Shriver and her two daughters.

A warm tingle rolled through Madi's chest. A feverish smile slowly ran across her face. A short chuckle escaped her lips before her dark amusement turned into a chorus of manic laughter.

"I say that girl truly is mad," the plump woman said.

Madi let out one last high-pitched scream and then surrendered the fight, falling limp in the man's strong arms.

Chapter 30

irvate Donovan grabbed Will by the collar and yanked him away from the wall. "Alright, rat. Who do you hold allegiance with? Sharpe? Pinkerton?"

Will stood silent and listened. All around, the riddling sounds of war penetrated their way through the thin walls of the Leister house. Gunfire popped in a drawn-out drone. Bombardments of heavy cannon fire pulverized the earth to dust. Shouts of rage rose in spirited yips with each charge of battling soldiers while sluggish yells of anguish fell with those meeting their premature demise.

"Answer me, boy," Private Donovan said, sneering through his bristly mustache that hid his tobacco-stained teeth. "Or I'll make certain you'll never see the likes of your sister again."

Will met the soldier's glare. "Go to hell."

"Why you – "

With a mighty, grunting heave, Private Donovan picked Will up by his shirt and tossed him onto the kitchen table.

Head over heels, Will tumbled to the floor, knocking down plates and cutlery in a cymbalic crash. He rose to his knees, steadied his head, and jumped to his feet.

Thunk-crack. A blindsided punch to the jaw.

Will rocked on one foot and tripped over the other, toppling onto an overturned chair. Groaning, he rolled onto his side and cupped his throbbing face. His chin swelled and grew into a knot of pins and needles. He swallowed down a small puddle of blood that tasted like pennies in his mouth.

"You know," Private Donovan said, tossing a chair aside. "This is nothing compared to what awaits you." He reared back and swung a hard boot into Will's stomach.

Oof. Will pinched his eyes shut and buckled into a ball as a deep cramp clenched his ribs. Above him, he could hear Private Donovan's cruel and bitter laughter, blending with the dithering sounds of war and its cacophony of death.

Will raised his tottering head and strained to look out the opened door. American and Dixie flags wrestled with the wind-filled sulfuric haze. Calvary units guided their trusted steeds across fields of war as infantry groups advanced enemy lines – the brunt of the war carried within the guns that were held strong in their fighting hands. But through it all, beyond this civil chaos and clamor, was Madi – defenseless, vulnerable, injured, and alone.

Will breathed in through his nose and exhaled. He slowly stood up and spat the remaining blood out of his mouth. Using the cuff of his sleeve, he wiped the lingering blood and spit from his lips and glowered at Private Donovan.

The soldier cocked his head. "What?"

Will planted his feet and balled his fingers into a tight fist; his fingernails digging deep into his sweaty palms.

"Oh, I see," Private Donovan said with a smirk. He set his rifle on the table and cracked his neck from side to side. "Come on," he gestured with a stiff wave of his hand. "Nothin' but a deadbeat, traitorous rat, anyway. Honestly, who do you think you are?"

Will puffed out his chest and jutted his chin. "A fighter."

Unleashing his full fury, Will lunged forward with a raucous roar. Private Donovan threw a fast punch.

Will dodged the blow and set a classic soccer kick in motion. He lifted his left leg and jumped high, swinging his right foot around and straight up into the soldier's face.

Smack!

The force and momentum sent Private Donovan careening backward into the wall.

"Come on," Will howled; his pent-up anger loaded within the

clutch of his two fists. "What are you waiting for?"

Bleeding from his nose and mouth, Private Donovan stumbled forward and returned a sloppy jab.

Will ducked and delivered a powerful right hook. *Crack* went the soldier's teeth.

Private Donovan teetered like a top and fell against the kitchen table, smacking the side of his face on its sharp corner.

A swelling roar soared over the home.

Will dashed out of the house, leaving the unconscious soldier behind. He vaulted over the porch railing and ran toward the road, pushing his way through the hordes of soldiers that advanced the area.

Battered snares and bugles mixed with sounds of cannon and gunfire. A mortar shell struck the picket fence with its mighty power, sending chunks of dirt and grass into the air.

Through the smoky violence, Will found Madi in the departing wagon, fighting and screaming in the arms of a large man. He darted around the burning fence and froze.

"Going somewhere," a mangy Rebel soldier asked, stepping through the raining soil.

"I'm not armed," Will declared, raising his hands in surrender.

The Rebel soldier smirked, revealing a set of chipped teeth. "All the better then." He raised his gun and fired.

A young Union soldier in a smudged-stained uniform jumped in front of Will and fired his own musket at the Rebel enemy.

Crack! Whizz!

The two bullets zipped toward each other, cutting through the smoky air at lightning speed. The Union soldier dropped his gun and buckled inwardly, grabbing his abdomen. He fell backward on stiff legs and collapsed against Will.

Will faltered under the man's weight and stumbled to the sodden ground; the gunning Rebel laying motionless on the muddy road.

"You – you saved my life," Will said.

The young soldier gurgled a cough, which sent a bubbling pool of blood out of his mouth.

"Just hold on," Will said as he frantically looked around the field. "I'm going to get you help. Just hold on."

The young soldier seized Will's wrist. "My mother," he rasped. He reached inside his uniform jacket and removed a crinkled, blood-stained envelope. "Give this to her," he said, handing Will the envelope with a shaky hand. The soldier coughed again. ". . . and tell . . . tell my brother that I was the one who saved the . . ." He breathed in sharply and fell silent; his fingers wrapped firmly around Will's wrist.

Will stared down at the young man, who stared back with lifeless eyes. A whir of gunfire crackled through the air in a rainstorm of hail. A repeating shelling pulverized the ground and punched holes in the surrounding landscape.

Will unlocked the soldier's fingers from his wrist and looked down at the envelope in his hand; its scripted name addressed to: *Evelyn F. DuBar.* Clenching the letter, he turned away from the horrid sight and covered his mouth with a hard fist, holding back the bile that was rising in his throat.

Will looked toward the muddy road. *Madi.* She was gone; taken away and now lost in the middle of this unfathomable and blood-soaked war. He couldn't protect her; keep her safe. Everything he had done; everything he had said had been nothing but a lie; his promise had been broken . . . again.

No. I'm not going to let it happen.

Will shot to his feet, tucked the envelope in his pants pocket, and ran with fervor determined to catch that wagon. He stormed through throngs of soldiers, shoving them out of his way with a rush of unexplainable strength. He dodged showers of gunfire and ducked under blasts of cannon fire as shards of rocks and splinters of wood pierced through his shirt.

Will hit the muddy road and ran full tilt; the cadence of his heart matching his rapid footfalls as he picked up speed. Fifty yards. He could see the back of the wagon, struggling to move through the thick mud.

Will gritted his teeth and pushed on. He was gaining ground. Twenty yards. Fifteen; he was going to make it – the wagon and Madi were in his reach.

A runaway horse galloped off the field and reared back with a squeal and nicker, forcing Will to change direction. As he stepped out of the animal's way, his ankle buckled on a cluster of protruding rocks buried deep in the mud.

Will stumbled and tripped, landing face down on the saturated ground. The pasty sludge and stagnant water entered his mouth and swam down his throat. The gritty liquid flew up his nose and burned the insides of his nostrils.

Will rolled onto his side, gagging and choking. Before he could stand up, a muddy boot kicked him square in his temple, rattling his brain underneath his skull. A burst of bright stars whirled around in Technicolor shades, blurring his vision. A sharp, stabbing jolt rang in his ears.

Will grabbed his head, wrenching in pain. He opened his eyes and found a shiny pair of black shoes stepping into his view, and Madi and the wagon were nothing more than a mere dot, disappearing beyond the smoky horizon.

Chapter 31

adi woke to a heavy clanking of the wagon's wheels and a faint hum of inaudible, hysterical chatter. She fluttered open her eyes and found the face of the scruffy, gray-haired man slowly coming into her blurry view.

"Let me go," Madi barked, squirming in his large arms that were wrapped tightly around her waist.

The man released his hold, throwing her down onto the wagon's bench. "No more funny business," he said with a jab of the finger. "You hear me?"

Madi huffed at the man and cowered against the front of the wagon, bringing her knees to her chest. She wrapped her arms around her legs and stared through tear-filled eyes at Mr. Jamison, who sat slightly hunched on his seat, snapping the horse's reins with fervor, taking her and the wagon's passengers far, far away.

|||||-|||||

For Madi, the trip down Taneytown Road was horrific and bumpy; a back-breaking, bone-jolting ride.

Several times, Mr. Jamison reduced the wagon to an agonizing crawl as it traveled over mud-filled holes in the road, and several times Madi contemplated the idea of jumping out and running back to find Will within this tangled web of war. But, as quick as the thought came, short bursts of gunfire and deep percussions of cannon fire would siphon through the trees and nip at what little mental and physical courage she had left.

Floating above the resonant sounds of war, Madi heard a faint but lively streaming melody of fife, accompanied by a rhythmic, *rum-*

tum-tumming. Using the back of her hand, she wiped her puffy eyes and looked past Mr. Jamison.

A small band of musicians was leading a parade of Union infantry – weapons at arms – in the direction of the wagon. Generals and lieutenants atop their majestic horses rode alongside a marching corps of soldiers. Though their feet kept time to the spirited melody, most of the men stared straight ahead, fixed on the impending battle.

At the front of the line, Madi noticed a young drummer boy, with shoulder-length brown hair that hung out from his disheveled cap. As he passed by the wagon, he looked up from his battered snare, jutted his chin, and gave a slight nod before leading the procession of men off the road and into the fiery pits of hell.

"Ladies," Mr. Jamison called over his shoulder as he brought the wagon to a halt. "We have arrived."

Madi watched as Tillie, Mrs. Shriver, and her daughters scurried out the back of the wagon and headed toward a two-story stone farmhouse.

The home's colossal windows were propped open; their lower sashes pushed up on their jambs. Five apple trees, in full bloom, lined a neatly manicured front yard that edged the dirt road.

"Little lady," Mr. Jamison said to Madi. "I suggest you go. You'll be safe here."

Madi looked at the encouraging driver and then at the imposing house, the vast field, and dense woods, even at the brave soldiers that now surrounded her. Though every rational thought told her to take shelter and hide, she couldn't will her legs to move.

Everything she had witnessed; she lightly touched her cheek. Everything she had lost; she looked back down the road. Madi remained – rooted to the wagon's wooden bench.

KA-BOOM!

A caisson from a distant cannon roared overhead and exploded in the adjacent wheat field, rocking the ground and shaking the wagon.

Another explosion followed; then another; and another.

Madi pressed her hands against her ears and ducked below the wagon's sideboard, squeezing her eyes shut from the fragments of dirt that fell in a dusty shower.

Make it stop, she cried. *Make it stop!*

A primal scream split through the thickening smoke and rising commotion. Madi clutched the side of the wagon and peeked over its wooden side. The plump woman and her pudgy daughter – huddled against one another – were screaming for help and pointing in the direction of the wheat field.

Through blurry eyes, Madi watched as four soldiers abandoned the procession and double-timed into the open field. They rushed over to a young soldier, who was withering on the ground, and picked him up by his arms and legs. As they ran past the wagon and headed toward the house, Madi caught sight of the wounded soldier. His burnt body convulsed beneath his torn and singed uniform. And behind his blood-covered face, his lips muttered a litany of silent prayers.

Madi felt her stomach harden. Her palms grew sweaty, and a roll of nausea, mixed with saliva rose in her throat. With a strangled gurgle, she cupped her mouth and pushed her way out of the wagon, tripping over the few remaining passengers.

Madi flung herself to the muddy ground and vomited.

"Good heavens," came Tillie's shrieking voice. "Madi."

Madi heaved again as her stomach rolled in waves. She lifted her bloody, tear-streaked face.

The world pulsated red. Mayhem. A plague of horrors. It was everywhere. Limping and crawling soldiers. Wounded men. Crying boys. Gut-wrenching gore and demise.

"Quickly. Inside," Tillie urged as she rushed toward the house.

"My brother," Madi shouted, rising to her feet. "We left him back there! And *you* did nothing. Nothing!"

A massive cannon blast shook the ground in a violent tremor. A stampede of soldiers converged on the road.

Madi staggered to her feet, looked all around, and then took off into the adjacent woods. Wind whipped against her ears. Sunlight flickered through each tree, striking her eyes. Leafy giants reached out and grabbed at her arms. Thick-skinned tree branches and vines snatched at her ankles while gray boulders sprouted from deep below the earth and blocked her way.

Madi bounded through a cluster of vines. A gnarled branch parted itself through the underbrush and lassoed itself around her ankle, pitching her into a pit of leaves, coiled brambles, and sharp stones. "Why?" she screamed, digging her fingers deep into the dirt. "Why are you doing this to me?"

A cool breeze plunged down from the canopy of trees and traveled through the woods, flowing ever-so-gently across the forest floor. Leaves rustled against its light touch. Thin branches bow against thick trunks and hummed in a legato scale, blending with the distant chorus of shouts and volleys of cannon and gunfire.

"*Maaaddddiii,*" the woods seemed to whisper.

Madi rolled onto her side and slowly opened her puffy eyes. "Hello?" she called out.

"*Maaaddddiii,*" the woods whispered again.

She sat up. "Is somebody there?"

The wind swelled around her and shot upwards, squeezing the trees together at their crowns. Their leafy tops blocked out any daylight, draping the forest in a dusky cape.

Madi rose to her feet and braced herself against a mighty oak tree from the sudden and unusual torrent. Thick strands of her hair banded together and whipped across her face. She moved the clusters out of her eyes, straining to see through the greyish, green tapestry. Behind a mountainous heap of stacked rocks stood what appeared to be a silhouette of a tall and lanky man.

J.B. Pierce

"Hey," Madi shouted. "O – over here! I – I need help!"

Without so much as a glance in her direction, the stranger placed a top hat upon his head and casually strolled away, ducking under a long row of evergreen trees that bordered the woods.

"No, wait!"

Madi pushed against the incessant wind and chased after the man. At the row of evergreens, she threw out her hands and stumbled blindly through their thick knitted fabric. As she broke through the lowing branches, her feet splashed against a small stream that wound past a deserted chicken coop.

The wind calmed, and the clouds parted, making way for the sun's bright, yellow face. Beyond the large open field, Madi watched as a burly man dressed in a gray uniform guided a white horse past a two-story colonial home. He cantered over to the stranger from the woods, who was now standing beside a red, distressed barn. The pair shook hands, exchanged a few words, and then as one, looked over at her.

"No," Madi breathed, grasping the pleats of her dress with her soiled hands. "It – it can't –" She whirled around and sprinted for the woods.

As Madi plodded back through the stream, a strong arm scooped her up by the waist. "Help!" she screamed. "Somebody, help me!"

"Well, well, well," came the growling voice of Bushy Beard. He tightened his hold. "Lookie who I found. Must be my lucky day."

The brute hoisted Madi up and onto his stolen horse and galloped back across the field. He entered the barn, plucked her off the horse like a petal from a flower, and flicked her harshly to the floor.

"Stay away from me," Madi said. She scurried backward on her elbows, fighting through the sharp pain that radiated from her bruised shoulder.

The barn door slammed shut.

206

Madi squinted against the slice of sunlight that found its way in between the eroded walls and saw the stranger from the woods standing at the door. He adjusted the black top hat on his head and fixed the long, black cape that rested on his narrow shoulders.

"Why hello, Madilyn," the man said, stepping further into the filtered light. "It's so nice to see you again."

"Who - who are you?" Madi asked with a tremble in her voice. "And how do you know my name?"

Bushy Beard jumped off his horse and hooted with laughter. "You were right, Fink. She is a naïve little lassie."

Madi looked at Bushy Beard and then back at the man, who stood in the beam of golden sunlight. He lifted the brim of his top hat with a bony, index finger, which wore a familiar tarnished ring molded in the shape of a skull. Its ruby red eyes winked at Madi.

"But . . . you - you can't be him," Madi said, cradling her shoulder as she stood up. "It doesn't make any sense."

Fink rubbed his pointed chin. "As I told you once before, it's all quite . . . " He paused; a sly grin spread across his menacing face. "How would you say it? Quite extraordinary really." He moved closer. "Are you ready to learn the truth, my dear?"

Madi bolted past Fink, running for the closed barn door determined to escape. Before the scream left her throat, Bushy Beard had clamped his meaty hand around her mouth, seizing her in his bulging arms.

Chapter 32

*W*ill breathed in deep and then exhaled, rubbing his forehead, clockwise - counterclockwise. His head throbbed like a second heartbeat, a relentless thumping that dug at his eyes with every pulse. He sat up; too fast. A soft groan escaped his dry lips. His whole body ached. His arms were like rubber and his legs felt loaded with lead. He didn't know why, but he could barely keep himself upright.

Will blinked a few times; focusing. A thin line of light streaked across the semi-darken space. Hovering over him was a curtain of plum velvet. It hung like a tent and draped vertically over four iron bedposts that trailed past sturdy and solid oak sideboards. Behind him was a majestic mahogany headboard, with three iron spindles. Two cornered footboards, sculpted with pewter curved loops, added to the bed's elegance.

Will slowly ran his fingertips against the satin-down comforter that he laid upon. *Where am I?*

A short *pop* like the splitting of wood punctured the silence.

Cautiously, Will crawled toward the divided curtain and swung his sore and heavy legs over the side of the bed. He raised a weak hand to the curtain, parting its smooth fabric. Slowly, he stood up. His bare feet hit a plush oriental carpet that surrounded the base of the bed.

"How are you feeling?" came a voice out of the darkness.

Will took a shaky step forward, catching himself on a three-drawer nightstand. "Who - who's there?"

"You've been asleep for almost twenty-four hours."

Will furrowed his brow. *I've been asleep for a whole day?*

A shadow moved through the dim amber light coming from a

large stone fireplace across the room. "Truthfully," the voice continued, "I'm surprised you're awake. That was a mighty blow to your head."

Will fought through the fog of confusion that plagued his thoughts. "Where am I?"

The stranger stepped away from the fireplace.

Will drew back and blindly slid his hand across the nightstand. His fingers latched onto a round metal tube. "Stop," he said, raising the heavy object in front of him. "Stay away from me."

"I can assure you everything is quite all right," the stranger said as he walked closer.

"I'm serious. Stay back, or – or I'll – "

"Please, if you may, set down the candlestick."

Will grasped the candlestick tighter in his hand. "No! Who are you? And what is this place? Where did you bring me?"

The stranger struck a match and held its tiny flame to a small pool of oil sitting in a cast iron hurricane lamp mounted to the wall.

Whoosh! The flame ignited the dark liquid, propelling a line of fire through an open channel of iron piping that ran along the walls of the room. One by one, seven individual sconces erupted in a kindling glow of incandescent light.

Will dropped the candlestick to the floor in muted wonder. Three brick walls coated in patchy stucco were decorated in industrial gears and clocks. A collection of framed photographs hung in a timeline of events. An iron-piped bookshelf, stacked with encyclopedias and world atlases, rose to the ceiling. A primitive sketch of the United States was tacked to an exposed wall of red brick and white mortar. A small globe sat atop a distressed executive desk; its matching swivel chair was surrounded by piles of weathered newspapers, hard-covered books, and leather-bound journals. In the center of the room sat an old steamer trunk. It separated the space between an exquisitely carved, walnut and leather sofa and two

Aubusson fabric parlor chairs that rested near the fireplace.

The stranger fanned out the match and adjusted a black derby hat that covered his crop of dark blond hair.

Will eyed the young man standing before him. Flashes of the Independence Day Fair and his grandparents' barn rushed through his head. "Eldon?"

Eldon smiled. "Hello, William." He walked over and placed a hand on Will's shoulder, giving it a squeeze. "Welcome home."

"Home?"

"I must say," Eldon began. "I never imagined I would ever see you again, especially in the midst of this God-awful war."

Will stood silent.

Eldon walked across the room to a narrow wooden table behind the sofa. "You didn't make my job easy," he said, stacking grapes, cheeses, and bread on a porcelain dish. He bit into a wedge of cheese and chuckled. "And you're welcome, by the way, for finding you when I did."

Will ran his hand through his hair. "Look . . . ah, Eldon. I'm – I'm a little confused here. You keep saying that you know me, but I sure as hell don't know you. And this . . ." Will looked around the room. ". . . this is *definitely* not my house."

Eldon popped a grape into his mouth. "Doesn't surprise me," he said with a mouthful of the fruit.

"What?"

"I said . . ." Eldon swallowed. "It is no surprise that you would not remember me nor this place." He walked over to Will and offered up the food. "You should eat something."

Will looked down at the plate that sat under his nose and then back at Eldon, who stood with a cocky smile on his face.

"No?" Eldon said. He plucked off another grape from its clustered bunch and tossed it into his mouth. "Suit yourself then."

Will pushed past Eldon, throwing his shoulder into the young man. He swiped his shoes and soiled shirt off a wooden armchair and stormed across the vast room. Lost, he stopped short in front of the fireplace and looked all around.

"The door's that way," Eldon indicated. He tossed a grape into his mouth and swallowed.

Will followed Eldon's pointed finger to a cherry wood-paneled door with an unusual brass knob on the far side of the room. With a huff and roll of the eyes, he marched back across the room, muttering under his breath. As he reached for the doorknob, his arm bumped into a square accent table, knocking over a round silver picture frame, shattering its thin glass.

Will picked up the frame and glanced at the black and white vintage image behind the cracked glass. He brought the photo closer and stared at the two people in the photograph.

The room began to spin.

Will dropped his shirt and shoes as a wave of nausea punched deep into his stomach. He staggered away from the table and looked up at the massive lit wall. A multitude of old photographs – family and individual, milestones and celebrations – hung in an undated timeline.

Will grabbed his temples as the thumping in his head returned with a vengeance. Black spots stained his vision, and his chest grew heavy. He clutched the frame in his sweaty hand, feeling his legs collapsing underneath him.

"Whoa, easy there, buddy," Eldon said, catching Will by the arms. "I gotcha."

"How can – where did – all the photos – " Will stuttered.

"Let's have a seat, shall we?" Eldon said, grunting under Will's weight as he led him to the sofa.

"Why are there so many pictures of . . . of *me*?" Will rasped, searching Eldon's face for answers. "I – I don't understand. Where did they all come from?"

Eldon straightened his vest, adjusted his hat, and looked hard at Will. "Trust me, William. As I told you once before; I would explain everything."

Chapter 33

The heels of Madi's boots chipped at the wooden floor as Bushy Beard dragged her across the barn. With a mighty shove, he flung her into a vacant horse stall; face-first into a pile of moldy hay.

Madi spat out the straw and scrambled to her feet, slipping on the clumps of hay. "Let me out of here," she cried, taking hold of the door's cold metal bars.

"Looks to me like you ain't going anywhere," Bushy Beard said, dangling a skeleton key between his chubby fingers. "So, I suggest you shut that mouth of yours."

Madi smacked the stall door with the palm of her hand. "Let me out, you creep! You can't do this to me!"

"As a matter of fact, Madilyn," came Fink's sinister voice. "*We* can do whatever we see fit."

Madi let go of the bars and stepped away from the door.

"No one leaves or enters this barn unless that request comes from me," Fink instructed Bushy Beard. "Understood?"

"Perfectly," Bushy Beard said, handing the key to Fink. He gave Madi a smirk, revealing a set of rotting teeth and then walked over to a rickety, four-legged stool near the entrance of the barn.

Madi watched as he plopped himself down like a heavy sack of flour, folded his arms across his belly, and leaned back, extending his thick legs in front of him.

"My apologies the accommodations are not better for you," Fink said as he dropped the key into a small pocket on his grey vest. He stepped up to the stall door. "But it was the best I could find under the circumstances. I'm sure you understand."

Madi cowered further back. The mere sight of Fink -his face

213

etched with a prominent arborescent flowering tattoo that branched out from the side of his neck and crept up and across his right cheek – made her skin crawl.

"Something wrong?" Fink asked.

"You tricked me?" Madi whispered.

Fink threw his hand to his chest. "Tricked you? I'm appalled that you would say such a thing."

"Well, it's true," Madi spat back. "At the Independence Day Fair, remember?"

Fink brought his hands together, each fingertip lightly touching the other. "You may be right, but then again, I had to. I cannot help that you are part of time's design."

"Time's design?"

Fink snickered through tight lips. "I'm sorry," he said, suppressing his amusement. "It's just I keep forgetting you really don't know the real truth."

Madi folded her arms tight across her chest. "Ask me if I care?"

Fink adjusted the top hat on his head. "You should, my dear. Your very life and those who you love depend on it." He scratched his pointed chin. "What's that familiar adage? Oh yes . . . once upon a time, a long, *long* time ago, three young men – a thinker, a fighter, and a charmer stumbled upon one another as if guided by fate. Their coincidental meeting – many years ago – spawned new alliances, and over time, they realized that each of them, together, had something essential, something worthy to give and contribute to humanity. Bounded by bonds of trust, they found a way to utilize their special talents. They devoted their lives to help those that were less than fortunate and whose lives were – " Fink paused. "– let's say, were less than favorable."

"So, they were like superheroes?" Madi said.

"Goodness child, no," Fink said sharply. "They were more than that." He leaned in closer. "They were guardians of *life.*"

214

"Guardians of *life*?"

"You see, these three men were part of the new revolution – an evolution of man and machine – that would slowly change the face and fabric of the country."

"You mean the Industrial Revolution?" Madi interrupted.

"Why yes," Fink replied. "Smarter than I thought, I see."

Madi shrugged her shoulders and looked away, slightly smirking to herself.

"But year after year," Fink continued, "tensions began to rise and halfway through the century, the country started to spin out of control. North and South. Compromises and controversy. The country was slowly dividing, crumbling itself to obliteration. Hope was all but lost for many. That is until these three – these three amazing young men – found a way to bend the laws of time."

Fink threw his shoulders back and tilted his head upwards toward the shaft of sunlight coming through one of the barn's dirty windows. He closed his eyes and basked in the spotlight like an actor on stage ready to take his bow.

"Are you saying they could time travel?" Madi blurted through the silence.

Fink flicked his eyes open. "Yes. Extraordinary, isn't it?" he said with a broad grin on his face.

"Cool," Madi replied.

"Though the Civil War began on April 12, 1861, the hope once lost on the eve of that fateful day was slowly being restored. All by the benevolent hands of NEVES [1]."

"NEVES?"

"The New Evolutionary Vigilante Elite Society. A first-class group of individuals who risked their very lives defending, protecting,

---

[1] NEVES – (nah' vess)

and guiding those who had the most need of deserved aid and prosperity. They were unstoppable. A prodigious faction. That is until the rise of the Nefarions."

"The who?"

"A secret meeting was arranged just north of the bordering woods near Little Round Top," Fink went on. "Through smoke and fire, the two groups met. Words were spoken. Trusts were broken. And while the Civil War raged on, a new war unfolded." Fink chuckled to himself. "But sad to say, in what some may say an ironic twist of fate, the fighter – the very founder and foundation of NEVES, protector and supreme guardian of life – could not be protected."

Madi slowly took hold of the metal bars. "He died?"

Fink flung himself forward and wrapped his long, thin fingers around hers. "I wanted to help; my intentions were forthright. Each and every plan I composed were methodical masterpieces, mapped out and scripted to near perfection. Our virtuous compassion for humanity and all we stood for could have changed the world." Fink's eyes burned red and turned glassy. "But it seems as though his time's design could not protect the plundering hands that sealed his fate."

Madi pulled her fingers out from underneath Fink's cold grasp. "You," she breathed. "You killed him?"

"He gave me no choice. All my ideas and theories, everything – rejected over and over again by *him*," Fink spat; his voice a raging quiver. "I was the pinnacle of the NEVES; equally important as much as he was, as any member was."

"While I made sacrifices for people I hardly knew, he stole the heart of the woman I *truly* loved and cared for. He tore my family apart down to its very core. And the friendship I thought we both had had all those years. . . " Fink lowered his head. ". . . I was played for a fool."

"That doesn't give you the right to kill someone," Madi said.

"Every day I would ask myself, why? Why had this happened to me? Why was I chosen? What made me so important, so special?" Fink shrugged, letting go of the bars. "But by then, my heart had withered, and my soul had hollowed itself into a deep pit of darkness. What I once had in my life had faded, disappeared from my grasp. I had lost everything and everyone I held dear. Until that night; that cold October night."

"With nothing left in my very being to continue on, I fell to my knees and looked up at the sky for a sign, vindication for my purpose in this world. Above me, the clouds churned and rolled in black waves while bright flashes of light sparked in their midst. A bolt of lightning struck the ground, setting fire to a nearby oak tree. And as I watched its branches burn through the pouring rain, the answer made itself known. It was then realized I needed one thing; the one thing to capture and change time."

Madi reached up at the necklace around her neck and slowly tucked its oak tree medallion inside the top of her dress; its bronze metal hitting warm against her bare chest.

"My purpose for life had changed. I was about to embark on a journey; a journey to fortify *my own* quest to rectify *my* own life that he ripped out from under me."

"But that's selfish," Madi said.

"And he wasn't?" Fink replied. "All those countless years I gave, following each and every bloody demand of his. It was enough. I had enough. It was my turn; my turn to be the fighter and take back what was rightfully mine." He looked up at the sky through a broken panel in the barn's roof. "When the lightning broke through the clouds and singed my body with its fiery hands, I saw my love and my life flash before my very eyes, but I wasn't letting go even to the very end."

"The welts," Madi whispered, staring at Fink's webbed face.

"I was dying," Fink continued. "I knew it; I had to be. But as it turned out, time's design had yet another plan for me." He stared down at his hands. "An indescribable power filtered in my body and coursed through my veins. The earth and its elements rose and fell with my every command. I couldn't believe it myself. I was part of it all: earth, wind, water, and fire. That is. . ." Fink ran his fingers over his scarred face and then flicked his eyes up at Madi from beneath the brim of his top hat. ". . . until you came along and changed everything."

"Me?" Madi retorted. "I didn't do anything."

"Ah, ah, ah," Fink said, waving a bony finger. "*Au contraire.*" He pointed at the chain around her neck. "The moment you found that timepiece and put it on, you resurrected me, brought me out from the depths of the earth that held me captive for so long, which I am eternally grateful. But, little did I know that giving you a remarkable gift - one that captures those moments in time - would reverse the chains of circumstance." Fink narrowed his cold eyes. "And now the camera, what I needed and fought for so long ago is lost . . . *again.*"

"I never would have lost that camera - that *stupid* camera - if you never gave it to me," Madi said; her voice rising with every word.

"How dare you?" Fink seethed.

"How dare me? How dare you? It's because of you that I'm here and my brother Will is gone!"

Fink plunged his shoulder against the door. "The *Will of Time* belongs to me, my dear. Every. Single. Piece. of it. And you're going to help."

"What if I don't?"

Fink peeled himself away from Madi's cell and traced the brim of his top hat with his fingertips. "Then, let me ask you this, Madilyn. How much is your life worth to you? Or William's for that matter?"

Madi stepped out of the sun's glare and into the cold shadows of her cell.

"Just as I thought," Fink said. He placed his top hat back upon his head. "Oh, and one more thing. You may want to think hard about where that camera is because by the time I return . . ." He looked at his pocket watch, which was hanging from his vest. ". . . in just a little under twenty-four hours, your very own time's design is up."

Chapter 34

"Okay," Will said, leaning back on the sofa. "I'm listening. Explain."

Eldon walked over to a large, oak sideboard with a low beveled mirror and opened its bottom cupboard. He pulled out a long-necked glass bottle, removed its cork, and started to fill two pewter mugs. "October 11, 1856," he began. "Though the Hanover Junction was complete, the railway from town would not be ready until the following year. So, by agreement, other arrangements were made. Once the carriage was packed, we took to the road although the weather . . ."

Will looked down at the frame still clutched in his hand as Eldon went on. He drew the daguerreotype out from beneath the shattered glass and studied the attractive couple glazed on the tintype. A young man dressed in a tailored suit and top hat sat poised on a Victorian parlor chair; an uncanny expression on his face. Beside him stood a beautiful, young woman in a long-checked dress and bonnet. But it wasn't the man that struck Will odd, but the woman with her mesmerizing, sable eyes that stared up from the photo with electrifying intensity.

Will dropped the photo and frame on top of the steamer trunk and pushed himself further into the sofa.

"Is something wrong?" Eldon asked.

"The young woman," Will said. "Who is she?"

Eldon raised a curious eyebrow and gave a sideways smile. He recorked the bottle and took the two mugs in his hands. "Anyway," he continued, ignoring Will's question, "since the weather gave us a bit of trouble, the trip took a day longer than expected. Not to mention poor 'ole Ace threw his shoe."

"Ace?" Will asked.

Eldon walked over to Will and offered up one of the pewter mugs.

Will hesitated.

"Go on. Take it," Eldon insisted. "It will help your head and your spirits."

Will puffed out his cheeks and slowly accepted the stein. He traced its smooth metal rim with his fingertips and sighed. Everything Eldon was saying didn't make sense. But yet, sitting here – surrounded by maps and books and the pictures on the wall; even the smell of the warm, waning embers in the firebox – somehow felt so . . . right.

"You *really* do look dreadful, William," Eldon said, relaxing back in one of the parlor chairs.

"Can you please stop calling me that?" Will muttered. "My name is Will."

Eldon crossed his leg over the other and gave a contrite nod. "But of course . . ." He raised his mug. "To you . . . the Will of Time."

Will looked up.

"Cheers," Eldon said with a wink before taking a hearty drink.

Will lifted the stein. The cool metal hit his lips, and he took a long sip. A burst of vanilla, clove, and white pepper, followed by a caramel flavor – crisp and dry – shocked his taste buds. "Oh my god," Will spat. "What the hell did you give me?"

"Old Overholt," Eldon beamed. "I've been saving it for you."

Will spat the remaining liquid out of his mouth. "Whiskey?" he sputtered, wiping his dripping chin with the back of his hand. "You gave me whiskey?"

Eldon nodded.

"But I'm 15!" Will blurted.

Eldon gave a quirky smile. "Right." He cleared his throat and continued. "As I was saying, 1856 was the first year for the fair's new

J.B. Pierce

location. When we finally arrived and settled in, we took to the numerous exhibitions of livestock and machinery. In all my days, I can never recall seeing such an audience. Thousands - upon thousands - of people came from the surrounding counties."

Eldon chuckled to himself and looked down at his mug. "By any means, the exhibits were interesting enough, but being young lads, you and I, we were more curious about the industrial exhibits - inventions of the revolution; the architects responsible for changing the world as we knew it. All the innovation; the intellect those men had." He paused and shook his head. "Simply amazing."

Eldon took another sip and continued. "As the day wore on, we couldn't help but entertain ourselves with the parade of sideshows in every corner of the fair. Honestly, William, I mean Will . . . some of those chaps and dames . . . they could really stir up the audience."

Will set down his mug and stood up from the sofa. "Look. This is all very interesting. Great story really; but honestly, *Eldon*," he mocked, "I don't see how this is helping me understand anything. Thank you for all that you've done for me, but I need to find my sister and get her back home to *2009* where we both belong."

"They have her," Eldon said matter-of-factly.

Will stopped short. "What did you say?"

"The moment Madilyn put on the necklace, they - "

"They what?"

Eldon swirled the remaining whiskey in his mug.

"What aren't you telling me?" Will persisted.

Eldon finished his drink and rose to his feet, setting his mug aside. "After the two of you were separated from Mrs. Leister's house, Madilyn jumped out of the wagon. She was tracked down in the nearby woods about half a mile away from the Weikert farm. I was planning to tell you. But - "

Will sprang forward and grabbed Eldon by the neck. "What do you know about Madi? Where is she?"

222

Eldon gripped Will's hands. "William, plea - please," he struggled to say. "You - you must calm down. With all that is happening . . . you're - you're not thinking straight."

"I told you to stop calling me that," Will shouted. He pushed Eldon backward across the room and slammed him against the wall, knocking the derby hat off Eldon's head. "It's Will! You got that! Will! Now, who has Madi? Who has my sister?"

"We're not at lib-liberty to say," Eldon said under Will's crushing hands.

"What do you mean *we*? Who are you talking about?" Will asked, feeling Eldon's pulse beating against his palms.

"I can't - br - breathe," Eldon wheezed; his face turning a deep shade of red.

Will released his grip, sending Eldon straight to the floor. He kicked at one of the parlor chairs, flipping it onto its side.

"Your name," Eldon managed to say as he rubbed his neck. "Your name is William James Parker; n-n-not Will Marshall."

Will stopped and looked back at Eldon. "Excuse me?"

"And your birthday," Eldon panted. "It's August 9. Correct?"

"Yeah. So, what - good guess."

Eldon placed his derby hat back on top of his head and staggered to his feet. "Though you'd like to believe you were born in the year 1994, which would rightfully make you fifteen. You, my dear friend, were born August 9, 1839."

Will let out a long, contemptuous laugh. "1839? You're crazy!" He swiped his soiled shirt and shoes off the floor where he'd dropped them and headed for the door. "And I'm not your *dear* friend," he threw over his shoulder.

"You are the firstborn son of Meredith and Stephen Parker," Eldon said. "You grew up in a large farmhouse just outside Gettysburg with your two younger brothers: Benjamin and Jeremiah."

Will stepped into his shoes and slipped his shirt over his head.

"Do me a favor, Eldon, why don't you take yourself and your asinine stories and shove 'em."

"I know about the scar," Eldon blurted.

Will looked down at his chest and slowly ran his fingers over his shirt, feeling the rigid line that marred his skin.

"And it's not from what you think or what you've been told."

"What about it then?" Will asked. "I mean, you seem to know so much about me. What story are you going to tell me now?"

Eldon adjusted his vest and walked over to Will. "In the course of numerous studies and a bit of trial and error, you and I – we – have found that life is meticulously constructed and scripted in a foundational code. Alongside this code, we also found that a single moral conviction is imprinted and rooted within each individual soul that places them on a path called, *impetus² existence.*"

"Impetus what?"

"Once the path is built," Eldon said, "a triune of three fundamental components – love, nurture, and knowledge – stimulate a catalytic increase – a driving force – of life's energy. Otherwise known as . . . *impetus existence.*"

Will shifted on his feet. "Is there a point to all this?"

"Yes, I was getting there," Eldon answered. "If one link of the triune is jolted, warped, or worse, broken, the mighty weight of shadow's hands smothers one's life, and like a plague, it slowly consumes a person's spirit in darkness and despair, which ultimately collapses their resolve. But you and I, let's say we have found a way to . . . " Eldon lowered his voice and stared hard at Will. ". . . to manipulate the cards that were dealt and more."

"With what? A necklace and a camera?" Will said with a contemptuous laugh.

"Yes. Deep within the two and working in tandem, lie a force and

---

² Impetus - /ˈimpədəs/

power beyond our wildest comprehensions. Yet, our remarkable discovery proved that one's *impetus existence* can be rewritten - skewed - per se. And because of you and your experiences alone - within and through passages of time -a window of innovation has opened wide and presented life with a gateway of monumental possibilities."

"What are you talking about - because of me?"

"Whether you believe me or not, but that minute that very moment when you let everything go and you open your mind to all the wondrous possibilities this life can bring, and you harness the courage to push against shadow's hands - the ones who have masked your own *impetus existence* for so long - it is then, you, my dear friend, will *finally* come to know who you *truly* are."

"And who's that?" Will asked.

Eldon smiled. "You're a living rarity, William; a guardian of life, a fighter - that I, that *we* - never knew could ever exist."

Chapter 35

*A*n ensemble of five hollow timbres chimed off the bedroom walls from a steel, industrial clock that sat on the stone mantle of the large fireplace. Like a caged animal, Will paced the perimeter of the room as an avalanche of thoughts flooded his mind.

Eldon - his story and theory of time travel. The necklace and the camera. The scar on his chest. *Impetus existence.* Madi. The fear in her eyes. The blood seeping from the gaping wound on her cheek. The sound of her pleading screams as she was carried out of the Leister house.

Will stopped in the middle of the room. *This - this is crazy. I gotta get outta here.*

As he headed for the door, his reflection bounced off a round mirror riveted on the wall above an elegant wash table. His shirt and pale face were heavily speckled and smeared with dried mud and blood. Strands of his hair hung in clumps over his forehead and skimmed the top of his eyelids. Even his ocean blue eyes seemed dull.

Will walked over to the wash table and rolled up his sleeves. He dove his hands into the copper bowl and scrubbed himself clean. He rinsed out his hair, pushing it up and off his forehead and washed his face. As he patted himself dry, a faint yet colorful glimmer reflected off the mirror.

Will set down the towel and followed the glimmer to an ornate double-door armoire that appeared to be built into the stucco wall. Its doors and mahogany arched top were carved in intricate detail, and its elaborate keyhole held a small skeleton key with a ruby macramé fringed tassel embellished with sapphires and emeralds and topaz.

Will reached for the key but hesitated; his hand hovering at the lock. He looked over his shoulder and listened. Only the ticking of the mantel clock softly echoed off the bedroom walls.

Will turned back to the armoire. He closed his fingers around the key and turned it one full rotation clockwise. A series of mechanical clinks and clanks knocked from inside unlocking the heavy doors. In an orchestrated and automated order, a set of shelves and drawers rolled out on metal rollers.

Neatly folded was a pair of grey slacks and a crisp, white dress shirt. A long, navy jacket adorned with a mandarin collar, button front closure, and shoulder straps hung on a wooden clothing rail. Will traced the jacket's unique rope detailing and skimmed his fingertips over the medallions, gears, and compasses that were attached to an assortment of silver chains.

The clock chimed. Half-past five.

Will looked beyond the picture window. The midnight sky was churning into a chilling shade of gray; a new day was on the horizon. Without thought, he quickly undressed, throwing his soiled clothes in a pile on the floor.

Will slipped into the slacks and shirt amazed at their tailored design that surprisingly fit him perfectly; even the black-laced shoes he found at the bottom of the armoire cradled his feet as if custom-made.

As he fit the jacket over his broad shoulders and buttoned the top button, an intense compression of internal heat rushed through his body. Will buckled at the knees and grabbed onto the armoire door, trying to keep himself upright. He pinched his eyes shut and grunted in pain as an assortment of memories flickered in his mind like a movie reel. Each colorful image – once crisp and clear – was slowly fading to gray; *school, soccer,* his *collection of friends;* his *father* and *mother; Nana* and *Grandpa;* the *hikes through the woods;* the *clubhouse;* even *Ma* –

Ring-a-ling.

Will breathed in deep. He lifted his head and searched the expanse of the room for the tinny ringing sound.

Ring-a-ling.

Above the bedroom door and fastened to the wall was a rectangular wooden block lined with four brass bells of different sizes. Below each bell was a thin metal nameplate: *front door, back door, library, NEVES staircase.*

Ring-a-ling. Front door.

A grinding of gears vibrated the armoire, popping open a hidden narrow drawer. Resting on a blanket of green velvet was a long-barreled rifle, ammunition, and a black leather belt with a knife in its holder. Will pushed through the internal heat and vanishing images that consumed his body and let go of the doors. He fitted the belt around his waist, stuffed his pockets with a pouch of ammunition, and grabbed the gun from its holster. Carved deep into the gun's wooden stock were two initials – *TS.*

Will turned to leave and heard an unlocking pop. He watched as a final drawer opened at the very bottom of the armoire, revealing the journal he took from Tillie's house and the two maps of Gettysburg. *What the –*

Ring-a-ling.

The bell rang again with agitated urgency.

Will stuffed the journal and maps in his pockets and ran out of the bedroom, leaving his soiled clothes behind. He rushed down the long hallway to the majestic staircase only to stop halfway down by the sound of two strong and arguing voices coming from somewhere on the first floor.

"Why was the door locked?" a loud voice demanded.

Will peeked over the handrail and down a spacious hallway that led to the back of the house. Beyond a large, arched threshold he noticed Eldon standing next to a tall, young man.

"No reason, really, a mere blunder," Eldon answered light-heartedly.

"And what is this nonsense that I am hearing?" the young man asked. "The locality of the parley – that you and I meticulously planned and plotted for months – is now to be called off?"

Will listened intently, trying to make out the stranger's youthful and familiar voice.

Eldon coughed, clearing his throat. "It – ah – it seems with the war waging – "

"That is no sound cause for stalling," the young man exclaimed, taking a step into the room. "You of all people should know that."

"Of course," Eldon replied. "But I think you should see this."

Will heard a rustling of papers. He leaned further over the banister, straining to catch a glimpse of the young man but all he could see was a shadowed profile against the dimly lit room.

"Who gave you this information?" the young man asked.

"Dorian. He brought this to my attention just before you arrived," Eldon replied.

"And the young girl? Who is she?"

"We can't say for certain."

"That I clearly see from the memo. What reason would be for her capture?"

"Before Dorian brought this to me," Eldon began, "he made his way through town, questioning the residents. However, with the unremitting battle, most have abandoned their homes. Those Dorian did speak with made claim to have seen her a few days ago with a teenage boy coming down Baltimore Pike. Witnesses alleged the pair took refuge with the Pierce family as the Confederates stormed the town on June 26. After that, nothing."

Will gripped the mahogany banister, fighting back the impulse to barge into that room and demand answers. *Madi. They knew where she was.*

"I respect your willingness to help," the young man said, "but what appears to be the case of a troubled orphan, I don't see the obligation to - "

"But - "

"We have more important issues at hand, Eldon. You know that, and this young girl, whoever she may be, is a setback that I - that *we* - don't have time for."

"You're wrong," Eldon said, shaking his head.

"I beg your pardon?"

"I know you disagree with me, but with all due respect, Smithfield, sir, you know damn well this could be done."

"How dare you speak to me like - "

"We have all the time in the world," Eldon blurted. He backed into the doorway, composing himself. "With your approval, let me send word to Wesley and Isaac. If they take the southern trail following *Plum Run* to the Parker Barn, they could rescue the girl before sunrise, and still be back in - "

"The answer is no!" Smithfield roared.

"They're going to kill her!"

Will stiffened and tightened his grip on the banister.

"By what means of proof?" Smithfield asked.

Eldon didn't answer; his silence added to the rocky tension.

"This conversation is over," Smithfield said. "You and I have labored too hard to jeopardize the parley of time's design. It's a war they want, so we shall give them one. Send out the call. We execute the mission at noon."

Will rushed down the staircase and quietly made his way across the grand foyer. He reached for the door handle and froze as the front door swung open wide. Like a shadow, he slipped into the darkness between the door and the wall and peeked through its narrow space.

A beautiful young woman with long, brown hair stopped in the center of the large foyer. She smoothed the sides of her black-bustled vest with her netted gloved hands and adjusted a brown belt that was wrapped loosely around her waist. "Eldon!" she called out, fumbling with the straps of a small cloth satchel.

"In the library," came Eldon's distant voice.

"Is he with you? Please tell me he is still here," the young woman said as she hurried down the hallway.

A gust of wind rushed through the opened door and whipped at her hair, sending a fresh scent of lavender straight to Will's nose. Spellbound, he stepped out from behind the door. It was her; the one from the photograph upstairs; the one from his dreams.

The young woman stopped in her haste and turned toward the opened front door. Will slid back into the darkness and held his breath, hoping he went unnoticed.

"Jules?" Eldon said, stepping out of the library. "Everything all right?"

Jules, Will whispered.

"Y - yes," she answered slightly befuddled "Everything's - everything's fine."

"Come," Eldon said, taking her hand. "Smithfield will be happy you're here."

Will stepped out from behind the opened door and snuck outside. He rushed down the flight of stone stairs and made his way across the front lawn, stopping at an iron fence at the edge of the property. He tightened his fingers around the gun and looked toward the sprawling woods. A brush of blood orange mixed with splashes of indigo painted the treed horizon. Subdued sounds of sporadic cannon fire echoed off the landscape. An aroma of sulfur hung in the humid air. Though the fighting in Gettysburg continued on, another conflict was brewing. Will was stuck within two worlds and battling two wars. It was up to him, and him alone, to make it to *Plum Run,* find the Parker Barn, and save Madi in time.

Chapter 36

"Wait!" Eldon yelled, sprinting up the staircase two steps at a time. He dashed down a long hallway, past Smithfield and Jules, and wedged himself within the frame of a large, oak door.

"For goodness sake, what are you doing?" Smithfield asked.

"Are – are you up for a game of poker?" Eldon panted. "Go back down to the parlor; play a hand or two."

"You cannot be serious? Do you have any idea of the time?"

Eldon extended his arm across the door, placing his hand on its frame. He looked at the second of the three watches attached to his wrist and squinted at its big and little hands. "Huh, would you look at that? 5:55." Eldon smiled. "Breakfast then?"

Smithfield rolled his eyes.

Jules strolled over to Eldon. She placed her hands on her hips, pursed her lips, and stared hard at him with questioning eyes. Eldon shifted uneasily on his feet. "He's hiding something," she said.

"What?" Eldon asked, surprised. "I most certainly am not."

Jules gave a smirk and then walked back over to Smithfield, placing her slender arm around his waist.

"She's right," Smithfield said. "Something's not quite right with you." He leaned into Eldon and sniffed. "You didn't? Tell me you haven't been into the whiskey."

"I wasn't," Eldon quickly answered, holding back a growing grin. "Well, okay. Maybe I had just . . . two."

"Geezus." Smithfield ran his right hand through his sandy, brown hair. "We've discussed this. You as well as I know that alcohol doesn't mix well in transit."

"Yes, I know. It's just – "

"Are you concerned about the jump during the parley?"

Eldon rubbed the back of his neck. "Makes me a bit anxious, I guess."

Smithfield placed a comforting hand on Eldon's shoulder. "Do not fear, my dear friend. All will go smoothly. You shall see, it will be over before you know it and everything will be back to how it should be. Now, get some rest; time is of the essence."

Smithfield took Jules by the hand and reached for the bedroom's doorknob. Eldon grabbed it first.

"What now?" Smithfield said with a huff.

"You can't go in there," Eldon said, guarding the door.

"Pardon me?"

"I said," Eldon paused; his stare never wavered. "I can't let you go in there."

"Is he serious?" Jules said; her arms folded tight across her chest. "You can't be serious?"

Smithfield stepped closer and fixed Eldon with a firm glare. "You will remove yourself from the front of this door."

Eldon held the doorknob tighter. He could feel a line of sweat beginning to form on his forehead under the brim of his derby hat.

"Maybe you didn't hear me clearly," Smithfield sneered. "Step aside. Now."

Eldon slumped his shoulders and lowered his head. He slowly released his hold on the doorknob and leaned up against the doorframe, letting Smithfield and Jules pass by.

"What in bloody hell!" Smithfield roared.

Eldon rushed into the room and slid to a stop, seeing Smithfield by the open and empty armoire. A bloody and mud-stained shirt dangled in his hands and a pair of soiled pants rested near his feet. "What's the meaning of this, Eldon? Who was in *my* house?"

"I knew it," Jules said curtly, fanning her face with her hands. "I knew he was hiding something. I could sense it."

Through the open picture window, a cool breeze dipped into the room and fluttered the sheer curtain wildly. Eldon hurried over and looked outside.

"Who's that?" Jules pointed out the window. She looked back at Smithfield. "Someone's wearing your uniform and . . . he's taking off into the woods."

"It's begun," Eldon whispered. He looked at the first watch on his wrist; *the gateway of time has opened its door.*

Eldon swiped his black trench coat off a metal coat rack near the window and slipped it over his arms. He hurried over to the primitive sketch of the United States and using two fingers, pushed in one of the bricks - the eastern coordinate - that jutted out from the stucco wall. With a winding of gears, each quadrant - north, east, south, and west - folded in on itself, revealing a hidden compartment of weapons and gadgets; books and journals.

Smithfield rushed over and seized Eldon by the arm. "What do you think you are doing?"

Eldon remained silent. He grabbed a single barrel pistol and a box of ammunition and loaded the gun's chamber.

Smithfield tightened his grip. "Seven years ago, you and I made a solemn pledge to watch over one another, to protect each other's very life. And now, after all the time vested, you go behind my back and bring a stranger into my home." He pointed at the empty armoire. "Who was here, Eldon? Who stole my uniform and gun? Is this your idea of loyalty and trust?"

Eldon swung the pistol upward, snapping its barrel into place. "Never in my life have I lost sight of the loyalty and trust we both had promised, and you know it. So, before you continue raising these false claims, I suggest you get your damn hands off of me and let me go." Eldon leaned in close. "Trust me, *my dear friend* . . .I'm saving your life."

Chapter 37

"Let me out of here!" Madi yelled as Fink made his way out of the barn. She grabbed the bars and pulled at them violently. She kicked at the door and continued to scream until her voice cracked and her throat turned raw. "I don't know where your stupid camera is! Do you hear me? I don't know where it is!"

"Hey!" Bushy Beard shouted from his stool. "How many times do I gotta tell you? Shut that mouth of yours."

"Make me," Madi shot back.

Bushy Beard jumped to his feet and stormed over to the stall like a bull, heaving in rage. "Whatcha say?"

Madi gripped the bars and gritted her teeth. "I said, make me."

Bushy Beard pushed his face against the bars. "Listen here, little lassie." A shower of spit flew out of his mouth with every word. "You're wasting your time. No one's gonna hear you or come and save you. So, either shut that trap of yours, or . . ." He raised a meaty fist. ". . . I'll shut it for you."

Madi dropped to her hands and knees and searched every square inch of the stall as Bushy Beard settled himself back on his stool. She pawed at the boards and dug at the dirt in every corner determined to find a way out before running out of daylight but only found a small hole on the top frame of the stall made by a scrawny barn mouse.

Nighttime dipped its fingers into the barn. Madi sank to the hay-strewn floor and brought her knees to her chest. A collection of faces nipped her thoughts and fell with each tear. *Nana. Grandpa. Her mother and father. Cassie. Will.* Everything she held onto and cherished. Everyone she cared for and loved. They were far, far away

- somewhere in time. A stream of tears slipped through her closed eyelids and dripped onto her dirty dress, for it was then Madi realized the life she once knew - its securities and comforts - would undoubtedly become her past, and this time and place would now become her future.

~

Daylight. A full day had come and gone since Madi had found herself thrown inside the horse's stall - a cold, damp space that stunk with the rancid odors of manure and mold.

Sometime in the early morning, while she was still asleep, someone had brought her breakfast - a plate of slimy scrambled eggs and a tall glass of sour milk. Though her stomach rumbled, Madi wrinkled her nose as she probed at the cold eggs with a metal spoon. She didn't feel like eating. What was the point? Twenty-four hours had passed, and she had no clue where the camera could be. Fink was right; her time's design was up.

A faint ray of sunlight broke through the clouds and sliced through the gap in the barn's roof. It passed over Madi's lap and hit the sidewall, creating a small burst of white light from behind a bundle of hay.

Madi set the cracked porcelain plate aside and shuffled over to the large bundle. With a labored grunt, she pushed the bale away from the wall, revealing a three-inch gap that stood between her and an open stall on the other side.

Madi laid on her stomach and pressed her face hard against the damp wooden floor. She squinted. On the other side was a single floorboard that sat an inch higher than the rest. From beneath the board, a white light flickered.

Madi blew the loose strands of hair out of her eyes and slid her arm through the rotten panel. She stretched, shoving her shoulder into the stall's wall only to find herself too far away; her fingertips barely skimmed the jutted board.

Madi brought back her arm and sat back on her knees. She placed both hands on the panel and pulled. The wood crumbled in her hands, sprinkling a cloud of fine dust to the floor. She gave the board a tug. *Creak.* She gave another tug. *Crack.*

The board snapped in half, breaking free from the corroded nails that held it in place. It sailed backward in an erratic arc and smacked Madi against her injured cheek, reopening her wound. She bit her bottom lip, stifling the scream that formed in her throat.

Ignoring the stabbing pain surging across her face, Madi quickly wiggled through the tight space to freedom. Once on the other side, she rolled onto her back – hardly breathing – and cupped her pulsating cheek. Fresh blood coated her fingers and trailed down her wrist.

Taking a deep breath, Madi crawled over to the jutted board. She wedged her thin fingers underneath and lifted. A single rusty nail that held the board in place squealed under pressure before popping free. Madi looked over her shoulder at the barn's entrance and froze.

Beyond a half-partitioned wall, she could see the soles of the Bushy Beard's leather boots. The brute crossed his feet – one over the other, mumbling in his sleep and snored on; a rhythmic buzz of sawing logs that bit into the silent morning.

Madi breathed a sigh of relief. She set the board down and turned back to the opening in the floor. Inside the earthly vault was a leather arm cuff with a rusty and cracked compass, a small book, a ripped marble bag, and a collection of metal American Revolutionary soldiers half-buried in the dirt.

Madi pushed the last of the soldiers aside. She pressed the palm of her hand against her heart, feeling a lightness flutter in her chest. A slow smile framed her face as she stared down at Fink's camera.

The barn door opened, spilling light across the wooden floor.

"You can't do this," came a man's pleading voice.

"Shh . . . Keep it down," whispered another.

Madi snatched the camera out of the hole and quickly replaced the board. She scrambled over to a slatted half-wooden wall and hid in its dark corner. Through the space between the slats, she watched as two young men walked into the barn and hovered over a sleeping Bushy Beard.

The first man, who had a crop of short dark brown hair, brought his finger to his lips, silencing his blond companion. Madi watched as he reared back his leg and then sent it forward, kicking the sole of Bushy Beard's boot.

"Wake up," the man yelled.

Bushy Beard woke with a start and teetered on his stool before toppling sideways to the floor with a heavy plop. The two men hooted in laughter.

"All right. Who was it?" Bushy Beard said, jumping to his feet. "Was it you, Benjamin?" he said, pointing to the young man with dark brown hair, "or this good-for-nothing brother of yours?"

"Fink requests to see you inside," Benjamin smugly replied.

"Is that right?" Bushy Beard snarled.

"Yeah, so get going."

Bushy Beard stomped closer. "I'll have you know – "

"I don't think you heard me clearly," Benjamin interrupted, looking up at the towering brute. "Fink has requested your presence. And that means now. Not later. Not tomorrow. Now. So, before he has all of our heads, I suggest you watch who you're talking to and geta-movin'."

Bushy Beard gave a harsh squint. "Just remember, I'm watching you –" He poked a hard finger into each man's shoulder. "Both you Parkers."

"And that, Jeremiah," Benjamin said, clapping and rubbing his hands together, "is how you take control of a situation."

Jeremiah? Madi shuffled to the opening of the wooden partition and peeked around the wall.

238

"Dammit, Benjamin. Why did I even allow myself to be duped by these men?" Jeremiah hung his head low. "What would Mother and Father think of me? Of us? I never should have listened to you."

"Hush," Benjamin hissed.

"But honestly brother, I - "

Benjamin seized Jeremiah by the arm. "This is not the time nor the place for your banter. That's all I need is for Fink to hear you."

Jeremiah shook his head and started for the opened door. "I can't do this anymore."

Madi ducked back around the partition and pushed herself against the wall, cradling the camera. A rap of footsteps echoed off the barn floor. They were close; real close. Madi could feel it. She pressed herself further against the wall and listened.

"All my life," she heard Benjamin say, "I needed to prove myself."

"Prove yourself? To who?" Jeremiah asked.

"It's just like you not to see it," Benjamin snarled. "I mean, all those years growing up, living day by day at *his* beck and call - "

"Who's?" Jeremiah interrupted. "Father's?"

"But of course, Father's," Benjamin scoffed. "He despised me and adored both of you when all I ever wanted was to feel important; like I truly belonged."

"Father was never like that; he loved us all equally."

"Horse shit," Benjamin spat, smacking the top of the partitioned wall.

Madi jumped and covered her mouth, stifling her yelp.

"You were always clinging to Mother's side or caught up in your own fantasy world, believing this and that," Benjamin said. "And as for William. Father's prized child. *Be more like William.* Father would say. *Watch and learn from William. William is refined and educated. He will be a man of greatness one day.* Blah, blah, blah."

"How dare you. How dare you speak ill of William," Jeremiah

seethed. "Do you not realize it has been seven years since he was last seen at the fair?"

"No tears from this brother," Benjamin said.

"You're becoming just like them."

"Those who you call *them* are the Nefarions."

"Nefarions? What good have they done for us?"

"They've taken us in and treated us like family," Benjamin replied.

"Maybe you. But certainly not I," Jeremiah said. "I had a family; *we* had a family who loved us."

"That's right," Benjamin snarled. "We *had*."

"Are - are you even listening to yourself?"

"Loud and clear."

Jeremiah huffed. "That man, who has taken presence in our home, comes up to you one day and fills your head with promises of power, and you trust him?"

"Yes," Benjamin answered.

"But why?"

"Because - unlike you - he saved me when I had nothing."

"I could not bring myself to follow the path you were taking," Jeremiah said.

"You are here now."

"Yes, but I thought we were going to war."

"We are," Benjamin answered sharply.

"When? Everywhere we go we find ourselves surrounded by it, yet we have not even fought a single-handed battle!"

"This," Benjamin said, holding up a small skeleton key. "This is our battle."

"For two years," Jeremiah began, "Two years we've been following Fink through sun and storm, wearing these ridiculous garments fashioned with metals and gears, chasing this and that, wasting time because some poor 'ole chap gave him the runaround."

"Fink is owed my loyalty and respect. He is my very own guardian of life, accepting me for what I am *without* judgment."

"He procured our house, then built his Nefarious headquarters in our attic while aiding the Rebel enemy all within Union lines. And now, he kidnaps a child; a child, Benjamin!"

"I'm sorry," Benjamin said, "but you and I, we have to do this."

Madi listened as the two men moved away from the partitioned wall. She carefully peeked around the wooden divider and saw Benjamin standing at her stall door.

Jeremiah placed his hand on the lock. "Wait. Tell me now. Do you truly believe that the necklace she wears and the camera she needs to find gives one the power to travel through time?"

"But of course," Benjamin said. "Why shouldn't I believe it?"

Jeremiah threw up his arms. "Because it's preposterous."

"I have nothing else to say to you."

"Let's say his assertions are correct," Jeremiah continued. "That one can travel through time. Can you not see the damage and corruption it would cause? Having the control to stop someone's demise or rewrite someone's life. History – the world itself – could be forever changed if this power falls within the wrong hands."

"Fink is a man of valor and good intentions," Benjamin stated.

"What if he isn't? What about our reputation if we are caught amongst his wrongdoings? We shall be tarnished as traitors, remembered forever as accomplices of evil. Please, I insist you stop while there is still time. If not for Father or William, for Mother. For me; the only brother you have left; bonded by blood."

Benjamin moved closer; his eyes cold as ice. "Our common surname we may share, brother, but the blood within *my* veins runs differently than yours. Now, move out of my way."

Jeremiah stepped back. "What? What does that even mean?"

"Whether you like it or not," Benjamin said, placing the key in the lock. "Our choices were made long ago."

The key turned with a *clink* and snapped in Madi's ears. She felt the stall door slam against the wall.

"I stand allegiance to the Nefarions and their cause," Benjamin said, "And so should – hey, where did she go?"

A chorus of shouts rang out behind Madi as she sprinted across the field of tall grass. How she escaped the barn, she will never know. It didn't matter. She was somehow free.

Madi gripped the camera and ran; ran faster and faster toward the woods; its arms wide open and waiting. She splashed through *Plum Run*, passed the chicken coop, and ducked under the multitude of evergreen trees, entering the vast and inhospitable woods, never looking back.

Chapter 38

A collection of faint cries and yipping shrieks rose with the sun and mixed with the subdued rumble of artillery that resounded off the trees. Gettysburg's last wave of war was rising to its final curtain call.

~

Will gripped the rifle in his hand and picked up his pace; each determined step forward propelling a surging stream of adrenaline through his veins. He trudged through the thickening woods amongst the rising humidity and pushed through banquets of ferns, plodding over the dense weeds and tangled vines that covered the ground in a lush green blanket.

A bundle of fallen tree trunks littered the forest floor. Will scaled over the lying logs and ducked through a veil of knitted greenery only to contend with a cloud of gnats hovering above a sparkling small stream on the other side. He waved the bugs away, disrupting their courting dance and eyed the stream's jagged outline that cut through the woods and looped around a cluster of large stones before disappearing into a vast, sun-drenched and grassy field. *Plum Run.* He had found it.

Will knelt down by the edge of the stream and set his gun aside. He cupped his hands and took a quick, refreshing drink. As he wiped his dripping lips with the sleeve of his jacket, a scent of lavender wafted in the air. *Jules?*

Will lowered his arm and looked out at the tree line. In the distance, an oncoming tide of translucent mist was rapidly weaving itself through the woods. Before he could move out of its path, the glistening vapor skated across the flowing water and coiled itself around his feet. Will shuddered and expelled an airy gasp as the luminous mist crept up the front of his jacket and slipped underneath his high collar. His breath quickened; his heart skipped a beat, and then, as cold as the mist once was, it turned warm and branched out to every part of his body.

Will loosened his collar and looked down at the shallow water. He leaned in closer, studying his reflection. An unusual growth of rough stubble covered the contours of his defined jawline and chiseled chin. *Impossible*, he murmured, running his fingers across his rugged face.

A twig cracked like the snapping of a whip. A crow shot out from a nearby tree in a crying caw, and a bullet whistled past.

Will dropped to the ground as another bullet zoomed past his face, hissing like an angry hornet. He tucked his rifle under his arm and crawled past a decaying tree stump, hiding inside a thick knot of hobblebush near the edge of the stream. Will positioned his loaded gun against his shoulder and took aim through the thicket; his finger hovering at the trigger.

From behind a cluster of tall boulders, he watched as a group of stealthy shadows emerged in a robotic march. Their green trousers and federal-style jackets, with collars and cuffs, trimmed in dark emerald, blended with the trees.

"The Berdan Sharpshooters," Will whispered to himself, recognizing the feared squad of men.

Moving as one unit, the sharpshooters patrolled the woods; the barrels of their weapons aimed straight ahead in their firm arms with full intent to kill any enemy within 200 yards. Their skill was dynamic; their actions were steady with each calculated maneuver as they executed their mission. They were exactly as Will had remembered: formidable assassins.

The lead sharpshooter – a robust, young man with coarse, black hair and tanned skin – sharply raised his hand, halting his force. He took a few steps forward, shifting the aim of his breechloader at the trees. He lowered his weapon. "We're clear."

Will watched as one sharpshooter walked away from the group and knelt by the edge of the stream. The soldier holstered his breechloader on his back and began to fill his canteen. At that moment, along and slimy shape with brown and tan scales slithered out of the water and into the hobblebush. Will clenched the rifle in his sweaty hands and shifted his weight on his elbows. He held his breath and bit his bottom lip as the snake's slippery body wound around his forearm and glided across his wrist, rustling the ivy.

The sharpshooter spun around on one knee, removing his breechloader from its holster, and aimed at shrubbery. He cautiously inched forward; the black barrel peeking through the hobblebush.

Will closed his eyes and pressed himself to the ground; the heavy smell of mud and moss drifted up his nose.

Boom! Boom!

The trees rattled and the ground vibrated. The snake slithered out of the underbrush.

"Left flank," shouted the lead sharpshooter. "Move! Move! Move!"

Will opened his eyes. The breechloader's barrel disappeared.

Bang!

Will peered through the dense shrub. The snake lay dead and the sharpshooter ran off, falling in formation with the rest of his squadron, who were retreating in the direction of the rising sounds of warfare.

Boom!

Another explosion hit the ground in a thunderous crash. Streams of smoke oozed through the woods like blood seeping out of a gaping wound, coating each tree, bush, and rock in a thick, murky haze.

"Help!" came a shrill call. "Help me, please! Somebody, help!"

Will's eyes searched the trees for the desperate voice. There. Behind him.

A young girl entered the woods in a frantic dash, dodging trees and ducking through low-lying vines. Chasing after her were two, young men with guns in their hands.

"Get back here you little brat," bellowed a third man as he broke through the tree line.

"Leave me alone," the girl yelled over her shoulder.

Will snatched his rifle out from the underbrush, scrambled to his feet, and took off, joining in on the chase.

Chapter 39

ldon raced out of the house and sprinted across the front yard, stopping at the fence. He took out a journal from his jacket pocket and flipped to a section bookmarked with a bronze, oak tree. He ran his finger across the page – a timeline of events – and read over his notes. A sound of thunder struck the humid air.

Eldon glanced at the first watch that was wrapped securely on his wrist and frowned. *Damn. I need more time.*

"Eldon, wait," came Jules' shrill voice. "We need to talk." She rushed down the porch steps and made her way across the yard; her hair whipping in the wind. "This – this needs to stop," she panted lightly. "All your comings and goings without any explanation. What is it that you are hiding?"

Eldon closed the journal and placed it back into his jacket pocket. "I'm sorry, but there are some things you just can't know."

"No. There are no secrets," Jules said. "Whatever it is, we are all in this together. That's the way it's always been . . . from the beginning."

The screen door opened with a *bang*, echoing off the house. "Would someone like to explain what the hell is going on here?" shouted Smithfield from the top of the porch steps.

Eldon looked up at Smithfield then back at Jules. "I must go."

"Eldon please," Jules begged.

"Listen, you must hold him back. Do you understand? It is imperative that he does not leave and attend the meeting."

"What do you expect me to do? You know he doesn't listen to anyone."

A clopping of hooves reverberated off the dirt road. "Isaac,"

Eldon said, nodding toward a young, black man perched atop a majestic, tan stallion that was heading toward the house. "Tell him you need help. He'll know what to do."

"But – "

"It will all make sense soon. I promise."

Eldon gave a quick adjustment of his derby hat, quickly kissed Jules on the cheek, and then ran out of the yard and into the woods, disappearing amongst the awaiting crowd of trees.

"Don't just stand there. Stop him," Smithfield yelled.

Jules ran over to Isaac, who was securing the horse to an iron hitching post, and whispered in his ear.

"Send out the call," Smithfield ordered as he made his way across the front lawn.

"My apologies, sir," Isaac said, stepping in front of the opened gate. He clenched the lapel of his jacket and stood straight. "But without Dorian and Wesley, who are presently absent at the moment, I am afraid that cannot be done."

"Who are you to tell me what to do?"

"I implore you to reconsider. It's not time," Isaac warned.

"Time or not," Smithfield retorted, loading his gun. He stared at the trees and narrowed his eyes. "I fear we have a traitor amongst us."

Chapter 40

rushing leaves. Snapping twigs. Swishing branches. Madi sprinted through the woods; her heart thumping against her tightening chest. She leaped over downed trees, ducked under low-lying branches, and sidestepped massive rocks that protruded out of the ground. Against the sound of her raspy breaths and frenzied movements, she could still hear the distant calls of her pursuers, yelling out to her.

Straight ahead, two tall trees - rooted at their bases - towered above the canopy of the forest. Madi slipped behind their sturdy trunks and hid, making herself small. Her lungs burned; her calves ached; her heart throbbed in time with her quivering body. And through it all, amongst the riddling sounds of war, she could hear Fink's venomous voice siphoning through the muggy air.

"Madilyn!" came his distant cackle. "You can run, my dear, but you can't hide."

Each word he spoke assaulted her ears and escalated her fear. Like a crazed wolf, he drew closer and closer, ruthlessly sniffing through the underbrush, determined to find her - his prey.

A low percussion of cannon fire rumbled through the trees. The scent of burnt powder hung in the air and nipped at her nose.

Madi opened her eyes to a blanket of sulfuric smoke slinking its way through the woods. Its ghostly stream was burying the forest in a white gloomy haze, creating an infinite labyrinth of trees, underbrush, and rock.

"Will," she whispered. "Where are you?"

An echo of gunfire popped and crescendoed in rapid sequence. Madi jumped at the assaulting sound and took off into the timbered maze, fighting against its unforgiving terrain. As she dodged a cluster of hobblebushes, a young man shot out from behind a tall, oak tree and seized her with his strong arms.

The woods spun like a merry-go-round, blurring in a mixture of grey, brown, and green. Madi flailed her arms and kicked her legs. As she was towed up and over a cluster of rocks, the camera slipped out of her unsteady hands and vanished in a patch of tall grass. "Help! Somebod – "

The young man cupped his powerful hand around her mouth and smothered her cries. "Quiet," he ordered through clenched teeth, stopping beside a dilapidated stone wall.

"I'm going to let you go," he puffed; his warm breath hitting against her ear. "But you must promise not to scream."

Madi sniffled, struggling to breathe beneath his suffocating hand.

He gave a quick and firm squeeze. "Do you understand?"

She nodded rapidly.

"Good. Now, stay here," he instructed.

Madi sucked in a breath as she was released. "Please," she muttered, grabbing the sides of her dress. "Please don't hurt me."

"I'm not going to hurt you," he replied, drawing back his double-barrel shotgun that hung loosely in his hand.

Through blurry eyes, Madi watched as the young man walked over to the patch of tall grass, reached down into its clustered bunch, and pulled out the camera.

"You can have it," Madi stammered, cowering back. "It's yours. Just please . . . please let me go."

The young man, in his cream-colored shirt and pin-striped navy-blue vest of chains, gears, and keys, casually walked back over to Madi and held out the camera. "I believe this belongs to you."

Confused, Madi looked up at the young man. As she met his two-colored eyes, a fleeting image of a sweet and caring five-year-old boy handing her a folded cloth full of warm griddle cakes flashed in her mind. "Jeremiah?"

"When I heard they captured a young girl with information about the camera, I knew it had to be you," he said.

Madi swiped the camera out of Jeremiah's hands and took off into the woods.

"I'm here to help you," Jeremiah called out.

Madi stopped in her escape and glanced over her shoulder. "Help me? Thirty seconds ago, you jumped out from behind a tree and kidnapped me."

"I let you go, didn't I?"

A colossal gust of wind blew through the woods, plunging below the trees. Leaves shivered in its wake. Branches rubbed against one another and cried out in eerie groans. Two muffled pops of gunfire clipped the air.

Jeremiah rushed over to Madi, grabbed her by the hand, and pulled her toward an underground hollow surrounded by the three-sided, dilapidated stone wall.

"Wait," she cried. "Where are you – "

"Not a sound," Jeremiah commanded, stopping below a canopy of tightly-woven vines and ivy that jutted out from the top of the wall of the dilapidated building. He flattened himself against the stone, holding his shotgun close and pointed up. ". . . or they will hear you."

Harsh footsteps. Crunching leaves. Snapping twigs.

Madi tucked herself into the stone wall and looked up through the awning of underbrush. Beyond the mesh of dense foliage, she watched as a young man, pistol hanging in his clutched hand, walked to the edge of the overhang.

"Where is she?" came the hissing voice of Benjamin. "I swear she went this way."

"What about that brother of yours Parker?" the gruff voice of Bushy Beard answered. "Where'd he run off to?"

"How should I know?" Benjamin said, scanning the trees. "I'm not his keeper."

Bushy Beard swatted at the low-lying vines near his feet. "You expect me to believe that flim-flam?"

"Silence, you fools," barked a sinister voice.

The wind stopped. The forest plunged in silence.

Madi clung to Jeremiah's strong arm and gulped down her breaths. *Fink.* He was here.

"How can I *think* with you two flapping your jaws at one another?" Fink pushed himself between the squabbling duo and rolled up his sleeves. "Honestly, where do you people come from?"

Bushy Beard took off his hat and placed it over his heart. "South Carolina, sir."

"It was a rhetorical question you moron," Fink said with a roll of the eyes.

"You – you Johnny Rebs," Benjamin said with a laugh. "You all are dumber than – "

Bushy Beard threw his hands against Benjamin's chest, sending him falling back into a tree. "Whatcha implying there, Bluebelly?"

"Enough," Fink snapped. He pointed at the woods. "Go. And don't come back until you find her. I need her to find that camera. I can't lose it *again.*"

Snap. Crack. Crunch.

Madi listened to the heavy tread of Benjamin and Bushy Beard as they disappeared into the dappled haze of the woodland trees.

"Oh Madilyn," Fink taunted. "Come out, come out wherever you are. I promise not to hurt you."

Through the knitted cover of branches and leaves, Madi saw the point of Fink's black boots step up to the edge of the wall; their tips hanging over the undergrowth.

"Fink," came Benjamin's yelling voice. "Quick, over here!"

Fink wheeled around. Dirt and crushed leaves sprinkled off the edge of the wall in a shower of soil. Madi covered her head and held the cough that rose in her throat.

"You found her?" Fink called out.

"Can't say for certain, but something just moved beyond those high rocks," Benjamin said confidently.

Fink stepped away from the edge of the wall. "You better be right about this, Parker."

Madi stood motionless, listening. Fink's footsteps faded and the lowing sounds of war slowly rose with the midday sun.

Jeremiah took her by the hand. "Come. I fear that we don't have much time."

Madi stole one last look above her before Jeremiah led her over to a small stack of stones. He sat down and pulled out a small, tied-up notebook and pencil from his vest pocket. "Why are you helping me?" she asked.

"Why should I not?"

"Because you're –" Madi hesitated. "– you're one of them."

Jeremiah looked up from the paper he was writing on. "Never." He quickly finished the note, tore out the page, and pressed it into her open palm.

"What's this?" Madi asked, looking at what appeared to be a coded message of geometric shapes, dots, and dashes linked or stacked together in various combinations.

"About a mile east from here," Jeremiah began, "you will come upon a large, stone farmhouse at the edge of the road." He placed the notebook back in his vest pocket and continued. "Go there. Ask for Mr. Jacob Weikert; he owns the farm. You must make certain he gives *that* note to a young man named Isaac Emerson. He will know what to do."

"I don't understand."

Jeremiah took Madi by the arm and led her to a clear path in the woods. "Stay straight with the seven mighty oaks. I will follow closely behind to make sure Fink and the others stay far enough away."

"But – "

A string of muted explosions suddenly shook the earth.

"You must go," Jeremiah warned.

Madi looked down at the note clutched in her dirty, blood-stained hand and then out at the vast woods. An echo of gunfire rang in her ears.

Jeremiah pushed on her arm. "Go!"

Madi gripped the camera and note and dashed out of the ruins and back into the heart of the woods. Dry, brittle leaves and small twigs crunched under her clumsy and frenzy footsteps. She stooped below low branches and avoided a cluster of protruding rocks, trying to stay on the path. She scaled a pair of covered mossy logs laid out in a large letter X, zigzagged through a cluster of split trees, and passed a huge boulder, protruding from the ground.

Headfirst through a web of greenery. Around a grove of trees. Sidestep another boulder. Sharp right.

A wave of fear plunged and knotted in Madi's stomach as she approached two familiar moss-covered logs in the shape of an X. "Oh, no," she moaned.

"Boo!" came a whoop of laughter.

Madi spun around and found Benjamin; a smirk on his face; his pistol aimed at her chest. "Going somewhere?" he asked.

Madi turned to run but froze as Fink stepped out from behind a large oak tree; his black cape fluttering erratically in the wind.

"Why hello, Madilyn," Fink said. "We've been looking for you. You didn't think that you could – the camera," he beamed. "You found it."

"Stay away from me," Madi warned, stumbling against uprooted tree branches that shot up from the ground.

Benjamin caught Madi in his strong arms and held her tight. He cocked back his pistol and pushed its barrel against her ribs. "I wouldn't put up too much of a fuss if I were you. I tend to have a shaky finger."

Loud quarreling rose from behind a stand of swishing ferns. Madi looked up to see Jeremiah tripping through the underbrush.

"Look who I found hiding in the trees, spying on us," said Bushy Beard, shoving Jeremiah along.

"Spying?" Jeremiah said. "You speak of nonsense. I was merely securing the area for you," he said, giving Fink a nod.

Fink folded his arms across his chest. "Go on."

Jeremiah pulled himself out of Bushy Beard's hold and fixed his vest that sat crooked on his broad shoulders. "In seeing that we were closing in on the girl," he began, "I felt it would be in the best interest of the group to have someone fall back; secure the area. I mean, you, yourself, made the claim that it was only a matter of time before the NEVES would – "

"What did you say?" Fink interrupted harshly.

"NEVES and the parley," Jeremiah said.

Fink stormed over to Jeremiah and threw a hard fist into his jaw. *Crack.* Jeremiah slumped like a wet rag and hung limp in Fink's stronghold.

"How do you know the meeting involves the NEVES?" Fink demanded. "You were never privy to that information."

"Leave him alone!" Madi screamed.

"Quiet," Fink threw over his shoulder. He lifted the brim of his top hat and stared at Madi's clutched hand. "And what do you have there, eh?"

Madi crumpled Jeremiah's note and stuffed it in her mouth.

"You little . . . " Fink threw Jeremiah to the ground and stormed over to Madi. "Spit it out," he demanded.

Madi pressed her lips together and defiantly shook her head.

With a lightning thrust, Fink grabbed her cheeks and squeezed, "I said spit it out."

Madi groaned from the pressure of Fink's bony fingers compressing against her wounded cheek. A stream of tears escaped from the corners of her eyes and ran down her face as she strained to keep her lips tightly shut.

"Isn't she a stubborn one?" Benjamin said.

Fink pressed harder. "I said . . . spit it out."

Madi puffed a cough through her nose. Colored spots danced in front of her eyes. Unable to bear the suffering any longer, she slowly opened her mouth.

Fink pulled out the wrinkled note and read the scrawled message, wiping his bloody and spit-covered fingers on the shoulder of her dress. His hand froze; his face contorted, turning into an unhealthy shade of purple. Fink balled the note in his fist, marched back over to Jeremiah, and grabbed him by his vest.

"Wait," Jeremiah pleaded as he was dragged across the ground. "I – I can explain!"

"You helping her?" Fink growled.

Madi looked down at Jeremiah. His two-colored eyes were glassy, and a thin line of blood trailed out of his mouth and ran down his chin.

"Answer me, you rat," Fink raged.

Madi stared, wide-eyed, at Jeremiah, willing him to say "no."

Jeremiah swallowed hard and hung his head. "Yes."

"He's lying," Madi said.

"I trusted you; took you in; and now, after all this time, you go behind my back and give her *this*." Fink shoved the balled paper into Jeremiah's face. "Not only does it expose me and everyone involved, but it reveals the true nature of this war? Whose side are you on, anyway?"

"It was never my intent – "

Fink yanked Jeremiah close and threw another hard punch into his face. Madi flinched. Benjamin snickered. Bushy Beard howled in a rumble of laughter.

Fink lifted Jeremiah's limp head by his hair and held the note up to his bleeding and swelling face. "How long? How long have you been helping *them*?"

Jeremiah's eyes rolled back in his head and a slew of inconsistent syllables left his swollen lips.

"Stop it," Madi yelled, fighting to break free from Benjamin's grasp. "You're hurting him!"

"You have no idea who I am or who you're dealing with." Fink clenched his fingers into a tight fist and reared back for a final blow.

"Wait," Madi cried.

Fink stopped; his fist hovering inches from Jeremiah's face.

"You can have the necklace and the camera. Just please," she pleaded. "Please don't hurt him anymore."

The wind calmed. The war paused in its assault. An unnerving silence hung over the woods.

Fink threw Jeremiah to the ground and walked back to Madi. "Empathy," he spat. "A pathetic representation of the weak."

Madi looked away, fighting back another wave of tears. In her short eleven years, she never imagined that she would have to make a choice – the choice to give up her life and the life she once knew to save the life of another.

"Now," Fink said, tapping his fingertips together as he eyed his prize hanging from Madi's neck. A hungry smile spread across his scarred face. "After all this time, it's finally mine . . . again."

Fink reached for the necklace. *Zzzap!*

A stream of white electricity shot out from the bronzed branches of the oak tree medallion. The sharp sizzle snapped in Madi's ears, and the scent of burnt skin wafted in the air.

"No!" Fink breathed. "It – it can't be true."

Madi opened her eyes and watched the tips of Fink's fingers bubble and blister.

"You want me to take a try at it, boss?" Bushy Beard asked. "I'll rip that necklace off her pretty little neck."

"You can't, you fool!" Fink snarled; his nostrils flaring with each heaving breath. "The prophecy must have been sealed the moment she put that damn thing on. She's the key. Only she can –" Fink whipped around. "That's it." A murderous grin formed on his face and his eyes became mere slits.

Fink ripped the camera out of Madi's hands and tossed it over to Bushy Beard. "Guard that with your life."

"With pleasure," Bushy Beard sneered, catching the camera in his meaty hands.

"Take it off," Fink demanded.

"What?" Madi asked.

"Th – the necklace," Fink sputtered with fury.

"No, Madi," Jeremiah rasped, slowly rising to his feet. "If – if you do, they – they win."

Fink turned to Jeremiah and kicked straight up into his stomach. "Shut up, you!"

"I said leave him alone," Madi yelled.

"Take off the necklace, Madilyn," Fink ordered.

Jeremiah coughed. "You can't, Madi. No matter what."

Fink pulled out a long-barreled pistol from his waistband, cocked it back with a *click*, and held it to the back of Jeremiah's head. "Do it now, or his blood will be on your hands."

Benjamin pitched Madi forward. "You heard him. Hurry up."

Madi looked over at Jeremiah. "I'm – I'm sorry," she whispered, "but I can't have you die."

Madi took a deep breath. She lowered her head and reached around her neck, taking the warm metal clasp in her cold fingers.

Chapter 41

"Drop the gun Fink," came a full and steady voice. "Or you'll be the one with a bullet in your head."

"You?" Bushy Beard roared, drawing his weapon from his waistband. "I told you to watch your back, boy."

"General Mills. Put down the gun!" Fink cried out.

"No," Bushy Beard spat. "This mudsill muggins made a fool of me back in town and – "

"That may be true," Fink quickly interrupted, pushing down on Bushy Beard's gunned hand. "But I can assure you, you will have time for your much-deserved revenge . . . soon."

Bushy Beard curled his lip with a grunt and grudgingly harnessed his gun into his waistband.

"Let the girl go!" the voice demanded.

The war unmuted. A reverberation of cannon and gunfire swelled in the distance.

Fink turned on his heels and spread his arms wide. "*William,*" he said with a snarky grin. "So glad to see you could finally join us."

Madi slowly let go of the necklace and looked over her shoulder. "Will? Will, help me. Please."

Benjamin grabbed Madi around the waist and pulled her back, covering her mouth with his dirty hand.

"It's been ages since I've seen you last," Fink said. "How've you been old friend?"

Will stepped out from behind the trees; his rifle aimed at Fink. "I'm *not* your friend."

Fink chuckled inwardly and scratched the side of his head with the barrel of his gun. "Funny. That's not how I remember it."

"William?" Jeremiah said softly.

Will shifted his aim. "Don't move."

"Good heavens," said Fink. "No need for dramatics. I mean, look at the poor chap. What on earth could he possibly do to you?"

Jeremiah staggered to his feet, coughing. He fell against a massive boulder and wiped his crimson-stained lips with the cuff of his sleeve. "How is it that you are standing here in front of us?"

Will glanced at Fink and then back at Jeremiah. "What do you mean?"

Fink bent at the waist and smacked the top of his knee, letting out a cackle that drilled through the rising acoustics of war.

Will pointed his gun back at Fink. "What's so funny?"

Fink's cackling reduced to a rolling snicker. "You – you never told them, did you?"

Benjamin lowered his hand from Madi's mouth and moved closer. "Will, please," she pleaded. "Help me."

Will knitted his brow but kept his aim steady at Fink. "Told them what?"

"I'm ashamed of you, William," Fink said with a dramatic pout. "Deserting those that truly cared about you; I mean, honestly, do you have no remorse?"

Will shifted uneasily on his feet. "I – I don't know what you're talking about."

"Of course, you don't," Fink said with a smirk. He snapped his cape theatrically to the side and back down again in a crack of thunder that punctured the air. "Well, there you have it, gentlemen." He looked over at Madi. "And young lady," he said with a sharp wink. "Without further ado, may I present to you the leader of the righteous; the defender of truth and justice; your guardian of life . . . *William J. Parker.*"

A blast of cold air shot down through the trees and struck Will hard with its icy spear. He buckled and swayed on his feet, faltering under the weight of the gun in his hand. He threw out his arm, steadying himself against his stiffening legs as a collection of canned voices warped and waned through his ears.

"His name is Will. Will Marshall," came Madi's squealing and distorted voice.

"I – I never stopped believing dear brother," Jeremiah said.

"Brother?" Bushy Beard scoffed loudly.

"No," Madi yelled. *"You're all wrong; tell them, Will. Tell them you're* **my** *brother."*

Will bit his lip and squeezed his eyes shut as their dithering voices dug deeper into his muddled consciousness.

"As a matter of fact Madilyn," Will heard Fink say. *"He's truly not your brother, but theirs: Benjamin and Jeremiah."*

"No," Madi yelled. *"You're lying. He's my brother; mine. Do you hear me? My brother!"*

The cold air dissipated.

Will slowly raised his head, blinking his eyes. The woods rippled in waves of green and brown. A high-pitched din surged in his ears. Will looked from Benjamin to Jeremiah to Madi. Each one of them tilted and then spiraled in a black tunnel; his future and his past collided head-on.

"No. It's not true," Madi said, stomping her feet. "I don't believe any of you." She looked at Will. "Tell them. Tell them who you truly are."

Will met her stark eyes. "I . . . I don't know."

"Can you believe it, Benjamin?" Jeremiah said. "William; our William has finally come home!"

"So . . ." Benjamin scoffed, harnessing his gun. He shoved Madi into Bushy Beard's arms and then stormed over to Will, grabbing him by the jacket. "The *infamous* fighting *hero* has returned?"

Will threw up his hands and cowered back at the growing fury in Benjamin's eyes.

"Brother, stop," Jeremiah yelled.

"No!" Benjamin spat over his shoulder. He looked back at Will with mounted contempt. "I've been waiting a long time for this very moment."

Benjamin ripped the rifle out of Will's hands in crazed disgust and tossed it amongst a bed of white trillium flowers. A twisted smile took shape on his weathered face. "I must say, when I heard the news of your disappearance, nothing pleased me more."

"Thank you, Benjamin," Fink interrupted. "But we have more pressing issues at – "

"Six months after your disappearance," Benjamin continued, "time stopped for everyone. No. I take that back. Life did. *Our lives.* With no word from you, Father vowed to Mother, to all of us, that he would search everywhere, travel far and wide, if he had to – just to bring you home." He grimaced. "It was a reminder of just how much he loved *you* and just how much he *truly* despised me."

"Spring came, then summer. Each and every bleeding day, Mother sat alone on the porch, staring blankly at the gravel path that led away from our home, waiting and waiting . . . and waiting for Father to return with *you*. But sadly, that never happened." Benjamin plucked out his pistol from the holster lying low on his hip and held it close to Will's face. "And do you know why?"

Will could barely shake his head.

"Tell him, Jeremiah," Benjamin ordered; the gun beginning to shake in his firm hand.

"Brother, please."

"Tell him!"

Jeremiah sighed. "Because – "

"Go on," Benjamin taunted.

"Because Father died while searching for you."

"That's right," Benjamin snarled. "Father died while searching high and low for his *beloved* William. Not even a month later, Mother – heartbroken and forlorn – fell silent, and became more distant; until finally, she followed in Father's path, leaving us alone. Because of you, I lost everything. A family. A home. I lost my dignity as a man when I became a vagrant on the streets begging for even the smallest piece of bread until stealing became my only option."

"Which was your choice," Jeremiah quickly replied.

"A choice I was forced to make," Benjamin snapped. "Where were you, Jeremiah, huh? Or you William for that matter? I rotted away in that filthy jail for nearly two years until a real hero came and saved me." Benjamin held his head high in allegiance to Fink.

"You're delusional brother!" Jeremiah said.

"No, you are!"

Will quickly glanced at Madi, then down at his rifle lying in the bed of white flowers, and then back up at her with serious eyes. She lightly nodded.

Benjamin turned back to Will. "Fink told me everything about you; all your lies and deceit, conning people into believing you were some righteous hero. A fighter for the unjust. A guardian of life. Bah! You may have had everyone fooled while you went on your merry ole' way, bouncing back and forth through time for – "

"What?" Jeremiah interrupted; his mouth open in disbelief.

"Oh yes, brother. All those years we believed William was gone. No. He was never really gone." Benjamin met Will, face-to-face and rested the barrel of his gun on Will's chest. "Isn't that right, *brother*? You knew exactly what you were doing, and where you were going each and every time."

"Father," Jeremiah whispered. ". . . and Mother. They both died because of – "

"HIM," Benjamin spat. "You hear that, William? The wrong was not righted by your benevolent hands. The wrong *lies* in them."

Chapter 42

A sharp, lone bugle call resounded through the trees. An uproar of quick yips and droned shouts filtered through the woods, which was followed by a steady volley of cannon fire that suddenly broke out in lowing valley.

Beyond a band of boulders, a thin Confederate soldier in a ripped and blood-stained uniform came wildly trampling through the underbrush. "Buford!" cried his desperate and shrill voice. "Buford!" The soldier ran straight toward the group and stopped. He bent at the waist and grabbed his knees. "Buford. Praise be, I found you," he panted. "It started. We have to leave . . . go. Now."

Through the mounting commotion of war and the soldier's frantic pleas, Will snatched up his rifle off the ground and quickly darted behind a nearby cluster of trees unseen.

"Who are you?" Fink asked the manic soldier.

"Shelton. Who are . . . *hey*, would you take a look at you? Ain't you dressed all fancy and such?" Shelton said, plucking at Fink's red suspenders.

"Will someone get this half-wit out of here?" Fink roared.

"Where'd he go?" Benjamin shouted, turning himself around.

"Who?" Fink asked.

"Me?" Shelton pointed at himself.

"No. William," Benjamin answered.

"Well, I'll be," Shelton said, slapping the side of his thigh as he looked at Madi. "Lookie who you found Buford! Isn't she the one that tried to steal your horse?"

"Fink," Benjamin said, running amuck with the gun in his hand as he searched the trees.

"You know him?" Fink asked Bushy Beard.

"Not at all," Bushy Beard replied tight-lipped.

"Yes, you do," Shelton said. "When we left home, you promised mama that – "

"Well, Mama ain't here now, is she?" Bushy Beard replied.

"Fink, are you even listening?" Benjamin said, grabbing his forehead. "William is gone!"

A barrage of gunfire pelted the trees like marbles fired from slingshots. Madi cowered in Bushy Beard's arms and screamed.

"It's happening," Shelton yelled in panic. "It's happening!"

"We got to move," Fink said, securing his top hat.

A wave of cannon fire rolled in like thunder and shook the ground in a violent tremor.

"What about William?" Benjamin yelled.

"We got the girl and the camera," Fink said. "We'll find him."

"But when?"

"In time," Fink answered, shoving Jeremiah forward. "Now, everyone, move out."

"Will," Madi screamed, twisting and turning in Bushy Beard's locked arm. "Help!"

Will slid back behind the tree and looked out at the enormity of the woods. His stomach knotted. His rapid breathing matched the beat of his racing heart. Worlds of war ensued him. Catastrophic chaos reigned. He placed his finger on the trigger and closed his eyes. In that sudden moment, his muddled thoughts became crystal clear; a luster of clarity. Somewhere deep inside an inner strength propelled outward and charged every inch of his body with absolute determination.

Will flicked open his eyes and set his jaw. *I got this.* In one fluid motion, he came out from behind the tree, aimed his rifle at Bushy Beard, and fired.

The bullet zipped out of the barrel and bit at the air. Around and around like a gyroscope, it flew before boring into the thick flesh of

Bushy Beard's shoulder. With a howl of pain, the brute released his hold, dropping Madi and the camera to the ground.

Benjamin raised his pistol and fired two erratic shots in Will's direction. Will dove behind a nearby boulder as the bullets ricocheted off the rock in a shower of sparks and stone.

"Stop shooting, you idiot!" Fink ordered.

Benjamin fired his gun again.

"Madi, run," Jeremiah yelled.

Fink grabbed Jeremiah by the throat and tossed him aside. Madi scrambled to her feet, swiped the camera off the ground, and took off into the woods.

"Don't just stand there," Fink said to Bushy Beard, "after her!"

Bushy Beard let out a drooling grunt and sprang forward, clutching his bleeding shoulder. "Get back here, you little Yankee brat!"

"Wait for me, Buford," Shelton said, waving his arm. "I'm coming with ya."

A shattering surge of thunder filled the air as a blitz of cannon fire fell on the woods. Will looked out from behind the boulder and watched in horror as a collection of cannonballs tore through the woods. They knocked down trees like bowling pins and drilled holes in the ground with a boom, boom, boom.

Before Will could scream a warning, the metal shell with its mighty force hurtled Shelton forward into Bushy Beard, engulfing the pair up in a fiery explosion. The shockwave rattled the earth, flinging Madi, and everyone, clear off their feet.

Will cowered against the boulder and covered his head as the multitude of thunderous percussions punched at the landscape. Rocks exploded on impact, sending slugs of shrapnel in the air. Trees snapped off their trucks, raining dirt and leaves in a dusty shower of burnt powder. One after another, the bombardment brutalized the woods until finally . . . silence.

Will wiped the dirt out of his eyes and looked around. Amongst the settling of broken branches and persistent white noise that rang in his ears, he heard a shallow moan. Through the dense smoke that spewed from the flaming hole where Bushy Beard and Shelton once stood, Will noticed a young man half-buried under a blanket of dirt, stone, and mulch. He rushed over and pushed aside the piles of ash and rubble. "Jeremiah?"

Jeremiah opened his eyes. A thin line of blood trailed out from his ear. "Will – William?"

"Don't talk. Save your strength. I'm going to get you out of here."

"All those years . . ." Jeremiah coughed. "How – how could you do that to our family, to me?"

"I'm sorry. I'll make everything right," Will said. "I promise."

"Is that the truth, William?" floated in Fink's sinister voice through the waning chaos.

Will wrapped each finger tight around his rifle and slowly rose to his feet.

Fink, with his black cape trilling in the breeze, walked through the mix of raining debris; Madi held hostage in his bony hand. "It's quite peculiar that it all has to end this way, don't you agree?" he said. "Brother vs. Brother. Truth vs. lies. This truly is a Civil War indeed."

"Will," Madi whimpered; the camera in her trembling hands. "Help . . ."

"Shut up," Fink spat.

Will raised his rifle. "Let her go, Marcus!"

Fink grinned wide. "Would you look at that?" he whispered to Madi. "He's finally remembering."

"You heard me," Will said, narrowing his aim. "Let her go!"

The sound of a pistol being cocked back snapped in Will's ears. "I don't think so," came Benjamin's cold voice. He pressed the tip of his gun's barrel hard against the side of Will's head. "Drop the gun. Now."

Outnumbered, Will relaxed his aim and lowered his arms. He uncurled his fingers, sending the rifle slipping out of his hands.

"Put 'em up," Benjamin ordered. "Where we can see them."

"What's this all about?" Will asked, surrendering. He glared at Fink. "What changed you over the years? How can you be so ruthless . . . so - so heartless?"

"Why, I could ask you the same thing, William."

"I never asked for or wanted any of this," Will yelled.

"And neither did I," Fink spat. He took a step closer; Madi still in his snake-like grip. "Years ago, I remember someone once had told me that 'we must accept the outcome of our lives whatever it shall bring.' That it was against convention to rewrite time's design for *personal* gain." Fink turned blazing eyes on Will. "But that never applied or held true for *you* now . . . did it, Sir Guardian?"

Will buckled over with an **oomph** as if he was punched in the stomach. He squeezed his eyes shut and grabbed his temples. A flash of scattered and sketchy memories drilled his thoughts. *His life as a child; the trips to the city; the barn; the letter; her face; her smell; the camera; the necklace; the piercing lights; the cold; the past; the future; the way she made him laugh.*

"I must say that I am truly saddened it had to come to this," Fink said. "I honestly thought our quest together would have been something grand; you and me."

"Just - just let her go," Will said, regaining his strength through the fading images. "She-she never did anything to you."

Fink yanked Madi by the hair, pulling her close. "That may be true, but it seems as though she holds key to the hands of time. So now it's my turn to avenge the wrongs that were done to me." Fink aimed his pistol at Will and smirked. "Say goodbye, William."

Chapter 43

rack!

Madi pinched her eyes shut and screamed in unison with the reverberation of the gunshot. *Will.* She didn't want to look; didn't want to see . . .

"Aires," Fink grunted, squeezing Madi's arm with his bony fingers, which burrowed deep into her skin.

Madi flicked open her eyes. Her breath caught in her throat. Will. He was still standing next to Benjamin, who had dropped his pistol to the ground and was cradling his bleeding abdomen.

Benjamin backed away with sluggish and jerky steps. He slumped against the trunk of a giant oak tree and looked down at his bloodstained hands. His body twitched. "You . . . you think you know," he said in labored gasps. He looked up at Madi with stark and vacant eyes. "You - you will never . . . you will never know the real - "

Fink aimed his gun toward the woods. "I know you are out there, Eldon. So, listen up. It all ends now! Do you hear me? I won't let this charade go on any longer. William has ruined and taken too many lives, especially mine. So, it's only fair that I *take* everything from him."

With a cackle like a jackal, Fink shoved Madi in front of him, pointed his gun at her chest, and pulled the trigger.

A puff of gunpowder. An orange clip of fire. A billow of smoke and flame rose in the air and haloed his devilish face.

Madi stiffened; her legs rooted to the ground; her breath bottled up in her lungs. Time stopped; the world paused, but her heart quickened. It pounded loudly in her ears as she watched the slaying slug soar out of the barrel, spinning, revolving through the air. In a blink of an eye, a tenth of a second, her life was about to be over.

Madi closed her eyelids. The world tilted. She was falling, falling to the ground. Not by the ripping force of the bullet but from the strength of a strong and powerful hand.

Wham!

Madi hit the ground hard and opened her eyes. She watched in horror as Will scooped up Benjamin's pistol, aimed it at Fink, and fired.

One.

Pop.

"Will!" Madi yelled covering her ears and shielding herself and the camera from the gunning discord. "No!"

Two.

Pop. Pop.

Chapter 44

bove the fading buzz of gunfire and her own heavy breathing, Madi heard a *snap, snap, snapping* of branches. She pushed herself up on her elbows and slowly stood up. A cold breeze swooped down from the trees and nipped at her cheek with a faint call of her name that rode on its tailwind.

Madi crept after the wind through the littered leaves and branches to a clearing of hollowed-out trees. There, she found Will sitting on a rotted tree trunk; his hands cupped lightly against his chest.

Madi took a wary step forward. "Will?" she whispered.

He raised his head ever-so-slightly and met her eyes.

"Will, what's – "

He swayed and then collapsed onto its thick trunk.

Madi ran to his side and fell to her knees. A puddle of crimson was seeping between his fingers. "No," she said with a numbed shiver; her eyes welling with tears. "No." She turned to the woods. "Help," she screamed at the trees. "Somebody. We need – "

In the smoky shadows, Madi saw a silhouette of a tall stranger lurking about like a menacing piranha out of water. Fink. She stared at him, and he incisively stared back at her. Then, without a word, he smoothly whipped around and floated away on his heels, disappearing into the charred abyss of the woods; his black cape curling upward behind him.

"Come on," Madi said, tugging at Will's arm. "We have to get you out of here."

Will arched his back and grasped at the hemline of her dress as an anguished moan escaped his drying lips. "I – I can't, Madi."

"Yes, you can," she said, rising to her feet. "You're a fighter. Now, stand up."

"I . . . " Will gasped in short staccato hiccups, and his body quaked and quivered.

"Please," Madi begged, kneeling beside him. "Please get up."

"I want - I need to tell you that - "A shallow gurgling filled Will's throat. He coughed, choking on a thick pool of blood that rose in his mouth and slipped through his drying lips. "I'm so sorry, Madi, for - f-f-for everything."

"Stop," she demanded, wiping away the blood that ran down his chin. "I don't want to hear this. You're not thinking straight."

"And . . ." Will took in a labored breath. "I'm sorry if - if I wasn't - if I wasn't there for you like - like I should have b-b-been."

Madi took the camera in her hands and held it high for him to see. "You were right about the barn. The camera - it was there. Now, we can go back home. You and me," she said, forcing a smile through her streaming tears. "Back to Nana and Grandpa, Mom and - "

Will silenced her words with a shaky, blood-stained finger. "Shhh . . ." he soothed.

"Please," Madi whispered in a broken voice. She wrapped her fingers tightly around his bloody hand and held it close to her heart. "Please don't leave me."

"It-it's okay. Everything will be . . ." Will inhaled sharply and slowly tilted his head to the side; a single tear streamed down his pale and dirty cheek.

The woods fell silent.

Madi blinked hard. Her body tensed; her heart froze in a frost of fear and anguish. "Will?" His name left her lips and took sail with the current, evaporating in an airy breath of smoke and ash.

Madi let go of Will's limp hand and skimmed her trembling fingers across the frayed bullet hole in the center of his corded jacket. Her cold fear melted and morphed into a blazing fire of fury that rushed through every square inch of her body. She grinded her teeth and clenched his strong shoulders. "Wake up," she wailed at his lifeless body. "You promised! You promised you'd get me back home. Wake up! You hear me! I said – "

High above the canopy of trees, brilliant flashes of light broke through the foliage and fell to the ground in a celestial shower of iridescent crystals. The incandescent rain extinguished the smoky haze in a hissing mist that coated the woods in a glaze of shimmering snow and ice.

Madi threw herself onto Will's bleeding chest and clutched his jacket in her fingers. Strands of her hair hardened in threads of icicles, and her tears crystallized on her eyelashes and cheeks. "Please," she muttered, shivering against the warmth of his stilled body. "You can't leave me. You can't . . ."

A sunburst of light fanned through the trees and reflected off the woods, casting a glimmer of divine iridescence. Needles of frost were stuck to branches and bark. Leaves and moss were tipped in ice. Microscopic star flares of blue and white swirled through the air in a mystic dance.

Madi breathed in a frosty scent of lavender and opened her eyes. Beyond the frozen trees, a river of misty wind was slithering through the woods. It traveled up her body and shrouded her neck. With a sharp click, the necklace unclasped itself and fell onto Will's chest.

Beneath the oak tree medallion, the opaque resin churned in a kaleidoscope of amber color. An icy liquid seeped out from its bronzed branches and fanned outward in a sphere of burning white, light.

Madi reached for the necklace.

A cluster of blazing tendrils rose from the medallion and latched onto her fingers. They climbed up her arm and one by one methodically braided around her entire body.

Fighting against the magical tether, Madi grabbed hold of the camera and held tight as she was thrust upwards with the force of a geyser. "No!" she screamed, wrestling within the tangled tendrils of voltaic power. "Put me down!"

On the ground below, two shadows, then three, then four, cloaked in dark coats, emerged from behind a gray translucent veil. They stood at Will's feet; and one - a woman with long, brown hair - knelt at his side.

"Get away from him," Madi yelled, twisting and turning about in the clutches of the banded branches. Her lone sobs bounced off her ears and dissipated in the whipping wind. "Get away from him!!"

Deep inside the camera, a surge of energy began to thump in a rhythmic pulse. Behind the glass lens, a faint white light grew bigger and bigger until it exploded in a web of icy lightning. The overpowering cold singed Madi's fingers, sending the camera plummeting to the ground. "No," she cried, grasping blindly through the air. "Will! Will!"

The trees parted, opening a funnel of darkness that quaked the sky and rippled the clouds in waves. An icy glaze coated her body in subzero armor, and a rush of warmth hit firm inside her chest, blanketing her heart.

Madi screamed Will's name one last time, gulping in a stream of brisk air as she was pulled away and sucked into a tunnel of darkness.

Chapter 45

adi threw her hand to her chest and sat up, gasping for air. She heaved in and out, trying to calm her racing heart. Her body shook in a cold sweat, and a relentless thumping pounded on the inside of her head.

"Madi?" came a soft voice followed by a light and hollow knocking. "Madi, wake up?"

Madi blinked several times and squinted through the strands of hair that stuck to her sweaty forehead. A sharp pinch caught her cheek. Grimacing, she bit her lip and touched her face. Her eyes went wide, and an impulse of emotion quickened her heart.

Madi threw the covers off her legs and jumped out of bed. She ran over to her dresser mirror and pushed back her damp hair. Taking a cautious step closer, she closed in on her reflection. A flush of adrenaline tingled through her body. She fell back into her dresser, sending her jewelry box to the floor with a jangled clatter.

A rattle of the door handle. "Madi, what's going on in there? Is everything all right?"

"Y-y-yeah," she answered as she slowly ran her fingers along the raised scar that lined her cheek. "Everything's fine. I'll – I'll be right down."

Chapter 46

"Well, there you are, sleepyhead. You had us worried."

Madi stopped in the doorway of the dining room to find her grandparents, fully dressed in their Civil War attire, sitting around the table, eating breakfast. The aroma of bacon, butter, and coffee hung heavy in the humid air and mingled with the glass chandelier that was covered in a thin layer of dust.

"Don't you look very pretty today," Nana said, pouring syrup from a ceramic pitcher decorated in small, intricate purple flowers.

Madi lowered her head and toyed with the seams of her ivory sundress. "Thanks," she replied with a watery smile.

"Doesn't she look nice, David?" Nana asked.

Grandpa looked up from his plate and smiled back. "Very nice. All grown up actually."

Madi felt her cheeks blush.

"You slept so long," Nana said with concern, taking a sip of tea. "It's not like you, especially on the first day of the fair. Are you sure you're all right?"

"Yeah," Madi said, taking her place around the table. "Just a little tired; that's all."

"I see your cheek is healing well," Nana said.

Madi stared blankly at her grandmother.

"You know, you and Cassie should be more careful with those boards. You're lucky you didn't need stitches."

Madi gave a slight smile and nodded. She picked up her fork and spun it in her fingers, staring absently at her breakfast plate - a mound of cold scrambled eggs. Like a ravaging riptide, the haunting images and sounds that consumed her mind and plagued her heart for so long came rushing back with a crushing and violent force of a tsunami. "I had a bad dream," she blurted, dropping her fork on her plate with a clatter.

Nana and Grandpa simultaneously looked up.

"And I've been having the same one for the past couple of months," Madi went on. "I don't know why, but I never told anyone, not even mom. But last night . . . last night was the worst. It felt so . . . *real*."

"I wouldn't let it bother you too much," said Nana. "That's why they're called – "

"It always starts with a storm," Madi interrupted. "And even though I'm sleeping, the lightning burns my eyes, and the thunder – the thunder roars louder than the wind, hurting my ears. Then it's over, and I'm running through the woods, tripping and falling, trying to get away as they chase after me." Madi grabbed the cloth napkin off the table, scrunching it in her cold and clammy hands; her leg rhythmically jittered beneath the table. She squeezed her eyes shut, trying to erase their menacing looks that coated their faces as they pursued her through the trees. "I can still hear their voices in my head," she whispered.

"It's okay, sweetheart," Nana said. She reached across the table and patted Madi on the hand.

"And just before I wake up, he's there, and he saves me."

"Who dear?"

"I – I don't know," Madi said, pulling back her hand. "But I yell out his name as I'm sucked up into the sky." She met her grandmother's worried eyes. "His name is Will."

Grandpa pushed back on his chair; its legs screeching against the wooden floor. He lowered his head and rubbed the back of his neck as he stood up. "I better get the truck packed," he said, wiping his mouth clean with his napkin. "We – ah – we don't want to be late."

|||||-|||||

Madi dried the last of the breakfast plates and placed them in the kitchen cabinet. She folded the dish towel and leaned up against the laminate counter, looking down at her sandaled feet. After she told Nana and Grandpa about her dream, she couldn't help but notice an unusual and somber shift in their mood.

"I remember it like it was yesterday," Nana began. She turned off the faucet and dried her hands on her apron. "Each and every detail. It was so hot and humid that day. In the distance, I could hear the thunder rumbling, but it wasn't until dinner time that the clouds started rolling in and turned the outside grey." She shook her head. "No. I take that back. It turned green."

"When the rain started, Grandpa went out to secure the barn and your mom and I finished cleaning up the dinner table. As we were putting away the last of the dishes, we heard a loud and rapid knocking at the front door. Shocked to hear such a noise, we both rushed to the hallway and found James on the porch, dripping wet from head to toe."

"James?" Madi said. "Who's James?"

Nana untied her yellow apron and slipped it over her head. "Maybe - uh - maybe we should get going."

"No. I want to know. Who is James?"

Nana slowly sat down in one of the kitchen chairs and stared up at Madi. "He was your mother's first husband."

"First husband - but - "

"I still remember the look on your mother's face when she saw him," Nana continued. "He was out of town for quite a while on a business trip, so we weren't expecting him until later the next day. It surprised us all to see him home early, but James - he was always full of surprises; you never really knew what he was up to. Anyway, he rushed into the house, grabbed your mother's hands, and told her to close her eyes. I watched as he reached into his pocket and placed a small key in the palm of her hand."

"Want to see your new home?" he whispered. Your mother opened her eyes and leaped into his arms. She was so happy. The happiest I had ever seen her."

Nana toyed with the ties of her apron. "By this time, the rain was falling in sheets, puddling in my flowerbeds, the driveway, even the road. Your mother grabbed her purse, hugged me goodbye, and went out with James into the pouring rain."

"Lightning was slashing, this way and that; and the wind . . . that's what worried me the most. You couldn't even imagine the sound it made. It howled and whistled louder than the thunder as it tore through the trees."

"Why didn't you stop them?" Madi asked.

"I tried. I ran to the car and grabbed the door handle, begging them not to go, to wait out the storm. Even Grandpa came running from the barn and tried to convince them into staying, saying it was too dangerous to leave. But they were young, and your mother and James were never ones to listen to reason. Before they drove off, I made your mother promise me to call the moment they got to the new house. She told me not to worry; that everything would be fine."

Nana lowered her head and wrung her hands together. "An hour later . . ." She breathed in deep. ". . . when the phone rang, the officer on the other line had told us there had been a terrible accident."

Madi sank into the chair across from her grandmother; her eyes wide. "Accident? Mom never told me about – "

"I don't even remember the car ride to the hospital," Nana whispered. "It was all a blur. By the time your grandfather and I got there, they were rushing your mother past me and into emergency surgery. Nurses were shouting orders; monitors were beeping erratically; doctors were being paged: CODE BLUE."

"I yelled her name, fought my way through everyone to get to my baby girl, but Grandpa held me back, insisting that I let everyone 'do their job'."

"Together we walked to the waiting area. Grandpa sat in silence while I paced the room and prayed. As the minutes rolled into hours, I noticed a young man was sitting all by himself in a darkened corner of the room. He looked up from a book he was reading and threw a quick wave. Realizing Grandpa and I were the only other people in the room, I waved back. And though he dressed a little odd, especially for being summer, I took a seat beside him, and we started talking. His voice was smooth as he spoke, and I found his words quite comforting. He had told me that he too was waiting to hear news of an old friend, who like your mother, was also in a horrible accident. *Dreadful,* he said, shaking his head. *Not wise for someone to be out in a storm like this.*"

"When the door to the waiting room opened, and I saw the nurse, I jumped to my feet. Every horrible outcome played in my head, but she turned away from me, looked at the young man, and said, *Mr. Fink? You can go back now.*"

"Without so much as a word of goodbye, Mr. Fink rose to his feet, placed the most peculiar decorated top hat on his head, and then strolled out of the room, whistling a soft melody to himself."

"But what about mom? James?" Madi asked.

"A few minutes later, a doctor came into the waiting room. *Mr. and Mrs. Douglas?* He walked up to us both and took off his surgical cap. *I'm Dr. Jancart, the trauma surgeon on call . . .*"

"I remember taking Grandpa's hand and together we stood up, holding onto each other."

When the tree came through the windshield, the doctor said, *it broke James' ribs, which pierced his lungs, causing him to go into cardiac arrest. I'm so sorry, but we did all we could do to save him.*

I fell into Grandpa's arms barely able to stand and cried. *My daughter -*

Alive. A few broken bones, cuts, and bruises, but all in all expected to make a full recovery . . . but unfortunately, we couldn't -

Nana stared down at her folded hands. There was a long pause. The sound of Grandpa starting the truck in the driveway cut through the silence.

Madi scooted to the edge of her chair. "Nana? They couldn't what?"

Nana looked up; her eyes full of tears. "They couldn't save the baby."

"Baby?"

Nana gave a watery smile. "Our sweet, baby boy. Our sweet, William."

Chapter 47

adi stepped out of the truck and into the hot summer morning. A large grandstand rose above the landscape, waiting to be filled by the hundreds of spectators for the upcoming reenactment. Beyond the vast battlefields, re-enactors – dressed in their period clothing – assembled on the fairgrounds, portraying their roles with the devotion of the past while people of all ages milled around the entertainment, entrenched in its living history.

"Madi?" Nana said, getting out of the pickup. "Are you all right? The whole ride here you were so – "

"I texted mom," Madi said, shutting the truck's door.

Nana adverted her eyes for a moment and slowly folded her hands across the front of her dress. "Was she upset I told you?"

Madi shrugged, kicking at the dirt path with the tip of her sandal. "Not really. She said that I'd probably have a bunch of questions and that we would all talk when her and dad – "

Nana pulled Madi close and hugged her tight. "I'm so sorry, sweetheart," she said, lightly kissing the top of her head. "I never meant for you to find out that way."

Madi sank into her grandmother's embrace. "Why wouldn't she tell me?"

Nana stepped back and lifted Madi's chin. "Your mother – she had her reasons."

"Madi!" a cheerful voice pierced through the somber mood. "Hey, Madi!"

With the back of her hand, Madi quickly wiped away her stray tears and looked beyond the parked cars and trucks to find her friend, Cassie Baines, waving and walking in her direction.

"There you are," Cassie said, beaming from ear to ear. "I was wondering when you were going to show up. Hi, Mrs. Douglas. Nice dress."

"Hello, Cassandra," Nana said. "And thank you; I like yours, too."

Cassie turned side to side, twirling the bottom of her cranberry-colored sundress. "Thanks," she said with a smile. She turned to Madi. "So, you ready? I was thinking that maybe we could – "

With a thunderous clap, a microburst of cold wind rolled across the fairgrounds. Like a tidal wave, it plucked away ball caps and top hats from the top of heads. It lifted dresses and skirts in a heap of fabric. Even Mr. Jacobs, who stood at the entrance to the parking lot, chased after the blue fliers that shot out from his tan canvas sack and fluttered in the air like scattering leaves.

Madi closed her eyes and held her breath as a cluster of churning dust swirled around her like a tornado. It whipped at her dress and tugged at her hair. Then, as quick and wild as the wind came, it was gone.

"What the heck was that?" Cassie asked, smoothing her hair.

Before Madi could answer, a delicate scent of lavender wafted in on a warm breeze, and she heard Nana gasp. Madi turned away from Cassie and watched as her grandmother walked to the edge of the parking lot and stared up at a wide, glistening contrail streaking through the clouds.

"What is that?" Madi pointed, squinting through the sun's harsh glare.

Nana jumped at the sound of Madi's voice. She let go of a vintage oak tree pendant attached to her lace collar, and with her gloved hand, she quickly dabbed away a few tears that slipped out of her eyes. She dug into her apron pocket, opened a small cloth change purse, and handed Madi a distressed fifty-dollar bill that was taped down the center.

"What's this for?" Madi asked.

"In case you and Cassie get hungry," Nana answered, "or if you need it to buy something."

"Nana, I can't take this. It's way too much."

"Take it," she insisted, firmly holding the bill down in Madi's hand. "Now, go have fun; your friend's waiting. I'll see you at the artillery show. You'll be back. 1:30."

Madi walked through the fairgrounds in silence alongside Cassie, who was still rambling on about the strange anomaly. It wasn't that she trying to ignore her friend, but after hearing about the story of her mother, feeling the strange, cold wind, and witnessing Nana's unusual behavior; it was all she could think about.

Cassie tapped Madi's arm. "Hey, are you even listening to me?"

"I'm sorry. It's just – " Madi stopped short. Across the dirt path, a large cream-colored canvas tent with a painted sign at its entrance: *The Battle of Gettysburg and its Stories In-between*, caught her attention.

"You want to check that out?" Cassie thumbed.

"Yeah," Madi answered and made her way toward the tent.

"Really?" Cassie muttered, following behind. "Seems kind of boring, if you'd asked me."

"Why good afternoon!" came a jolly voice as the girls lifted up the tent's heavy canvas and stepped inside. "You're right on time!"

A pot-bellied man dressed in a crisp Union uniform and a cheesy grin spread across his round face stood at the front of a small crowd. "You ladies missed the tour, but the presentation starts in a few minutes." He reached into a basket, sitting on the top of a three-legged stool and handed over two folded brochures. "Here's some reading material for you both to look at, and . . ." The curator scratched his bearded chin and scanned the rows. "I see a few empty chairs scattered throughout the tent, but. . . ah, right there, back row. Three opened seats."

"Thanks," Madi said.

"My pleasure," the man said, tipping his slouch hat.

The girls locked arms with one another and made their way toward the back of the tent, giggling to themselves.

"Ladies and gentlemen, boys and girls," the curator began.

Madi and Cassie quickly shuffled into the row and quietly took their seats.

"Welcome to Gettysburg, Pennsylvania; home to one of the greatest battle sites of the American Civil War. I invite you to sit back and relax while I take you on an adventure; an adventure of sacrifice, sorrow, and . . ." He bent at the waist, narrowed his eyes, and whispered, "secrets."

Madi sat back on her folding chair and opened up the brochure, tuning out the curator as he briefly recapped the three-day battle. She stared at each black and white photograph, transfixed on the vacant expressions of soldiers and families, individuals and couples. Below each photo, brief captions recounted the personal sacrifices soldiers made within the trenches of the most horrific war on American soil. Inside, stories were shared of heroic citizens, like Tillie Pierce, who helped the wounded after she left her home with her neighbor, Mrs. Henrietta Shriver, and her two young daughters – Molly and Sadie. A full page was dedicated to the sub-cultural societies of the NEVES and Nefarions as well as the rise and fall of the Parker family, whose lives were intertwined with both groups and torn apart at its roots through greed, lies, and betrayal.

"Excuse me miss," came a brush of a smoky voice, "but is this seat taken?"

"It's all yours," Madi mumbled as she finished reading the brochure.

"Thanks," the stranger said, sitting down. "It feels good to finally rest for a moment. I've traveled pretty far to get here today."

Madi placed her elbows on her knees, cupping her chin in her hands and stole a sideways glance at the stranger sitting beside her. He was a young man, most likely in his early twenties, with a crop of sandy-brown hair that hit just above the ears. He stared straight ahead, making no sudden movements and listened intently to the curator and his story. But for Madi, it wasn't his unyielding behavior that she found odd or long, navy jacket, which was decorated with chains, gears, and keys. It was the long, bronze necklace he wore loosely around his neck; its opaque resin slightly glowed in amber beneath an ornate oak tree medallion.

"And that, ladies and gentlemen, brings me to my final story of the NEVES," the curator said.

"I just read about that in the brochure," a middle-aged woman in a Gettysburg Got Ghosts? t-shirt spoke out from the second row. "So, it's true then? The battlefield hauntings?"

"Well, to this day," the curator began. "Many claim to have seen the seven spirits of the NEVES walking around town, making their way across the battlefields, or wandering through the adjacent woods along the fairgrounds that lead to the property line of the Parker Farm, which I'll have you know is now owned by our generous sponsors of this historic tent: the Douglas Family."

The crowd applauded with a soft roll of clapping.

"The NEVES are sly, smart," the curator went on, tapping his temple. "It's like one minute they're there, and the next thing - *poof* - gone - vanished into thin air."

"I don't know about you," the young man said, nudging Madi's arm, "but they sound fascinating."

"If you were to ask me personally," the curator continued. "I like to consider the NEVES more as guardians; prodigious guardians of a legacy, who at one time before their collapse and demise, left a mark on the world as they protected the very essence of history and of life."

The curator picked up a black and white poster-sized, photograph and raised it above his head. "As you can see here, these two objects are what many historians dedicate their lives to finding. They hope one day when these remarkable pieces of history are found and brought together, a door through time will open and reveal the true story and nature behind the secret lives of the NEVES, which you can read more about in the brochure."

"Wow." Cassie pointed. "Hey, Madi. Take a look at that!"

Madi raised herself higher on her chair and stared at the poster that showed a black, rectangular camera and a long, bronze necklace with a glowing ornate, oak tree medallion. A puff of air popped in her throat. *No way. It can't be.*

Madi spun on her seat toward the stranger beside her and froze. "Wait a second," she said, looking down the row and behind the chair. "Where did he go?"

"Who?" Cassie asked.

"The guy; the guy that was sitting next to me."

Cassie leaned forward. "What guy? No one was there."

"Yes, there was. He was right – " Madi looked down at the seat. A long, white strip of paper with four colored photographs sat in the middle of the chair. Her heart started to race.

Fingers trembling, Madi picked up the photo strip and stared at a sequence of four photos. "It wasn't a dream after all," she whispered.

Madi turned to Cassie, smiling wide. "He's alive."

"Huh?"

"Will's alive!"

"Who's Will? What are you talking about?"

"Right here," Madi said, holding up the photo strip.

Cassie giggled. "What are you saying, silly? The paper is blank."

Ignoring her friend, Madi climbed onto the seat of her chair and scanned the crowd. *Where is he?*

"Child, I insist you sit down," said a plump lady in the next row, who sat close to her chubby daughter. "You're going to fall on your head."

"Miss?" said the curator, stopping his presentation. "Is something wrong?"

The crowd stirred from the sudden commotion and at the same time, turned around in their seats.

"I can't believe it! Wait until I tell – " Madi stopped short. At the front entrance of the tent, obscured by the sunlight flittering in from the outside, stood the young man in the long, navy jacket. "There," she pointed. "He's right there!"

The stranger fixed his high collar and then quickly ducked under and out of the tent's heavy canvas door as the crowd and Cassie looked in the direction of Madi's pointed finger.

"Miss," the curator said. "Please. You must sit down."

"No, wait," Madi yelled.

"Umm . . . Madi," Cassie said, taking her by the hand. "Are you okay? You're acting kind of weird."

Madi looked at the bewildered faces of the crowd and then back at her friend. "I – I gotta go." She scrambled off her chair and raced past the rows of spectators, heading toward the entrance of the tent.

"Madi!" Cassie shouted. "Where are you going?"

"I can't explain right now. But I will . . . I promise."

Madi burst out of the tent and slid to a stop by a small parade of musicians, playing their fife and drum to a circling crowd of spectators. She looked through the musical mob and caught sight of the young man, weaving in and out of the scores of people making their way up and down the dirt paths. "Wait," she yelled.

Madi clutched the photo strip in her hand and took off. She side-stepped a group of rowdy teenagers, who stopped at a nearby hot dog stand, arguing about who was going to pay for lunch and zigzagged through groups of Confederate reenactors, making their way to the battlefield. As she dodged out of their way, her ankle buckled and she fell, forward, bouncing off the round belly of a tall, burly man.

"Watch it," the man barked in a southern accent.

"Yeah," heckled a slender man, tugging at his grey trousers.

"I'm – I'm sorry, mister," Madi replied.

"Hmph," the man answered with a grunt, struggling to pull up on the belt around his Confederate uniform jacket that bulge against his stomach. He scratched his chin beneath his thick, bushy beard. "Best be more careful there, little lassie, 'cause next time . . ." He leaned in close and flicked the side of his nose. ". . . you might not be so fortunate."

Lightning flashed. A rumble of thunder thrummed in the distance, beating against the sky in a climactic roar. Both men and Madi looked up. Rolling in from the west was a shelf of grayish-green clouds. Little by little, they crept across the sky like a giant amoeba, swallowing every inch of summer blue.

"You see that, Buford?" the slender man said to his Confederate comrade. "It's happening. A storm's a-coming. We – ah – we should get going."

As the two men scampered off, the thickening clouds burst under pressure like a giant water balloon, dropping a volley of rain to the ground. Madi cowered against the downpour and squinted through the pouring rain. "No, no, no," she said in a panic, spinning around. "Where'd he – "

Standing at the tree line, Madi noticed the young man staring in her direction. He shook his head and then stepped off the dirt path, disappearing between two, large oak trees. "Hey," she waved. "Stop! Wait."

Madi ran as fast as she could through the rain to the tree line, splashing mud up and onto her sandals. She turned at the pair of mighty oak trees, crossed onto the secluded dirt trail, and froze.

High above, the trees' thick vines and foliage slowly began to

J.B. Pierce

intertwine with one another in a knotted, leafy pattern, blocking out the pelting rain.

Impossible, Madi murmured, marveling at the earthly anomaly.

She looked back at the fairgrounds. Beyond the entrance of the path, the heavy rain continued to fall, soaking the ground. Flags that once fluttered lightly in the summer wind hung heavy and limp. Sporadic groups of people plodded through the growing mud as they searched for shelter from the storm.

Trembling from the growing cold, Madi raised her arm and reached out at the wall of rain that fell just beyond her sandaled feet. As the tip of her fingers hit the waterfall of water, it rippled, like a skipping stone on a pond, distorting the flags, tents, and people.

"Pretty amazing how that works, isn't it?"

Madi jumped at the voice. She spun around, finding the young man standing behind her.

"But? How – where– " Madi looked back at the curtain of rain and then down at her clutched hand. Slowly, she held out the photo strip. "Where did you get this?"

The young man gave a sideways smile. "From you. It was your idea, remember?"

"Me? But – "

"I'm – I'm sorry," he chuckled. "You must forgive me. It's just that . . . I guess the journey back affected you more than I thought."

Madi looked down at the teenage boy in the photo strip and then up at the young man standing before her. His long, navy jacket sat upon his broad shoulders and light stubble highlighted his defined jawline.

Madi took a tentative step closer and looked hard into his piercing blue eyes that stared down at her. At that moment, a sequence of memories flooded her mind – *trips to Nana and Grandpa's, horseback riding in the fields, hiking through the woods, finding the clubhouse.*

"Will," Madi cried. She threw her arms around his waist, closed her eyes, and listened; the cadence of his strong heartbeat sang sweetly in her ears.

Will stepped out of her embrace and lightly cupped her cheek with his warm hand. "Hello, Madi. It's so good to see you again."

Madi wiped her watery eyes. "I can't believe it! I can't believe you're real." She took Will by the hand. "Come on! Let's go home!"

"Madi, wait," Will said, pulling back.

"Mom's never going to believe this. And just wait until Nana and Grandpa see you. Hey, can we finish the clubhouse? Cassie's fun and all, but – "

An icy gust of wind whooshed through the woods, covering the path in a frosty mist. The subzero temperature glazed the nearby trees and nipped at Madi's bare, wet arms, sending a shiver down her spine.

Snap. Crack. Crunch.

Madi cowered into Will as another young man, wearing a black derby hat and trench coat, appeared out of the woods; a black, rectangular camera was in his hands. "My apologies, Smithfield, but I'm afraid it's time."

Madi looked at Will, confused. "Smithfield? But your name is . . ."

Will took the camera from the young man and nodded. "I'll be just another minute."

"As you wish." The young man tipped his hat and threw Madi a wink before stepping back into the shadows of the trees.

"Good 'ole Eldon," Will said. "Got to hand it to him. Always watching out for me; keeping me on course."

Madi let go of her trembling arms and looked down at the photo strip. "I don't understand," she mumbled; her mind a dusty cluster of questions. "I thought it was all – "

"A dream?" Will finished.

Madi touched the scar on her cheek. "But it wasn't. Everything happened; you and me; the barn; the town; the war."

"It did," Will answered.

Madi shook her head. "Nothing is making any sense."

"It's complicated," Will said. "I promised I would get you home, remember?"

Lightning flashed and sifted through the tightly laced trees. Thunder rumbled and vibrated the ground.

Will looked up at the churning clouds. "I have to go."

Madi furrowed her brow. "Where are you going?"

"Home," Will said somberly.

"Then, let's go," Madi said, reaching for his hand.

Will stepped back toward the trees. "I'm sorry, but I can't."

"What do you mean, you can't?"

Will ran his hand through his hair and sighed.

"It's me, isn't it?" Madi asked. She grabbed Will by the wrist. "Listen, I'll – I'll change. I'll leave you alone. I won't bother you if we have to share your room again at Nana's, and we don't have to finish that stupid clubhouse if you don't want to. We can – "

Another clip of thunder rolled through the woods, rattling and quaking the ground.

Will looked over his shoulder to the trees where Eldon stood patiently waiting. "I'm sorry, Madi, but I have to go before it's too late."

"No," she said, wrapping her arms tight around his waist. "You're staying here with me. I'm not letting you go this time."

"I wish it could be different," Will said, holding her close. "But I made my choice – a long, *long* time ago – and by my choice, I'm forever bound to the hands of time."

Madi looked up at Will; trails of tears ran down her face and dripped onto his jacket. "What does that even mean?"

Will wiped the tears from her scarred cheek. "Goodbye, Madi. I won't ever forget you."

Madi closed her eyes and held Will tight never wanting to let go. "Please. I don't want to lose you again."

A cold gust of wind broke through the trees. Leaves and branches quivered in a winding whir. A bolt of lightning shot down from the clouds, striking the edge of the path with a startling flash. Its voltaic current charged the trail and pitched Madi to the ground. "Will," she cried scrambling to her feet.

The cold wind whipped at her hair and toyed with her dress. Madi stared up at a black and hollow abyss that sat high above the trees. It siphoned itself up and into the darkness. Then, with a thunderous clap, the funnel closed and Will was gone.

"Goodbye," Madi whispered.

The wall of rain at the entrance of the dirt trail slowed and then in a wave, lowered melodically to the ground. The trees stepped aside, making room for the warming sun. Madi breathed in a gentle mist of lavender that mixed with the remaining tears that ran down her cheeks. She looked down at the photo strip in her hand and watched as the glossy images of her and Will fade and morph into an embossed message. Gently, she traced the elegant, script with her fingertips and smiled, reading each handwritten word.

"Together we have shared if only awhile;
forever remember me."
The Will of Time.

If you enjoyed reading *The Will of Time,*
here is a sneak peek of book 2 . . .

THE POWER OF WILL

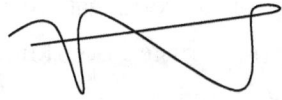

* * *

A scent of must and dampness hung stagnant in the dank air. William gasped, expelling an airy cough. His body shook in spasms from a warm surge of internal energy that rushed from the tips of his toes and ascended fast through every vein and artery like a tidal wave.

William forced his heavy eyelids to open. Lifting his shaky hands, he wiped the tears off his cheeks. He strained to take in his surroundings. The room was small and square. A dimly lit candle sat crooked in its pewter holder and barely held the flame. Its wax dripped slowly onto the hardened puddle on the floor. A metal washstand with an enamel basin held medicinal bottles and a used roll of bloody muslin. A glass syringe (half-full with a clear liquid) and a pair of rusty scissors sat next to an hourglass that ran out of time. A.

"Hello," William rasped.

On the opposite side of the room sat a three-legged stool near a six-panel, wooden door with a rusted doorknob. William tried to sit up but fell back, heaving in and out. He ran his fingers against the rough wool and burlap beneath him. *Come on, remember. What was the last thing that happened? And how did I end up here?*

William swallowed hard. *I can do this.* He propped himself up on his elbows. A sharp burning stabbed his chest. He curled his body, knees to his chest, from the sudden pain.

"Hello?" William coughed. "Eldon?"

Grinding footsteps broke through the eerie silence. A rattle of a chain. The clink of a bolt unlocking.

William watched as the doorknob slowly turned. The door squealed open. A tattered, black booted foot stepped inside the room.

"Eldon," William began, "I don't know what you think you are doing, putting me down here in this hole of a place like this, but – "

William looked up. His breath caught in his throat. His heart pounced beneath his ribcage. He stared at the finger adorned with a skull ring; a glare of menacing ruby red eyes.

"Why, hello, William." Fink removed his black, top hat and narrowed his chin. "It's so nice to see you – alive – yet again."

Beyond the Story

Over the years and through my intensive and extensive research while writing *The Will of Time*, I have come to learn and appreciate moments in time as well as the many people of our American history – those remembered (and those sadly forgotten.) I have read compelling and heartwarming stories, both authentic and unaltered; I have studied their simple, yet complicated lives.

If you, like me, would like to go beyond the story of *The Will of Time* to those moments and people that lived, breathed, and experienced those times in our history, look to the information below.

WORKS OF NON-FICTION

Alleman, Tillie (Pierce). *At Gettysburg: Or, What a Girl Saw and Heard of the Battle, A True Narrative.* New York: W. Lake Borland, 1889

Anderson, Tanya. *Tillie Pierce: Teen Eyewitness to the Battle of Gettysburg.* Kansas City. Quindaro Press, 2013

Gudmestad, Nancie. *The Shriver's Story: Eyewitnesses to the Battle of Gettysburg.* Gettysburg. The Shriver House Museum, 2008

QUOTES

Gaelic Proverb - Cha tèidnìsambithsandòrndùinte. "Nothing can get into a closed fist."

American Ballad. *Home, Sweet Home.* Written by American lyricist John Howard Payne & English composer Sir Henry Bishop. It was first produced in London in 1823 for an opera & became popular in the United States, especially during the Civil War.

INTERNET WEBSITES

http://www.berdansharpshooters.com This website gives historical information about Hiram Berdan and his sharpshooters during the Civil War as well as information for the Company "C" 2nd Regiment of U.S. Sharpshooters.

https://www.battlefields.org This website, American Battlefield Trust, gives an in-depth look at many of the people, events, and battles before, during, and after the Civil War.

https://www.gettysburgdaily.com/gettysburg-female-institute-artillery-projectile This website, The Gettysburg Daily (January 16, 2009), gives a pictorial and editorial description of what the Seminary for Young Ladies during the Battle of Gettysburg.

http://yorkfair.org/our-history This website provides current and historical events that happened at the York Fair in York County, Pennsylvania.

http://www.foodtimeline.org/foodpioneer.html This website provides a timeline of American foods in the 19th century.

http://gettysburg.stonesentinels.com/battlefield-farms/leister-farm-meades-headquarters & https://npsgnmp.wordpress.com/2015/01/08/the-widow-and-her-farm These two websites offer a detailed description of Lydia Leister's farm (General Meade's Headquarters) before, during, and after the Civil War.

https://www.gettysburgreenactment.com This website is dedicated to the annual reenactment held at Gettysburg, PA. This event showcases the three-day battle through thousands of devoted reenactors and historians.

PHOTOGRAPHS

The photographs - taken by Bethany Brown, Jenn Davis, and J.B. Pierce - that appear in conjunction with this book were all reenacted and shot at the various locations listed below.

*Additional images of the characters and their adventures can be found at jbpierce.com and on Facebook, Instagram, and Twitter.

TERMS AND THEIR DEFINITIONS

(Fictional & those of historical significance)

Impetus Existence (fictional) - /ˈimpədəs/ /igˈzistəns/ - a force of energy that stimulates life

NEVES (fictional) - /nah'vess/ - seven chosen individuals who protect and guide those who have lost their way and purpose in life

Blue-belly (historical, American Civil War) - Noun. a Union soldier

Johnny Reb (historical, American Civil War) - Noun. another term for Rebel - Confederate - soldier

Rebel (historical, American Civil War) - Noun. a person who rises in opposition or armed resistance against an established government or ruler; slang name given to Confederate soldiers

Abolitionist Movement (historical, American Civil War) - The belief that slavery should be abolished. In the early nineteenth century, increasing numbers of people in the northern United States held that the nation's slaves should be freed immediately, without compensation to slave owners - dictionary.com

Griddle Cakes (historical, American Civil War) - Noun. a flat cake, such as a pancake or a johnnycake, that is cooked on a griddle.

HISTORICAL LOCATIONS OF
INTEREST/INSPIRATION

Larimer Mansion – North Huntingdon, PA – The Larimer Mansion Farm was built on the King's Highway circa 1790. It was the homestead of Gen. William Larimer, Jr. one of the founders of Denver, Colorado. Historical figures, such as William Henry Harrison and Aaron Burr visited the home.

Today, the Larimer Mansion is privately owned and runs as a Bed and Breakfast. For more information: www.larimermansion.com/

Braddock's Trail Park – North Huntingdon, PA – One of the largest parks in North Huntingdon historically tied to Braddock's Military Road and known for its beautiful array of wildflowers, nature, and hiking trails as well as its scenic waterfall.

For more information: https://www.township.north-huntingdon.pa.us/Facilities/Facility/Details/Braddocks-Trail-Park-3

West Overton Village – Scottsdale, PA – The village of West Overton began in April 1800 when Henry Overholt (distiller of Old Farm Pure Rye Whiskey), his wife and twelve children emigrated from Bucks County, Pa, to Westmoreland County, Pa, settling with other Mennonites who resided in the Jacob Creek area. It is also the birthplace of Henry Clay Frick.

For more information: https://www.westovertonvillage.org/

Old Brush Creek Cemetery – North Huntingdon, PA – This cemetery with headstones dating as far back as the late 1700s sits off of Route 30 in Westmoreland County, PA on Leger Road.

For more information: https://www.pa-roots.com/westmoreland/townships/northhuntingdon/oldbrush.html

Round Hill Park and Farm Exhibit - Elizabeth Township, PA - Round Hill Park and Farm Exhibit - opened year-round - showcases farm animals and includes other amenities such as soccer fields, spray park, shelters, and walking and bridle trails within its 1,101 acres. For more information: https://www.alleghenycounty.us/parks/round-hill/index.aspx

About the Author

J.B. Pierce grew up in McKeesport, a small mill town 20 miles outside of Pittsburgh, Pennsylvania. When she wasn't dancing or singing, she was orchestrating cheesy haunted houses (that were never really scary) or setting up a backyard carnival with Bingo and Pick a Duck (yes, everyone was a winner). Entertaining was in her blood. She was always conjuring up something (even one-act plays), ready for the smallest of spectators – me, myself, and my make-believe audiences. As she grew older, J.B. graduated from California University (of PA) with a bachelor's in Elementary Education and continued her academic career by receiving her master's degree in Curriculum and Instruction from Gannon University. Though the grass and sheets disappeared over time, she found a new stage and audience: eager and energetic 5th graders. With each reading and grammar lesson and through every moment of our American history she has shared, a new show emerged, and her imagination was sparked back to life – *The Will of Time.*

For more about J.B. Pierce, visit her website at jbpierce.com; join her email list at j.b.piercebooks@gmail.com; follow her on Instagram (jbpierce) and Facebook (jbpiercebooks), and leave a review on Amazon!

Acknowledgments

As many of you know, *The Will of Time* has been an ongoing project since 2009. Through the ups and downs, revisions, and writer's block – *The Will of Time* has continued to evolve into an adventurous and heart-warming story about selflessness, love, and courage. What it once was to where it is today, could not have been done without the enormous amount of support and love from the many people that have followed and helped me along the way throughout this writing journey.

To my husband Jim: I cannot thank you enough for your love and support and patience you had with me over the years as I took on the idea of becoming an author alongside being a wife, mother, teacher, and photographer.

Braden and Brinley, the loves of my life: You bring me so much joy and laughter. You may not see it now, but you both are an inspiration to me and will always be my two main characters in my best-selling story – the story of us, our family.

Mom. When you called me back in 2009 with an idea to collaborate and write a book, I never knew what adventure awaited me, awaited us. Over the years, you have been the backbone of this project, supporting, teaching, guiding, and mentoring me through Will and Madi's adventure. Thank you for calling me that early fall morning. If it weren't for you, the world would never have known *The Will of Time*.

And to all my students and fans (past and present): Every enthusiastic comment, harsh criticism, or critique as well as creative idea you had ever given, I want you to know that each was taken wholeheartedly. You are (and were) my first real audience. You truly inspire!

www.ingramcontent.com/pod-product-compliance
Lightning Source LLC
Chambersburg PA
CBHW051938220626
47052CB00004B/707